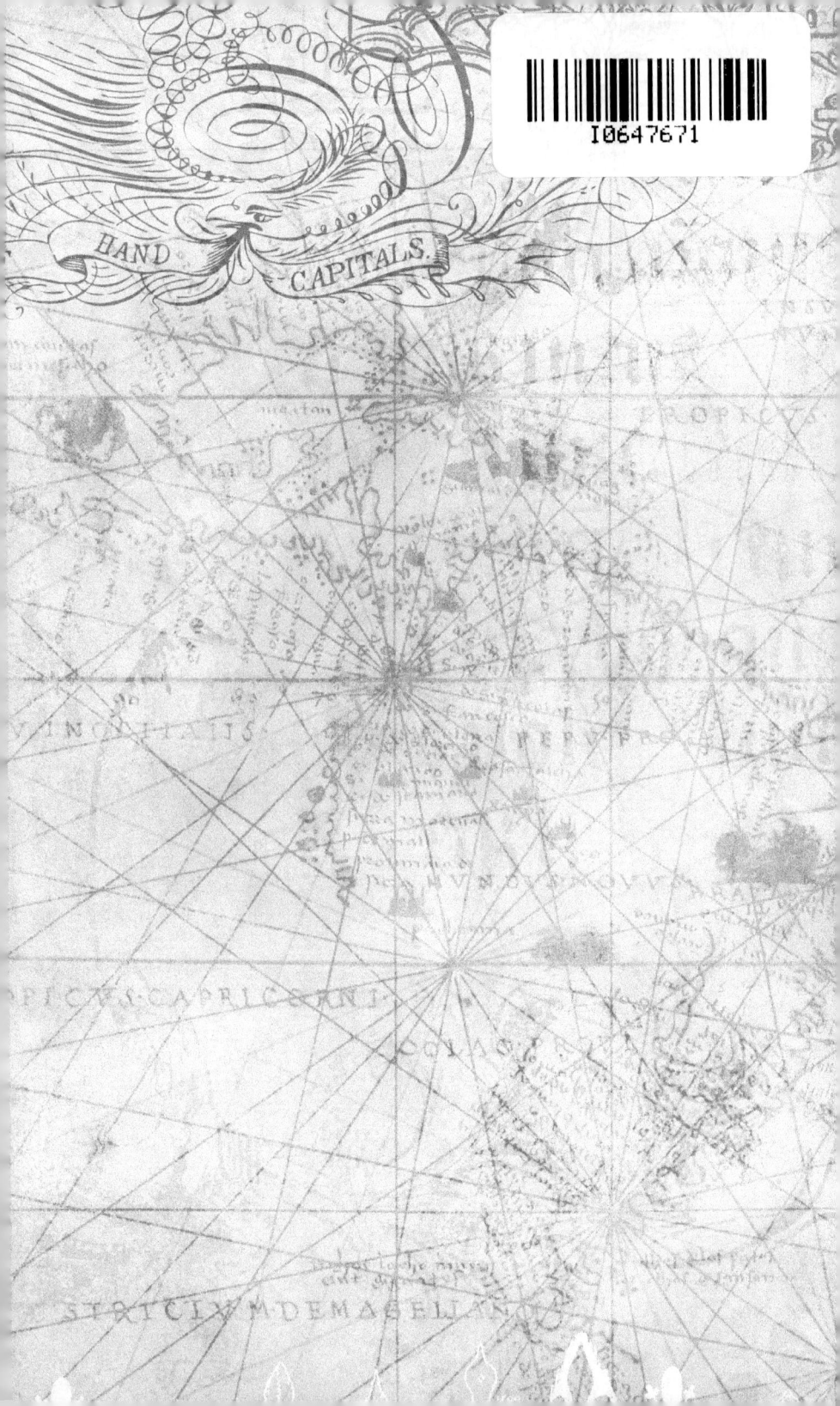

The Viscountess Interrogates

A DOMINION EROTIC MYSTERY

Cameron Quintain

Circlet Press, Inc.
Cambridge, MA

Chapter One

The dance floor smelled like sweat and nitrous oxide. Most of the people fled when the plants burst through the floor, but Severin and several others were caught up by the long, powerful vines that writhed like snakes. They were lifted into the air and left dangling there as the clinging vines ripped and shredded their clothing. The it was dpounding dance music was replaced by cries of anguish.

Under the flickering lights, two women sauntered through the chaos. One of them had light green skin and blood red hair. She wore nothing but clinging vines with small white flowers. Her companion was wearing only a pink tutu, striped knee socks and a red bow tie. Her skin was chalk-white with red dots on both sets of cheeks and over her nipples. Above her wicked grin, her eyes glittered with a crazy light.

Severin tugged on the vines, but found them as tight as any bondage he had ever been in. Now that he was actually here, he was beginning to think maybe a trip to a dominion with actual supervillains wasn't such a good idea. Still, it was too late to turn back now.

The green woman, known as Honeysuckle, was grabbing jewelry and wallets from the captives. Her partner, the Clown Queen, walked past the row of prisoners with a baseball bat on her shoulder. She paused to yank the thong panties off one of the prisoners whose dress had been torn off by the vines. The woman screamed and kicked feebly against the vines.

"Don't worry sweetheart, I'd need a weed whacker to get in there." Clown Queen snickered and gave a sharp tug on the woman's thick pubic hair.

Severin was trying not to stare too hard at the pale curves of the nearly nude body. When she glanced his way, he instinctively lowered his gaze to avoid eye contact. She strolled up to him casually. Just when he thought she might not have noticed him he heard her squeaky voice call out.

""Hey Honey, I think we've got a live one."

"Let's find out." Honeysuckle turned to look at Severin. Her eyes narrowed as she focused her concentration on the plants.

Severin gave a little scream as fresh vines snaked up his pants legs. Sharp thorns cut into the fabric, tearing away his pants and underwear, exposing him to the two women.

Clown Queen glanced at him then winced. "I guess you're only a boy wonder."

"We can still have some fun with him," Honeysuckle announced, coming closer. Severin felt overwhelmed by the sweet scent that was rolling off of her. His arms and legs were yanked apart by the vines so he hung spread-eagled.

"Hey Honey, you go out for a long one, I'll see if I can hit a home run with these balls." Clown Queen tapped his genitals with her baseball bat.

Severin realized with shock that she was serious. He was on the verge of using his Safeword when there was a loud crash. A figure burst through the window of the nightclub and landed in a shower of glass.

The newcomer was tall and powerfully built with long dark hair held back from her face by a metal tiara. Her body was encased in a tight, brightly colored leather corset and a glowing rope hung from her belt. She was exquisitely beautiful and moved with power and grace. Her well-toned body gave the impression of immense power that went beyond her slender frame.

"All right Princess, now it's really a party," Clown Queen shouted, charging forward with the bat.

Princess reached down very calmly and took the rope from her waist. With a flick of her wrist she sent it lashing out, the end of the glowing rope settling around Clown Queen's neck. With a yank of her arm it tightened like a leash.

Clown Queen made a little high pitched noise and screeched to a halt. Her legs splayed out to the side, forcing her into a split. She went down so fast that her shaved pussy smacked into the floor audibly.

"Thank you, Princess," Clown Queen murmured a dazed expression on her face.

Severin had never seen someone drop into Subspace so suddenly and so violently.

"Too bad your rope of submission doesn't work on someone who is part plant." Honeysuckle approached the Princess while long vines with sharp thorns rose up to wrap around her wrist.

The plant woman used the vines like a whip, lashing out at the Princess, drawing blood in a half dozen places where the thorns cut her.

Princess took an involuntary step backwards. She was suddenly breathing harder and her skin was growing flushed.

"The aphrodisiac on the thorns was Clown Queen's idea," Honeysuckle explained. She sent the whip hissing out again, but Princess nimbly dodged it.

As the whip drove her back, she was unaware of the plant that had sprouted behind her. It was like a Venus flytrap, but monstrously large. It leaned over, splitting in half, opening a mouth so large it could encase the Princess' entire head.

While the fight had been going on Severin had been struggling with the vines. When Honeysuckle was no longer concentrating on them the vines became more like plants and less like living steel cables. He swayed back and forth in the vines wrapped around his torso while he freed his arms and legs.

By the time he had pulled himself free Princess was inches from the Venus flytrap.

"Behind you!" Severin called out.

He was looking around trying to find something to use as a weapon when someone grabbed him from behind. He felt a hard, naked body pressing into his own, erect nipples grinding against his shoulder blades as Clown Queen wrapped one arm around his throat and grabbed a handful of genitals with her other hand. Apparently when Princess dropped her rope it lost its power.

"I like you. You're a glutton for punishment," Clown Queen giggled, chewing on his ear. "How about I take you home and make you my piñata?"

Severin watched as Princess spun and cut through the stem of the Venus flytrap with a single karate chop. But by turning she had exposed her back to Honeysuckle's whip. As the plant woman lashed out, Princess pivoted, raising her arm so the cruel lash wrapped around her forearm.

Bracing herself, Princess pulled on the thorn whip with all her strength, yanking Honeysuckle off her feet and launching her through the air so hard that the plant woman crashed into a wall and slid to the floor.

Princess wiped the fresh blood from her arm as she approached the fallen woman, pinning her to the floor with a bright red boot.

"Hey, I've got a hostage over here!" Clown Queen called out cheerfully while giving Severin's balls a cruel twist. He tugged at the elbow that was bent across his neck. Although she didn't look well-muscled, the Clown Queen had a grip like iron. Severin felt he could get enough air to use his Safeword, but he decided to wait it out to see what would happen.

"You're finished, Clown Queen. Let him go." Princess took a step forward.

"I'm afraid I have to agree with that sentiment," a new voice said.

Everyone turned to see a beautiful woman in leather stepping gingerly through the open window. She had long dark hair and pale skin, with a strong, clear face. She wore a leather jacket over a corset that was set with steel. Thigh-high boots and long opera gloves completed the picture. From her belt hung a single-tail whip and a flogger.

Severin had been so wrapped up in what was going on, he hadn't felt her approach. As soon as he saw her he felt his heart race and his desire grow. Her familiar dominant energy swept across the room, matching his own submissive energy until they fit together like a Yin/Yang symbol.

"Viscountess," he breathed, his voice a reverential whisper.

Clown Queen felt his cock rise against her hand. "Hey, what's she got that I don't have?"

"Stay back, sister," Princess warned the Viscountess. "She means business."

"So do I." The Viscountess unclipped the single tail called Tears-Like-Rain from her belt. "She has something that belongs to me."

"The man?" Princess glanced at Severin as if noticing him for the first time. "If that's all you want, I can get you a dozen like him."

"I'm sure, but I rather need him."

"Hey, still got a hostage here!" Clown Queen gave him a painful squeeze. "If you two don't quit yakking, I'm gonna stick my hand up his ass and work him like a sock puppet."

"I'm sure he'd enjoy that, but business before pleasure." The Viscountess approached them, brandishing her whip.

"Take the right, I'll take the left." Princess put on a burst of speed, scooping up her rope as she raced past.

Clown Queen wasn't sure which way to turn. As she hesitated, Severin slipped from her grasp and threw himself to the floor at the feet of the Viscountess. Princess spun her lasso and caught both of Clown queen's wrists, pinning them together.

Once again Clown Queen gave a gasp and sank to the floor, landing heavily on her knees.

"Thank you for your assistance," Princess said to the Viscountess.

"No, thank you. You saved his life," Viscountess snapped her fingers and pointed to the Princess. "Slave, she's got sap on her boots. Get rid of it."

Severin immediately prostrated himself on the floor, bringing his face to the bright red leather boots. His tongue crept out to lap at the drops of sap. It was sticky and sweet, and some of it required sucking on the boot to get the sap off. A few inches away from him Clown Queen was slowly masturbating.

"Thank you, that was most kind." Princess gave a dazzling smile. "You two aren't from this world are you?"

"No, I'm afraid not. On our world things work a bit differently."

"There's something about your aura that attracts people from my universe. That's why those two singled him out. It can be very dangerous for people from your world, the Vanilla World, to travel here."

"He has a Safeword if he remembers to use it."

"Sounds like a certain Air Force major I know." Princess chuckled. Suddenly she swayed and Viscountess had to reach out and steady her.

"Are you all right?"

"I'll be fine. That aphrodisiac is powerful stuff."

"Maybe you should sit down."

"Perhaps I should fly you back to my island and we can explore the differences in our worlds."

"Um, that's incredibly flattering, but..."

Severin regretted that he was still on the floor cleaning the boots. He couldn't remember the last time the Viscountess was at a loss for words and he wished he could see the expression on her face.

"An important case has come up and I need his help," the Viscountess explained.

"Ah, then in your own world you are a superhero, too."

"Hardly, but we do try to help people whenever we can."

"Then I won't keep you."

Severin couldn't resist any longer, and looked up in time to see the two women kiss.

"You must come back to my world sometime." Princess raised her boot, wet with his saliva and wiped it across Severin's face. "And do bring your slave. He seems delightfully submissive."

"I promise I shall."

The Viscountess slapped her thigh twice and Severin heeled, crawling next to her as she headed for the door. Severin saw Princess drag Clown

Queen over to where her partner lay in a tangle of vines.

"It's time I taught you two the art of loving submission," Princess informed her captives.

Outside the nightclub the police had cordoned off a large area, keeping the crowd back with police cars and wooden sawhorses. The reporters in the crowd began snapping pictures as soon as they appeared. At home, a naked man and a leather clad woman would have been practically invisible with the Blindfold hiding them from anyone who wasn't kinky. Here in the Dominions there was no Blindfold. The reporters just assumed they were a new superhero team and started calling out questions immediately. One of them wanted to know what the Viscountess' name was. Another asked if she were planning any other team-ups.

Inside the cleared area made by the police sat a cart pulled by a woman wearing only a leather body harness. She gave a snort of happiness at the sight of Severin and the Viscountess and stamped one foot.

"You owe her at least a half an hour of oral sex," the Viscountess informed him. She removed the last shreds of his clothing and replaced it with his collar, ankle and wrist cuffs. "We've been searching for you for hours."

The feel of the leather on his body sent a wave of deep and passionate submission through him. When she attached the leash he felt complete. Her dominant energy flowed down the leash into him.

"Honestly, Severin," the Viscountess teased. "I don't see how you get yourself into these situations."

"It wasn't easy," the slave admitted. "You only gave me three days' vacation. I had to use most of the time figuring out where they were going to strike so I could get captured. Fortunately, their MO is pretty simple, which is why they get caught so easily."

"I think those two enjoy getting caught almost as much as you."

"I was this close to learning what loving submission was when you interrupted."

"It looked more like you were close to singing soprano." The Viscountess gave him a gentle shove to the floor of the cart. "Unfortunately, it's back to the Real World for us. We have a client, and when I tell you who it is, you won't believe me."

Taking a towel from a small travel bag, the Viscountess wiped the sweat from the pony girl's face and pushed a sugar cube past her bit.

"Ready for one more jump, Blossom, back home?"

The pony girl snorted and tossed her head.

"Good girl." Viscountess checked the butt plug holding the pony tail in place and gave an affectionate pat on the tattoo of small flowers on the pony's thigh.

Once inside the cart the Viscountess took the reins in her gloved hands and snapped them smartly against the slave's shoulders. The pony slave trotted forward, the bells on her harness jingling.

As people in the audience snapped pictures with their cell phones, the pony cart accelerated. When the Viscountess brought the whip to bear, the slave increased her stride.

The space cleared by the police wasn't very big. They were going faster and faster, heading for a row of wooden sawhorses.

Just before they reached the barrier, the world seemed to blur and fade away. The uneven pavement under the wheels became a smooth surface. Lying on his back, Severin looked up to see the night sky change into a pearlescent grey.

With the cool wind of the void blowing in her face, the Viscountess leaned back in her seat and pressed her boot heels deeply into Severin's chest.

Chapter Two

Half an hour later Severin was kneeling in front of the couch with the long legs of the pony slave draped over his shoulders. He lapped up the sweat and sweet juice that flowed from her and sucked greedily on the tender flesh.

Once she was out of the pony headspace she seemed less like a horse and more like the college volleyball coach that she was in the rest of her life. Of course she was an extremely aroused volleyball coach, since it took a great deal of sexual stimulation to travel the void between Dominions. She'd been turned on all night, but probably hadn't been able to climax, even though the leather strap that passed between her legs must have driven her arousal continually higher.

Severin's experienced tongue tasted several layers where she had gotten wet, dried off, then gotten wet again. She was already flowing like a fountain as he ran his tongue up and down her labia.

The Viscountess sat in the large comfortable chair enjoying the sights and the sounds. They were back home now, not only in their own world, but in the elegant Boston brownstone she shared with her two slaves. Blossom the pony slave was on loan from the Duchess, who trained the finest dog and pony girls on her farm. Sadly, there just wasn't room in the city for the Viscountess to keep her own pony slave.

On the couch the slave shifted her weight and managed to slide a pillow under her ass, lifting herself up so Severin could get a better angle. The scent and the taste of her overwhelmed him, and he ignored the ache in his jaw and put his tongue to work again. From the way her flesh trembled he felt that he had already given her a few orgasms, but she wasn't satisfied, so neither was he.

The Viscountess sipped hot chocolate and rested her feet on the back of Sklavin, the strapping German beauty who was her house slave. Sklavin was on all fours wearing only her stockings and corset. Her large, pear-shaped breasts hung freely, the iron rings that pierced the nipples moving slightly as she breathed.

Blossom let out a low moan and she tightened her legs against

Severin's head, shutting off all sound. For a split second it felt like her powerful thighs would crack his skull, but she sighed and settled back into the couch.

"Are you satisfied?" Viscountess asked.

Severin murmured something that was lost in the flesh his face was buried in.

"I wasn't asking you, Severin."

"Yes, Viscountess." Blossom shifted her position to take pressure off her back. "Thank you for that."

"It was his pleasure, I assure you. Do you need some dinner?"

"No, Viscountess, just sleep."

"I'll have Sklavin show you to your room; it's on the second floor." The Viscountess gave Sklavin a kick, signaling her to rise. "Will you be returning to the stables?"

"No, Viscountess, I have some time off. A friend is going to pick me up tomorrow, if that's all right."

"Of course. I may not see you tomorrow. Just think of my house as yours, and give my love to your owner."

Blossom looked half asleep as Sklavin gently guided her towards the stairs. Severin twisted around on the floor, hands still held behind his back by the wrist cuffs. The scene with Blossom had brought back his erection, harder than ever.

"I see you've gotten hard again. I assume Blossom gave you permission for that," the Viscountess commented upon seeing him.

"No, Viscountess."

"I'm certain I didn't give permission."

"I'm sorry, Viscountess." Severin knelt, looking down at his own naked body, his stubborn cock showing no sign of getting any softer. "I was thinking perhaps you might be aroused by tonight's activities, and you might need me to..."

"Oh, I see, you got an erection just in case I might have need of it. Honestly Severin, you're so thoughtful," the Viscountess chuckled.

When Sklavin came back into the room the Viscountess pointed out the situation. The German slave looked at him and glared disapprovingly.

"We unfortunately have business to discuss tonight." The Viscountess glanced at her cup. "Would you like to finish my hot chocolate, Severin?"

"Yes. Thank you, Viscountess."

The Viscountess handed the cup to Sklavin. "Help him with this, my dear. I've noticed the whipped cream is gone, but I'm sure Severin will enjoy providing a substitute."

"Yes, Viscountess," Sklavin replied in her husky purr.

The German slave knelt next to Severin and grabbed his cock in one hand, holding the cup of hot chocolate in the other. She pumped him hard and painfully, several long strokes that made him come very quickly. Just as the semen began to appear, she dipped the head of his penis beneath the liquid. He gasped more in surprise than pain as he squirted his seed into the hot chocolate.

"There, that should aid your concentration." The Viscountess leaned back in her chair. "By now I'm sure you're dying to know who our client is."

"Yes, Viscountess." Sklavin didn't free his hands, but brought the cup to his lips, feeding him a little at a time. The Viscountess had enjoyed making him eat his own come ever since he admitted to her that he had a problem with that. It wasn't a hard limit—in fact it wasn't much of a limit at all, since he was getting quite used to it. The hot chocolate was delicious.

"Imagine if you will, the Executrix and I after making love are lying in bed, just the four of us, me, her, and two slaves, when suddenly there is a fifth person in the room. She was naked except for a mask, boots, and gloves."

Severin froze. It could only have been a Kamen Girl, the strange band of naked, masked mercenaries. Their powers were legendary and included the ability to leap from one dominion to another without using pony slaves or permanent gateways.

The first time he had seen a Kamen Girl she had nearly kidnaped him. He and the Viscountess eventually kept her from completing her mission by destroying a dangerous fetish object she had been hired to recover.

"The masked woman said that the leader of their order wishes to hire us. There will be two Kamen Girls meeting us in Victoria at one in the afternoon to take us to their headquarters. That's eight in the morning our time."

Severin swallowed more hot chocolate, then turned his head so he could talk.

"Why Victoria?" Severin asked.

"That's one of several questions I have. They seemed to prefer Victoria, and it's very convenient for us."

Severin nodded. There was a permanent Gateway to Victoria very close by. They had gone through it several times in their most recent case.

"Do you think it's a trap?" The Viscountess asked, seeing the expression on his face.

"It's hard to say. They may still be angry at us, but if they can just appear in people's bedrooms, why would they bother to set traps?"

The Viscountess frowned. "What do you know about their home?"

"No one knows anything. Supposedly only Kamen Girls have ever been there."

"I checked with the Duchess when I picked up Blossom. None of her pony girls can find it, and she doesn't know anyone who can. Now, finish your chocolate and tell me everything you know about them."

Severin did as he was told. When he was done with the chocolate his arms were freed and he sat on the floor at her feet, mere inches away from her boots. The leather boots smelled even better than the chocolate.

"We know they're mercenaries who hire themselves out to the community for either money or favors. They have a reputation for being hard to beat." Severin vividly recalled the slim Japanese beauty in the red mask who had tried to grab him. She had been built like a fitness model and was as limber as a gymnast. "The group is all female, and until recently I thought that they were all Japanese."

"The one that I saw was clearly not ethnically Japanese. She was black."

"Apparently I was wrong about their ethnicity," Severin admitted. "We know for a fact that they travel the Dominions by opening a portal and stepping through. That's very different from how the pony slaves operate. A pony slave fades from one reality to another through the void. The Kamen Girls jump from one to Dominion to the next without passing through the void."

"Actually that sounds more efficient," the Viscountess pointed out.

"Not necessarily. Kamen Girls lack the precision of a pony. If you wanted to get from here to Paris, you could get a girl from Duchess and she could take you through the void and bring you back in Paris. The Kamen Girls can't do that sort of thing."

"One of them appeared in the Executrix's bedroom."

"I have a theory about that. I think they make up for their lack of control by manipulating the Blindfold. The same way Vanilla people can't see us when we do public scenes, the Kamens can't be seen unless they want to be seen. Sort of like kinky ninjas."

"That was an uninspired metaphor. You get three strokes for that."

"Thank you, Viscountess." Severin lowered his head. "Unfortunately the Kamen Girls value their secrecy. I haven't been able to find out any more than that."

"That's hardly satisfactory. We may be going into the lion's den tomorrow and we need every scrap of information we can get."

"We could always tell them no."

"Then we'd never know what they want. Unfortunately curiosity is one of my few vices. I'd like to hear what they have to say, and the chance to visit a secret private Dominion doesn't come along every day."

"I agree, Viscountess."

"I'm so glad." The Viscountess rose to her feet, unclipping the single tail known as Tears-Like-Rain. "I believe I promised you three. Head down, ass in the air."

"Yes, Viscountess."

Severin immediately moved into position, raising his hips to provide her with a clear target. He kept his legs spread, aware of how vulnerable he made the most sensitive part of his body. Tears-Like-Rain was one of the few whips that he truly feared, but he knew better than trying to defend himself from her punishment. She knew he wasn't deep enough into Subspace to get any pleasure from this.

The first stroke cut high on his right buttock. It was a clean, sharp pain that made him gasp a little. He was better prepared for the second stroke, and took it almost without a sound. For the third, she waited, letting the pain soak in and positioning herself. When it struck he jumped a little, almost leaving the floor. She had crouched down and put it just where the curve of his ass started, so close to his balls that he could feel the rush of air as the stiff leather struck.

Severin took a deep breath, allowing the pain to fully register. He could feel himself slipping deeper into Subspace, and knew that if she chose to continue the punishment he would be able to handle it better. She had only promised him three strokes, but the actual number was up to her, and he had no right to complain.

She seemed to read his mind and chuckled softly, dragging the leather across his back.

"More slave?"

"Yes, Viscountess," he replied, perhaps a little too eagerly.

"Up, on all fours."

He moved into position, keeping his gaze focused on the carpet. She walked around him and sent a blow across his shoulders. He shuddered with pain and heard the sound of clothing rustling. Before he could process the sound another blow came, followed by another. The pain swept through him with breathtaking speed.

Between blows he heard the distinct sound of leather garments being removed. Severin lost count of how many times the leather hissed across his flesh. Through the haze of pain he heard Sklavin re-enter the room.

"Up, kneel, face me," the Viscountess said. When he had gotten into position he saw that she was gloriously naked, the whip still dangling from her hand. "Sklavin, he still has chocolate on his cock, would you be a dear and take of that."

"Yes, Viscountess," Sklavin purred in her husky German accent. She put herself on the floor and sucked him into her mouth. Her clever tongue went to work on him with passionate enthusiasm.

The delicious pressure made Severin groan with pleasure. Just the sight of her head bobbing up and down was usually enough to arouse him, but as she continued to work, he noticed that he had not yet fully responded. When she knelt next to him Sklavin took him in her fist and began pumping, but he had barely managed half an erection.

"Something wrong, Severin?" The Viscountess asked. She sounded as if she were trying to keep from laughing.

"I'm sorry, Viscountess," Severin gasped. "I don't know what's wrong."

Actually he knew perfectly well what was wrong. The two comic book villains had worked him into a fever pitch. After that, being brought off into the hot chocolate was enough to leave him completely drained. He was in Subspace and very excited, but he wasn't quite able to demonstrate that physically yet.

"What's the matter, Severin, don't you find me attractive anymore?"

The Viscountess stepped closer to him, reaching down to touch herself. She was clearly aroused; moisture glistening as her fingers gently stroked the red lips of her labia. As the scent of her reached him he lost control, leaning forward to take her with his mouth. This earned him a hard slap across the face.

"I hardly think you've earned that privilege," she informed him coldly. She added something in German that sent Sklavin from the room.

In a few minutes the slave returned from the second floor bedroom with a dildo harness, some lube, and a familiar dildo. Severin recognized Penetrator, the sleek and powerful dildo that was one of the Viscountess' favorites. Often Severin had been on the receiving end of Penetrator, but he had a feeling that this night was going to be different.

He was ordered to lie on the floor after Sklavin had put the dildo harness on him. Penetrator was jutting upward with its base right next to his own cock. Its cruel hardness seemed to mock his limp flesh.

The Viscountess stood over him, letting him see every inch of her as she slowly bent her knees and lowered herself on to the dildo. A shudder of pleasure went through her as the cock slipped inside of her. Her pleasure reflected back on Severin, who squirmed under her. He reached up to touch her only to have Sklavin grab his wrists and lock the cuffs together. The cuffs were then attached to his collar, bending his arms across his chest. He couldn't touch her, or even feel her as she rode him, her face a mask of pleasure.

"Fuck me, slave," she growled, not even opening her eyes.

Without the use of his arms, Severin couldn't brace himself on the floor. The best he could do was try to catch his heels and drive his hips upward. The raw flesh on his shoulders and ass burned as he rubbed against the carpet. He saw her rocking back and forth as he thrust his hips and he knew that it was taking all his strength to drive the cock into her. He felt exhausted in seconds.

"I said fuck me!" The Viscountess raked her fingernails across his ribs. Severin moved his arms so his nipples would be available. She took advantage of them at once, grabbing and twisting. "Go on, pretend like you're man enough to fuck me!"

Her sneering words struck him hard. Severin whimpered and felt tears welling up in his eyes. Gritting his teeth with determination he thrust his hips up again and again. She laughed, crushing him down with her weight as Penetrator filled her entirely.

Sklavin reached around from behind, kissing her owner's cheek. Her hands reached around to stroke her and in a few seconds there was an orgasm that sent a wave of energy through Severin. He sank into her pleasure like a warm bath.

With her knees on the floor to take some of the weight, the Viscountess began riding him even harder, slamming into him. He tried to thrust up to match her movements, but she was fast and not yet tired.

Each time she rose up on the cock and slid back down her ass hit his erect penis.

Severin was surprised to discover he had a cock of his own. Her humiliation of him and the sight of her had done its job.

"I'm in the mood for a bit of double penetration," the Viscountess informed Sklavin.

The German slave grinned wickedly and reached down to manipulate his cock. Severin felt cold lube on his cock, then warm flesh sliding around him as the Viscountess lowered herself down on him. As she rocked back and forth he felt her sphincter tighten and release the base of his cock.

She was grinding down into him, twisting around cruelly as if there was no difference to her between the artificial penis and the real. Sklavin hugged her tightly, pressing herself against the Viscountess, the big, pierced clit pushing against the base of her Mistress's spine. The slave's hands reached around, still slick with lube, and began to stroke her mistress.

The faces of the two women, both wrapped in ecstasy floated before Severin. Forgetting his exhaustion he continued to thrust upward, trying to lift both women with only his pelvis. He was determined not to let them down, vowing to service both of them if it was the last thing he did.

Abruptly the Viscountess had a series of three orgasms that struck almost simultaneously. The force of her pleasure ran through Severin like an electric shock. Seconds later Sklavin squeezed her eyes shut and gave a soft cry. The power of her submissive orgasm trickled into the pool of feminine power generated by the Viscountess.

Severin continued to thrust upward, although his efforts were growing more and more feeble. His cock, now suddenly smaller, worked its way out of his owner's ass. He realized that he had gotten an orgasm of his own, but hadn't noticed it because he had been concentrating so hard on his mistress. The limp dick flopped back and forth, just inches from where Penetrator proudly held his ground.

Gradually the Viscountess slowed her movements. She smiled dreamily and leaned forward, catching her weight on her hands. She gave Severin a long, slow kiss, then rose majestically off the dildo.

"Thank you, my pets, that was quite satisfactory," she announced. "Sadly we have no more time for play. You have to shower and shave Severin, and we both need our sleep. Now clean me up."

As soon as Sklavin had freed his hands, Severin got to his knees, heading towards the pussy, still flushed with pleasure that peeked tantalizingly at him. The Viscountess clicked her tongue disapprovingly.

"Sorry Severin, that wasn't the part of me that you soiled." She patted her ass and smiled.

"Yes. Thank you, Viscountess."

The Viscountess stood, hands on her hips while the two slaves went to work. Sklavin got the plum job of cleaning out her pussy, while Severin was covering the rear. Not that he minded, of course. There was no part of her body that he didn't worship, but the sounds of her being licked by Sklavin were going to drive him crazy.

He shut his eyes, trying to block out all sensory input except for his tongue. He ran it up and down the crack, finally circling her asshole. Along with the ubiquitous lube, he could taste himself on her. As his tongue probed more deeply he was filled with the memory of being inside this perfect body only seconds ago. The pleasant thoughts made it possible for him to ignore some of the less pleasant things he was tasting inside of her.

The Viscountess shifted her weight back and forth, sometimes making it easier for one of them, and sometimes the other. Finally she took Sklavin by the hair and pressed her close. The slave's pierced tongue was hard at work and in a few seconds another, final orgasm rippled out, sending waves of power into the room. The energy washed off the walls, flowing back into the two slaves. Sklavin and Severin shuddered, giving soft sobs of submission at almost the same time.

The Viscountess clapped her hands for them to stop and turned to stride from the room, heading for the second floor bedroom.

Later Severin stood in the shower trying to remain as motionless as possible while Sklavin ran an antique straight razor over every inch of his body. He had already shaved his own face before entering the shower, but the Viscountess was very strict about keeping his body free from hair. It was a mark of ownership with her, since she hadn't tattooed or branded him.

It didn't help that every mark left by the whip throbbed and ached under the hot water. Just trying to stand still was a challenge.

Sklavin covered him with a layer of shaving crème and took her time razoring it off. She made sure to make it as excruciating as possible for him, reminding him about how only little boys had no hair. She shaved under his arms and teased his nipples with the cruel steel. By the time she got to his genitals he had actually gotten another erection. Severin looked down at the lump of flesh, buried under white foam as if he had no idea how that had happened.

"Too bad you didn't get that earlier," Sklavin teased, tapping his cock with the razor. "Maybe you could have gotten in her pussy instead of her ass. Her pussy was so delicious tonight."

"You're a cruel woman, Sklavin."

The crow's feet at the corners of her eyes crinkled as the mature slave smiled at him. She reached over and yanked the faucet, sending a blast of cold water across him. Instinctively Severin turned away from the icy stream, but that only exposed the welts on his ass and shoulders to the water. As he cried out and twisted under the brutal torrent she smiled smugly and folded her arms across her ample chest.

He withered quickly under the icy stream. When he had shrunk down completely Sklavin glanced at him and shrugged. "Now we continue with no shaving crème," she announced, bringing the straight razor to bear on him. "Please do not move, unless you'd like to lose something valuable."

Severin took a deep breath and managed to resist the urge to thank her for the punishment. Although they were both slaves, Sklavin was a woman and automatically superior to him in this household. Although she was very submissive, she had a dominant side and occasionally liked to show off. She couldn't possibly top him like the Viscountess, but he was too submissive to resist her.

Severin whimpered softly as she yanked on his limp cock and dragged the razor across it. Sklavin ignored him, humming softly while she worked.

An hour later Severin crawled into his owner's bedroom. His body was scrubbed and shaved—or to be accurate scraped—clean. He found that the Viscountess was already asleep.

He looked at her, face pressed into a pillow. He relished the opportunity to gaze at her for as long as he wanted. When they were in public he tried not to make too much eye contact with her, but now that she was asleep he could drink in every detail of her face.

Of course Severin thought about more than her face. The sight of a single breast, visible under the silk sheet reminded him that she was utterly naked. He thought about her, every inch of her.

Forcing himself to look away, Severin realized sheepishly that he had been staring at her for almost half an hour. With a sigh he turned off the lamp by the bed and curled up on the circle of carpet on the floor.

The welts that the Viscountess had given him were still pleasantly painful, but the irritated skin from the razor was another matter. The punishment hadn't been given to him by his owner, so he had a harder time dealing with it. Severin twisted around on the floor for several minutes before he finally fell asleep.

Chapter Three

The next morning Severin and the Viscountess were at the old brick building which housed the Gateway to the Dominion of Victoria. They were still buzzing with energy from the Scene the night before. Once inside, the Viscountess glanced at the grandfather clock and did some quick calculations. The clock was set to Victoria time, which was the same as London in the Real World, and it read noon. They had an hour until their meeting.

They were greeted by Tiffany, a tall brunette transvestite who curtsied and smiled at the sight of them.

"Good afternoon, Viscountess. It's so good to see you again. Why, it's been nearly a month." Tiffany was a picture of feminine beauty, blurred only by a slightly husky voice and Adam's apple.

"It's good to see you, Tiffany. I'm afraid I'm here on business again. We have an appointment in an hour."

The Viscountess had worn a leather cat suit, with her usual tools hanging from the belt. To better fit with the spirit of the Dominion they were visiting, she elected to wear a greatcoat over the outfit. After Tiffany draped the coat over her shoulders and buttoned it, the Viscountess looked the picture of swashbuckling elegance.

"You look superb, Viscountess. And for you, slave?"

"Nothing. He will be naked, of course."

"An excellent choice."

The two women laughed while the Viscountess removed all her electronic devices and left them in a tray. Holding her cell phone in her hand she glanced over at Severin.

"Perhaps Victoria wasn't just chosen for its convenience. We can't take photographs or record anything."

Severin nodded. The same thought had occurred to him. "Perhaps that's how they keep their secret headquarters a secret."

A few minutes later they had stepped through the gate and were walking down a street that was a replica of London in the 1890s. Of course it had a great deal more naked people than the real London. Historians would also point out that it smelled a great deal better than the real thing, too. In this reality there was zero chance to catch typhus or any venereal disease since they didn't exist.

The Viscountess made her way across the busy sidewalk to the curb where she caught the eye of a passing cabbie. The hansom cab was pulled by a strapping pony boy, the bell in his Prince Albert piercing making a dull clang as it slapped against his bare thigh.

"Where to, Ma'am?" The cabbie tipped his hat.

The Viscountess gave an address in Limehouse which made the driver stare.

"Oh, I wouldn't go there if I were you, Ma'am. Even in broad daylight that place is dangerous."

"Unfortunately, I have a meeting."

"Even so, you must watch your step. If them heathens get a look at a white woman like you they might not be able to control themselves."

"I shall have to take my chances," the Viscountess said breezily. "Besides, I have Severin to protect me."

"Ha, that's even worse. Them slant-eyed witches get their hands on him, they know things to do to a man that will have him screaming like a dammed soul."

Severin looked eagerly at the Viscountess, but she dashed his hopes with a glare.

"Business before pleasure. Now get in the cab."

The hansom cab made its way through the streets of London heading for the waterfront and Limehouse, London's notorious Chinatown. In the real London, Limehouse was a slum about two blocks long, but in Victoria every salacious rumor was true and the neighborhood filled several blocks of dark twisting alleys filled with opium dens and brothels stocked by white slaves.

The Viscountess glanced down at Severin who was trying to make himself comfortable on the floor of the cab despite the bumpy ride.

"Did you enjoy your little session with Sklavin last night?" she asked casually.

Severin glanced guiltily at his naked body, wondering what had given him away.

"Yes, Viscountess," he admitted.

"I couldn't help but notice that you had a touch of razor burn. I need you in top form today, not distracted. I'm sure you know that I didn't give my permission for any more punishment."

"Yes, Viscountess." Severin hung his head, knowing Sklavin was now going to be punished just because they had been having fun in the shower.

"Relax Severin." She gave him a playful kick. "I just need you to focus today. We have no way of knowing what to expect from this case."

"I'll do my best."

"I have no doubt that you will."

The Viscountess rested her feet on his shoulder. Severin turned his head to press a kiss into the sole of her boot.

They were deposited in front of the Jade Pagoda, a rather disreputable-looking bar.

"It doesn't look open," Severin commented.

"I'm told that it never closes."

"You've been here before?"

"Sadly, no." The Viscountess shook her head. "When I trained in Victoria I never got to Limehouse, but even then this place had a reputation."

Inside the bar was dark and dingy. The air stank of opium and hashish. It was clearly still being cleaned from the night before. A slender white woman wearing only a shift was in the process of sweeping the floor. She startled as they entered.

"You shouldn't be here." The woman glanced around nervously.

Before the Viscountess could answer, there was a clicking sound as a Chinese woman walked through a beaded curtain. The woman with the broom lowered her eyes and hurriedly went back to sweeping.

The newcomer was tall and willowy, encased in a very tight silk dress that showcased her body with expert style. Long blue-black hair cascaded all the way to her waist like an inky waterfall. Her face was a perfect mask that looked as if it had been carved from ivory. Beneath her bangs, jade green eyes considered the Viscountess and Severin as if they were merchandise on display that she was considering buying.

"I am Pain Toy," the woman announced. Her voice dripped like honey. Severin resisted the urge to drop to his knees, but he did shuffle closer to his owner. "It is rare for us to have visitors this early. Perhaps you have come to experience the thirty-three vermillion gates of ecstasy?"

"Sadly, no, we've come to meet with someone. Have you seen anyone with a mask this afternoon?"

"Yes, of course, they are in one of our private rooms." Pain Toy made an elegant gesture to an unassuming door near the bar.

"Then I'm afraid we must be going. It's been a pleasure meeting you." The Viscountess spoke pleasantly. Pain Toy had a dominant manner but had not yet raised any of her energy. It was impossible to tell how powerful she was, but she had Severin shivering with her voice alone.

"Perhaps next time you can be persuaded to stay longer." Pain Toy gave a mocking half smile.

"Perhaps."

The two dominant women exchanged bows. As Pain Toy turned away she noticed the woman with the broom. Raising one arm casually Pain Toy revealed that the tips of each of her fingers was encased in long, sharp claws of gold. When she lowered her arm the gold claws caught in the neck of the woman's shift, tearing it all the way down. The flimsy material fell to the floor, leaving the woman naked.

The woman hugged the broom to herself, as if the thin wood could hide any part of her. She lowered her head, the unwashed hair falling across her face. Pain Toy glanced at her, then turned to the Viscountess.

"This creature was like you once, so proud, so confident she could not be broken. I managed to change her mind."

The exquisite face of the Chinese woman slipped into a whiplash sneer as she turned and went back through the beaded curtain with a sensuous, almost serpentine grace.

As they headed to the door, Severin glanced back at the swinging beads.

"I'm sure she's a sweet, innocent girl at heart," he murmured.

"You're incorrigible, Severin," the Viscountess teased. "Perhaps next time you can get a look at her vermillion gate."

The door led to a hallway with several openings on each side of the wall. The doorways had curtains to provide some privacy in the small rooms. In the first room they saw a huge Asian man who was stripped to the waist snoring on a low cot. The distinct sound of two people making love came from the next room.

Standing in the doorway they saw two figures entwined on a cot trying to wiggle a double ended dildo into themselves. They were so lost in their work that they didn't notice the Viscountess and Severin. They were wearing nothing but boots, belts, gloves, and their full head masks. With their trim, well-muscled bodies they looked like the sexiest Mexican wrestlers ever.

They were definitely not Asian. One of them was pale and slender with legs like a dancer and a blonde ponytail coming out of a hole in her mask. The other was slightly heavier with darker skin and full breasts. It was impossible to guess her exact ethnicity.

Seeing two Kamen girls side by side for the first time, the Viscountess noticed that both their masks were unique. The blonde had a burnt orange colored mask, while the other was a deep purple. In addition, the mouth and eye holes had different shapes. Neither mask matched the red one she'd seen on the first Kamen Girl. Did each of them have a unique mask, or did the different types signify ranks in their order?

Suddenly realizing they had an audience, the two women broke apart, the blonde making a little squeak of surprise.

"Don't stop on my account," the Viscountess smiled.

"Sorry, we were just—" the darker skinned Kamen Girl started.

"Trying to become aroused?"

Ponytail nodded. "We have to be turned on to take you back to our Dominion."

"So you have your own Dominion?" The Viscountess asked conversationally.

"Very few outsiders see it," the blonde explained. "We can take you there as soon as we, um..."

She broke off and glanced at her fellow Kamen Girl.

"Perhaps we can be of some assistance?" The Viscountess offered.

"You don't have to," the darker woman protested.

"Nonsense, Severin will be more than happy to lend you a hand." The Viscountess assured them. "Besides, we don't want this to take all day."

The Viscountess snapped her fingers and pointed at the cot. Severin immediately dropped to his knees and approached the two women. When they didn't tell him to stop, he took the long dildo and began to twist it around, sliding it first into one woman and then the other.

The double ended dildo was an instrument that worked better in theory than in practice. Since this one was made without modern materials it was even harder to work with. At least there was plenty of lube.

The Kamen Girls seemed a little surprised that Severin was so eager to help them. After a few seconds of him sliding the dildo gently in and out of both of them, they sighed and settled in next to each other. Pressing their masked faces together they shared a deep kiss.

After a few minutes a shimmering portal appeared in the air. The blonde Kamen Girl slipped off the dildo and got to her feet.

"If you'll just come with me please. Take my hand and whatever you do, don't let go."

She reached out and took the hand of the Viscountess. They took two steps together and were gone. The portal folded in on itself and was gone.

A second portal appeared just as they vanished. The dark-skinned Kamen Girl got to her feet.

"So what happens if I let go?" Severin asked her.

"Just don't." The purple-masked woman grabbed his wrist with one hand, and took his forearm with her other hand in case he slipped away from her. She walked backwards into the portal and Severin stumbled forward.

There was no feeling of travel or the slight tingling of passing through a Gate. Severin took a step forward and suddenly everything was different. The air was wrong, the light was wrong, even the gravity was off.

Pulling himself free from the Kamen Girl, Severin turned and looked back the way he had come. He knew he wouldn't see the bar in Limehouse, but he was unprepared for what he did see. There was a rocky plain behind him that went for about a hundred feet, then dropped off. The land literally came to an end where there was a translucent barrier of some kind. Beyond the barrier was the shimmering endless void between Dominions. Apparently this Dominion was so small that its edges showed.

Looking the other direction Severin realized that there were much more interesting things to see. For instance, there was the huge ziggurat of glass and stone that loomed up in front of him. Above the stepped pyramid, a reddish sun hung in the sky.

The area between them and the ziggurat looked like slave girl boot camp. Trails wove between obstacle courses and gym equipment. On one side naked women crawled through the mud trying to pass under wires strung low to the ground. They had to practically bury themselves in the mud to get under them. As Severin watched, one woman's ass brushed the wire. There was a shower of sparks and a high scream as the woman drove herself deeper into the mud.

There were three lines of naked women in front of benches that had a series of dildos jutting up from them. Each of the dildos was larger than the next. The women had to straddle the bench, lowering themselves onto the shafts until they were in all the way, then move on to the next dildo. From the way everyone was cheering and clapping it was obviously a race between the three teams. Masked women encouraged them with blows from bamboo staffs and provided lubricant for the dildos.

"This must be the place," the Viscountess commented as she watched a woman twisting around, trying to impale herself on a sizable dildo.

"Do you notice the trainees don't have masks?" Severin pointed out. "They don't even have boots or gloves."

"Apparently you earn your mask here." The Viscountess turned to ask a question of the pair who had brought them there, but both women had dropped to one knee and had their heads bent.

Severin saw what the Kamen Girls had seen and pointed it out to the Viscountess. In the distance, from the base of the ziggurat, a litter was borne on the shoulders of four Kamen Girls. The litter had an awning which hid its occupant.

As the litter drew closer they admired the women who carried it, four women who jogged in an easy rhythm. Although every Kamen Girl they had seen had been in good physical condition, these four were in a class by themselves. They looked like they'd just stepped off the stage of a woman's bodybuilding competition. Sweat rolled off of their rock-hard bodies.

The sight of the litter being carried on their shoulders made Severin think of something. He picked up a rock and experimentally tossed it. The stone fell to the ground with a thump.

"All right Severin, what have you found?"

"I think the gravity here is slightly higher than the earth. Also there's less oxygen in the air."

"Is that good or bad?"

"It's good for them. This is a perfect place for physical training. They get used to the higher gravity so they'll feel light on their feet on Earth. The low oxygen makes their cardiovascular system work more efficiently, giving them a lot of energy. Of course it's bad for their visitors. Under these conditions running up a flight of stairs would feel like a marathon for us."

"I'll keep that in mind."

The four women came to a halt and dropped to their knees. They gently laid the litter on the ground. The woman in the great chair atop the litter slowly rose to her feet. She was using a staff to stand, but there was a majestic grace about her.

Like the others she was virtually naked, but the body she revealed was far different from what they had seen. The hair streaming from beneath her faded mask and the tuft of hair between her legs was snow white. Her body appeared not so much aged as weathered. Her muscles seemed like valleys and crags carved by the wind. Thin blue veins marked her the way a river marks a map. The only part of her that seemed frail were her breasts, which were long and thin, hanging down to her ribs.

Severin found her oddly fascinating. She was clearly old enough to be his grandmother, but she was a woman of power and confidence which naturally attracted him. He swayed on his feet, feeling the urge to kneel. The Viscountess noticed this and took his leash, giving it a soft tug, bringing him to the ground.

Supported by her staff the old woman came forward. Behind the mask, her clear sharp eyes took in the two visitors.

"I am known as The Crone," she said.

"I am the Viscountess, and this is Severin."

The Crone bowed slightly to the Viscountess, who returned the bow. The elderly Kamen Girl held out her boot and allowed Severin to kiss it.

"I'm glad that you have come. Please follow me to the Hanging Garden where we may speak freely."

The Crone turned from them and began walking towards the ziggurat. Despite her staff and the higher gravity, she made very good time. The Viscountess pulled Severin to his feet and the two of them had to scramble to keep up. The four bodybuilders and the two Kamen Girls who had brought them over stayed behind, kneeling as still as statues.

As they walked, they saw a group of naked women jogging the perimeter of the Dominion. They ran in a line next to the cliff that marked the edge of their world, their arms pinned behind their backs, wrists tied to the opposite elbow.

That must make thirty women we've seen here in training, Severin thought. With all that manpower, what on earth did they need the Viscountess for?

Separated from the training grounds by a stone wall, the Hanging Garden turned out to be a grove of trees with long gnarled branches. From the branches hung numerous women bound with rope in intricate patterns that sank deeply into their flesh. They were eerily silent, swaying only slightly, like huge fruit.

They hung like ornaments from trees, some high and some lower. When The Crone walked down the path she pushed one of the women, deliberately making her swing into another captive. That woman swung into another and another, setting off a chain reaction.

"It's a specialized form of shibari," The Crone explained. "The ropes constrict a series of pressure points that place them in a deeply meditative state, as well as making them wet."

She patted between the legs of one woman where the rope sank deeply between her pink lips. The woman moaned softly, but her eyes were glassy, oblivious to everything around her.

Severin pondered if this was the sort of meditation that helped the Kamen Girls stay in a semi-aroused state and channel their energy into teleportation. He was pondering so hard that he failed to notice a taut ass that swung into the side of his head, knocking him off balance.

"Steady on Severin, we're not out of the woods yet." The Viscountess pulled on his leash, keeping him on his feet.

The center of the Hanging Garden was a perfectly mundane flower garden. Bees hummed as they went from one flower to another and birds splashed in a stone fountain. In a circle of mosaic tiles there was a simple stone bench. Next to the bench there was a woman wearing a black mask highlighted by gold.

The woman had a lean, well-muscled body with small, firm breasts. Hair the same color as her mask streamed out below the leather hood. From the golden brown tone of her skin and the glimpse of her eyes through the hood, Severin thought she might have been Asian. She was standing at attention while The Crone approached, then stepped forward.

"Grandmother, I must ask that you reconsider this." She glanced at the Viscountess and Severin. "You cannot bring outsiders into this."

"We have discussed this. The decision has been made." The Crone glared at the other masked woman.

"You can't—"

"Enough!"

The Crone suddenly no longer needed the staff for support. As she straightened there was a swell of dominant energy that flowed from her towards the woman in the black mask. The other woman gave a little gasp and swayed. She looked as if she were trying to summon her own dominant energy to counter the power washing over her.

Whatever she was trying, it didn't work. The power of The Crone was not to be denied. A tiny sob escaped the black mask. The woman's body trembled. Her nipples were stiff and drops of moisture appeared in the triangle of black pubic hair. As if in slow motion, her legs bent and she went down, finally kneeling before The Crone.

Severin felt his cock harden with a suddenness that was almost painful. He was suddenly mesmerized by The Crone's deeply lined flesh, her pendant breasts, and found himself sinking to his knees.

When the Viscountess felt Severin go down, she tightened her grip on his leash. Her own power flowed down the leash into him, bolstering his strength. He could not kneel without her permission, and that knowledge gave him the strength to regain his composure.

"You overstep your authority, woman." The Crone savaged the younger woman with her glare. "You will not argue with your elders. Now you will do penance."

"Yes, Grandmother." Her voice was shaky.

"Place both thumbs inside yourself as deeply as they will go."

The black masked woman hesitated, which made The Crone stamp her staff on the paving stones. The other woman jumped and gasped as if she had been struck. She brought her trembling hands down between her legs and began working her thumbs into her dripping pussy. Her arms were stretched across her chest, squeezing her breasts together. Tears streamed from the eyeholes in her mask and her humiliation hung like a cloud around her.

The Crone left her like that and turned to sit on the stone bench. Severin felt a spark of power as she glanced at him and knew that she was fully aware of the effect her power had on him.

"Please forgive the interruption," The Crone went on. "We find our-selves faced with a crisis that is unique in our history. As you can see the course ahead is not clear and there has been some dissension."

The Viscountess nodded. She glanced at Severin to make sure his head was clear. Satisfied with what she saw, she made a circular motion with one hand. Severin dropped to all fours, taking a position behind her. The Viscountess took a seat on him, sinking her full weight on his shoulders and resting a hand on the back of his head.

"I hope that we can be of some assistance." The Viscountess spoke pleasantly. "You must understand that we know very little about your organization. The single encounter we had with one of your number was somewhat unpleasant."

"It was unpleasant for her as well." The Crone gave a thin smile.

"She tried to kidnap Severin."

"She made a mistake. She failed to kidnap him, and you prevented her from fulfilling her mission."

"I did more than that, I saved her life. If it wasn't for me, she'd be a urinal right now."

"She has been punished for her failure." There was a sharpness in The Crone's voice and a bit of her dominant power flared.

"I'm sure you haven't gone to all this trouble just to talk about the past," the Viscountess said coolly, crossing her legs. She felt Severin tense and relax beneath her as she shifted her weight,

"Indeed not, we face a grave crisis."

"What sort of crisis could you possibly have that your people couldn't handle?" The Viscountess glanced around at the dozens of women hanging like ripe fruit all around them.

The Crone lowered her head a moment before answering.

"We are powerful, it is true. We are also a very proud organization. A crime has been committed that strikes at the very heart of who we are. It threatens our very existence."

"I see," the Viscountess said, trying to draw her out.

It was obvious this wasn't coming easily to the old woman. She leaned on her staff even though she was sitting down.

"There is an object of great power. It is what enables us to pass from one world to another without being pony slaves. This object has been stolen by one of our sisterhood."

Kneeling, her thumbs still thrust deep inside herself, the black mask woman stiffened. Even in the depths of her submission, she still resented the secret coming out.

"Is this a Fetish item?"

"Not in the way that you mean. It is not a whip or a dildo. It is the living heart of what makes us Kamen Girls."

The Viscountess felt Severin's muscles tense beneath her and knew that he was following every word with interest.

"I don't want to be disrespectful." The Viscountess chose her words very carefully. "You are a secret order and I respect your right to secrecy. Now you tell me your most sacred item has been stolen and you want me to recover it."

"That is so."

"Then you must know that you have no choice but to tell me everything. There is nothing in the world more intrusive than a criminal investigation. If I am to proceed than it must be all or nothing."

"If I agree to tell you everything, do you agree to return to us that which has been lost?"

"Before I answer I must know why you have sent for me. You have an army of powerful women at your disposal. What do you expect me to do that they can't?"

The Crone chuckled and spread her arms to take in the hanging women in the garden.

"The ones that you have seen are still in their early stages of training. It would be fortunate if five or six of them proved worth enough to don a mask and join our order."

"And the ones who have their masks?"

"I could flatter you by saying that they lack your wisdom and experience."

"I'd prefer the truth."

The Crone sighed again.

"At the present time there are very few of us who know what has happened. Call it vanity or pride, but I wish to keep the theft from as many of our order as possible. I would hate for them to know how foolish their elders have been."

"I can't guarantee to keep your secrets. When I investigate I must be free to ask questions and follow where the answers lead."

"I suppose I can do nothing but rely on your discretion."

"I'll try and cause you as little trouble as possible. It goes without saying that anything I learn will be kept in strictest confidence. I have never betrayed a client's secrets."

"If I didn't know your reputation you would not be here. I take it you speak for your slave as well?"

"Severin would no more betray me than my right hand would betray my left." She patted his ass familiarly.

"So be it." The Crone planted her staff and rose to her feet. "I suppose I have no choice but to tell you everything."

Chapter Four

They left the garden and walked a stone path towards the glass and stone ziggurat. The Crone moved fast enough that the Viscountess and Severin had to work to keep up. The black masked Kamen girl was allowed to remove her thumbs and follow them, which she did, keeping her head meekly lowered. Before she lowered her gaze Severin caught a glimpse of her eyes and knew that she still resented them. Somehow the woman blamed the Viscountess and Severin.

They passed many flowers and a water garden where a bound woman meditated while water cascaded over her head. The flowers seemed to be tended by novices who were supervised by older, possibly retired Kamen Girls.

"Our order is open to women only," The Crone explained. "Both those who are born women and those who come into their womanhood later in life. We accept women from many different lands."

"Until recently I thought you were all Japanese." The Viscountess said.

"A natural mistake. Our founder was from Neo-Nihon and the name Kamen means mask in Japanese."

Severin noticed that not only were they not all Japanese, they weren't all trim, athletic martial artists either. One of the women who came by pushing a wheelbarrow filled with transplanted flowers was definitely on the heavy side. Her massive breasts hung down to the rolls of her stomach. Her mask was white with a pattern of green vines running across it.

"Are you a religious order?" Viscountess asked The Crone.

"We consider ourselves a spiritual order, but we follow no religious path. We seek to empower women, to bring out their strengths. The sacrifices are great. They lose their homes, their names, their faces and must remain naked for the rest of their days. We hide nothing, conceal nothing."

"Except your faces."

"It symbolizes the loss of self. The old face is replaced with a new one that becomes one's true face. All else is naked, for we have no fear of exposing ourselves. We conceal nothing, those that hire us know that we have no secrets when we venture into the worlds."

"You said many of your trainees fail?"

"Yes. We are brutal and uncompromising, but there is no shame in failure. We send the candidate home after a simple ceremony that lightens the burden of their memory."

"You erase their memory?" the Viscountess snapped.

"Not erased. We merely soften the details. If our enemies felt a failed novice could reveal our secrets they would be targets. It's for their safety as much as ours."

A thought occurred to Severin. He jostled the leash, making the Viscountess glance at him. When she saw the intention on his face, she nodded, giving him permission to speak.

"Is that why no pony slave can come here? A pony can return to any Dominion they've ever visited. You've never brought a pony slave here, and your students have had their memories, um, softened."

"It's true," The Crone admitted testily. "No pony slave can find our location. Those students who might get pony training after leaving us find they cannot remember enough to make their way back."

"You talk as if there were no gateways to this world." Severin went on.

"There are none. This world was formed from the ether by the sheer will of our founding members. It can only be reached by the power of the Kamen Girls."

"Then we're trapped here until one of you takes us home."

"You are not trapped." The Crone sputtered in anger. "We would not do that."

The Viscountess stepped neatly between the two.

"He's being intolerably rude, and I'll make sure he's punished for it," the Viscountess said with a smile. "But he has brought up an interesting point."

"This is our home, not a prison. If you wish to leave at any time I or one of my sisters can open a portal for you."

"I apologize if he insulted you. Each Dominion has its own rules and it's important that we understand them."

"Of course." The Crone sighed and spread her arms, encompassing everything. "When it was made there was nothing here. All of it had to be built or bought with the fees paid for our services. To build our pyramid, stone was brought here and put into place with our own hands."

Severin had a brief erotic vision of sweating masked women

dragging massive blocks of stone into place like Egyptian slaves while The Crone cracked a whip over them. Apparently the Viscountess sensed what he was thinking, for she gave him a sharp stomp on the foot to snap him back to reality.

The open front of the ziggurat was supported by massive pillars. As they entered Kamen Girls scurried past trying not to stare at the strangers in their most private sanctuary. They were too well trained to stare or ask questions.

"I've noticed each mask is very different," the Viscountess said, trying to start the conversation again.

"No one can control the face they are born with, but if they pass their tests they gain a new face, which they are allowed to choose. We have leather smiths to make the masks, boots, and gloves, but often they prefer to make their own. Usually the new name and the new face they gain match each other."

Moving deeper into the structure they passed a small alcove where a woman lay on her back on a stone slab, her legs widely spread and chained to the ceiling. Her legs had been drawn up so high that only her shoulders and head were on the slab. Candles had been inserted into both her pussy and ass. The candle in her ass pointed straight up, its wax slowly dripping down into her the valley between her cheeks. The candle in her pussy was at an angle, sending the burning wax across her belly. A masked woman stood nearby with a cane in her hand.

"What is the slave nature of the candle?" the masked woman asked.

"I don't know," the woman gasped.

Her instructor gave her a series of sharp blows on the soles of her feet with the cane. She cried out and squirmed, causing more wax to cascade across her.

"I've always found the Kamen Girls to be rather dominant, but I noticed your training consists of a great deal of submission," the Viscountess pointed out.

"To be a Kamen Girl means you have won the right to define yourself by your own terms. We are dominant and submissive. We are what we need to be to accomplish our goals."

In the alcove the training continued.

"Does the flame not dominate the candle?" the trainer asked.

"Yes." The woman replied only after she had gotten a cane stroke to the soles of her feet.

"Then what is the slave nature of the candle?"

"The candle submits to the flame and is consumed by it."

"What does the submission produce?"

"Light and heat," the woman guessed, looking across her naked body at the twin flames.

"And?"

"I don't know."

That response earned her three very hard strokes on her ass. Severin whimpered in sympathy. With her legs stretched like that the skin would be pulled tight and he knew how much it would hurt. She gave a little scream and despite her bondage she jumped so hard that the candles sent wax cascading across her flesh.

The masked woman carefully broke off each candle from the wax that held it in place. She brought the flames low across the naked flesh, sending a rain of hot wax down.

"Light, heat, and pain." The instructor concluded. "True submission always produces light, heat, and pain. Your slave nature is the same as that of the candle. Your submission provides the light of wisdom, the heat of your passion and pain, it is always painful to truly submit."

The group moved on. They descended a gently curving spiral staircase carved from stone.

"When they have passed all their trials the novices have earned the right to come here, to enter the sacred heart of our temple." As The Crone spoke she descended the stairs, taking her time with them. The Viscountess slowed to match her pace.

At the bottom of the stairs they faced a sealed doorway. The room was lit by torches on the walls. The Crone reached up gently and touched a hand to the cheek of the woman in the black mask.

"Child, do you know why I humbled you earlier?" The Crone asked.

"Because I questioned your orders?"

"No child, I love you too much for that." The Crone leaned over and gently kissed the leather clad cheek. "Think about why I humbled you."

The woman in the black mask hesitated. She opened her mouth, then closed it again before answering.

"Because my pride means nothing compared to the crisis we face."

"Indeed." The Crone beamed at her then turned to the Viscountess and Severin. "I wanted Black Masque here to tell you the rest of it. She is our greatest expert at creating portals. On a good day she could take you to a dozen different Dominions in the time it would take you to harness a pony slave."

You could take us there and strand us, Severin thought. He had nearly been kidnapped by a Kamen Girl and was still a little leery.

"So they call you Black Masque?" The Viscountess asked casually, running her eyes up and down the taut, golden-brown body.

"Yes, Viscountess. Most of us wind up with names based on our masks." She gestured to indicate the leather hood covering her face as if somehow it hadn't been noticeable before.

"Are you the only one with a black mask?"

"No, there are others. There aren't that many colors to go around," she admitted. "But the gold highlights are mine, and others must call themselves something else."

She seemed proud of both her mask and her name. The Viscountess wondered if the Kamen Girls ever fought over their colors or titles.

"Our powers..." Black Masque began to speak, but hesitated. "It's very hard to explain."

"Start at the beginning. Tell them everything." The Crone spoke sharply, a hint of her dominant energy rising to the surface.

Black Masque stood with her legs open and her arms behind her back in almost the military parade rest stance.

"You need to understand that part of our origin is in myth, so bear with me. The first Kamen girl and her companions were all trained pony slaves from Neo-Nihon. They were tired of being used as mere transportation, and liked to explore. One day they found this Dominion. We like to say that they formed it from sheer force of will, but it might be that it had been recently abandoned when they found it."

The Viscountess nodded. There were a lot of theories as to exactly how Dominions were formed and as far as she was concerned one theory was as good as another. Philosophy was Severin's department.

"They wanted to form a sisterhood, a powerful order of women. They recruited from all across the Dominions, but since most of their recruits weren't pony slaves they spent a lot of time ferrying them in and out. They knew to be successful they had to find a new way to travel."

She broke off again. As she reached the heart of her story the words were coming more slowly.

"As we talk we can walk the Path." The Crone gestured to the door, which slid open revealing a narrow, dimly lit hallway. "For those who have passed their training this is the final test. They must walk the Path and face traps as well as surprise attacks. For today I think we can dispense with the challenges."

The Crone passed through the door and the three of them followed. The hallway twisted about and turned as they walked. The Viscountess instinctively kept track of the turns as if she worried about getting lost.

"It's a labyrinth, not a maze," Severin whispered to her. "There is only one path with no dead ends."

If the two Kamen Girls had heard him they didn't answer. The Viscountess spoke up to fill the silence.

"So they were seeking a new way to travel?"

Black Masque nodded. "In some distant Dominion they found a spell or ritual and constructed a hollow crystal globe."

"We call it the Sphere," The Crone added. "To embrace the Sphere is the final test of a Kamen Girl."

"What did they do with the Sphere?"

"As the founder grew old she somehow passed a portion of herself into the Sphere at the time of her death. As each of the founders reached the end of their lives they did the same. It was filled with wild energy. Those who touched it felt as if they were receiving powerful electric shocks, but they also discovered that they could open up portals to other Dominions. It was like the power of a pony slave, yet different."

"We leap from one Dominion to another without passing through the void." The Crone confirmed what Severin had guessed. "We merely have to visualize the Dominion to open a door there."

"And be aroused," the Viscountess added, remembering the pair on the cot in Victoria.

"Yes, of course, we must all be aroused to achieve our goals." The Crone chuckled.

"Does your power have any limitations?" The Viscountess asked.

"Our method of travel lacks precision," Black Masque admitted. "And we find it very difficult to reach the Real World, despite its central location."

The Viscountess noted that they said nothing about making themselves invisible, although she was fairly certain that Severin had been right about that as well.

The winding path finally reached a wall. The way was blocked by a massive circle of stone that was carved like a Mayan calendar. A Kamen Girl was bound across it, her arms and legs spread wide, held with heavy iron staples at the wrists, ankles, waist and neck. It looked as if the metal had been driven into the stone and she had been there for years, but that didn't seem likely. Beneath the mask her eyes were half closed. She made no sound, no motion, as if she were unaware of their presence.

"As with all things it is pleasure that is the key, pleasure and pain." The Crone spoke knowingly. She struck Black Masque behind the knees, sending her to the floor. The younger woman knelt awkwardly, her body stiff. It looked as if she was going to resist, but the dominant energy of The Crone was too much for her.

As Black Masque's body relaxed Severin sank to his knees, his cock beginning to swell. The Crone ran her staff up and down the firm body of the younger woman. When she raised the staff and brought it down sharply on Black Masque's ass the sound of wood smacking against flesh filled the small stone chamber. Severin felt his cock twitch with each blow.

"No man has ever served the pleasure of the guardian," The Crone explained. "And since you are our guest I can hardly ask you to perform such a service."

"Thank you." The Viscountess inclined her head to the older woman.

The staff left bruises rather than welts. As her tight cheeks began to darken, Black Masque sighed and shifted her weight. There was no fight left in her now. Her fingers crept forward to touch herself only to have her hands driven back by sharp blows from the staff.

The Crone, who by now was herself aroused, nipples hard at the ends of her swaying breasts, rubbed the staff between the other woman's legs. Black Masque moaned and leaned into the hard wood. With a dry chuckle The Crone placed the dripping end of the staff against the back of her masked head and pushed her forward. Black Masque shuffled forward on her knees, her head moving between the legs of the woman on the stone circle.

As the energy of the Scene filled the room, the woman had slowly come out of her trance. She took a deep breath, her breasts rising and falling for the first time since they had entered the room. Black Masque pressed herself into the woman, using her fingers to hold the guardian's lips open so that her tongue could get to the clitoris.

After a few moments of licking and sucking the bound woman began to stir. She could barely move a muscle, but she managed to tense and relax, making tiny movements with her hips as her belly pushed against the iron band pinning her to the stone.

A low moan came from under the mask. Her breath suddenly came in rapid gasps and her whole body seemed to shiver. Just as the orgasm struck her, a grinding sound came from the walls and the entire stone disk rolled to one side. They saw the smiling face of the Kamen Girl roll past as she vanished into an alcove in the wall.

"That's an excellent security device." The Viscountess commented wryly. "I'd install one in my own house, but I'd have to take out a wall."

"It serves our purposes." The Crone chuckled.

The two Kamen Girls entered, Black Masque getting unsteadily to her feet. They were followed by the Viscountess and Severin, who crawled after his owner. The room was small and round, lit by torches. There was a fountain where the weary Kamen Girls could refresh themselves with cool water. In the center of the room was a round depression on the floor where something was obviously missing.

"This is where the Sphere was." The Crone leaned heavily on her staff.

As she was speaking, Severin crawled along the rim of the depression. He was shaking himself out of his submissive state and trying to reactivate the detective portion of his brain.

"Your guardian must have seen who took it?" The Viscountess asked.

"The guardian only saw the mask of the woman." Black Masque shot back angrily. "However, when we went to question her we discovered that her mask had been stolen while she was asleep. She awoke with no mask. A thief had taken it to place over her own mask so she could get through undetected. Once the thief had the Sphere she used a portal to escape. When I catch up with her—"

"How big was it?" Severin asked, cutting off Black Masque, who shot him an angry glare. He didn't see her face, but he felt a surge of her dominant energy.

Before Black Masque could say anything more The Crone spoke.

"It is fifty-five centimeters in diameter and weighs about four and a half kilograms."

Severin nodded. He imagined a crystal sphere about the size of a beach ball and roughly ten pounds.

"Explain to me how it works," the Viscountess asked. "Your initiates pass all their tests, make it through the path and past the guardian, then what?"

"Here they ready themselves for the ordeal." The Crone explained. "When they are mentally and physically prepared, they lay their naked body across the sphere and let the power flow into them."

"It's incredibly painful," Black Masque said wistfully. "It's like electricity, but worse. You can feel every nerve in your body ignite. Your skin feels like you've been dipped in acid."

"Sounds invigorating." The Viscountess smiled.

"Some do not make it all the way through," The Crone admitted. "That is the purpose of our training, to make it through this final test without passing out. If you succeed you are truly a Kamen Girl."

"Does it do anything besides give you the power to make portals?"

"Isn't that enough?" The Crone responded.

From the floor Severin looked up at the three women. "Is the power to make portals permanent, or do you have to renew it?"

The Crone and Black Masque gave each other a quick glance. Clearly Severin had hit on something they were holding back.

"It must be renewed once or twice a year." The Crone said after a pause. "Depending on how often you use the portals. Giving women the ability to hold and retain the power they need is another function of our rigid training."

"So it's not just the new recruits who need it. Some of the older Kamen Girls must be in need of a recharge." The Viscountess guessed.

The Crone nodded and sighed. "It's true. The loss of the Sphere is the end of us. We cannot graduate new recruits and one by one those that already have the power will grow weaker. We have already recalled everyone who is not on assignment so they can be here in case we have to evacuate."

"How long do you have before things get bad?" Severin asked.

"We do not squander our power. It will be weeks, perhaps a month before problems arise. Once the power starts to fade there is no way to replenish it without the Sphere. Everyone must be taken to a nearby Dominion. When the last of us has lost our power no one will be able to find this world again. Anyone who stays behind as her power dwindles will be here forever."

There was a note of finality in her voice. The Viscountess sensed that The Crone was planning on being the one woman left behind.

"Let's hope it doesn't come to that."

"We've got to get the Sphere back!" Black Masque insisted.

"We'll do our best."

"That's not good enough."

The Crone made a soft noise in her throat and Black Masque bit back whatever else she was going to say.

"You said someone had her mask stolen?" The Viscountess continued diplomatically as if Black Masque hadn't spoken.

"She is known as Skye." The Crone explained. "She hasn't left her room since that night. I'm afraid she's taking it very hard."

"We'll have to speak with her."

"Of course."

They left the chamber heading back into the labyrinth. Behind them the stone door rolled back into place with a grinding sound.

The private chambers were in the middle of the ziggurat. To reach them the group went to the center of the structure where there were elevators. They had to pass through a large communal area where about thirty Kamen Girls played cards, wrestled and read books. About half the naked women glanced up to look at the group as they passed and Severin felt their eyes on him. He found himself staring back at the sea of lovely bodies and wound up crawling slowly enough that the Viscountess had to tug on the leash to make him keep up.

"Problem, Severin?"

"I'm sorry, Viscountess; I just realized I'm the only man in this entire Dominion."

"Don't let it go to your head." The Viscountess wrapped the chain around her hand, drawing the leash so short his hands almost left the floor. "Technically you're a slave and not a man at all."

"Yes, Viscountess." Severin lowered his head and crawled as fast as he could. Black Masque had turned her head to look at them and gave a little snort of laughter.

Skye had a room halfway down the hallway. When The Crone rapped on the door with her staff a soft voice said to come in. The Kamen Girl was sitting on the edge of the bed looking as if she had in that same position for days. A tray of uneaten food sat on a desk next to the bed.

When she saw the Viscountess and Severin, Skye looked startled and got to her feet, but The Crone calmed her.

"We have asked outsiders to investigate." The Crone explained soothingly. "You need to tell them everything that happened."

From his position on the floor Severin looked up at the naked woman. She had short dark hair and a body that was so lean she didn't seem to have an ounce of fat on her. Apart from the fact that she was older than twenty-five she looked like she would be at home on an Olympic gymnastics team. She looked helpless and vulnerable without her mask.

She looked from one face to another before she spoke. Her shoulders shook as if she were trying to cry but just didn't have the strength any more.

"It's all my fault," she blurted out.

"Nonsense," The Crone immediately told her.

"I've betrayed my sisters, the order, everything I believe in."

"That kind of talk is getting us nowhere." The Viscountess said briskly. She took the Kamen Girl by an arm and gently guided her to a chair. "Tell me everything you can about the night your mask was stolen."

Skye glanced up at The Crone, who nodded.

"I'd just gotten back from a mission and made my report."

"What mission?" Severin asked from the floor. Skye gave a start, as if she hadn't known he could speak.

"Nothing special, Gaius Claudio in Roma was throwing one of his parties and wanted a certain wine from Victoria. I was really just delivering groceries."

"What happened after you made your report?" The Viscountess prompted her gently.

"A few others had just returned, too. We were in the lounge on the twenty-third floor."

"Who was there?" Severin wanted to know.

"Tiger Mask, Papillion, Red Lightning, and someone else, um white mask with sequins."

"Blanca," Black Masque put in.

"Oh, you were there too," Skye remembered.

"I just stopped by for a moment," Black Masque immediately said, sounding a little too defensive.

"So what did you do there?" Severin brought her back to her story.

"Nothing, we talked, ate some snacks, I had a drink. Just two glasses of wine, but that must have been what did it." Skye's shoulders slumped again. "After I got back here I saw Jolly was still out on a mission."

The Viscountess glanced at the nearby bed which was neatly made.

"I tried to read, but I started to feel really sleepy. I went to bed and drifted off. I remember lying there and feeling like I was floating, I wasn't sure if I was asleep or awake. Those two glasses of wine did me in. I heard someone come into my room. I felt them pulling my mask off, but I couldn't stop them. I just lay there drunk out of my head. The next thing I knew it was ten hours later and Black Masque was shaking me, demanding to know where the Sphere was."

"I should have known it wasn't you," Black Masque said by way of apology.

"But it was me! If I hadn't gotten drunk..."

"You weren't drunk." Severin stated flatly. Everyone looked at him. "This wasn't the first time you had wine was it?"

"Of course not. My mother was French, I think I had it in my baby bottle. That's why I was hired by Gaius."

"And you've never passed out before?"

"No, never."

Severin nodded. "Stealing a mask from a sleeping woman, even a drunk one, is very risky. I'd say the thief made certain by putting something in your drink. It could have been an old-fashioned mickey, but it sounds more like rohypnol, or what they call a 'roofie' in the Real World."

Skye blinked her eyes several times. Her face was blank, as if she had no idea how to respond. Severin continued talking.

"Alcohol increases its effects. The thief was counting on you being helpless. It wasn't your fault."

"Then who is the thief?" The Crone asked.

"Someone who had access to her drink, which gives us four suspects. Five counting you." Severin glanced up at Black Masque, who was gritting her teeth beneath the mask. "How many people knew that Jolly was out and Skye would be alone?"

"Everyone," the Crone admitted sadly. "There is a board with all the names and locations of women on assignment."

Viscountess ticked the names off on her fingers. "Tiger Mask, Red Lightning, Papillion, and Blanca. Each of them had the opportunity to put something in her drink."

"They are all above suspicion," the Crone declared.

"Yet they are our only suspects," the Viscountess said gently. "Can we speak with them?"

"Perhaps. I'll have Black Masque check on them."

Black Masque bowed and started to exit the room. She paused in the doorway and looked back, catching the eye of the Viscountess.

"Do you seriously consider me a suspect?" Black Masque demanded.

"Everyone who was in that room is a suspect," the Viscountess reminded her. "But I think we can find you if we need you."

With the tension broken Skye began to cry again. The Crone went to her and hugged her.

"Relax, my dear. These people will find the Sphere and your mask." The Crone made a point of making eye contact with Severin. "Thank you for everything you have already done."

Severin bowed his head in response.

They left Skye to rest and went down to the garden again while waiting for Black Masque to return.

The sun above their heads seemed larger and hotter. The Crone saw that the Viscountess noticed this.

"It's nearly noon here. Our Dominion has regular days and nights. In another six hours it will darken and we will be lit only by the light of the void."

As they talked Black Masque approached them. She had some papers in her hands and the expression under her mask was not a good one.

All four of the suspects were away on assignments. Like the rest of the Kamen Girls, they had been sent a message that they should return to their home when they were finished.

"I don't think we can wait that long," Viscountess decided.

"You're assuming they are actually coming back." Severin reminded her. "All they have to do is take off and wait until the rest of their sisterhood runs out of juice to track them down. They've got the Sphere; they can waste as much power as they want."

From the expressions on their faces it looked as if neither Black Masque nor The Crone had thought of that possibility.

The Viscountess looked through the papers and found that they contained the details of the cases the four Kamen Girls had been assigned to. Unfortunately, there wasn't much to go on.

"Thank you for this. If Severin has no more questions I'd like to get started on this right away."

"No, Viscountess," Severin said from his usual position at her feet.

"Then we can send you back to Victoria or any Dominion you please," The Crone offered.

"Why not back to my home?"

"It takes a great deal of energy to reach the Real World. In addition, we might have to make several trips to get you near your home. It would certainly be a waste of our resources."

"So, I guess it's back to the Jade Pagoda." The Viscountess smiled.

"I'm certain that can be arranged."

Chapter Five

It was dark on the streets of Victoria, but when they reached home it was just after noon. Sklavin prepared a sandwich for the Viscountess and boiled a hot dog for Severin, placing it on the floor at his owner's feet. He was hogtied and lying on his side, which would make getting the hot dog into his mouth quite a challenge.

"What do you think, Severin?"

Severin had managed to get the hot dog between his lips by using his tongue, but once he bit into it, the hot dog slipped from his mouth and rolled away. "I think wearing masks hides their faces and makes it easier for them to lie to us. Also that military style training gives them very stiff posture, making it hard to read their body language."

"You think they're lying to us?"

"No, Viscountess, their story sounded too true." Severin looked mournfully at the hot dog, just out of reach. "But when we talk to those four, one or more of them is going to be lying to us."

"Are you certain it's one of them?"

"I'm certain that someone put something in Skye's drink. Those four had the opportunity."

"What about Black Masque?" Viscountess asked after she finished more of her sandwich.

"She looks mad enough to spit nails."

"I agree. It wouldn't be the first time the guilty party has drawn attention to themselves so they'll look less guilty, but in this case I'd like to give her a wide berth unless we have some evidence implicating her."

Severin hit on an idea for the hot dog. Wriggling across the floor he managed to shift his weight enough to roll over on his stomach. His face was pushed against the hot dog and he started nibbling it.

"Having problems Severin?" the Viscountess called from above.

"No, Viscountess," Severin spoke into the floor as he continued to eat away at the hot dog.

The Viscountess took the opportunity to glance at the papers they had been given.

"Apparently Tiger Mask is in some Dominion called the Wasteland. Ever hear of it?"

Severin nodded. "I've heard of it. It's a post-apocalyptic world—after the collapse of civilization."

"And people find this sexy?"

"It's a brutal world where only the strong survive."

"Still not seeing the sexy."

"Let me put it another way. The strong dominate the weak. Rape and slavery are a way of life."

"Sounds dreadful." The Viscountess sighed. "It also sounds very macho. Are there any dominant women?"

"There's no restriction against it, so there must be a few." Severin was trying to get to his knees. Seeing him flop back to the floor, the Viscountess hooked a finger in the ring on his collar and pulled him to his knees. Now that he was stable he looked up at his owner. "Thank you, Viscountess. From what I've heard, the Dominion has a pretty bad reputation. It's become one of those places where almost anything goes."

"But the Safeword must still work."

"Sure, for all the good it does you. It's the sort of Dominion people go to who want to do things and not get caught."

"Wonderful. Do you know any way to get in, or do I have to call Duchess for another pony girl?"

"I'd hate to bring a pony girl there. I doubt there's any secure place to keep her. If you just tie her up someone is bound to come along and steal her."

"That means you need to find me a Gateway."

She unlocked his wrists and ankles, allowing him to stand and stretch. When he felt up to it he went to the computer and started to work. After a few minutes in front of the screen he heard her behind him. She fed him another hot dog by hand as his fingers flew across the keyboard.

"If it's any consolation Severin, one of the Kamen Girls we're after is in the Real World. We shouldn't have too much trouble tracking the others down," she informed him.

"Where are the others?"

"That would be telling."

He could feel her grin even without look at her.

Severin emailed two people and sent instant messages to three others.

While he was waiting for a reply he used the computer to videoconference someone who gave him an idea about a message board that was hidden behind the Blindfold.

It seems that everyone had heard of the Wasteland, but no one actually knew how to get there. By dinner time he was still waiting for answers. Sklavin made pasta for dinner with mushroom sauce. The Viscountess had hers with wine at the table. Severin ate his with water from a plate on the floor.

Wanting to be in top form for their trip to the Wasteland, the Viscountess ordered her two slaves into the basement for an after dinner punishment. Severin had a spreader bar separating his wrists and another on his ankles. Sklavin stripped in front of him, slowly, teasingly. When she was sure she had his attention she attached a chain to her nipple rings. Putting the center of the chain in her mouth she pulled up her breasts so that the tender flesh of the undersides was exposed.

Severin groaned and squirmed in his bondage. By mainstream standards, Sklavin was a normal middle-aged woman, one that he had seen naked hundreds of times, but he found the raw sexuality that she exuded more arousing than any "sex kitten" type could be. It was no wonder that her porn films were still considered legendary years after her retirement.

The Viscountess took her time unlocking the three padlocks and slipping them from the labia rings that sealed the German slave's pussy tightly. The dominant woman ran her fingers inside the already dripping pussy, gently stroking. Sklavin bucked her hips, trying to get the Viscountess to focus on her clit.

"Don't worry, I haven't forgotten about you," the Viscountess teased Severin.

She went behind him and came back with a small case of clothespins. They had rubber tips so they held fast once put into place. Each of them also had a hole from which weights could be hung.

With lightning speed, she grabbed his penis and pinched up as much loose skin as she could. She caught the skin with the clothespins, deftly moving around his cock, applying them on all sides. He was still limp when she touched him, but now he had begun to grow. As his cock started to swell it was twisted out of shape by the clothespins.

"There. This should help you focus." She added clothespins to each nipple.

"Thank you, Viscountess," Severin said. His voice barely showed the pain, but the clothespins were insidious; the agony was going to build slowly.

Lying on a mat on the floor, Sklavin spread herself, lifting the labia rings to show glistening pink flesh. She slid three fingers in, making a wet slurping sound.

Severin stared at her as if mesmerized. His cock had slowly, stubbornly continued to swell, despite the clothespins. As it grew, the pressure on his trapped flesh increased as did his pain. There wasn't enough loose skin to let him get an erection.

"Enjoying yourself?" The Viscountess asked pleasantly as she continued her work. She began attaching small lead weights to each of the clothespins. The weight increased slowly, dragging his cock down and stretching it until it pointed to the floor. The skin pinched by the clothespins was stretched cruelly. As the pain radiated through him Severin's mouth dropped open in a silent mask of agony.

"As you know the key to dealing with weights is to be very still," the Viscountess reminded him as she attached weights to the clothespins on his nipples. When she felt he was in sufficient pain, she nodded. "The only way you can endure this is to keep the weights from swinging like this."

She brought up her boot and gave the weights dangling between his legs a playful kick. Severin let out a small scream as the heavy lead swung back and forth. He felt as if his cock was going to be torn out. What flesh he could see around the clothespins was bright red with trapped blood.

"Excellent. Let's begin, shall we?"

The Viscountess crossed behind him leaving him guessing what she was doing. He got his answer a few seconds later when a heavy wooden paddle smacked his ass with a sound so loud it echoed off the walls. The sound of wood hitting ass was immediately followed by a scream of pain from Severin. When the paddle connected, he couldn't stop his body from lurching forward, sending all the weights swinging.

"You're not keeping very still, Severin," the Viscountess laughed. "Let's try again shall we?"

She was on the other side of him now, swinging from a different position. By turning his head he was able to see her bracing herself, using both hands to swing the paddle. When the second blow came, it was as bad as the first, possibly worse. In trying to keep still and not let the weights swing, Severin had simply knocked them off their course and made them tug and twist at odd, painful angles.

There was a third blow, then a fourth. She altered her position each time, noting how the sweat rolled off his body and the tears flowed down his cheeks. By the time of the fourth blow his muscles had started to twitch and she chose to give him a break.

"Just relax and enjoy the show," she informed Severin. Sklavin was still masturbating furiously. She had a dildo now and was driving it in and out at great speed. Her low, guttural moans and the overwhelming scent of her passion helped Severin endure his ordeal.

Just as it looked as if Sklavin might come, the Viscountess reached down and took the dildo from her hands.

"Don't think you're getting off so easily," the Viscountess informed her. "I noticed the razor burns on Severin's body this morning. You did a Scene last night without my permission."

Sklavin opened her mouth as if to protest, but she finally simply nodded.

"Yes, mein herrin, I'm sorry mein herrin."

The Viscountess went to an umbrella stand and returned with a thin cane in her hand. Sklavin gave a little gasp when she saw it, since she knew what was coming.

"I give you a great deal of freedom in this household, Sklavin. Do not forget your place. Now present your breasts."

With only a moment's hesitation the slave reached up and lifted her heavy breasts. The tender flesh hung off the edge of her fingers, the nipples weighed down by iron rings and the chain that linked them. The Viscountess tapped her cane a few times at the base of the breasts, setting up her stroke. Her arm rose and fell, the cane whistling down. When it struck there was a loud smack and a hiss of pain from Sklavin.

Severin felt immediately guilty. He had really enjoyed the punishment in the shower and now Sklavin was being punished for it. He also felt guilty that he was enjoying watching it.

The second stroke came in the middle of the breasts. This time there was a little cry and Sklavin's body began to shake. The slave took a deep breath, trying to maintain her composure while tears began to run down her face.

The Viscountess tapped the cane at the spot where Sklavin's breasts hung over her hands. The last blow was going to hit very close to the nipples.

The arm of the Viscountess rose and fell a third time. This time

Sklavin let out a gasp of pain and fell to the floor, rolling into a fetal position. The Viscountess waited until she had stopped sobbing before bending down and wiping the tears from her cheeks.

"Danke, mein herrin," Sklavin fell back into her German as she turned her head to kiss the hand that had punished her.

"You're welcome, and I'm sure we won't have any problems with this in the future."

"No, mein herrin."

The Viscountess went upstairs to get some water for her slaves. As she passed the computer screen she noticed that an instant message had popped up and she couldn't resist reading it. Apparently one of Severin's friends had come through with information on the Wasteland and instructions for how to get there, as well as a warning:

> The Wasteland is a Dominion where people
> like it rough. They pride themselves on
> never using a Safeword. Anyone visiting
> had better brace themselves and be
> prepared for a bumpy ride.

That was fast work, she thought. Severin definitely deserves a reward.

Returning to the basement, the Viscountess gave Severin some water. She let him drink his fill, holding the glass to his lips. He tried his best, but ice water still trickled down his hot skin, which made him twitch and set the weights swinging.

"Tell me, slave," she began in a conversational manner. "If I were to perform one sex act upon you, what would you most want it to be?"

Severin blinked. It was obviously a trick question.

"You may do whatever you like to your slave," he stated diplomatically.

She chuckled and gave the clothespin on his right nipple a light tap.

"Seriously, Severin, what would you like me to do to you?"

"Um, oral sex," he said hesitantly.

"I'm sorry, what was that again?" She leaned very close to him, letting him feel the warmth of her body. The fact that she was still fully clothed somehow made it even sexier.

"A blow job."

"Details, Severin." She brushed against his cock, making the weights bounce.

"If you could defile your perfect goddess mouth with my tiny, disgusting cock...?" He was guessing; he had no idea what she was after.

The Viscountess beamed. "Why Severin, when you ask me like that how can I refuse?" She dropped to her knees and faced his tortured cock. "Too bad about the weights, but I suppose it can't be helped."

She leaned in and began to run her tongue up and down his shaft. His body shook with pain each time her tongue found one of the clothespins. Viscountess removed some of the weights so that the cock bobbed upwards, still trapped by the clothespins.

"Join me, Sklavin," she ordered.

The German slave knelt facing the Viscountess. They took turns licking the length of his cock while he sobbed and whimpered. At one point the two women kissed, keeping his cock between their mouths as they tongued each other.

The sight of the two women with their mouths wrapped around his cock was almost too much for him to bear. It was exactly the way he had always imagined it—except for the clothespins. The pain that radiated through him made it hard for him to focus on anything else. The sensations that coursed through him were so great that he felt as if he would explode.

At the command of the Viscountess, Sklavin went behind Severin. The German slave licked around the base of his balls, then drew his testicles into her mouth. He could feel a powerful suction and her tongue moving his balls in their sack.

Severin made an inarticulate gurgling noise. The Viscountess laughed and removed the clothespins from his cock. The sudden rush of pain turned the gurgle into a soft whimper. She was still smiling as she leaned forward, taking his head firmly in her mouth.

The sight of his cock vanishing into her mouth and the sensation of her tongue touching him blotted out everything else.

"I'm going to come," he warned her.

"I'll be rather disappointed if you don't," the Viscountess commented, leaning just far enough back that her teeth only caught him a little as she spoke. She went to work on him again and in a few moments his body twisted in his bonds as orgasm struck him. Come dribbled from the head of his cock and the Viscountess sucked hard, drawing out every last drop.

As his twitching body calmed, the Viscountess rose regally to her feet and kissed him very hard on the lips. He opened his mouth to her and tasted his own sperm as she spat. He almost choked as it hit his tongue, but she emptied her mouth into him. Only after he had swallowed every drop did she suck hard, drawing his tongue into her mouth. She bit down on the tongue just as Sklavin started to apply her teeth to his testicles.

Severin sobbed and whimpered. A few stray drops of come dripped onto the floor.

After what seemed like a very long time, the Viscountess broke off the kiss and smiled at her slave.

"Do you know why I did that Severin?"

"Because you enjoyed it?"

"Very true," she laughed. "But there's another reason. That was your reward for a job well done."

Severin blinked, still half-blinded by sweat.

"While we were down here, someone responded to you and gave us directions. We know now how to get to the Wasteland."

Severin sighed. He was still trying to wrap his head around everything that had just happened.

"It was nothing," he mumbled.

"Good," the Viscountess smiled sweetly. "I'll remember that next time I feel like being generous."

She began to carefully pull the clothespins off his nipples. As the blood rushed back to his trapped flesh he cried out again.

Chapter Six

There were entrances to Dominions in various places on the Earth. Some were located in the backs of gay bars or strip clubs. Others were in comic book stores or old buildings. Many of these permanent Gateways, like Victoria's, had gatekeepers who helped with the transition to the new world.

The Wasteland apparently had a junkyard.

Following the instructions in the message the Viscountess and Severin arrived at the gate of what appeared to be an abandoned junkyard. There was no sign of life and what few lights there were flickered on and off. All they could make out through the fence was debris and huge mounds of rusting cars. The gate was closed, but not locked, so they made their way inside.

So many of the messages had stressed how dangerous the Wasteland could be that the Viscountess had ordered Severin to wear clothing and removed his collar. There was no sense in drawing too much attention to him by letting him go naked. For her part the Viscountess wore a long coat over her cat suit and placed her six foot bullwhip on her belt next to her other tools. The bullwhip was not a Named Fetish object, but it was loud and impressive when she used it. She kept other items they hopefully would need in the coat's pockets

Severin's hiking boots crunched broken glass as they slipped through the fence. Although every instinct told him to walk behind his owner, he felt the uncertainty of the situation called for him to take the lead.

They took the broadest path between piles of old cars and appliances and soon found there was so much debris built up that they were cut off from the rest of the city. A few lights cast a yellowish glow over the scene.

Abruptly they heard barking and two naked women rushed out of the shadows on all fours growling and snarling. Their bodies were lean and hard like greyhounds and it was impossible to tell much more about them since they were also covered in dirt. Both of them had shaved heads and heavy metal collars with spikes.

Their movements were so animalistic that for a split second they really seemed to be dogs. Both the Viscountess and Severin froze instantly. The two women scrambled around them on their hands and knees, growling and sniffing them.

The dog on their right barked loudly, making them jump slightly in the opposite direction. That set both of the dogs barking and snarling as they shuffled forward on their hands and knees. The Viscountess and Severin found themselves being forced down a sort of alley between mounds of old cars.

"Do you suppose they're the gatekeepers?" the Viscountess whispered, afraid any loud noise would set the dogs off.

"Either that or Timmy's fallen down a well."

They were gradually forced down one path and around a corner. If either of them deviated from the path one of the dogs would growl at them and snap their teeth.

They found themselves facing the front end of an old van that was sticking out of the junk pile at an odd angle. The hood and badly cracked windshield were visible, but the rest of the van was buried in junk up to the front doors. The dogs barked excitedly. One of them got up on her knees and pawed at the door.

The Viscountess and Severin glanced at each other. Severin shrugged.

Carefully the Viscountess opened the door. She removed a flashlight from the pockets of her coat. There seemed to be nothing unusual about the interior, but as she played the flashlight around she saw something that made her pause. There was no junk visible through the rear windows.

Followed closely by Severin, she made her way back. When they got to the rear doors both of them felt the familiar tingling sensation. They were about to enter a Gateway.

Throwing open the rear door, they saw that they were in a junkyard, but not the same junkyard they entered. Both of them knew that they were in another Dominion. The crisp, clear air of the desert filled their lungs. The objects on this side of the van had been stripped clean of anything that might be useful. The mounds of wrecked cars were smaller and more scattered. Above them the moon hung large in the sky, not obscured by layers of smog.

They made sure to close the doors to the van behind them before starting out. This junkyard was set on the edge of a small town. Many of the buildings were abandoned and decayed. Torches provided illumination in some parts of town, but there appeared to be electricity in others. Two searchlights stabbed into the sky, rotating back and forth.

"What do we know?" The Viscountess asked.

"Tiger Mask was hired to fight on behalf of a group of women. From the looks of the place, it's probably some kind of gladiatorial match."

"Any more clues?"

"The file was very sparse, but I say we should head for the searchlights. If the fight isn't being held there, they should know where it is."

Viscountess nodded. The lights came from the center of town, where several fires burned.

The road into town was partly covered by blowing sand. An old, bullet-ridden sign once declared what highway this was, but the details had long ago rusted away. There was a fairly high-tech windmill on either side of the road. Each windmill had a naked woman tied to the blades, her arms on one and her legs spread on the two others. Their faces were relaxed in deep submission as they turned slowly and mournfully in the breeze.

Faces peered out from cracked windows as they went deeper into the city. They heard loud music and the sound of an engine from behind them. The Viscountess and Severin managed to get out of the way just as a pickup truck went roaring past them. The music sounded like arena rock from the eighties, but the distortion in the speakers made it hard to tell. Perhaps that was when their apocalypse had occurred and it was the only music they had left.

The back of the pickup truck had been made into an iron cage with welded bars. Women wearing nothing but rags clung desperately to the bars, trying not to be injured by the reckless driving. There was another woman stretched across the hood of the truck like a prize deer they had killed. There was a blanket protecting her from the heat of the engine, but Severin still winced in sympathy.

Two blocks ahead of them, a makeshift prison had been set up with barbed wire. The sobbing and screaming women were dragged out of the back of the truck and forced through the gate. Men with rifles looked down from rooftops into the barbed wire pen.

The Viscountess walked in front, Severin slightly behind her. She kept up an even pace, and tried not to pay too much attention to what was happening around her, but couldn't help seeing the woman chained across the hood being set free. They gave her some water and what looked like a snack bar.

When she was finished eating, the leader grabbed her by the hair and forced her to look at the holding pen where the rest of the prisoners were being kept. The woman wailed in anguish and gave her attacker an unexpected elbow in the ribs, breaking his grip. She ran a few steps, but was brought down by three men and pinned to the pavement. What few scraps of clothing she had left were torn away. During the struggle she was hit hard enough that her lower lip bled.

They were preparing to gang bang her as the Viscountess and Severin walked past. One of the men glanced up, saw The Viscountess, and grinned from ear to ear,—or to be accurate from one ear to the stump where he had lost his other ear. He had a shaved head and was wearing a motorcycle jacket, no shirt, and torn denim pants. He held a two-foot machete in one beefy hand.

"Hey boys!" he called to the rest of the men. "Looks like we got another volunteer."

"Sorry, no," the Viscountess nodded politely to him. "I'm just passing through."

"I didn't say you could fucking pass."

He came at her, fingering the machete. The woman who was their first victim had finally been pinned and she twisted her head to see what was causing the delay. She glared when she saw the Viscountess. Apparently she was not happy with the competition for the men's attention.

The Viscountess let her dominant energy spike to the surface. The would-be attacker halted as solidly as if he had hit a brick wall. His own dominance flared, breaking like an ocean wave against her indomitable will.

They were close enough now that she could talk without his friends hearing. Very casually the Viscountess opened her long coat and showed the flagellation instruments hanging from her belt. He stared at them and tried to laugh, but it didn't quite come out right.

"Either I can Safeword and walk away, or I can make you apologize on your knees in front of you friends. Which is it going to be?" she asked sweetly.

The big man licked his lips nervously. The rest of the gang was still egging him on. Carefully he extended his arm, bringing the point of the machete towards her throat, but not close enough to be an actual threat.

"That's right, cunt! Take your asshole friend and get out. The next time I see you, you're the one who's going to be across the hood of the truck."

The Viscountess backed away, pretending to be intimidated by him.

Severin stuck close to her. He didn't have to pretend to be afraid; the bald man was quite a bit taller than him and his arrogant manner reminded Severin of way too many schoolyard bullies he had encountered.

On the pavement the gang's victim was raising her hips and grinding them against the man on top of her, trying to get him to stop staring at the Viscountess.

As the Viscountess and Severin retreated from the Scene they saw the man with the machete go over to their victim and put a boot on each of her wrists, crushing her arms to the ground. The man on top of her rose long enough to grab her legs and force her knees to her chest. He held her there while yanking open his pants and letting his sizable cock swing free. The woman let out a shrill scream as he penetrated her.

As the sound of the assault faded behind them the Viscountess sighed.

"I suppose it's a prejudice, but I prefer the more genteel and civilized form of slavery in Victoria," she admitted.

The building with the searchlights loomed ahead of them. It was apparently some sort of civic center which had once held sporting events—and apparently still did. A great many letters were missing from the sign, but it distinctly said "FIGHT" with the few letters that remained.

As they walked, a figure was keeping pace with them, scurrying in the shadows. He was thin with a sallow face and patchy facial hair. As soon as the Viscountess became aware of him she noticed that his gaze was riveted on the sidewalk where she walked.

"May I help you?" She came to a sudden halt.

The man hesitated, stumbling a few steps. He tried to raise his eyes, but wasn't quite able to.

"You must be new here," he said hesitantly.

"How can you tell?"

"Your boots. They're so nice and new. No one's made new boots here in decades." He licked his thin lips. "At least not like that."

"You're welcome to take a closer look if you'd like."

The words had barely left her lips before the man threw himself to the pavement. He pushed his face closer to the leather boots, but she took a step back, keeping him at a distance.

"I see they've gotten dirty," he said, unable to take his eyes off them.

"How unfortunate," the Viscountess spoke in a distracted voice, as if she were barely aware of the man groveling at her feet. "If only there were some way to clean them."

"I could..." The man licked his lips again and began to crawl forward, his whole body pressed to the pavement.

"Your tongue on my boots?" The Viscountess gave a little snort of laughter. "I think not. Still, I suppose you may be able to clean them, if you can answer a few questions."

"Of course, anything."

"What do you know about that building up ahead?"

The man lifted himself up from the sidewalk far enough to get a good look at the building.

"Oh, that's Cherub's place. She runs half the town. Everybody goes there for entertainment."

"And what can you tell me about her?"

He squirmed uncomfortably.

"She's very um, well very beautiful, but I think she's a mutant. She's short, a midget or something, but she's powerful."

"You mean she's a dominant?" The Viscountess was delighted at the idea of finding another dominant woman in the Dominion.

"Not as dominant as you of course," the man hastily spoke.

"What can you tell me about this fight?"

"I don't know, I mean I don't know the details. Some girls who turn tricks for the Boss Man want out, and they have to fight for it."

"Boss Man?"

"Oh, he's well... I don't think you'd like him. He runs the part of town that Cherub doesn't."

"I see. So he and the girls who want to be free have both picked champions?"

"Yeah. That's the way I hear it. Some girls tried to get out from under the man before, but it didn't go so well for them."

"Thank you, you've been very helpful."

With great cruelty she made as if to walk away from him. "Your boots!" he sobbed.

"Of course." The Viscountess smiled indulgently. Before coming she had filled her pockets with anything that might prove useful on their trip. Reaching into a pocket she withdrew a silk handkerchief and let it flutter to the ground. "You may clean my boots with this. Give them a nice shine, but you'll have to provide your own water. Neither your fingers nor your tongue may touch the boots."

"Oh thank you, thank you," he murmured, getting immediately to work. He spat on the top of the boot and began using the handkerchief to polish the black leather. Slowly, carefully, with great reverence he made his way around first one boot, then the other. By the time he was done, both of them shone like new.

"I think that will do for now. You may go."

He held up the handkerchief, now filthy with mud.

"You may keep that."

"Oh, thank you, mistress."

As they walked past he stayed on the sidewalk, pressing his lips to the silk and drawing some of the delicious dirt into his mouth.

From inside the civic center came the sound of drums and flutes. The big glass doors leading to the lobby had long ago been smashed, but the metal security gates had been slid aside to show the interior. The food court area was now a bar. Naked girls danced to acoustic music in cages on platforms. Most of the musicians were female and naked as well.

The lobby area was filled with tables and mismatched chairs. There were dozens of people visible through the haze of cigarette and marijuana smoke. It looked like a dimly lit sea of leather, spikes, and odd haircuts. There were sequins and more than a little body paint, too, and at least one feather boa.

"So this is where heavy metal bands go to die." Severin murmured under his breath. That earned him a quick elbow to the ribs. "Thank you, Viscountess."

The Viscountess concentrated, expanding her dominant energy until it filled the room. She got an instant response from several of the women, and a few men. Then in the back of the room there was flare of female dominance, a power that was easily the equal of hers.

The other dominant woman emerged from deep in the room where she had been in shadows, watching the door without being seen. It took her a few minutes to get to them, which was fine since it took the Viscountess and Severin a few minutes to process what they were seeing.

There was a very tall woman walking toward them. She had broad shoulders, wide hips, and breasts that jutted out like the figurehead of a ship, supported by powerful muscles. Her arms were pulled behind her back and the only thing she was wearing was a hockey mask over her face. The truly odd thing was that she wasn't the most interesting of the group that approached.

There was a naked man scrambling to keep up. A ring in his nose was attached to a belt around the tall woman's waist with a chain so short the man couldn't possibly get to a standing position nor to kneeling one. His long, thin cock lay flat across balls that had been stretched so far that the sac hung halfway to his knees and slapped his thighs as he tried to walk. He wasn't the most interesting either.

There was a sort of body harness attached to the tall woman. The harness held a chair. The person in the chair was no taller than a child, but she was clearly a fully grown adult. She was wearing what Victoria's Secret would produce if they made a kindergarten collection.

Severin accidentally made eye contact with her and immediately regretted it. He dropped his gaze to the floor, but she had already burned an image in his mind. Cherub wasn't as powerful as The Crone, but her dominance had a cunning cruelty to it, and she had already sensed that Severin couldn't resist her.

The Viscountess and Cherub locked eyes as the tall woman approached. Several people saw this and got out of their way. The music trailed off and finally stopped. Cherub's pretty face smirked as she glanced from Viscountess to Severin.

"We don't get a lot of your kind in here," Cherub said.

"Too bad. You could use more dominant women in this town."

The Viscountess was braced, ready for Cherub to challenge her. Although the little dominant was keeping her power up, she wasn't actually pitting herself against the Viscountess. Perhaps she was waiting for the Viscountess to challenge her. The Viscountess decided not to rise to the bait and continued the conversation.

"You've got a nice place here." The Viscountess ran her hand down the length of one of the bars on the cage. The dancer inside shivered as if she could feel the touch of the Viscountess.

"I'm glad you like it." Cherub leaned back in her little chair, reaching up to toy with the nipple rings on the heavy breasts of the tall woman in the hockey mask. "I've got an empty cage if you feel like dancing a few numbers."

"Care to join me?" Viscountess smiled.

After a split second Cherub smiled as well.

She turned in her chair and caught the eye of the lead musician. The music started up again and the women in the cages returned to dancing. Cherub tugged on the nipple of her human mode of transport and the tall woman came forward. Over the sound of the music they could talk without being heard.

"I like you," Cherub said.

"Thank you."

"That doesn't mean I'm not going to totally fuck with you."

"Of course," The Viscountess nodded.

"I'm Cherub. This is Chair." She gestured to the tall woman's masked face. "And this disgusting piece of shit is Wormcock."

The man chained behind her kept his face as low as he could with his nose still chained to the other woman's belt.

"I am the Viscountess; this is Severin."

"For a boy like that, he's got a lot of clothes on."

"What makes you think he's submissive?"

Cherub gave a snort of laughter. "You've got him on a leash even when he's not on a leash."

"I need some information."

"And I need to see your boy naked." Cherub grinned wickedly. "See how it works, honey? We don't have any money, so we use the barter system here. You have to give to get."

The Viscountess glanced at Severin to see if he was willing to go along with this. She felt pretty certain she knew what his answer was going to be. After all, she had felt him slipping into Subspace almost as soon as Cherub had approached them. Severin nodded his consent and reached into his pocket for his collar. The Viscountess gently took it from his hands and placed it around his neck. As soon as it was in place Severin felt a rush of relief as everything was right with the world again.

"Let's go to my private table where we can talk." Cherub gave another hard yank on a nipple and Chair turned towards the back of the room.

Cherub's table had an open area around it where no one was sitting, but it was hardly private. From this spot they could see both the doors and the large inner doors that lead into the civic center. Men with batons were posted to keep anyone from trying to get an early seat for the fight.

Wormcock reached up and unlocked Chair's wrists. The big woman gently lifted the chair from her body harness and placed it on the table. Cherub unbuckled the leather seat belt and squirmed into a more comfortable position, her sandaled feet swinging back and forth.

The little dominant offered a seat to the Viscountess, who graciously accepted. Severin stayed standing behind her.

"He's still wearing clothes," Cherub pointed out.

"And he will remain wearing them until we've come to terms." The Viscountess smiled. "I need to talk with someone and I think you can help me with that."

"Depends on who you're looking for."

"Someone who is going to fight here. When is that fight, by the way?"

"Two hours. Boss Man isn't even here with his crew yet."

"I think the person I want to see is with the women who are going against him." The Viscountess leaned forward. "What can you tell me about them?"

"Depends, how naked can your boy get?"

The Viscountess glanced at Severin and nodded. He began slowly removing his clothes. As more and more of him was exposed Cherub's lascivious smile grew even wider.

"I want him for an hour." Cherub announced.

"Thirty minutes," the Viscountess said casually. "I don't think we have an hour to waste."

"All right. Half an hour, but I get to work him like a government mule."

"Done."

The two dominant women shook hands on the deal.

So much for not drawing attention to myself, Severin thought. He stood naked except for his collar. He could hear snickering laughter coming from the men in the room. All the submissives in the room were female except for him and Wormcock.

"See wormy, that's what a real cock looks like," the little vixen teased her slave. "I'll bet he has a pair of balls that actually work too."

"I noticed you've done some stretching on your slave," the Viscountess commented.

"That wasn't me, it was his original owner. He used to have to drag weights behind everywhere he went. I don't mind the stretching, but eventually she broke something inside him. We had kind of a disagreement about how he should be treated."

"I have a feeling she didn't take too well to that."

"You can ask her yourself. She's in the third cage on the left."

Cherub grinned wickedly. She was still admiring Severin's naked body.

"We don't get a lot of sub-males around here. I think all the alpha males drown them at birth." Cherub leaned forward as if she was sharing a secret. "The War wiped out about two thirds of the male population, and the numbers haven't really come back. All the mutants and so forth make it pretty hard to repopulate."

"If there aren't enough men, why aren't there more dominant women? It seems like you could have taken over the world."

"In some towns the women did take over, but gangs of men put women in their place wherever they could. A lot of women like my mother went along with it. It was better to obey and know where your next meal was coming from than fight back and risk starving."

"You seem to have done all right."

"I got lucky, plus I got a few friends."

Standing behind her, as solid as a statue, Chair cracked her knuckles.

"We can talk more later." Cherub got to her feet. "Right now I want to see that boy of yours sweat."

"Help yourself. The clock is ticking."

Cherub walked across the table to where Severin stood. He noticed that she had trouble walking and winced inwardly. It was impossible to imagine how hard her life must have been in this male-dominated Dominion. No wonder she was a fierce ball of dominant energy. She probably had to be at the top of her game every day of her life to keep out of that rape pen down the street.

She put her hands on her hips and sneered at him.

"So what kind of things do you like, boy?"

"I enjoy pain and humiliation. I enjoy being a slave to a woman. I've been trained to serve and take punishment in a variety of different ways. Perhaps you should just start with me and I will let you know if there are any problems."

"Oh honey." Cherub grinned. "You are going to be so sorry you said that."

Chapter Seven

Severin was on all fours. There was a bit between his teeth buckled behind his head with reins coming off of it. On his back was a simple leather saddle with stirrups, and a butt plug with real horse hair had been lovingly and painfully pushed into his ass.

Cherub approached him wearing spurs on her sandals. Apparently the man outside had not been lying about the lack of boots in this place. She also had on a cowboy hat and carried a short riding whip. Severin could tell that it was a real whip, designed for use on animals, and knew that it could do serious damage to him if she wasn't careful.

"Ride 'em cowgirl!" someone shouted.

Cherub turned to them and waved her cowboy hat while the men hooted and jeered. She put a foot in a stirrup and swung into the saddle.

Severin barely felt the weight on his back. He was used to being crushed into the floor by the women who dominated him, but compared to them Cherub was as light as a feather. As she settled onto him he saw that she was almost exactly the right height to make this kind of pony riding work. Normally when women rode him like this it was awkward because they never knew where to put their legs. Cherub's legs were almost perfect, which she proved by kicking back her heels and driving the spurs into his groin.

Severin gave a little scream into his bit gag and surged forward while the crowd roared with laughter. He knew the spurs weren't actually sharp; he had seen the Viscountess inspect them and give her approval. But even blunt, the little pieces of metal hurt.

He carried her across the floor, keeping his head down. He only knew when to turn when she yanked on his bridle. She brought the whip down on his ass, urging him to go faster. He scrambled around the room as fast as he could, the drums and flutes providing musical accompaniment to his suffering. Not only did she not hesitate to use the spurs, she quickly discovered the trick of leaning forward in the saddle and bringing the spurs to bear on his balls. The first time she did it he jumped so much he almost left the floor.

Severin went back and forth around the room wherever she steered him. Cherub was laughing and talking to people, but it seemed very far away to him. He didn't realize how tired he was getting until sweat ran into his eyes, blinding him.

Cherub laughed and brought the whip down again. It hissed across his ass with a burning pain and he surged forward. He moved at full speed for only a few steps until his exhausted body began to slow.

"Come on boy, faster!" she called, kicking with the spurs.

He surged forward, but again began to slow. Cherub pulled up abruptly on the bridle, forcing him to rear back. Severin pawed the air with his front legs. He tried to whinny into the bit, but he wasn't sure how convincing it sounded.

He could feel Cherub shifting her weight. He could visualize her rubbing her thong panties across the saddle. When he went down to all fours she didn't urge him to crawl again, but began to rock back and forth. Severin caught the rhythm of her motion and rose to meet her. She wrapped her legs around his chest, pressing herself down as much as she could. She pulled back on the reins, steadying herself while he bucked under her. Her orgasm built slowly at first, then came all in a rush and he felt a wave of sweet dominant female energy sweep across him.

"That's a good horsie," Cherub cooed to him. She gave a gentle slap with the whip and guided him deeper into the club, back to her table. When they arrived she dismounted and removed the saddle from his back, forcing him onto his knees and tying the reins around the table leg.

She was still flushed with excitement and Severin took certain pride from the wet stain on the front of her panties. Her tiny breasts had come free of the lace bra, but she didn't seem to notice. Her power was fully manifested now and she towered over him.

Without any warning Cherub began to whip him. She was hitting him not as a rider hits a horse, but as a woman punishes a slave. Severin writhed under the lash, twisting around, even though he knew every movement simply exposed new flesh for her to strike.

The crowd watching had grown quieter now, struck silent by the simple, elegant brutality of the beating. Riding him had been fun and games, but suddenly this was for real. Severin felt as if she were proving her right to own this building, her very right to be a dominant woman, by reminding every man there what she was capable of.

The braided leather slammed into him again and again. His back and shoulders grew warm and raw under the beating. Tears were flowing freely now and he struggled to keep still.

Severin couldn't see Cherub's beautiful face growing dark as she whipped him. The blows came faster and faster and she seemed to be lost in a kind of trance as she beat him. The Viscountess, who had been watching while enjoying a cool drink, came to her.

"That's enough."

Cherub caught herself in mid-stroke. She let the whip fall from her hand. It took her a minute to catch her breath before she could answer.

"Time's up?" she asked.

"I say it is."

Cherub glanced at Severin's back and finally nodded.

"You're right." She wiped her brow and glanced at Severin again. "Thank you for letting me use your slave."

"You should be thanking him."

Cherub unwrapped the bridle from the table leg and took the bit from his mouth. Severin was still trying to get him eyes to focus when she leaned in and kissed him on the mouth. He was still too much in Subspace to respond.

"Thank you," she told him. "I've always dreamed of doing that to a guy, but Wormcock has a bad back."

Severin nodded, not quite sure what to say.

Chair got her mistress a cool drink while the Viscountess ran ice from hers across Severin's back. The touch of sudden cold made his whole body shake.

"Are you all right Severin?"

"Yes, Viscountess."

"I see you enjoyed yourself." She reached out and playfully tugged on his erection. "How was she?"

"Good. She's very powerful." Severin looked up to the table where Cherub was back in her chair being tended to by Chair. The sight of her disheveled form made his cock twitch involuntarily.

"I'm glad her height wasn't a problem."

"Height?" Severin frowned.

"Never mind." Viscountess sighed. "Go to the bar and get some water. Cherub says they have it waiting for you."

"Thank you, Viscountess."

Severin started to crawl away, but when the Viscountess saw his ass she ordered him to stop. The plug was still in his ass, but clearly he had forgotten about it. Gently she worked the plug free and set it aside.

"Oh, thank you, Viscountess."

"You should probably stand up, that'll make it easier, and feel free to put your clothes back on."

Grabbing the back of the chair Severin managed to get to his feet. It had originally hurt him to be on his knees, but now standing hurt almost as much. The skin across his shoulders felt tight as he put his shirt and pants back on.

At the bar the burly bartender had a glass of cold water ready for him. Most of the people seemed to be drinking various forms of home-made alcohol. Probably water was scarce in this Dominion.

Severin heard an odd humming sound and turned in time to see an odd figure float up to him.

"I enjoyed your little show," the man said.

The newcomer seemed to not simply be wearing latex, but as if his entire body was made of latex. Muscles and veins were visible on his shiny black flesh as he shifted his position. He was seated on a large floating chair with a high back. The back of the chair had a large metal ring mounted on it big enough that a person could stand on the bottom of the ring and reach up to touch the top. The arms of the chair were made from the same dull, silvery metal. It was covered with tiny, intricate designs that looked to be part writing and part artwork. Some of the de-signs glowed with a faint yellow light. The entire thing must have been very heavy, but it floated a few inches off the floor, bobbing slightly like a balloon.

The latex man had a companion, a strikingly beautiful blonde kneel-ing on the large footrest facing forward. with her arms were pulled back, each wrist attached to tone armrest. She seemed to be kneeling rather comfortably all things considered. She had superb muscle tone, healthy tanned skin and high, firm breasts. Her shoulder-length blonde hair seemed almost too bright in the dimly lit room, and the hair between her legs was exactly the same color. The woman's head was down, not making eye contact, but Severin could still make out her sharply chiseled features.

"Thank you, I'm glad you liked it," Severin managed to say. He drank some water to give himself time to think. There was something off about those two, but he wasn't certain what it was. "My name is Severin. I be-long to the Viscountess."

"I am known as Abraxus," the man announced. He did not introduce the girl. "I see that like me you have come from far away."

"That's true," Severin admitted. "We came for the fight."

"Indeed, it should prove interesting."

Abraxus interlaced his long, thin fingers across his chest. He had an odd, distant smile on his face. Something in the way he said the word "interesting" sent a shiver down Severin's spine.

"Well, if you'll excuse me sir, my mistress has need of me." Severin bowed and backed away.

"Of course." Abraxus made a fluttering dismissive gesture to send him on his way.

As Severin turned to go he noticed that Abraxus brought one hand down across the armrest of the chair. Several of the lighted areas changed colors and the chair turned to float after Severin.

Severin was still drinking his water as he returned to the Viscountess and Cherub. His owner glanced over his shoulder and saw Abraxus, who was keeping his distance.

"Friend of yours, Severin?" The Viscountess eyed the latex man warily.

"Not exactly. He calls himself Abraxus."

"I've seen him here before. I don't know where he comes from, but whenever he shows up there's always trouble." Cherub scowled.

"I have a bad feeling I know where he's from," Severin muttered. He glanced back at Abraxus and saw him idly petting the blonde, as if he didn't have a care in the world.

"Don't keep it to yourself," the Viscountess encouraged him.

"Notice how much they stand out? Their color seems almost too bright. It reminds me of the heightened reality of the Comic Book Dominion."

"How did they get here?"

"I think it's more important to ask why they're here. He looks like a man who's up to something."

"Sadly we have no time for another mystery. Our primary concern has to be finding Tiger Mask." The Viscountess glanced at Cherub. "Mistress Cherub here has just been telling me about tonight's fight."

"Boss Man keeps a lot of girls as whores. It's a tough life, about as brutal as he can make it," Cherub explained.

"Why do they put up with it?"

"Some of them don't. He has ways of getting rid of troublesome girls that you really don't want to know about. We have a deal. I don't mess with his whores and he doesn't bother any of the property I own."

"Then who does mess with him?"

Cherub grinned. "There's a new pimp in town named Rowdy. She's just starting out, but she's good. She's hard, but fair, and she's offering vacations and health care. Six of Boss Man's girls want to jump to Rowdy's stable."

"I'm sure he's not taking that very well."

"They each picked a champion and they're going to fight it out tonight. There aren't a lot of rules, but I'm here to see that nothing goes too badly wrong. If this Tiger Mask loses, then the six girls have to stay with Boss Man and Rowdy joins them. He likes to make examples of girls who cross him; it's not going to be pretty." Cherub hesitated and the compassion that she kept carefully hidden came to the surface. "I wish I could help them, but I can't afford to cross the Boss Man openly. They've already agreed to whatever punishment he says, no limits, no Safeword, just for a chance at being free."

Instead of responding immediately, the Viscountess clenched her teeth. Severin could see the jaw muscles working as she brought herself under control. When she spoke it was with a cool voice that lacked the anger she was obviously feeling.

"I'm afraid there are aspects to your Dominion that I do not like," she stated.

"Hey, it's home," Cherub grinned.

The Viscountess turned to Severin, hoping that he would continue the conversation.

"Where can we find Tiger Mask?" he asked.

"She's in back, working out. Come on, I'll introduce you." Cherub tugged on a nipple and Chair took her away. Wormcock shuffled behind them and the Viscountess and Severin followed.

The locker room of the civic center had a well-equipped gym for the sports teams, which was surprisingly intact. Near the benches were a group of nervous, scantily clad women. They were wearing tube tops or halter tops and had either short skirts or tight shorts that showed off their curves. They were smoking and talking quietly amongst themselves.

As soon as the group entered, one woman got to her feet who was not like the others. She was of average height, but looked bigger because of the football shoulder pads that she wore. They were all she wore except for a black X of electrical tape across each nipple. Her jet black mohawk was spiked up like the crest of an angry lizard. In back the mohawk became a pony tail that fell to the small of her back. Her sharp eyes were banded by a strip of black paint across her face like a mask.

In the back of the room a naked woman was pounding a heavy bag with her fists. She had on a yellow mask with three black lines on each cheek.

The woman with the shoulder pads raised an aluminum baseball bat, but Cherub spoke to calm her down.

"It's okay, Rowdy. This is the Viscountess and Severin. They're friends."

Rowdy relaxed somewhat, but was still on guard. The Viscountess stepped forward and bowed her head to her fellow dominant.

"Cherub told us what's going on tonight," Viscountess explained. "We wish you luck."

"Thanks," Rowdy grunted. "I'm hoping we won't need it. Tiger Mask there can take down about anybody I've ever seen apart from Boss Man himself."

"You were lucky to find her." Severin spoke up. Both the Viscountess and Cherub turned to him in surprise when he started to speak. "Kamen Girls aren't always easy to hire."

"We got lucky. This creepy guy in a floating chair just showed up with her one day."

"Really?" The Viscountess raised an eyebrow. "And he did this out of the goodness of his heart?"

"He said he wanted to help, and frankly I don't care why he did it." Rowdy glanced back at the women. "If it wasn't for him, I'd be fighting myself. Don't get me wrong, I'm tough, but Boss Man knows me and can come up with something I can't handle. This Kamen Girl is a stranger."

"I do wish you luck." The Viscountess assured her. "If you don't mind I'd like to speak to Tiger Mask."

"It's all right with me," Rowdy shrugged.

Rowdy talked to Cherub while the Viscountess and Severin approached the fighter. She was pummeling the heavy bag with lightning jabs that were so fast it sounded like a machine gun. The sweat glistened off her bronzed body as she pivoted; bringing one leg up for a kick that rocked the bag on its chain.

When she saw them, she paused and bowed. She was no taller than five and a half feet, but she packed a lot of muscle into her compact form. Severin noticed the sweat dripping off the nipples on her tiny breasts and felt his cock twitch inside his pants.

Tiger Mask put her feet together and bowed from the waist, Japanese style. The Viscountess returned the bow and Severin dropped to his knees.

"My name is the Viscountess and this is my slave Severin. We'd like to ask you a few questions."

Tiger Mask hesitated, her face impossible to read under the yellow mask. "I'm sorry," she finally said in slightly accented English. "I already have a job here."

"It's not about a job," the Viscountess explained. "The Crone asked us to investigate something."

Tiger Mask gave a start, losing her rigid military posture for a split second.

"I'm sorry, I must go."

She turned back to the heavy bag, but the Viscountess took a step forward.

"This is important."

"This is important, too!" Tiger Mask snapped, looking past her to Rowdy and the six women. "Those people are counting on me."

"I understand. Perhaps after the fight..."

"Perhaps."

Tiger Mask ignored them and went back to her workout.

"She certainly sounds guilty about something," Viscountess said under her breath as they walked away.

"Nah, it's too easy," Severin replied.

Looking at the group of frightened prostitutes, the Viscountess shook her head.

"It's as if they don't know they can Safeword."

"We can Safeword and go home," Severin reminded her. "Don't forget they're Denizens of this Dominion. What seems out of control to us is just normal for them. I'm sure if things were really outside the norm they'd Safeword."

They had just reached Cherub and Rowdy when a woman came from the bar with a message. Boss Man had finally arrived.

"Come on, you're not going to want to miss this," Cherub informed them.

Outside of the civic center Boss Man was making his entrance. First came a team of six pony girls in two rows of three. They were not the well trained pony slaves that the Viscountess and Severin were used to. They didn't all have bits or bridles, and instead of body harnesses they had chains locked around them. Instead of running in an easy rhythm with precise footwork, they stumbled and dragged their feet, trying to lug the massive weight of the vehicle their master was riding in. By the time they got to their destination they looked as if they would collapse.

Boss Man wasn't riding in a cart or a carriage. He was riding in a Cadillac. The huge piece of Detroit steel had been lovingly restored, but since gas was still a problem it had been retrofitted for slave power. The chains that bound the slaves were attached to the front grill of the car. The driver sat on a chair on the hood with the reins in his hands and a buggy whip, which he had been using frequently.

As soon as the car rolled to a stop the driver jumped off the hood and went around to open the back door so his passengers could exit.

The first person out was a slave. She crawled out of the back of the car, making her way painfully onto the pavement. She was plump and pretty, but her face was showing the signs of strain as she tried to move. Her limbs were caught in leather sleeves that bound her arms and legs bent, her hands against her shoulders and her feet to her thighs. There were little pads on the sleeves so she could walk on her knees and elbows, but such movement was very difficult. Her heavy breasts swayed back and forth as she crawled, making it hard for her to maintain her balance.

"I think I know her," the Viscountess said to Severin.

The slave's leash was held by the man who exited the car after her. He was simply huge. He stood over six feet tall and had shoulders as wide as the average door. His skin was an unhealthy white and he had no visible hair. His elephantine grace seemed barely human.

Dominant energy rolled off him in waves. He stood on the sidewalk and studied the people who had gathered. There was no question he was master of all he surveyed. Only Severin, the Viscountess, and Cherub seemed unaffected.

"This Dominion clearly has a knack for benevolent mutations," Severin commented.

The last person from the limo seemed nondescript compared to the other two. She was a slender brunette with a very beautiful face, wearing a silk robe that she hadn't bothered to tie, leaving most of her body visible. She was rail thin, but her breasts seemed a bit large for her narrow waist and obvious lack of body fat.

"That's the fighter?" Cherub couldn't help gasping.

It was true; the woman looked more like a starving supermodel than a fighter. She seemed as if she would be challenged by a stiff breeze.

Cherub and Boss Man exchanged formal greetings and the pimp was escorted inside. The tension between the two dominants, one so huge and the other so small, was so thick it was almost visible in the air.

In the lobby, Boss Man paused to climb into an extra-large chair. The woman with the bound limbs caught up to him while the woman in the robe followed with a blank expression on her face. Everyone watched him with a mixture of envy, fear, and desire.

He grunted a command to the woman on the floor. She balanced precariously on the stumps of her legs and leaned her face into his crotch. Boss Man opened his pants and unlimbered what looked like a long albino snake, but was in fact his cock. He began feeding the massive organ into the woman's mouth. She choked and twisted, trying to keep the cock in her throat and still keep her balance.

"That's a very large penis," the Viscountess admitted.

"If he ever fucked me with it, he'd rip me in half," Cherub shuddered. "He's threatened to enough times."

"It looks too big for him to get a full erection," Severin pointed out. "Not that it seems to be slowing him down."

The noises the woman was making grew louder and more intense. Boss Man thrust his massive body, sending the cock even deeper inside her. She made a high-pitched noise, and then fell backwards. As she hit the floor the cock sprayed semen like a fire hose, covering her face and chest. Boss Man roared with laughter and kicked her away.

With some difficulty she managed to regain her knees and elbows. By this time Cherub had opened the doors to let the audience in. The sea of moving people cut the woman off from her master. He got to his feet and headed for the arena, the frail woman following him, leaving his other slave behind.

The Viscountess took a rag from the bar and went to her at once, restoring her vision by wiping her eyes clear of come.

"There, that should help," the Viscountess said soothingly. "I had a silk handkerchief, but I'm afraid I lost it."

"Thank you," the slave said.

"Ah, you can talk. I thought you were a dog."

"I'm not a dog; I'm a quadruple amputee."

"Oh, I see." The Viscountess shifted her position so the crowd wouldn't kick the girl and knock her over. "I'm not sure if you remember me, but I topped you at a party in San Diego about two years ago."

"I remember." The slave blushed and looked down at her bound arms. "You're not going to tell anyone about this, will you?"

"You've nothing to be ashamed of. But don't worry, your secret's safe with me. I just came for the fight."

"I hope you're not betting on the hookers to win."

"Why?"

"Boss Man has someone who's bound to win. It doesn't matter who they get to fight."

Severin was close by. The Viscountess caught his eye and he immediately knelt next to her so he could hear the slave speak.

"Who did he get?" the Viscountess asked.

"She's called Ess Model. She's some kind of robot."

"She's an S Model android," Severin guessed. "Do you know what she's programmed for?"

"The guy in the chair said she was a pleasure unit, but that she has to obey any order she is given. Believe me; I saw her beat up two guys without even blinking."

Severin and the Viscountess exchanged worried glances.

"Um, thanks for the help, but I've got to get back to him. If he gets pissed, he'll kick me like a football."

"Thank you for everything." The Viscountess laid a friendly hand on the slave's shoulder as she hobbled away on her knees and elbows.

"This is bad." Severin said unnecessarily.

"Do you think that girl is really an android?"

"It could be. We think of this Dominion as being low tech because they've forgotten how to build things, but the tech level might be high enough to support a humanoid android."

"It supports a floating chair."

"Actually I'm thinking the chair may be magic."

"That doesn't help us, Severin. I have a bad feeling Tiger Mask isn't going to make it out of this fight."

From down in the arena came the roar of the crowd. They were stamping their feet in anticipation of the fight. If they were going to stop this fight, it might already be too late.

"Think of something." The Viscountess ordered. "And think of it fast."

Chapter Eight

"There's nothing I can do," Cherub told them when they had explained why they wanted to stop the fight. "Hiring a robot isn't actually against the rules. I warned you, we don't have a lot of rules here. I promise I'll call the match before anyone gets killed, but beyond that there's nothing I can do."

"I understand," the Viscountess declared.

She returned to Severin who was looking across the audience.

"I found Abraxus," he pointed. "He's got a box seat."

"I'll bet he does."

As they made their way through the audience they heard the sound of a bullwhip crack. Naked women, who before had been tending bar and dancing in cages now began to run in something like a giant hamster wheel. It went faster and faster, filling the air with ozone. When it hit the right speed the lights suddenly came up, illuminating the arena.

In the center was a ring set up for a wrestling or boxing match. Suspended above it was a large cage made of chain link fence pieces. The crowd went crazy, howling their glee at the top of their lungs.

"Apparently it's a steel cage match," Severin said, leaning in close so the Viscountess could hear him.

Under the hot lights, Chair carried Cherub into the center of the ring. The big masked woman unbuckled the chair and lifted it high over her head while Cherub spoke into a microphone.

"Ladies and gentlemen, and assorted perverts!" Cherub shouted. "Tonight we have a special event. It's a fight to the finish between Tiger Mask and Ess, with the freedom of six women on the line."

The crowd roared its approval.

"The fight will go on until we have a winner. There will be no weapons. There will be five minute rounds. The first fighter to surrender loses."

As the crowd stamped their feet and shook their fists in the air the two fighters entered the ring. Tiger Mask looked hard and fit. Ess stepped in front of the audience without a stitch of clothing on, glancing about as if she had gotten lost on the way to a tea party.

Chair carried Cherub to her large raised chair at the edge of the ring. Rowdy and the prostitutes were gathered in one corner near Tiger Mask, ready with water and rags. Boss Man was in the opposite corner, but didn't look as if he had any support supplies for his fighter.

"Let the battle begin!" Cherub shouted into the mike.

The cage descended slowly, sealing the entire ring inside the chain link fence cube. The fence sat just outside the ropes of the ring. As soon as the cage thudded on the floor, guards came forward to lock the winch. No one was coming out until there was a winner.

Wormcock was keeping track of the time. He signaled Chair who rang a bell.

As the fight began, the Viscountess and Severin finally reached Abraxus. The blonde girl was free of her restraints and was kneeling between his legs. The last time Severin had seen Abraxus, the man's crotch had been completely smooth, but now a cock-shaped protrusion jutted forth. It looked more like a shiny latex dildo that an actual living penis and the blonde was running her tongue up and down the length of it.

"I'm the Viscountess," she announced herself. "I believe you already know Severin."

"Ah, the famous Viscountess." The black face slid into a tight smile. "I am familiar with your work. I heard about the incident involving the Black Jade Dragon Dildo."

"I've been hearing about your work as well. You arranged this whole thing."

"I? Of course not. A brutal thug of a man, captive women yearning to be free—I had nothing to do with that. Perhaps I may have provided a few introductions here and there."

"Why?"

"Why not?" he chuckled. "I'm sorry, but I've always found why to be a tedious question."

"So this is all some game to you?"

"Hardly. I consider it an experiment."

"How so?" the Viscountess shot back.

The first round had started and he had to lean over in his chair to look around the Viscountess to see the action. This caused his cock to pop out of the mouth of the blonde girl who scowled and shifted her position to start sucking again.

"I think you'll agree that knowledge is the most important thing in the universe, in many universes," Abraxus added with a chuckle. "The only way to gain knowledge is through exploration and rigorous experimentation. I've always been fascinated by the Kamen Girls, but I've never found a way to test their abilities. Likewise I find the female robots that were produced here before the collapse to be remarkably versatile, but I'm not sure how successful they can be outside the bedroom. When the opportunity arose to test one against the other, how could I refuse?"

The crowd was even louder. The Viscountess and Severin couldn't help but turn to watch the action.

In the cage Tiger Mask was squaring off against Ess. Except for the Kamen girl's mask, both women were naked and of similar height, but Ess looked frail and helpless. When the Kamen Girl launched a series of powerful punches, Ess took the blows without any apparent effect, then swung an arm and knocked Tiger Mask to the mat.

Tiger Mask jumped up, kicking and punching. She was already breathing hard and sweating, but her opponent neither breathed nor had to perspire. Her skin was too perfect, smooth and unblemished, almost shiny. The high breasts were unnaturally perky. As the fight continued Ess was becoming more animated. Her face showed bright excitement as she casually blocked every blow the Kamen Girl sent at her.

Thinking quickly, Tiger Mask threw herself to the mat. She swung her legs around, catching Ess behind her knees. Android knees worked a lot like human ones, and the android crashed down.

Tiger Mask was on her in an instant, pinning her. After a few seconds of struggle Ess braced her heels on the mat and arched her back, throwing Tiger Mask off. The Kamen Girl was fast, catching herself and launching back with both feet. Her feet slammed into the android's head, ripping the skin of the forehead.

Ess got to her feet, unconcerned by the apparent injury. Artificial blood drained down from the wound, then automatically shut off when it seemed that it would block the vision in one eye. Under the flap of torn skin the bone in her forehead was clearly metallic. The sight of this sent the crowd into a deafening frenzy.

The Viscountess turned back to Abraxus and glared.

"Are you seriously going to tell me that you don't care who wins?" she demanded.

"It's important to remain impartial." Abraxus explained. "But obviously you care about the outcome. Perhaps we can work out a deal."

"What kind of deal?"

"I can bring this to a halt with a word."

"What do you mean?"

"The android was programmed to obey me before she was programmed to obey her new master. She has hieratical programming. If I give her the command to stop it will supersede the command to fight and the lovely Tiger Mask will go on to fight another day."

"And what would you charge for this service?"

He smiled and pushed the blonde girl off of himself.

"Merely a favor, nothing more. You travel a great deal and are developing a reputation among some very powerful people. I foresee a day when I will want to call on you for a favor and I need to know that you will grant it."

"What sort of favor?"

"There's the rub." Abraxus chuckled. The cock that had sprouted from his crotch now shrank back down, vanishing into his latex skin until he seemed to be completely neutered. "You never know what I want until it's too late."

"I take it she owed you a favor," the Viscountess glanced at the beautiful blonde.

"She does, and she's still paying it off."

The Viscountess glanced over at Severin.

"How are we doing?" she asked her slave.

"I'm ready when you are," Severin shrugged.

The Viscountess turned back to Abraxus and regarded him with regal disdain.

"I'm afraid I have to turn down your generous offer," she informed him. She then leaned in closer so no one else could hear. "I also think you're not as impartial as you pretend. If you didn't want to see those women punished by the Boss Man, you would have given the android to them."

Abraxus gave a start, as if he couldn't believe that anyone would question the purity of his motives. A yellow light throbbed in his eyes. Just as the Viscountess stepped away she caught a glimpse of the blonde prisoner grinning from ear to ear and knew that she had scored a hit against Abraxus.

They went down the steps toward the huge cage.

"Super villains," Severin chuckled. "They always talk too much."

"You actually have a plan?"

"Of course I have a plan. I can't guarantee it will work however."

"It's better than being an ornament on a floating sedan chair," the Viscountess pointed out.

"I have a feeling he would have a much different way to use you," Severin commented. "But that's a point well taken."

In the ring Tiger Mask was trying to get an arm lock on Ess. The android simply twisted her body and sent the Kamen Girl flying into the chain link fence. As she slid to the mat the bell rang marking the end of the round.

The exhausted Tiger Mask collapsed in her corner where Rowdy pushed some water through a hole in the fence. Tiger Mask was gasping as if she had run a marathon and it was only the end of the first round.

"Let us talk to her," the Viscountess said to Rowdy. "Severin has a plan."

The female pimp turned to the Viscountess and the dominant saw fear in the other woman's eyes. All their hope of freedom was slowly vanishing. Rowdy nodded, and stepped down so Severin could get to the edge of the ring.

Severin pulled himself close to the Kamen Girl. "Listen to me. You've got to make her come."

Tiger Mask turned and stared. "This isn't a catfight. She's killing me in there."

"And she'll stop if you can turn her on. Try it. You've got nothing to lose."

The bell rang. Tiger Mask got to her feet and went to the center of the ring. Ess walked slowly and carefully. The wound on her forehead still showed her metal skull, but she felt no pain or discomfort.

Tiger Mask threw a punch, which Ess easily blocked. Grabbing the arm that was used to block, the Kamen Girl twisted, throwing the android to the mat. In a second she was on top of Ess, pinning the android's wrists to the mat. Tiger Mask leaned down, pressing their two naked bodies together. The Kamen Girl's leg slid between the android's thighs.

With her superior strength Ess should have tossed Tiger Mask aside, but she did not. For precious seconds they were locked together. Finally, Ess broke free, but when she got to her feet she looked slightly dazed and was a bit unsteady.

Tiger Mask used the leg sweep again to bring Ess to the mat. The two of them were grappling, rolling across the mat. Each was trying to get a grip on the other; it looked as if they were somehow one person instead of two. The more they contorted, the more they twisted and turned on the mat, the more obvious it became that their struggle had become more sexual than combative.

"Don't fuck her, kill her!" Boss Man roared, lumbering to his feet.

"How did you know that would work?" Viscountess asked Severin.

"Abraxus gave me the idea when he mentioned her programming. She was programmed for sex before anything else."

"But she was ordered to fight."

"She has no choice but to follow those orders, but that doesn't change the fact that she's built to give and receive pleasure. Expressing herself sexually will override all other commands." Severin explained. "Obedience and sexual expression are the first two laws of sexbots."

"Sexbots have laws?"

"Yes, it's kind of like Asimov's three laws of robotics, but completely different."

"Really, so what's the third law of sexbots?"

"I don't remember, but I think it's don't kill anyone."

Oblivious to the irony, Boss Man screamed "Kill her!" again.

The two naked women were rolling around on the mat. Ess tried to break free, but Tiger Mask grabbed her arms and pined both the android's wrists to the small of her back. With her free hand Tiger Mask reached between the android's spread legs and began to stroke the clitoris.

Ess flopped on the mat, but despite her vastly superior strength she was utterly unable to free herself. Apparently her programming only allowed her to fight back for a limited time before succumbing to someone's advances.

When the Kamen Girl released her, Ess got to all fours, but wasn't able to stand up. The Kamen Girl took her and threw her on her back. Kneeling between the android's legs, she began to finger the pussy, now revealed to the crowd as dripping wet. Tiger Mask fucked her with one finger, then with two, then three fingers. Faster and faster she fucked her. Tiger Mask's powerful arm moved as fast and as hard as when she had been punching the heavy bag.

Ess cried out, a loud high-pitched noise. She had another loud orgasm that wracked her whole body with spasms and shouted something, but nothing could be heard over the sound of the crowd. When Tiger Mask was finally tired, she stopped. Ess tried to sit up, but flopped helplessly on the mat.

The deafening roar of the crowd was cut off by the ringing of the bell. It took several minutes to restore order. Finally, one of Cherub's guards had to fire precious bullets into the air to get everyone's attention.

"I declare Tiger Mask the winner!" Cherub shouted into the mic. The crowd went wild again, even louder than before. The huge cage was lifted to the rafters.

Rowdy and the women were hugging and kissing while Tiger Mask stood to one side and watched. Boss Man was trying to get to Cherub, but was held back by her guards. It was impossible to hear what he was saying, but his body language accused Cherub of cheating.

Viscountess and Severin were approaching Tiger Mask to talk to her when they saw Boss Man, having given up on Cherub, stalk angrily into the ring holding a length of chain. His slave flopped onto the mat next to him, trying to keep up.

"I'm sorry I failed you," Ess said.

Before she could rise from the mat, Boss Man slammed the chain across her body. Ess cried out in pain as she was programmed to do.

Seeing the beating sent a white hot surge of rage through the Viscountess. Without even thinking about it, she leapt between the ropes into the ring.

"Stop that!"

"She's just a machine," he sneered.

"I don't care. She's your slave and she did her best. You have no excuse for treating her like that," the Viscountess declared.

Chair had brought Cherub down to the ring. The little dominant slipped from her perch and went forward on her imperfect legs.

"She's right," Cherub declared. "You don't treat anyone like that. Not in my place."

"Maybe it won't be your place much longer."

His dominant energy rose up. Viscountess and Cherub felt it as if they were standing too close to a bonfire. He was powerful and he liked controlling women. His cock stirred in his pants in anticipation.

Before anything else could happen, Tiger Mask slipped easily between the ropes. She fell into a fighter's crouch next to the Viscountess. Rowdy joined her, baseball bat in hand. The prostitutes were right behind her.

"You think I'm afraid of you," Boss Man declared. Even as he said it he could feel himself being overpowered by the wall of angry women. Severin gasped as the rising tide of female dominance in the room swept through him. Dominants couldn't join their energy—each one at a different wavelength—but each of these women were individually angry at Boss Man, and each of them challenged his power.

Boss Man might have backed down, but he heard jeering from the crowd. His anger surged and he swept back his powerful arm to strike with the chain again. The chain went back, but it did not come forward. Over his shoulder he saw that the end of the chain was tightly gripped in the teeth of his amputee slave. He knew he could yank her into the air with a sweep of his arm, but the sound of a long bullwhip uncoiling caught his attention.

The Viscountess had her whip out, and Chair, who was almost as tall as Boss Man had a baton in her hand.

"It's over," Cherub told him. "Get off my property."

Boss Man gave a disgusted sneer and threw the chain to the ground. As he stalked out of the ring, he saw Abraxus floating ringside on his chair.

"This is your fault!" Boss Man roared. "You set me up."

The huge dominant male rushed Abraxus. Before anyone else could move, the pretty blonde suddenly rose to her feet. She caught one of Boss Man's wrists between her thumb and forefinger, forcing him to halt. She gave a gentle smile and a slight turn of her wrist.

There was a loud crack of breaking bone. Boss Man screamed and fell to the floor, clutching his arm, while the blonde sank back to a kneeling position.

Ignoring the interruption, Abraxus floated over to where the Viscountess stood.

"I'm afraid I find the results of this experiment inconclusive," he informed her.

"I'd say you've learned something important." The Viscountess smiled down at him. "You've learned not to piss me off."

Abraxus laughed. It started as a small chuckle, but after that he seemed to throw caution to the wind and let loose a full belly laugh. When he was done laughing he pressed something on his armrest and gestured to the blonde girl. She rose and obediently went to the back of the chair, placing herself inside the large ring.

As soon as the naked woman stepped into the ring, manacles grabbed her wrists and ankles, pulling her into the shape of an X

"You are correct, Viscountess. I have indeed learned something, and as I've said, all knowledge is valuable." Abraxus ran his fingers across the glowing symbols on his armrest.

Two mechanical arms emerged from the back of the chair. Each of them ended in distinct phallic shapes, dripping with lubricant. The mechanical arms positioned themselves, then slowly forced themselves into the blonde girl, penetrating both her pussy and her ass. She cried out and twisted in her bonds. The metal arms moved like pistons, in and out, faster and faster. As they built up speed the girl gasped and rolled her head from side to side.

"Until we meet again." Abraxus nodded to the Viscountess.

His chair floated up into the air like a balloon and then faded from view. Severin realized with a shock that he was fading into the void as if he were in a cart pulled by a pony slave.

Everyone stared for a few seconds at the space where he had been and the huge room, still teeming with people, was oddly silent.

"I hate that guy," Cherub muttered. Chair picked her up and began positioning her on her perch.

From the center of the ring Ess sat fawn-like, gazing around her. Apparently she sensed she didn't need to display the bruises from the chain any longer, since her skin returned to its normal healthy, almost shiny look.

Hesitantly Rowdy took a step towards the figure who looked so much like a frail, helpless woman, but wasn't.

"I can help you," Rowdy said gently. "I can get you clothes, a place to stay."

"I don't need clothes, or a place to stay." Ess spoke in a soft, placid voice no doubt calculated to make her more appealing.

"But you should have them."

"Why?"

That one stumped Rowdy. The pimp with the Mohawk looked over her shoulder at the other women for some suggestions.

"Try acting more dominant," Severin suggested.

Rowdy stood straight and raised her power. Behind her the prostitutes gave little contented sighs as they felt her strong energy wash over them. Ess hesitated for a second, then crawled to Rowdy's battered work boots and kissed them.

"How may I serve you mistress?" Ess begged.

The Viscountess leaned in close to Severin. "If she's only a machine, how can she pick up on our auras?"

"I don't know. She has to be sensitive to it in some way. That's what separates a high tech Dominion from one like ours. In our world science has its limits."

Rowdy bent and gently lifted Ess to her feet. The android leaned into her for a kiss, but Rowdy stopped her.

"You need to learn to take care of yourself," Rowdy told her.

"Of course," Ess smiled broadly. "If it pleases you."

"It does."

Rowdy gave a signal to the prostitutes who surged forward, enfolding the android in a sea of friendly hugs and kisses. Ess looked a little dazed as she tried to process it all.

As the group was leaving Viscountess saw Tiger Mask leaning against the ropes. Sheepishly the Kamen Girl came forward.

"I suppose you're here about Abraxus," she said.

"Abraxus?" the Viscountess asked.

"I deliberately lied on my report. Abraxus is the one who paid me, not Rowdy, but for some reason he wanted to keep it a secret. I should have known that he was up to something."

"That's not why we came." The Viscountess assured her. "Severin and I are here about something completely different. Why don't we sit down so we can be more comfortable?"

Behind her mask, Tiger Mask's eyes narrowed in suspicion and curiosity, but she did take a seat in the rows now empty of spectators.

"Tell me what this is about," Tiger Mask insisted.

"You were in the lounge on the twenty-third floor a few days ago with some others. Did anything unusual happen?"

"I don't know."

"Who else was there?" Viscountess prompted.

"There was Skye, Red Lightning, Papillion, and Blanca."

"Was Black Masque there?"

"Maybe, I don't know."

"Just tell us what happened." Severin suggested.

Tiger Mask looked from one to the other. "Nothing happened. Nothing unusual, anyway. We were eating and drinking. Skye was telling how in Roma she took a wrong turn in this guy's villa and wound up in the vomitorium. I can't believe what some people are into."

"Anything else?" the Viscountess smiled in sympathy.

"The usual rumors and gossip. The flu's been going around again; Blanca made fun of Red Lightning for busting up her leg, which she didn't appreciate. Papillion found this great pastry at a place in Paris in Europa Dominion. That's all I remember. I was sleepy and went to bed."

"How long were you there?" Severin asked.

"An hour, maybe longer."

The Viscountess was allowing Severin to ask the questions. "Where did you go then?" he continued.

"To bed."

"Do you have a roommate?"

"Not any more. I snore." Abruptly Tiger Mask got to her feet. She stood rigidly and fixed them with her dark eyes. "I appreciate all the help you've given me, but I think I have a right to know what's going on here."

Severin glanced at the Viscountess, passing the lead to her.

"After you went to your room, something was stolen from the temple," The Viscountess chose her words carefully. "Severin and I were called in as an outside agency to investigate."

"I don't... Wait a minute, you think I stole something?"

"It's a possibility. We're talking to everyone who was in that lounge."

"Oh." Tiger Mask shrugged. "I guess that's what I get for not having a girlfriend. I slept alone that night. I'm pretty sure Blanca and Papillion went off together. They've been an item for a while now."

"What about Red Lightning?"

"I don't know. I've never really talked to her."

"Have you been contacted by the Kamen Girls yet?"

"Yes. They want me to come right back, no side trips."

"If you talk to The Crone, she may be able to explain what's going on," The Viscountess reassured her.

"Yes, well, I'd better check in with Rowdy to make sure she's satisfied before I go."

Tiger Mask bowed stiffly and left. She seemed happy to see the last of them.

As soon as she left, the Viscountess and Severin exchanged glances.

"What do you say?" the Viscountess asked her slave.

"She sounded believable," he sighed. "But by her own admission she has no alibi."

"She said Black Masque wasn't there."

"She may not have noticed her. Tiger Mask was exhausted and in the middle of a meal. Plus we're asking her to recall a conversation from days ago, right after she'd gotten punched in the head. I wouldn't be surprised if the details are fuzzy."

"She didn't ask what was stolen. Isn't she curious?"

"I think it's their training. You notice how formal she was, as if she were in the military," Severin replied thoughtfully. "Besides she probably knows she can find out what's happened as soon as she gets back. That place must be a hotbed of rumors by now."

"Be that as it may, that still leaves us with one down and three to go." Viscountess glanced around the building. "For now I think I prefer the pre-apocalypse. Let's go home."

As they turned to say their goodbyes, they saw the nameless slave who had belonged to Boss Man struggling towards the stairs on her knees and elbows.

"Where do you think you're going?" Cherub asked. From her chair she was clearly enjoying the sight of the slave's full ass and heavy breasts that swung back and forth tantalizingly as she crawled.

"Home, I guess," the slave answered. "He was my master and I'm not good for very much."

"What do you mean?"

"I'm not exactly the kind of slave who dances in cages in case you hadn't noticed."

She raised one of her bound arms, crushed into the leather sleeve and waved it in the air. When she looked up at Cherub she saw a wicked grin on the face of the little dominant.

"Oh, I wasn't planning to put you in a cage." Cherub glanced down at her slave and barked an order. "Wormcock, get my saddle and spurs. I feel the need for another ride."

Looking up from the floor, the slave began to grin as well.

The Viscountess and Severin left quietly so as not to disturb the happy couple.

Chapter Nine

The Viscountess and Severin both slept late the next day. In the afternoon the Viscountess wished to cleanse herself of the grime from the Wasteland and spent some time luxuriating in her sunken bathtub. Severin rolled aside the enema stand and knelt next to the tub so he could bathe her.

"I couldn't have handled the Wasteland without you." The Viscountess sighed as the sponge passed across her. "Sadly, we have to get to the rest of the Kamen Girls before they get back and hear the rumors. We'll cover more ground if we split up. Are you game for some solo action?"

"If it pleases you." Severin lifted her hair and rubbed the sponge across the back of her neck which made her almost purr with satisfaction. "We've got weeks until they start running out of energy, but I'd like to get this wrapped up long before then."

"My sentiments exactly. Let's see, we have someone called Papillion in Las Vegas, Blanca in the Hospital Dominion, and Red Lightning in Europa. I've always wanted to go to Vegas, and it's in the Real World so it shouldn't be that difficult. Do you think you can handle Europa without me?"

"Europa?" Severin asked.

"Yes, it's sort of a historical mash-up combining the Venice of Casanova, the France of the Sun King and the Marquise De Sade, and the Rome of some of the more decadent popes."

"I take it you've been there?"

"The Duchess and I visited it on our Grand Tour. Red Lightning is supposed to be in Venice. Fortunately, I know someone there. I'll write a letter of introduction for you to Bonaventura."

"And he is..." Severin prompted as she raised her leg. He trailed the sponge down the length of her leg and began to wash her foot.

"He's quite a character. I'll warn him to be on his best behavior." The Viscountess presented him with the other leg. "Between the two of you, I'm certain you can handle it. Then we can meet up to compare notes and go to the hospital Dominion."

The Viscountess reached down and began to stroke herself between her legs. She raised her hips; her warm, wet body rose from the water. Severin had been trying to concentrate on the bath and ignore her body, but it was no longer possible. He pressed kisses against her foot, the only part of her that he could easily reach.

Laughing, the Viscountess pulled her foot from him. "You can find a better spot to kiss me that that," she teased, separating her lips with her fingers in case he wasn't getting the idea.

Severin immediately changed position and leaned over into the tub. Just before he reached her, she let herself sink beneath the water.

"Sorry, darling, you're going to have to decide what's more important to you, oxygen or giving me pleasure."

By way of answering Severin took a deep lungful of air and dived beneath the water. He managed to plaster his mouth over her clitoris and went to work with his tongue. His mouth was full of bath water, but when he gulped it down all he could taste was her. With his head submerged he felt as if he were diving into some unknown world.

Just as he was getting a smooth rhythm going Severin felt himself running out of air. He kept at it until his lungs burned, but finally he had to pull his head out with a great splash of water.

"Severin..." the Viscountess started to say something, but before she could continue he had gotten his wind back and dove down a second time.

This time Severin attempted to expel a small amount of air, then trap the air with his mouth over the clit. This was almost successful. He managed to get more suction on the clitoris, but the air bubbles made the Viscountess squirm. As she shifted position, the slave had to leaned further over to keep his mouth in position.

Suddenly he toppled forward, landing in the tub and sending a wave of water to the floor. The Viscountess cried out and tried to get out from beneath him even as he tried not to land on her. Both of them wound up standing in the tub with most of the water on the floor. Mistress and slave were laughing so hard it was difficult for either of them to speak.

"I'm so sorry," Severin stammered.

"Are you all right?" the Viscountess asked at almost the same time.

"I'm fine," Severin insisted. "Did I hurt you? I'm so sorry."

"No darling, I'm fine." She glanced around the large bathroom at the rapidly spreading pool of water. "I was joking, you know. You don't have to risk your life to please me."

"I just thought—"

"I know what you were thinking, and I'm terribly flattered."

At that moment Sklavin came to the door, skidded to a stop in her high heels and stared at the mess. The Viscountess was quick to reassure her.

"We're fine, Sklavin. Get a mop and bring it here. Severin has some cleaning up to do."

Later, after dinner and a light whipping, Severin went on the computer to research the real Venice. He wasn't sure how much the Dominion would resemble the real thing, but he knew that Victoria's version of London followed the actual map of London with very few deviations, so he assumed that it would be the same with the European cities in Europa.

After a few hours research he went to the bedroom to curl up on the floor. The Viscountess had fallen asleep reading. He gently took the book from her hands and slipped a bookmark in place. She murmured something and rolled over, turning her back to him. With a sigh he lay down on the floor and drifted off to sleep.

The gateway to the Europa Dominion was not only easy to find, it actually had a sign. Europa Clothiers appeared on the surface to be a specialty clothing store that specialized in vintage costumes. It was very popular with steampunk and renaissance faire fans, as well as the fetish community.

The array of clothes was staggering. The scent of velvet, leather and silk filled Severin's nostrils as he entered the store on his leash. The Viscountess had time to see him off since it was still several hours until her flight to Vegas. She hated borrowing a pony girl for such a short hop, and besides, asking Duchess for another girl so soon would seem like she was taking advantage of their friendship.

Inside the store there was a group of women trying on bodices for the coming faire season. Three of them were kinky enough to pierce the Blindfold. They glanced up and grinned at the sight of Severin on his leash. Their friends were not sure what they were smiling at. The Viscountess gave the women a nod of acknowledgement while Severin kept his head down.

The woman who ran the store was elegantly attired and carried herself with the air of royalty. She had a cool, glacial dominance that made Severin's cock twitch. This was a woman who could whip a man until he bled without ever raising a sweat.

"I'm the Viscountess, and this is Severin."

"Of course." The woman favored the Viscountess with a smile. She spoke clear, precise English, but there was something formal about her speech, as if she had learned it from a book. "I am Miss Ghiacciato. I take it your slave will be traveling to Venice?"

"That's right."

"And you're allowing it to wear clothing?"

"I thought it would be best."

"We'll see." Miss Ghiacciato looked him up and down, a tiny sneer curling the edge of her mouth.

"Is anything wrong?" the Viscountess asked casually.

"Not at all." Miss Ghiacciato turned to the Viscountess and her cold expression instantly warmed. "It's simply that some people were meant to wear clothing and some people were not. I can dress him, of course, but even well-tailored clothes will look wrong on someone of his nature."

"He's really only making a short visit."

"Yes, well..." Miss Ghiacciato paused and frowned as if trying to imagine him with clothes and failing. "I suppose there's something to be done with him."

She lifted a riding crop from the counter and slapped the wood with a loud crash. The sound of the noise sent two men scurrying from a back room. The store had several doors that lead off to storage areas and rooms with sewing machines where the clothing was made. The two men were dressed in suits and ties, but they came into the room as meekly as if they were collared slaves. She gave them a series of rapid fire orders, partly in French and partly in Italian. Miss Ghiacciato spoke both languages as well as she did English.

As the men ran off to gather clothes, Miss Ghiacciato produced a tape measure and began to carefully measure Severin. She took her time, moving her hands familiarly across his body and jotting down the results on a small notepad. After doing his inseam, she stretched the tape down the length of his flaccid cock, then wrapped it around to check his girth. She made notes of both numbers. Next she passed the tape around his testicles, measuring both how wide they were and how low they hung.

There was something arousing to Severin about her cold indifference to him. Being treated like a piece of meat spurred his cock to swell. Miss Ghiacciato glanced at his organ and gave a tiny, almost imperceptible shrug before glancing back at the Viscountess.

"Do you wish him to pass for upper class?" the clothier asked.

"Nothing too fancy."

"I believe we can come up with something."

Miss Ghiacciato went to her two minions and gave them the measurements. As they carried out a fevered multi-lingual discussion the three young women in brand-new bodices shyly approached. Apparently they had sent their Vanilla friends on ahead.

"Good afternoon ladies," the Viscountess greeted them.

"Um, sorry, I was just..." the boldest one suddenly got very shy. She was a voluptuous beauty whose corset displayed a lavish amount of cleavage

"Just what?" the Viscountess asked. She put a slightly harsh tone in her voice and let some of her dominant energy rise to the surface.

"Wondering if we could punish your slave," the young woman blurted out. The two behind her giggled and a very thin brunette snapped her chewing gum.

The Viscountess cocked her head to one side as if to get a better view of the trio.

"That was very rude," the Viscountess informed them. "Who trained you?"

"No one trained us. I'm dominant," the curvaceous woman insisted.

"Really? How interesting." The Viscountess put her hands on her hips. Her dominant energy spiked suddenly. Severin shuddered and sank to his knees. The leader of the three young women managed to stay on her feet, but her face flushed and she found herself looking at the floor unable to raise her eyes. "Just because you have power doesn't mean you know how to use it. A few simple lessons from someone older and wiser will help before you embarrass yourself by approaching a stranger, let alone doing a public scene. Do you understand me?"

"Yes, Ma'am," the leader said, still looking down.

"And the rest of you?" The Viscountess turned her steely gaze on the skinny brunette and the short woman with red hair.

"Yes, Ma'am," they both said.

If the three of them were capable of raising any dominant energy to resist her they were showing no signs of using it. The subtle waves of submission that the Viscountess had been sensing from them now flooded the room. They had fallen into Subspace without so much as a whimper.

"As for you..." The Viscountess glared at the skinny brunette. The bodice squeezed her narrow body, giving her an androgynous look. "It's quite rude to snap your gum during a conversation. Take the gum from your mouth."

The young woman hesitated for a second, then reached into her mouth with trembling fingers and took out the well-chewed wad of gum.

"Now stick it to your forehead."

The woman's hand seemed to move of its own volition as she stuck the grey mass to the center of her forehead. Apparently their submission wasn't completely without a whimper, since she was making small high-pitched noises in her throat. By the time her arm fell to her side there were tears welling up in her eyes.

"Humiliating isn't it?" the Viscountess asked casually. "Think of the suffering you could have saved yourself if you were only a bit more po-lite. I hope you'll remember that in the future."

The brunette nodded, her ability to form words having temporarily left her.

"Now on your knees, all of you!"

They dropped very quickly to their knees. The redhead moved so rapidly that her golf-ball sized breasts popped out of the bodice, her nipples pink and hard.

Miss Ghiacciato came from the back room and paused. She inhaled deeply, absorbing the heady energy in the air.

"Forgive me," the Viscountess said to her. "I didn't mean to start a Scene in your establishment."

"No need to apologize, it's quite all right. Please continue. If you'll allow me to borrow Severin, we can begin dressing him."

"Certainly."

The Viscountess unclipped his leash from her belt and handed it to Miss Ghiacciato. The cool blonde drew him to his feet. The seamstress noticed that his cock had gotten quite hard when his owner's dominant energy rose and took the time to do a few more quick measurements.

As Miss Ghiacciato led him into the back room, the Viscountess or-dered the three young women onto their hands and knees. She went to each of them and carefully lifted up their skirts. Beneath their histori-cal-style skirts they wore very modern underwear. One by one the Viscountess pulled their underwear down, leaving them exposed and vulnerable. They obligingly raised their knees so the underwear could be pulled down to their ankles.

"If any of you are uncomfortable with this, please Safeword now," the Viscountess informed them. Tears-Like-Rain was twitching against her thigh, but she knew the wicked single tail was too harsh for the trio. She took Hornet's Sting from her belt and felt the moose hide strands splay out, eager to be used.

"No Ma'am, um, I mean please..." the one who had first spoken stumbled over her words, but there was no sign of a Safeword in the sentence.

The Viscountess drew back and let the flogger hiss through the air. The leather strands smacked hard against the creamy white backside of the curvaceous woman. Her fleshy cheeks quivered and turned red at the first blow.

At the sound of the flogging Severin turned his head to watch. He expected a tug on his leash, but instead Miss Ghiacciato stopped and simply cleared her throat. The sound was as menacing as a bullet being loaded into the chamber of a gun. Severin lowered his head and hurried after her.

The Viscountess moved from one woman to the next. She used simple, solid strokes, making sure that the wrap around didn't strike their pussies when she hit their inner thighs. They sobbed and moaned, the leader shaking all over. The redhead was so turned on she reached up to play with herself, which earned her a sharp rebuke from the Viscountess and extra strokes.

As she flogged them, the Viscountess explained a little about courtesy and how to address fellow dominants and submissives.

"It's all about respect, really," she informed them while delivering a hard blow to the leader. The Viscountess noticed that the skinny brunette couldn't take much of a whipping on her ass, and the redhead was bucking her hips so wildly she'd have to be tied down for a further beating. The Viscountess decided to focus the rest of the punishment on the chubby beauty who had been so rude.

"Do you even know what you did wrong?" the Viscountess asked her. She teased the thongs of the flogger across the red cheeks.

"I shouldn't have talked to you," the girl sobbed.

"You have every right to talk to me, but you should introduce yourself, then enquire about myself and my slave and see if he is available. In fact, he is rather busy now, which is a pity since he loves public Scenes and I'm sure he would have enjoyed submitting to you under other circumstances."

"I'm so sorry, Ma'am," she gasped as another stroke of the flogger burned across her quivering flesh. She sounded very sincere in her apology.

"I am the Viscountess. You may address me as such."

"I'm sorry, Viscountess."

The Viscountess placed her boot next to the girl's head, gently lifting it until the tear-stained face was visible. All three of them were crying now.

"I'm sorry, Viscountess," she repeated. She started to kiss the boot and the Viscountess let her worship only the toe of the boot before she removed her foot.

She repeated the process with the other two. Each apologized and added their kisses to the tear-stained leather.

The whole Scene might have gone on longer had Severin not emerged from the back room at that point. He was wearing a long brocade coat over a tight vest and a linen shirt. His breeches were tight and his polished leather shoes had heels on them. He walked awkwardly, as if he were on stilts.

"Severin, you look marvelous," the Viscountess greeted him. "How do you feel?"

"Like a mummy. It reminds me of the time you had me in a straight-jacket."

Miss Ghiacciato swept past Severin, giving him an icy gaze.

"Madame, there is a limit to what even I can do. Perhaps in dim light he might get by, but one simply cannot make a lion from a mouse."

The Viscountess frowned and examined him. Severin shuddered under her gaze. He was doing his best to wear the clothes, but somehow they simply didn't hang on him properly.

"You may be right," the Viscountess admitted. "I'm afraid I shall have to send him naked."

"Very good."

Miss Ghiacciato gave a quick order. The two attendants emerged from the back room and took the clothes from him in a fraction of the time it had taken to put them on. Once he was naked again Severin knelt at his owner's feet.

"I don't want you to be accused of trying to pass yourself off as a dominant. Honor's very important in Europa and I don't want you getting into trouble." She handed him the letter. "You look very tempting like that. Fortunately for you I've instructed Bonaventura to keep his hands off you."

"Then he's gay?"

"Quite, but since that word hasn't been coined in his Dominion he simply calls himself a sodomite."

"I see."

"He's a marvelous guide. You should be able to find him every day at the public punishments in St. Mark's Piazza."

"The Venice Gate opens to St. Mark's," Miss Ghiacciato explained.

The Viscountess gave Severin a detailed description of Bonaventura and allowed him to glance at a map of Venice to give himself a passing familiarity with the city.

Severin studied the map, but when he glanced around he saw the three girls lined up with their heads against the wall. Their hands were behind their backs, holding up their skirts to display their red, punished asses. He was still admiring them when the Viscountess excused herself and went to the trio.

"I hope you've learned your lesson," she told them after giving them permission to move.

"Yes, Viscountess," the leader said.

The Viscountess gave the leader of the girls a slip of paper. "The people on this list will be more than happy to talk to you about etiquette and protocol."

"Thank you, Viscountess," all three of them said.

The Viscountess leaned over and kissed the leader on the cheek. "Now run along. I'm sure your friends are waiting."

The three of them lowered their skirts, stepping out of their underwear and leaving the panties behind. As they left Severin noticed that the skinny brunette still had the gum stuck to her forehead. Pressing her head against the wall had flattened it to a disc. Severin wondered how long it would be before she was able to remove it.

"Once again my apologies," the Viscountess said to Miss Ghiacciato when the three had left.

"Think nothing of it; it was a pleasure watching you work." Miss Ghiacciato smiled warmly as a spark of attraction leapt between the two women. "Perhaps we can get together again when we have more time so I can study your technique."

"I think I'd enjoy that very much."

Severin remained quiet, with his head down while the two women flirted. Finally, the Viscountess turned to him.

"Are you ready Severin?"

"Yes, Viscountess. Are you ready for Las Vegas?"

"I believe so," The Viscountess adjusted his collar so the tag identifying him as her property was in front. "Do you have any tips for my interrogation?"

"Just follow your instincts. Try to ask about the conversation in the lounge without mentioning the missing Sphere or the drugged drink," the slave suggested.

"Wouldn't they already know if they stole the Sphere?"

"But they don't know that you know. They also have no reason to think that you've discovered the drugged drink. The more we can get them to talk before they have a chance to go home the better."

"Understood. Be careful Severin. Bonaventura will take good care of you, but it's still a new Dominion for you, and I'm not sure how many of your favorite fetishes you'll find there."

"I'll be fine. Have fun in Vegas."

"I intend to."

The Viscountess stepped back and extended her foot. Severin got to the floor and passionately kissed the boot.

Miss Ghiacciato produced a large ornate brass key. "If the slave will accompany me, Venice awaits."

Chapter Ten

Severin stepped out onto the large plaza and was immediately over-whelmed by the sights and sounds. It wasn't as busy as Shinjuku in Neo-Nihon, but it was a lot like stepping into the middle of a circus. The area was packed with people. Most of them were dressed in the same elaborate eighteenth-century style that his own body had rejected, although he saw a few naked slaves. One naked woman was playing a violin. She had a cloth on the paving stones in front of her to collect coins.

In the center of the plaza stood a platform where the public punishments were taking place. Two men and a woman were chained to posts being flogged. It was a serious beating; the strands of the floggers were old and stiff, easily able to draw blood. As the blows fell and the cries from the victims increased, the cheers from the crowd also increased.

The Viscountess had said that Bonaventura would have a good seat for the festivities, but that he wouldn't be able to afford the best seats. Clearly the best view was from the balconies that overlooked the square, but those were packed with a glittering throng of people, some of them masked. The next best view was from the back of a cart that some enterprising soul rented as a viewing platform

It didn't take long for Severin to notice a striking figure leaning against the rails. The man watched the whipping with an insolent air while enjoying a gelato. His clothes were exquisite and made what Severin had attempted to wear look like rags. The breeches were so tight it seemed he shouldn't be able to move, but he looked as casual and natural as if he had been born in them. He wasn't particularly handsome, but he had an animated face and sharp, clever eyes.

Severin approached. After one particularly nasty stroke of the whip, the man flinched and glanced away. When he turned his head he saw Severin and the sight of Severin's naked body seemed to perk him up a great deal.

"Excuse me, are you Achilles Bonaventura?"

"Indeed I am." He forced his gaze away from Severin's crotch and made eye contact. "I don't believe we've met. I never forget a, um, face."

"My name is Severin, I belong to the Viscountess. She told me to give you this letter."

Bonaventura leaned out of the cart and plucked the letter from Severin's hand. The Venetian read it with some interest. When he was done he handed the gelato to the person next to him and slipped nimbly under the rails of the cart to land on the street. Along the way he scooped up a tricorn hat and a walking stick that very likely concealed a sword. He moved with amazing grace despite his layers of clothing.

"It appears I am at your service. You must tell me how the Viscountess is doing."

"She's quite well." Severin hesitated, not quite sure if his next question was going to be rude. "How do you know her, anyway?"

"We had a few adventures a while back. Charming girl. I tell you, if I were the sort of person who could fall for a woman—and I assure you, I'm not—" He gave Severin a suggestive wink. "Then she would be the sort of woman that I would fall for."

Severin wasn't quite sure how to respond to that, but it was just as well since Bonaventura was still talking.

"So you have come to infiltrate the party of Duke D'Agostini?"

"I'm really just here to talk to the Kamen Girl."

"But the letter says she was hired for security by Manzoni the diamond merchant."

"Exactly. I need to find this Manzoni. Does he have a shop nearby?"

"He has a shop, but he isn't in it. He's getting ready for the duke's party. Tonight he's going to debut his new collection. The whole town is talking about it."

"All right, so how do I get into the party?"

"That is simple. All you have to do is arrive with me. I am never turned away from a party." Bonaventura favored him with a smile. "Of course once you find your girl, you're on your own. Interrogating women, masked or otherwise, isn't something I have much practice in."

"I think I can handle that part."

"Excellent! Then let us be off. We have time for some coffee and relaxation before the gala begins."

"Sorry to take you away from the whipping."

"It's an uninspired bunch today. Perhaps next week we'll have more lively miscreants." He glanced over his shoulder to see one more blow from the heavy flogger before turning his full attention to Severin. "Is this your first time in Venice?"

"It is, but I've heard of St. Mark's Square."

"We simply call it the Piazza. It's the center of Venice—some say the center of the world. I've travelled the world, but always I return here."

They made their way across the brightly decorated paving stones past vendors of various kinds. A black cloud of pigeons flew up, momentarily obscuring their view, but Bonaventura continued walking, ignoring the birds. With their backs to the huge church, Severin saw bright blue water at one end of the square. The scent of the sea had been in the air the whole time, but Severin hadn't noticed it with everything else to take in.

A group of nuns, their bodies tightly covered except for their faces, walked past. They looked at Severin and giggled, nudging each other in the ribs. Were nuns dominant or submissive here? It could go either way, but he decided to keep his head down and not take chances.

They passed between two huge columns. One of them was decorated with the statue of a winged lion, the other with the statue of a man with a whip who was subduing a naked woman.

"The fellow with the whip is St. Theodore; he was the patron here before St. Mark took over. I'm a little fuzzy on the history of the statue, but I think the naked woman represents sin or something."

There were more boats that Severin could count in the lagoon. Bonaventura navigated past people selling trinkets of all kinds and zeroed in on a gondola whose boatman jumped to attention at the sight of them. Bonaventura called the man by name and flipped him a coin before turning to help Severin. He guided Severin to a bench in the back of the boat.

The wood was smooth under his ass and the air felt good on his skin. The boatman knew his job and guided the boat easily through the water. The long, lean gondola glided smoothly away from the docks and into one of the stretches of canals that filled Venice.

"Listen to me prattle on," Bonaventura sat on a bench of his own. "I've only been to a few cities and you've probably been to a hundred different worlds."

"Not quite that many," Severin admitted. It always felt uncomfortable talking about the Dominions with someone who was born in them. "I take it the Viscountess described how she traveled here."

"Yes, all those different worlds, and you just leap from one to another like a flea jumping from one person to another in the Piazza."

"That's a pretty good metaphor."

Bonaventura glanced up and caught the eye of a young man walking across a bridge. Just as the gondola went under the bridge Bonaventura winked at the man, who blushed and looked quickly away.

"If it's all the same to you," Bonaventura announced lazily. "I shall be satisfied with one world."

The gondola slid silently across the dark water of the canal. It was literally a street made of water, splashing against buildings on both sides. Severin knew about the famous canals of Venice, but somehow being there was so much more impressive than seeing pictures.

They passed an open area with a dock where two men were vigorously fighting with swords while a few other men cheered them on. Severin sat up in alarm, but Bonaventura glanced at them and shrugged.

"It looks like someone's made fun of Antonio's vest again." The Venetian shrugged. "We'd be spared a great deal of bloodshed if he'd only find a decent tailor."

Following his instructions, the boatman steered the gondola to the coffee shop whose dock lead to stone steps. Bonaventura flipped him a coin and stepped onto the stone as easily as if he were stepping across a muddy puddle on the sidewalk. Severin tried to follow just as casually, but he started to lose his balance and Bonaventura had to steady him.

"So tell me, this Kamen Girl of yours, do you know what she looks like?" the Venetian asked conversationally.

"Only that she will be naked except for a mask."

Bonaventura had a good laugh and informed Severin. "It's a lucky thing you didn't come at Carnevale when 'naked except for a mask' describes about a third of the population."

Inside the shop the atmosphere was rowdy and smoky. There was a riot of conversation going on in several languages. Bonaventura stared wistfully at a card game as they entered, but steeled himself and went to a table in the back.

The sounds of the voices made Severin think of something.

"I want to compliment you on your excellent English."

"Really?" Bonaventura grinned amiably. "And here I was about to compliment you on your Italian."

"I'm not speaking Italian," Severin protested.

"I can assure you I'm not speaking English. This must be one of those tricky things that happens when you jump worlds."

Severin nodded, a little excited about discovering a new fact. "Each of us hears the language that we're the most comfortable with. But if I want everything in English, why can I hear the people at the bar speaking in Italian and French?"

"Perhaps because they're not talking to you," Bonaventura suggested. "Or perhaps it's simply that they come from the France and Italy of your world, and therefore encounter only people speaking French and Italian."

"That's a good theory."

A waiter came with a cup of coffee for each of them.

"It's the best coffee in the world, or if it isn't, just keep adding sugar until it is."

Severin sipped the coffee and found it surprisingly good. He added sugar anyway and lamented to his host that there was no cream for it.

Bonaventura caught the eye of a handsome young man and produced a coin. The young man was at his table instantly with an eager expression on his face.

"May I help you sir?"

"Yes, I'll take some," Bonaventura told him. The man grinned and made the coin vanish. In the space of a few seconds he was on his knees, opening the front of Bonaventura's breeches. "Don't worry Severin, I'll find a boy for you, or perhaps you'll take this one when he's done with me."

"Oh no, that's quite all right," Severin informed him. The sounds of sucking and slurping coming from under that table made him uncomfortably aware of his own nakedness.

"It's no problem at all. I'm sure they have another boy on duty."

"Really, I'm fine, thanks."

"It's a perfect way to relax before the night's festivities." Bonaventura shifted in his seat, giving the young man better access. "Is anything wrong?"

Severin hesitated before answering. The fact was he did feel uncomfortable with male-on-male sex. He had no problem watching it, but participating in it was another matter.

"Nothing's wrong. I simply prefer to have sex with women," Severin said as diplomatically as he could.

"Really? One of those, eh. I'd never have guessed by looking." Bonaventura took a sip of his coffee. "It's always seemed to me that if you want a proper sexual partner you should look for one who has an intimate knowledge of your body. I ask you, what does a woman know about a cock?"

"Excuse me?"

"Oh, she may be quite well practiced at oral sex, don't get me wrong, but how can she understand the subtle intricacies, the delicate complexity of the male organ without possessing one?"

"It seems to make sense when you put it that way."

"The sheer logic of the argument is overwhelming."

"But the heart is not logical," Severin explained. "I love women as much as I love being whipped."

"I suppose it takes all kinds." Bonaventura shrugged. Apparently at that point the young man applied his tongue to the delicate complexity of his cock, for he sighed and leaned back in his chair.

Severin sipped his coffee for a few minutes while Bonaventura's breath came in rapid pants. Finally, he sighed and relaxed in the chair. The young man came out from under the table dabbing at his face with a handkerchief.

"You were superb, as usual." Bonaventura tossed him a second coin.

"Thank you, sir." He turned to leave, but noticed Severin. "If your friend would like I can..."

"Alas no," Bonaventura held up a hand signaling the young man to stop. "My friend has an illogical heart."

The young man didn't seem to quite understand that, but he nodded and smiled and went on his way. He vanished almost at once in the swirling mob of people.

Bonaventura finished his coffee and put the mug down with a theatrical flourish. "Good coffee, good conversation, and excellent sex. If heaven isn't at least half this good, I have no intention of dying."

Severin raised his mug in salute.

Venice at night was a sea of candles and torches. The light reflected off the white walls and the water of the canals. The gondola took them into the Grand Canal, a wide superhighway of water that curved gently through the ancient city. They were clearly moving into a better part of town now. On one of the side canals the lavish home of the Duke D'Agostini glittered as the light reflected off the white marble of the palace-like structure.

As the gondola slid noiselessly up to the dock, Severin saw that the private dock was lit by torches held aloft by women wearing nothing but body paint. Severin wondered how they could hold the torches outstretched for more than a few minutes until he saw that each woman was encased in a wrought iron framework which held her limbs in place and supported the weight of the torches, giving the illusion the women were holding them. The metal had been painted the same white as the women's bodies, making them look like ancient Roman statues.

As soon as he saw the guests with their jewels sewn with gold thread into the fabric of their clothing, Severin knew that they had made the right decision to send him in naked. Bonaventura took it all in stride, hopping off the boat, acknowledging the servants, and exchanging quick smiles with the other guests who were still on the dock. He noticed Severin's discomfort and slipped an arm over his shoulder.

"Relax, my friend," Bonaventura whispered. "Just pretend as if you belong here and no one will question you. I escaped from the Bastille that way. Funny story, remind me and I'll tell you about it."

They entered the great house. Bonaventura seemed to know everyone, or at least pretended to. Severin noticed the obvious class distinction. There were wealthy guests at the party and the elaborately dressed servants with their innumerable buttons and powdered wigs who served them. Below them were the naked slaves, both male and female, who moved about doing their duty as if invisible. Protocol was clearly very important here. The servants provided food and drink while everything sexual was done by the slaves.

Severin realized that although a dozen people had hugged Bonaventura or clasped his hand, none of them had given Severin more than a passing glance. He realized the wisdom of making this journey naked. He never could have pulled off passing as a rich man, and he wasn't even sure he could pass as one of the liveried servants. Hopefully as a mere slave he could do what he had to do and slip out unnoticed.

"Enema?" Bonaventura offered. He gestured to a room where elegant men and women lay on couches while servants prepared various mixtures and sent them through rubber hoses in their asses.

"Sorry, no. I'd like to look around on my own a bit."

"I hope you won't mind if I..."

"By all means, continue." Severin bowed to him and Bonaventura returned the bow.

Moving deeper into the vast building, Severin navigated his way through the many rooms. The gathering was much less kinky than many parties he had attended, but there was an air of corrupt decadence about the whole event. There was something terribly sexy about the glimpses of naked flesh beneath the elaborate clothing as people unbuttoned their breeches or flipped up their cumbersome dresses. Many of the women wore pannier under their dresses that served to widen their hips and made their torsos look unnaturally small.

Severin noticed two men engaged in an intense conversation. Between them a woman wearing only an iron collar knelt, giving each man a hand job. Their conversation never lagged, as if they didn't notice her. She had a cock in each hand and was furiously pumping. When one of them was ready to come she leaned in and opened her mouth, gulping all of it neatly down. She then repeated the process with the other man. The men were still talking as the slave closed their pants and left.

As Severin entered a new room he saw an elegant woman with an open fan across her chest. When she saw that he had noticed her she lifted the fan, exposing her breasts which were lifted and displayed by the corset. Her hoop skirt was completely open in the front, showing off her stocking-clad legs and what lay between them. She had thick pubic hair and a prominent clitoris which rose from the hair like a dolphin leaping from the ocean.

"Ah schlavo," she said as she saw Severin. "You are not familiar to me. Do I know your owner?"

She extended a foot encased in a tightly buttoned calf boot. Severin dropped to his knees and kissed her foot.

"No, mistress. I am Severin, I'm traveling without my owner, but in the company of another."

"How extravagant that your owner allows you such freedom," she chuckled. "I am the wife of Duke D'Agostini. You may stand."

Recognizing the name of his host, Severin scrambled to his feet. She was exposing herself, but he didn't get the feeling that she was a slave. She was a powerful beauty, but she wasn't giving off either dominant or submissive energy. He kept his gaze on the floor just in case.

"You may look at me. I give you my permission." She seemed vaguely amused by him. Severin brought his eyes up, taking in every bit of her. She fluttered the fan, using the breeze to make her nipples hard. "Perhaps you are wondering about the dress? It was a gift from my husband."

"I see." Severin tried to sound non-committal.

"He recently caught me with another man and decided that since I never hesitated to flaunt my attributes he should have my dressmaker provide assistance."

"You look quite lovely in it."

"Thank you. I must tell you that in addition my husband has decreed that since I have played the part of the donna immorale it would be wrong of me to deny his guests or their companions anything they may desire."

"I see," Severin repeated. He noticed over her shoulder a small commotion at the back of the room.

"Perhaps I could order you." She snapped her fan shut and used it to stroke his penis.

Severin bowed to her again. This was a Dominion where manners counted a great deal and he knew he has to tread carefully. "I'm very sorry."

Behind her Severin saw a short, squat man with a diamond pin on his lapel entering the room. He was accompanied by a Kamen Girl.

"Surely your mistress need never know," Duchess D'Agostini teased.

"A thousand pardons, I mean no disrespect, but I'm afraid I'm unworthy of your precious time. If you will excuse me..." Severin kept bowing as he backed away from her and maneuver toward the diamond merchant. The Venetian beauty flared her nostrils and gave him a last look of contempt.

Apparently Red Lightning wasn't just the security for the jewels, she was also the display case. She had a heavy necklace of diamonds draped around her neck and a jeweled bracelet on each wrist. Teardrop diamond earrings glittered on each nipple, hung from wire since her nipples weren't pierced. She walked with a stately elegance behind the man who had to be Manzoni the diamond merchant.

People clustered around Manzoni, shaking his hand and admiring the latest designs. Severin felt sorry for Red Lightning as she stood very still, allowing people to handle the diamonds and cop a feel at the same time.

After a while the crowd thinned around the Kamen Girl. Manzoni was talking loudly a few feet away, surrounded by people. Severin took the opportunity to slip next to the masked woman.

"Excuse me, my name is Severin and I'd like to ask you a few questions?"

The woman turned and stared at him as if he had two heads. She had what Severin had come to think of as the standard body type for Kamen Girls. Average height with a slender, hard body. Her mask was silver and had, not surprisingly, red lightning bolts arcing across the top of her head, meeting on her forehead.

"I'm working." Red Lightning said coldly. She ignored him and smiled at the guests, encouraging them to take a look at the diamonds.

"The Crone has asked me and my Mistress to look into something. This will only take a few minutes."

Red Lightning regarded him again and finally nodded. "I'll get a break in about ten minutes. You can talk to me while he loads me up with another batch of diamonds."

Severin waited, trying not to look too impatient while Manzoni made small talk, bringing every conversation back to the fine quality of his diamonds. Finally, Manzoni excused himself and left the room, followed by Red Lightning. Severin noticed that she walked with a limp, favoring her right leg.

There was a secure room with a heavy lock that Manzoni opened. Inside were several heavy leather cases with padlocks. Manzoni paused on the threshold, realizing that Severin had followed the two of them.

"It's all right, he's with me," Red Lightning told him.

"Ah, very well," Manzoni peered over his glasses at Severin, but apparently wasn't worried by what he saw. "I'll be back in a few minutes. Enjoy yourselves."

When he had left, Red Lightning locked herself and Severin in the room. Obviously Manzoni thought there was something going on between the two of them, but Severin didn't try to correct him. The reason for the locked door was clear when Severin saw that the cases contained dozens of pieces of jewelry. Even in the candle-lit room the diamonds glittered. There had to be several million dollars in that tiny room.

"You wanted to talk, so talk." Red Lightning went to a small table and poured herself a glass of wine.

"When you came back from your last mission you were in the lounge on the twenty-third floor." Severin spoke carefully, trying to keep his voice neutral. "Skye was there, Tiger Mask, Blanca, and Papillion."

"If you say so."

"Do you remember anything about what happened while the five of you were talking?"

"Why are you asking me these questions?"

"My Lady and I have been asked to investigate something that happened that night. I'd like to know what happened in that lounge. It could be very important."

Red Lightning finished her wine before answering. "Nothing happened. I mean I don't remember anything happening. We just talked."

"About what?"

"Stuff." She shrugged. "There's a nasty bug going around. Papillion almost got caught stuffing her face with French pastries."

Her voice trailed off, apparently unable to recall any more. Severin decided to prompt her. "I noticed that you walk with a limp. Did anyone mention that?"

Red Lightning's eyes flared with anger.

"Blanca! She has no right talking like that. What has she ever done? She said I fell down a flight of stairs."

"So what really happened?"

"I was thrown down the stairs by Mariabots in Megalopolis—you know like the ones from that movie."

"I'm familiar with them." Severin had a mental image of the shining metal female robot from Metropolis. He had no idea there was even one Maria robot out there, let alone enough to attack a Kamen Girl.

"I could have died," Red Lightning told him. She turned her back and filled her wine glass again. "Look, I'm sorry; it was just an ordinary, boring conversation."

"Was Black Masque there?"

"Sure, she stopped by, said hello to everyone; she always likes to get a feel for how a mission went, something beyond the written report."

"Did anyone tell her anything unusual?" Severin asked.

"No, nothing. I suppose you were expecting some kind of crazed lesbian conspiracy or something, but we're really very dull."

"Do you know what order people left in?"

"I'm not sure. Tiger Mask and Skye left. I went after them so Blanca and Papillion could go muff diving in peace."

There was a knock at the door.

"If you have any other questions, they're going to have to wait," Red Lightning informed him. When she unlocked the door, Manzoni was standing on the other side.

"All done, you two?" the diamond merchant asked by way of greeting. He seemed disappointed that he didn't find them sweaty and disheveled.

"Just one question." Severin put in. "I noticed you haven't asked me what I'm investigating."

"Why should I?" Red Lightning smiled beneath her mask. "I'm going back as soon as I'm done here. When I get there I can ask someone I trust what's going on."

Severin had no response to that. He left the two of them alone.

Manzoni began picking out fresh diamonds to drape her with.

Severin returned to the party. It was becoming a bit wilder now, and he noted various people has lost some of their clothing. He hunted until he found Bonaventura. The Italian adventurer was in a side room surrounded by a small crowd of people. Another guest of the party was bent over a chair, his wrists tied together and the rope running through a pulley in the ceiling. His coat and shirt had been thrown over his shoulders and his pants and underwear at his ankles. The man's ass showed every sign of a spanking and his erect cock bobbed up and down as Bonaventura methodically rogered his ass.

"Ah, good evening Severin." Bonaventura greeted him. "I hope your evening has been as successful as mine."

"I found the person I had to talk to."

"Excellent. I'll be done with this rascal in a moment." He gave a sharp spank to the man, who gasped and jumped.

"You don't have to hurry on my account," Severin informed him. "If I can get one of those gondolas I can make it back to the Gateway without any problem."

"Nonsense, I can't have you wandering the streets at night. If brigands were to come upon you the Viscountess would never forgive me."

"If you insist."

"I do. Besides I think I have sufficiently driven home my point." Bonaventura thrust deeply, until his hips were against the man's red ass cheeks. "Unless of course our friend has some further criticism of Voltaire's conclusions in Candide."

"No," the man gasped. "You're quite right about the subtlety of his arguments."

"I'm so glad we could reach an agreement like gentlemen."

Bonaventura reached into a pocket and plucked out a handkerchief. Reaching around, he got a grip on the other man's cock while using his free hand to brace himself with the rope holding the man's wrists. Spreading his legs for better balance Bonaventura began a vigorous pounding, driving himself into the man again and again.

Much to the amusement of those in attendance the man cried out as he was fucked. He squirmed, pressing his own cock into Bonaventura's hankie. A squirt of come gushed out and was caught by the hankie before it could ruin his shirt. A moment later Bonaventura sighed with satisfaction and slowly withdrew his cock from the man's ass.

A servant came forward with a tray containing a cloth and a bowl of warm water. As one man held the tray another servant dipped the cloth into the water and efficiently wiped Bonaventura's cock clean. The adventurer tucked himself into his pants and tossed the servants a few coins before turning back to the man who was still in bondage.

"We shall have to discuss Socrates next," Bonaventura teased. He leaned in close to Severin. "Just a typical literary conversation. I'm sure you have them all the time on your world. Are you familiar with Voltaire?"

"Not, uh, intimately." Severin admitted. He glanced over at the man and noticed that no one seemed to be in a hurry to take him down. Someone was admiring Bonaventura's work through a monocle.

The two men made their way through the people towards the exit. The party had grown more crowded as the evening progressed. They were almost to the door when Severin felt a powerful burst of dominant female energy ripple through the room.

Almost against his will Severin turned and found himself face to face with the Duke D'Agostini and his half-dressed wife. Her eyes smoldered with fury.

"I believe that you have come here under false pretenses," The Duke announced.

Severin froze, rendered momentarily speechless. Bonaventura stepped forward smoothly and took charge.

"I beg pardon your grace, to what do you refer?"

"Your companion, the schlavo. He has come to interrogate my guests."

A small crowd of people had gathered, hanging on every word that was said. Severin could see Red Lightning in the crowd, but as always the face of the Kamen Girl's was impossible to read under her mask. Still, there seemed to be only one way the Duke could know why he had come here.

"There's no insult intended," Bonaventura assured the angry man.

"Ah, so you are together, then?"

Bonaventura glanced at Severin. Apparently the Venetian was willing to go along with the assumption if it would help. For a second Severin was tempted to say that they were together. Bonaventura's reputation would probably help calm the situation. It would be an easy lie, but he had many gay friends back home, and he knew the difficulties they went through. Pretending to be gay just to get out of a tight spot seemed like an insult to his friends.

"Bonaventura is only my guide," Severin explained. "Any fault that was made was by me alone."

"He's owned by a very powerful woman," Bonaventura added helpfully.

"She has sent me here to investigate a crime. I meant no insult to you or your guests."

"No insult?" Duke D'Agostini scowled. "Yet you call my guests criminals. Bah, I am done with you. If you were a man I would challenge you to a duel, but since you are not, I will leave this to my wife."

His wife stepped forward, hands on her hips, her bosom heaving with agitation.

"Perhaps you wish to accuse me of something as well?" she asked in a haughty tone.

"No, mistress."

"Padrona!" she snapped.

"I'm sorry, Padrona."

"In our country when someone of your station insults their betters they are whipped. Tell me, does this mistress of yours allow you to be whipped by other women when you have angered them?"

Severin hesitated. Again it would be easy to lie and say the Viscountess did not allow him to be whipped by others. It would be even easier to Safeword and simply leave. Unfortunately, he wasn't sure if that was the right thing to do. Technically Red Lighting was working at the party and wasn't a guest, but her employer Manzoni may have been the one who complained. Severin may not have felt that he did anything wrong, but by the rules of this Dominion he may have been out of line.

As he was thinking this Severin became aware of the powerful waves of dominant energy rolling off of Padrona D'Agostini. She may have been playing the whore earlier in the evening, but now her true nature was coming to light.

"She does allow me to be punished by other women," Severin admitted.

"Then will you submit to me and accept my punishment?"

Feeling as if he had no choice, Severin sank to his knees. He heard a murmur of excitement pass through the room as he prostrated himself before her.

"Come," she said curtly and left the room in a swirl of fabric. Severin followed on his knees with Bonaventura and the rest of the group following close behind. Apparently Severin was the hit of the evening.

She led him into a garden where there was a block of smooth stone with rings set in it. Severin was commanded to place himself across the stone, which he saw had recesses for his arms and legs. Bonaventura volunteered to tie his limbs into place.

"You should be in for quite a treat," the Venetian informed him. "Normally she's only dominant in private with her husband. You must have brought out the beast in her."

"Lucky me." Severin tried to twist around on the hard stone, but any way he moved his stiff cock was still pressed painfully into the stone.

The functional sculpture was just large enough that his head was free. He looked around at the glittering, well dressed guests and felt more naked than ever. The position was familiar to him from being on a spanking bench, but the solidness of the stone made him feel more helpless than usual.

If this had been a beating from the Viscountess he would look forward to a delicious power exchange as their energy flowed together, but that only happened when a couple were very familiar with each other. Padrona D'Agostini, beautiful, powerful and dominant as she was, was a stranger. Severin would probably find the whipping painful and possibly exciting, but it would leave him drained rather than energized like a session with the Viscountess.

A servant arrived with a tray of flagellation instruments. Padrona D'Agostini fingered several of them before deciding on a short riding whip whose tip splayed out into several strands. She passed it through the air a few times to get the feel of it and held it before his face.

Severin looked at the smooth, well-worn leather and nodded. He had been hit with worse. When he tried to relax and make himself ready for the beating he found the stone he was bound to was too cold and unyielding to offer him any comfort. Perhaps the uncomfortable position was part of the punishment.

She turned out to have a smooth, even hand with the whip. The first few strokes went across his shoulders lightly, but she moved to his ass and let loose with her full strength. Severin squirmed beneath the impact, feeling the heat grow inside him.

The Italian beauty paused to let the pain sink in fully and pinched his ass cheeks.

"Pity," she murmured. "We could have been making love even now, but you seem to prefer this."

When she walked to the front of the stone block she passed her hand in front of his face and he saw that a finger was wet. The scent of her reached his nose. He groaned instinctively and pulled against the ropes which made his tormentor laugh.

At this moment Manzoni arrived, holding an elegant flogger in his hand.

"If you will forgive me, signora," he executed a little bow. Severin saw that Red Lightning was near him, still decked out in glittering gems. "If I might make a suggestion, perhaps it would amuse you to use this item of my own creation."

She took it from him and swung it through the air. Perhaps it was Severin's imagination, but he thought he saw the whip glitter as it passed through the air.

It was not his imagination. "This flogger has tiny diamonds woven into the strands of leather," Manzoni continued.

"Thank you, sir, this is marvelous." The dominant woman turned her dark eyes on Severin's body. "Are you prepared?"

"Yes, Padrona."

The whip came down very suddenly across his shoulders. Although floggers were made of many individual strands of leather, when they struck it felt like one solid piece. Severin took the force of the blow and was pleased to find that it was well within his pain tolerance. Two more blows showered down on his shoulders before she paused.

As he shuddered against the stone Severin felt a burning sensation as the pain of the flogger sank in. This was the sort of slow burn he associated with the cane. After the flash of pain from the strike his skin still tingled where he had been hit.

Nearby Duke D'Agostini winced in sympathy. Apparently he had some experience both with the stone block and his wife's fury.

As the pain increased Severin gasped and writhed in his bonds. The sweat running into his eyes momentarily blurred his vision. He thought he caught a glimpse of Abraxus in his floating chair with the naked slave girl at his feet. He looked absurdly out of place in glittering Venice.

Severin blinked his eyes to clear them and saw that there was no one there. It must have been a trick of the shadows caused by the flickering lights. Soon the rain of blows made him concentrate on nothing else but the pain building in his back.

Just as the pain was reaching a critical mass Severin heard her announce "Enough!"

She walked around to the front of the stone block where he could see her beautiful face, her breasts heaving with exertion. Her prominent clitoris was swollen and flushed with excitement.

"I told you I would get satisfaction from you one way or another," she laughed. "I take it that you enjoyed it as much as I did."

"Yes, Padrona."

She laughed and gave an order to some of her maids. As the women untied Severin he saw Red Lightning smirking at him under her mask. She was enjoying this far too much not to have had a hand in it.

"Bravo, Severin," Bonaventura congratulated him. "I'd call for an encore, but I'm not sure you could take it."

As Bonaventura helped Severin down from the stone whipping block Severin saw that the Venetian was paying close attention to Severin's erect cock. Since everyone at the party was looking at him, there wasn't much point in being modest.

The maids applied some salve to his back and ass which made him feel much better. Several people approached Severin and complimented him on his performance. He saw Bonaventura slip off with Padrona D'Agostini and confer with her about something.

By the time the maids were done with him, Severin saw Bonaventura return with a sealed letter.

"What's the letter?"

"Something for your owner. It's nothing to worry about."

On the gondola trip back to the Gateway, Bonaventura held forth on the history of Venice, speaking of the scandalous affairs that went on behind the darkened windows. Severin shifted, trying to make himself comfortable. He could see the appeal of this strange, almost magical city.

When they reached the Gateway, Bonaventura dismissed himself with a bow and pressed the letter into Severin's hand.

"If you or your lovely mistress seek to return, you will find me at your disposal," he announced with a flourish.

"Thank you for everything." Severin tried to imitate the bow, and didn't quite succeed. Bending over made his shoulders sting again.

Farewell Bonaventura, farewell Venice, Severin thought as the door closed behind him. One day he would have to find out what kind of adventures the Viscountess and the Duchess had with Bonaventura anyway. But first he had to find out what was in the letter.

Chapter Eleven

While Severin journeyed through old Venice the Viscountess took a very different trip, flying cross country to Las Vegas. With her typical Teutonic efficiency, Sklavin had arranged the reservations and the limo that would take her to her destination.

The searing desert sun cast everything in Las Vegas in a slightly unreal light. Through the tinted glass of the limo the Viscountess saw pirate ships and pyramids, sky scrapers and even the Eiffel Tower.

The big black car—driven by a handsome, submissive chauffeur—slid to a halt in front of a large building designed to look like it was made of ancient stone. Two huge statues of lions with the bearded heads of men flanked the wide glass doors. The exterior walls were a bright blue mosaic showing various animals both real and imaginary.

"Welcome to the Hanging Gardens of Babylon." A man wearing only a loincloth and a cloth on his head held in place by a metal circlet greeted her and opened the door of the limo. Another man dressed in a similar manner was already taking her luggage out of the trunk.

"Thank you."

The Viscountess tried to take everything in. The sidewalk was packed with tourists who weren't batting an eye at anything they saw. It was like being in a Dominion where there was no Blindfold. Apparently the reputation of the hotel for adult entertainment was so strong that they had no qualms about openly advertising. A glittering marquee announced Slave Poker, Nightly Punishments. There was a wooden sandwich board showing scantily clad girls in chains advertising Slave Girls of Babylon, Every Night at 9, 10, and 11.

She followed her luggage through the glass doors into another world. The massive atrium was much cooler than outside despite being filled with sunlight. There were plants of all descriptions, from towering palm trees to long vines that hung down from platforms so cleverly designed that they seemed to float in midair. Water flowed everywhere, dripping into pools on the floor. The Viscountess made her way around them and saw that there was a large front desk to one side of the atrium and a row of shops and stores that looked disturbingly ordinary on the other side.

The Viscountess stepped aside to allow a couple with two children to move past her. They were dragging enough pieces of luggage to take care of a small army and trying to find the desk through the massive greenery. An almost-naked woman nodded and smiled to them as she pointed out the desk. As the family walked away, the father turned to ogle the woman, which earned him a sharp rebuke from his wife.

As the woman approached the Viscountess it was clear that she wore nothing but leather thong panties and metal caps on her nipples. There was a metal collar around her neck and thin chains that connected her collar to metal bands at her wrists and ankles. The chains were very light and long enough to allow freedom of movement. Clearly they were for show rather than restraint.

She knelt on the stone at the feet of the Viscountess and looked up at her. The Viscountess stared back at her, not entirely sure what to say.

"It's a lot to take in, isn't it?" the woman grinned. She was very attractive in a polished, professional sort of way. "I'm Chelsea, I'm one of the concierges for our special guests."

"I'm the Viscountess."

"I know. Your room is ready; you just have to sign in."

A young couple came past. Both of them looked admiringly at Chelsea's bared breasts.

"I notice you're not using the Blindfold," the Viscountess pointed out.

"It's not necessary in this part of the building. The Hanging Gardens is famous for its slave girls."

"I saw the sign outside. You perform nightly?"

"Oh I haven't been on stage in years. I'm in hospitality now. The Slave Girls of Babylon is a pop music show with some mild S&M themes. It's mostly for tourists and goes along with the whole ancient Babylon motif. Of course the hotel and casino is filled with lots of kink-only features."

"Please rise and tell me all about it."

Chelsea started to her feet and the Viscountess helped her.

"Thank you, Viscountess." The concierge gave her a professional smile. "All of our special rooms come complete with bondage gear and some instruments of punishment. Many of our guests have to fly in and can't bring their own equipment. The suites have their own dungeon, but of course any guest can use the dungeon facilities on our main floor. You'll find that it's very well equipped."

"Sounds wonderful."

The Viscountess gave her name to the woman behind the desk and was given a plastic card key for her room.

"If there's anything I can do to make your stay more pleasant," Chelsea said suggestively. "Please don't hesitate to ask."

"Thank you." The Viscountess ran her gaze down the long legs and trim, well-toned body. Chelsea might not dance any more, but she still kept in shape. No doubt it was a job requirement, like her perfect teeth and expertly styled hair. "As a matter of fact there is something I need. I'm trying to reach one of your guests. There should be a Mr. Redmond who is staying here."

"He's not one of my guests, but I can look into it. Why don't you get settled and I'll be in touch." She favored the Viscountess with a well-practiced smile.

The room turned out to be quite nice. It came with a comfortable bed, a small cage, and a reinforced wall with chains. An assortment of whips, floggers, and paddles—along with wrist and ankle cuffs—hung from hooks.

By the time the Viscountess had finished unpacking the phone rang.

"Mr. Redmond is staying in one of the suites with his bodyguard," Chelsea informed her.

"What can you tell me about him?"

"The privacy of our guests is our chief concern."

"That was an order. Tell me about Redmond." She put just a touch of power into her voice and heard a quick intake of breath come through the phone.

"He's staying here for the week. According to his concierge he was supposed to spend the time with a submissive, but she got sick and cancelled at the last minute. He's been in a pretty foul mood and he's been working his way through our professional submissives. They tell me he's pretty rough."

"Sounds like a challenge."

"If you want to meet with him, he's been in our special gaming room every night by seven."

"Special gaming?"

"Casino games for our more sophisticated guests, with a kinky theme."

"I see. That sounds fascinating."

"Will there be anything else, Viscountess?"

"No, that will be all."

As the Viscountess hung up the phone she pondered her options.

Redmond was a fixture on the Chicago S&M scene. He had made a fortune in construction and had a reputation for pushing the boundaries of the women he was with. He had never gone too far with anyone, but he had a hard time keeping a submissive partner for very long and most of the women in the Chicago scene had learned to be wary of him.

It seemed typical of him that he would hire a Kamen Girl to be his bodyguard. It was very unlikely that he was actually in any danger while on vacation, but it probably stroked his ego to have such a powerful woman at his beck and call.

The Viscountess had a light dinner at a restaurant called the Ishtar Gate, then dressed for an evening at the casino. The special gambling area was down a long corridor filled with statues of Mesopotamian gods. This was one of the areas hidden by the Blindfold to protect unwary tourists looking for the floor show.

A dark-haired beauty wearing only body paint and gold jewelry in her piercings opened the door for the Viscountess as she approached. The Viscountess suspected the woman had been put on light duty to recover, since as she turned she revealed a back that was well marked by the whip and an ass with deep purple bruises.

The glass doors opened onto a lounge area where drinks and snacks were served. To the right was a polished and well equipped dungeon with a great deal of expensive equipment. It could hold quite a few people, but only a few of the stations were in use. A naked man was being whipped by two women dressed for the stage show while another woman, presumably his wife, snapped pictures. There was also a woman in her underwear with pads attached to her who was being given electric shocks by a circle of giggling friends. A bachelorette party?

To the left was the casino. In many ways it seemed ordinary. There was a wheel of fortune, but in this case gamblers who put their money on the double payout risked strokes from the riding crop in addition to losing their money. The women who ran the games were all glossy and beautiful, dressed in leather body harnesses which gave them a slightly dominant appearance while hiding none of their charms.

It wasn't difficult to spot Redmond. He was sitting on a couch giving a spanking to one of the hotel workers, his big, powerful hands smacking the girl's ass with a great deal of force. A Kamen Girl stood by him. She had an elaborate butterfly on her face mask; her eyes peered from spots on the wings. She seemed to be observing the spanking with a professional curiosity.

The Viscountess sensed she was being examined with interest. From another entrance in the back of the casino a voluptuous woman entered. She had skin the color of chocolate and wavy black hair that tumbled to her shoulders. She swayed when she walked, her breasts shifting enticingly under the flimsy dress. Behind her was a woman with lighter skin, almost the color of caramel and blonde hair. The combination of blonde hair and slightly dark skin was strikingly beautiful. The blonde was naked except for her high heels and body glitter that sparkled as she walked.

The dark woman sent out a wave of dominant energy. The Viscountess raised her own power to counter it. Their eyes met and neither of them flinched.

"It is a pleasure to meet you," the woman said in slightly accented English. "I am Dona Samara."

"I am the Viscountess."

"I am here on vacation from Rio."

She added something in Portuguese which made the blond come out from behind her and sink gracefully to her knees. The Viscountess extended a foot and permitted the slave to plant a kiss on the toe of her black patent leather high heels.

"Your slave is lovely and quite well trained."

"You are very kind to say so. She is escrava Lia. That is what we call slaves in my country, escrava."

The exquisite blonde submissive was very well trained. She rose from kissing the shoes of the Viscountess and slipped back to kneel at her owner's feet with a grace born of long practice.

While they had been talking Redmond had finished with the spanking and dismissed the woman. She took a moment to catch her breath, then picked up her drink tray and left the room. The Viscountess wondered if she had really done something to deserve the spanking, or if Redmond was simply enjoying the fact that the hotel's staff was trained to cater to their guests' every need.

"Please excuse me for a moment, Dona Samara." The Viscountess smiled and bowed her head in respect to her new acquaintance before making her way to the couch.

Redmond had already noticed her and liked what he saw. The spanking had raised his dominant energy and as the Viscountess came closer to him, his desire for her almost made the room crackle with energy. She made sure her dominant aura was up, but unlike Dona Samara he did not seem to notice or respect her power.

"Good evening. I'm known as the Viscountess."

"I'm Master Redmond."

They did not shake hands. The Viscountess had an absurd notion that she should extend her foot for him to kiss, but she thought better of it.

"It's a pleasure to meet you," the Viscountess said smoothly. "If you don't mind, I'd like to speak with Papillion for a moment."

He glanced up, as if he had forgotten she was standing there.

"She's working," Redmond said curtly.

The Viscountess looked at Papillion who nodded. "Like he said, I'm working."

"Perhaps another time."

As she smiled and walked away the Viscountess knew that she had piqued both their curiosities. Hopefully that would pay off.

The casino was beginning to fill with people. A young couple wandered in from the lounge. The dominant man was leading a woman dressed entirely in white on a leash. She had a matching white patent leather waist cincher and collar, with white thong panties. Her high heels were white as was her stockings, which were held in place by ruffled garters. The fact that she was wearing a wedding veil strongly suggested that they were on their honeymoon.

The woman, a slender strawberry blonde, was attractive in a conventional sort of way. She might have been the hit of her cheerleading squad, but she clearly had a lot to learn about being a submissive on public display. Her arms were folded defensively across her bare breasts and she kept looking around the room to see if anyone was watching her. It probably didn't help her nerves any that almost everyone in the room was.

While everyone was checking out the newlyweds, a new dealer entered the room. She took her place at an empty table and set up with brisk efficiency, quickly announcing, "Ladies and gentlemen, we are ready to begin slave poker!

Redmond's head came up at the announcement. Apparently this was the big event since people immediately move from the other tables. They seemed eager to watch, but no one took a seat at the table.

The brochure that had been in her room said any of the dealers would be more than happy to explain any game, so the Viscountess asked her about it.

"I'd be happy to explain." The dealer smiled. She had the same coolly professional aura of submission that the Viscountess had noticed in

Chelsea. Somehow she managed to seem deferential and in charge at the same time. "We require at least four players, but we can take up to six. The game is seven card draw poker with a few unique variations."

She opened a small box and displayed chips of six different colors. Several people were paying attention to the explanation.

"There are different colors for each player, and each chip is worth one stroke. All players are issued exactly the same amount to start. Chips that are lost go to the house, while the winner of each hand gets his own chips back. When a player's chips are gone, that player is out, and one hundred strokes are delivered in the lounge in front of an audience."

The dealer glanced meaningfully toward the well-equipped punishment room. Everyone was silent, absorbing what she had said. Finally, the newlywed man asked what several people had been thinking.

"A hundred strokes with what?"

"A flogger, sir. I think you'll find we're firm but fair in our punishments. The flogging is usually delivered by one of our women, but anyone who prefers a male may request one."

"You're leaving out the best part," Redmond put in; apparently he had heard the spiel before.

"Of course," the dealer gave him a slight smile and addressed those who were listening to her. "All the players who drop out are punished with a flogging until it's down to the final two. At that point the game becomes winner take all. The loser will belong to the winner until midnight. It's hoped that some activity will take place in the lounge, but it's entirely up to the winner. Naturally, all limits will be respected by order of the house."

There was a visible stirring in the audience as everyone contemplated the possibilities. A hundred strokes of the flogger was a formidable punishment, but to be owned by a stranger for hours, possibly serving in public, was another story entirely.

The Viscountess knew from experience that a hundred strokes from a single tail or a cane would have her laid up for days, but she felt she could take even the heaviest or the stingiest flogger without too much trouble. The hours of slavery that were a possibility were more problematic, but she saw that Redmond was eager to play. He was already scanning the faces of the crowd to see who else was interested.

"For those dominants who wish to play," the dealer continued smoothly. "Your submissive may volunteer to take the punishment in your place."

There was a bit of murmuring from the crowd as this point was made. Dona Samara exchanged a few quick words with her slave, then stepped forward, her dark smoldering eyes fixed on the Viscountess.

"Would you care for a game, my dear?"

"I'd be honored," the Viscountess smiled. "Of course since I have no submissive with me I'll have to take the risk myself."

"In that case it would be unfair of me to ask Lia to take my place. I, too, shall place myself on the table."

Dona Samara smiled and smoothed the dress across her generous hips, just in case the Viscountess had failed to notice her curves. Escrava Lia cast her a glance that seemed to say she would be more than willing to take the punishments and possibly that the submissive thought her mistress shouldn't be risking herself over something so foolish.

"With two such lovely ladies at the table I guess I can't lose," Redmond chuckled. "I've been waiting three nights for enough people with the guts to play."

"Let's hope you still feel as eager when the game is over." The Viscountess met his gaze and let her dominant energy flare.

Redmond smiled, as if he was amused by her attempt to intimidate him. He also glanced at Dona Samara. It could not have been more obvious that he was mentally picturing her stripped, bound, and at his mercy.

"Last night poor Mr. Redmond couldn't get anyone interested in a game," Dona Samara confided to the Viscountess nodding her head toward the door. "He had to take out his frustration on one of the dealers."

The Viscountess glanced at the woman who was on door duty, the one with the welts and badly bruised ass. Dona Samara had seen Redmond in action and was clearly sending a warning to her how rough he could be.

The Viscountess appreciated the warning, but it seemed to her that the only chance she had to get to Papillion was to have Redmond under her thumb, and the poker game seemed to be the best way to accomplish that. It bothered the Viscountess that Dona Samara would risk placing herself at the mercy of a man she didn't like. If this went badly and Dona Samara wound up with Redmond, the Viscountess knew she was going to feel very guilty.

"That makes three. We require at least four players," the dealer looked around. Several people were backing away, eager to watch, but not participate.

"I'd like to play," the newlywed stepped forward. "My wife, uh, slave will take the punishments."

He glanced nervously over his shoulder for confirmation and saw that his bride was covering up her chest with her arms.

"Sandy," he hissed. "Do I have to cuff you?"

"No," she squeaked. When she lowered her arms her breasts bobbed embarrassingly before they settled down. She blushed deeply and looked at the floor.

"Sorry," the husband apologized.

"Nothing to be sorry about," the Viscountess said graciously.

"We don't get out a lot. There's not a lot of S&M clubs where we come from." He was visibly nervous, but not blushing as much as his wife. "I'm Ray and this is Sandy. We just got married."

"Congratulations," the Viscountess said.

"You're a very lucky man," Dona Samara added. Sandy made the mistake of glancing up at her just as she sent out a wave of dominance tinged with Sapphic desire. The Viscountess felt the air crackle with erotic energy. Sandy lowered her gaze just in time to see her nipples grow hard and a spot of moisture appear on the tiny thong she wore.

Ray sensed that something had just happened, but he didn't seem to know what. He leaned over and kissed his bride on the cheek after whispering something in her ear.

"I'm fine," she whispered back just loud enough to be heard.

"Anyone else?" The dealer looked around and saw no stepping forward. "Excellent. It looks like an exciting game. Shall we begin?"

Chapter Twelve

They each took their seats, Dona Samara beside the Viscountess, then Ray and Redmond. Lia and Sandy stood behind their owners just as Papillion stood behind her employer. The slaves both seemed nervous, but as usual the Kamen Girl was impossible to read.

The Viscountess mentally reviewed everything she knew about poker. She had been pretty good when she had played it in college, but hadn't had much experience since then. During her time as a professional submissive she once made the mistake of joining a game of forfeit poker where sexual acts were used in place of chips. For weeks after she had been paying off sexual favors to the rest of the players.

She missed Severin deeply. She could have used his advice on whether this was a good idea or not. Perhaps if he had been there he would have thought of some clever way of getting to Redmond.

The major flaw in her plan was that she absolutely had to win and make sure Redmond came in second. If he won her she had no doubt he'd be merciless, although there still might be a chance for her to have a conversation with Papillion. All the other outcomes would be entertaining, but weren't going to get her any closer to solving the Kamen Girls' problem.

After a few more rules were explained the dealer went to work with cool efficiency. Each player had to ante up a one-stroke chip, and then two cards were dealt face down. The third card was dealt face up. The player with the lowest card placed two one-stroke chips in the pot as the bring-in. Going clockwise around the table, each player then had to fold or stay in the game by adding two more chips to the pot. Any player could raise at any time after the bring-in.

The mathematics of the game were clear to the Viscountess. They only had chips worth one hundred to put in the pot, and each hand would cost at least eleven chips to stay in long enough to get all seven cards. If someone raised they could drive the cost of the hand up rapidly. Unlike poker involving money, slave poker looked like a fast game. There was a crowd waiting and the casino wanted to give them a good show without having to wait hours for the game to end.

On the first hand the Viscountess folded after only four cards, deciding the hand wasn't worth trying to build on. Dona Samara followed on the next round, and when Ray suddenly raised, Redmond folded as well, giving the modest pot to the newlywed. On the second hand apparently everyone received such bad cards that no one raised. Redmond went all the way to the last card and still won with only a pair of threes.

The Viscountess studied each of her opponents. Ray's eagerness and nervousness showed, but Redmond was keeping his face carefully controlled. Dona Samara sipped her rum and Coke, seemingly at ease, but she watched the other players more than the cards.

Redmond and Ray were the two most aggressive players. As their piles of chips grew, the Viscountess began pondering higher bets. Apparently both she and Dona Samara had the same idea. They both stayed in after the buy-in. Unexpectedly Ray raised by ten chips, the highest raise so far.

Redmond raised as well. The Viscountess looked at her hand and tried not to sigh audibly. She had a six, eight and nine of clubs, not quite a straight flush. If she stayed in to get her last cards it was going to cost her. Ray raised fifty chips. Redmond matched it and raised ten more. The Viscountess folded.

Dona Samara stayed in another round, then, apparently not getting the cards she had hoped for, folded. The two men kept going until the final card. Finally Redmond called. Ray sheepishly turned over his cards to reveal that he had nothing. There was a Jack, Queen and ten of spades, it could have made a royal flush if he had gotten the right cards, but he didn't. Redmond had three nines and took everything.

Dona Samara frowned as she watched Redmond rake in his winnings. The Viscountess wondered if Dona Samara had noticed what she herself had noticed. The normally unflappable Redmond had taken to nervously tapping his cards on the table while running out the very low hand.

The stack of chips belonging to the house was showing a great deal of Ray's colors, but there was quite a bit of Dona Samara and the Viscountess as well. Even Redmond had given up a few hands.

Two more hands passed with no one willing to raise. The Viscountess counted out her ante and threw away worthless cards. On the next hand Dona Samara raised moderately. Ray dropped out at once, still burned from his last loss. The Viscountess met her raise and Redmond raised yet again.

The Viscountess had two fours. Two of a kind had been a winning hand in previous rounds, but with both Dona Samara and Redmond raising it seemed unlikely that both of them were bluffing. She decided to play it safe and fold.

Redmond was tapping his cards again. Perhaps taking this as a good sign, Dona Samara began to raise recklessly. After Redmond raised her again she startled the onlookers by putting everything she had into the pot. For her it was all or nothing.

The entire room seemed to be holding its breath. Redmond had more than enough chips to match her. When Dona Samara revealed her hand she was holding a very respectable flush, five hearts.

Still showing no emotion, Redmond showed his hand: four of a kind.

There was a split second of surprise on Dona Samara's face before she composed herself. Graciously she rose to her feet.

"It appears I should have stuck to Blackjack," she said, getting a small laugh from the crowd.

"It is customary for the losers to remove their clothes in anticipation of the punishment," the dealer informed her.

"Of course." Dona Samara flashed the dealer a smile. She nodded her head and began to peel off the tight dress. As every inch of her dark body was revealed, Redmond began to show real emotion. He was obviously enjoying her humiliation.

For her part Dona Samara acted as if she was a queen being mildly discomfited by commoners. When the dress came off her shoulders her large breasts rolled free, drawing a murmur of appreciation from the crowd. When she forced the dress past the curves of her hips it fell to the floor. She bent at the knees, picking the dress up and draping it over her slave's arm. Two dealers in leather harnesses with floggers on their belts came to escort her to the next room.

Before she left, she flashed a warning glance at Viscountess. The Viscountess nodded her understanding. Redmond was a pro at this. He had suckered her into betting high with the card tapping trick.

Many people left to watch the punishment, but there were still quite a few there to witness the rest of the game. The loss of the first player seemed to add to the nervousness Ray displayed. He gradually lost the rest of his chips until the last few were wasted just anteing up, then he too was out.

"It's okay honey," Sandy put a comforting hand on her husband's shoulder. A good part of the crowd was waiting to see her shimmy out of the thong and waist cincher. She didn't disappoint them. Although she tried to be as bold as Dona Samara, her hands were visibly shaking by the time she was down to her stockings and high heels.

Her husband got to his feet and hugged her. Although this served to cover her up, no one seemed to mind. The bond of affection between them was so strong it seemed to radiate from them.

Redmond took his gaze off Sandy's ass long enough to gaze at the Viscountess. The Viscountess prided herself on her ability to read people, but she didn't need any of her skills to know what was going on in his mind. He wanted her, and he wanted her badly. In his mind she was already stripped and bound; the rest of the game was just foreplay for him.

As she felt the dominant energy washing across her, the Viscountess raised her own power, matching him and meeting his challenge openly.

"I hope I don't ruin the rest of your vacation, Mr. Redmond," she said casually. "I don't think you're going to be in much shape to do anything after I get through with you."

"Funny, I was about to say the same thing to you," Redmond said with a sneer. He seemed very confident, but there was an odd look that passed through his eyes. The Viscountess saw fear in him. Despite his bravado, there was a part of him that was afraid of being dominated by her.

The Viscountess kept her poker face intact while the next hand was dealt. He had perhaps forty chips remaining, and the Viscountess half that, but she did not seem to notice that there was an issue. She made strong bets, forcing him out of the first two hands almost at once.

"Are you all right with anal penetration?" the Viscountess asked while the next hand was dealt. There was no rule against talking, but it had been a very quiet game so far. "I just want to get limits established right up front."

"I've got no problems. How about you?"

"You mean with your penis?" the Viscountess chuckled as if the thought amused her. "I'm certain it's not going to be an issue."

Redmond glared at her and couldn't think of a response.

On the next hand, the Viscountess found almost nothing she could use. By staying in she was able to get three of a kind, which wasn't a great hand, but she practiced his trick of tapping the cards on the table as if she were nervous. He folded at once.

"I assume there'll be no problem with golden showers," the

Viscountess said casually while glancing at her cards for the next hand.

"No," he stammered. "I mean yes, there is a problem. That's one of my limits."

"I see." The Viscountess sounded a little smug, as if she had just scored a point on him. Actually golden showers were a limit for a lot of people and she had no intention of doing it with a stranger, but it was fun watching him squirm.

Redmond stayed in the hand, getting more cards and raising her by ten. The Viscountess matched that and raised. She glanced up and made eye contact with the dealer.

"Can we have some more ice brought into the lounge?" she asked the dealer.

"I'm certain that can be arranged."

"Good." The Viscountess glanced at Redmond. "Testicles can swell tremendously," she explained to him. "Of course, I've heard the ice is pretty painful all by itself."

The Viscountess had a two and three of hearts, but she also had a two of clubs. There was a possible three of a kind, or maybe a straight flush. Either way it was worth building on. Redmond raised her and she met his raise. He had lost badly enough that their chip count was almost even.

Redmond had faith in his hand and continued raising. As the cards came in the Viscountess saw her hand getting better and better. There was another six and two more twos. She had four of a kind.

The Viscountess placed the rest of her chips in the pot. Redmond only hesitated a moment before he put all of his chips in as well.

Redmond revealed a full house, eights and kings. It was a good hand, but not good enough. When the Viscountess showed her cards, Redmond's face was impassive for a few seconds. He kept looking at her cards and at his, as if he could change them by sheer force of will.

He got to his feet without making eye contact with anyone. The Viscountess was still waiting for him to respond to her in some way when he turned to face Papillion.

"You take it for me," he ordered.

"That's not what you hired me for," she immediately snapped.

"You were hired to do what I tell you to do," he began, but he must have realized how lame that sounded because he cut himself off. "Look, you're my bodyguard, aren't you supposed to take a bullet for me?"

The Kamen Girl looked at the dealer who shrugged.

"You're free to take his place if it's consensual," the dealer reminded her.

Papillion looked next at the Viscountess, who was trying to make herself look as innocent as possible. It was somewhat difficult as she had just so clearly topped Redmond during the last game. The last thing she wanted to do was scare off Papillion when she was so close to getting a chance to talk to her.

Apparently Papillion was satisfied with what she saw. She put her hands on her hips, her hard body rigid with tension.

"I guess you've got me until midnight. Before you ask, I don't do golden either."

"Neither do I on the first date."

The Viscountess glanced up to say something to Redmond, but he was already leaving the room. He seemed to be willing to forget the whole thing ever happened. Papillion glared at his retreating back.

The Viscountess rose to her feet and addressed the crowd who had stayed to the end of the game. "I'm afraid my session with this young lady is going to be in private," she announced. There was a murmur of disappointment and the people started to drift away.

The Kamen Girl started to kneel in front of her—a touching gesture of submission from such a powerful woman. Reluctantly the Viscountess reached out and took her arm, keeping the woman on her feet.

The Viscountess leaned in close to whisper, "There's no need for that. All I want to do is talk to you."

"Talk?" the eyes behind the mask widened in surprise. "You went through all this just to talk to me?"

"Yes."

"You risked being enslaved and whipped just to talk?"

"I'm afraid so."

Papillion opened her mouth and closed it again. It took her a few seconds to come up with a response to that.

"I guess I belong to you until midnight, so if talking is what you want, that's what you'll get."

"Excellent. Let's go to the lounge."

They had to pass through the bar to get to the lounge. A few people who had watched the game congratulated the Viscountess as she walked past them. Two very aroused submissive men knelt to offer their greetings by kissing her boots. Several people of both genders gazed jealously at the hard body of the Kamen Girl.

As the crowd of people who had seen the game dispersed the Viscountess noticed something moving through the crowd. There was a black shape moving away from her. It reminded her very much of the floating chair that had belonged to Abraxus, but what on earth would he be doing here?

The crowd blocked her view, and he was gone, if he had ever been there at all.

The lounge area beyond the bar was crowded. The first thing they saw when they entered the room was the newlywed couple. Apparently Ray had decided not to let his wife suffer for his poor poker skills after all. He was stripped and bound with arms and legs spread so he was stretched between two posts. One of the dealers was behind him whipping him Florentine style, a flogger in each hand. She struck quickly and with great precision, the blows seeming to rain down on him in a continuous stream as he twitched and writhed. No one seemed to be counting the strokes, but his back was already red and the rest of him has a faint gleam of sweat.

Sandy was kneeling in front of him, looking up at him with adoring eyes.

"Just a few more," she said encouragingly. He opened his mouth, but instead of saying something all that came out was a gasp of pain. Seeing that he was close to breaking, she leaned in and took his cock in her mouth, sucking it to distract him from the pain.

A few feet away Dona Samara sat in a chair enjoying the show. Her body was flushed from her own punishment and the lap dance she was getting from escrava Lia. They were both naked, and the body glitter from the slave had rubbed off on the mistress, glittering like diamonds on velvet.

Dona Samara glanced up at the Viscountess and the Kamen Girl and guessed what happened.

"I should have known he'd chicken out."

"It's too bad everyone's not as brave as him." The Viscountess nodded her head toward the newlyweds.

Escrava Lia said something in Portuguese. The Viscountess suspected it had something to do with Redmond's mother.

The Viscountess and Papillion sat on a couch where it was quiet enough for them to talk. The woman in the butterfly mask was still nervous, pressing her hands into her thighs instead of sitting comfortably.

"I need to ask you a few questions. I've been hired by The Crone to investigate an event that occurred after you returned from your last mission."

"Why? What happened?"

"Please tell me what went on in the lounge on the twenty-third floor. I think you and a few other Kamen Girls had all returned at about the same time. Can you describe what went on?"

"We talked, and ate—really nothing happened."

"What can you remember about it?"

"I don't know." Papillion looked down at her lap. Although the Viscountess wasn't trying to dominate her, the Kamen Girl was putting out very submissive energy. She almost looked guilty about something.

"Just describe what you can recall."

"Let's see. Kabuki had the flu, and we were worried because when one of us gets sick, it pretty much runs through the whole group in no time. Skye stumbled across two people doing a Scene in a vomitorium, which wasn't exactly what I wanted to hear when I'm eating."

She seemed reluctant to go on. The Viscountess wracked her brain for any scrap of information she had gotten about the conversation in the lounge. Tiger Mask had said that Blanca made fun of Red Lighting because of a leg injury, and there was also something about a pastry.

"Tell me what Blanca said to Red Lightning."

Papillion stiffened slightly. The mask may hide her facial expressions, but her naked body had no way of covering up a physical reaction.

"Blanca really went after her about the limp. She shouldn't have done it. I'm sure it happened just like Red Lightning said, but Blanca was angry at her for going after me."

"About what?"

There was such a strong aura of submission coming off of her that the Viscountess felt her dominant power rising almost of its own accord. She reached out and grabbed the light brown pony tail that streamed out the back of the mask and twisted it, forcing the Kamen Girl to look up from her lap.

"Tell me everything."

"Blanca was just trying to defend me. I was talking about something that happened in Paris, in Europa."

"So what happened in Europa?"

Papillion gave a little sob. Her breasts rose and fell as she drew in a deep breath.

"I thought it was funny. I was following this guy. I'd been at it all day and I hadn't eaten. When he went into a bakery the smell almost drove me nuts. As he went out I scooped up a pastry and ate it, but I guess I didn't make it invisible fast enough since someone saw it floating in midair."

"Go on," the Viscountess said gently. Apparently Severin had been right about them becoming invisible.

"Everybody laughed and Tiger Mask said I should have eaten it so they could see it vanish one bite at a time. Then Red Lightning started in on me about how becoming invisible is our greatest secret and anything that jeopardizes that puts us all at risk. She was right and I know it. I just can't believe The Crone hired you to come after me for one little pastry."

"I'm not here about the pastry."

"Then why?"

"Something happened later. Did you notice anything unusual about Skye, or anything she ate or drank?"

"No. Why? Did something happen to her?"

"She'll be fine. Is there anything else you can remember?" The Viscountess released her hair and smoothed out the pony tail.

"I don't know what you want me to say. I've grabbed a snack there a hundred times. It was just like any other day."

"I know." The Viscountess reassured her. Papillion's guilt over the pastry was making her very vulnerable. It was hard to believe she'd ever do anything like steal the Sphere. "I'm sure when you return it will be explained to you. How much longer is this assignment?"

"Until the end of the week, unless he gets bored and decides to go back early." The Kamen Girl hesitated as something occurred to her. "You're not planning on talking to Blanca, are you?"

"Yes I am. Is that a problem?"

"She's not very fond of you or your slave. She and Crimson Shadow trained and got their masks together. I've heard her go on and on about how you two humiliated Crimson and she'd like a chance to get back at you."

Crimson Shadow must have been the Kamen Girl who tried to kidnap Severin, the Viscountess realized. They had never known her name. She decided to change the topic.

"I've heard you and Blanca are a couple."

"Yes, we've been together for about a year."

"And after you left the lounge where did the two of you go?"

"Back to her room. She knew her roommate was out."

"How long were you with her?"

"Until lunch the next day."

The Kamen Girl shifted on the couch. She was still uncomfortable talking about this with outsiders.

"Thank you, you've been very helpful."

"I guess you have me until midnight."

"I told you all I wanted was to ask you a few questions. Why don't you spend the rest of the evening relaxing and enjoying yourself?"

"Thank you, Viscountess." Papillion brightened considerably at that suggestion and left quickly, before anyone could take advantage of her submissive state.

As Papillion left, the Viscountess saw Sandy saying goodbye to Dona Samara and escrava Lia. The pretty blonde also said farewell to the Viscountess.

"It's so nice meeting you," she gushed. The newlywed hadn't bothered to put her waist cincher back on, but was holding it up across her chest. "We're just heading back to the room to, um."

It was fairly obvious what they were going to do. Her husband was in the process of trying to get his underwear on over his erection.

"Have fun," the Viscountess smiled. "It was nice meeting you as well. Please let me know if you're ever in Boston."

"I will, thanks."

She scampered back to her master who chided her for covering herself up. He took the waist cincher and thong from her and cuffed her wrists behind her back. Once the leash was attached, he led her towards the elevator.

Dona Samara joined the Viscountess in watching the newlyweds leave.

"I wouldn't mind having either one of them on my leash," the Brazilian beauty commented. She had put her dress back on and her dominant energy was starting to build up again.

"I'd prefer to have both of them at once. Two can serve as easily as one."

Dona Samara gave a little snort of laughter. "I saw you with the masked woman. If that's your idea of a hot scene maybe it's good that I didn't win you."

"That was business." The Viscountess explained. "Now that it's done I'm free for the rest of the evening."

"Don't get too attached to being free."

Dona Samara sent a spike of dominant energy into the Viscountess. It washed over her, enveloping her with a suddenness that made her shudder.

It would be sweet to submit to her, and her slave, the Viscountess thought, but as appealing as the thought was, she also wanted to have the two exotic beauties at her mercy. She raised her own dominant energy, matching Dona Samara.

"You're bluffing," the Viscountess told her simply.

Dona Samara was a powerful dominant and perhaps on another night she could have taken charge of the Viscountess, but as it was she had already revealed her weakness. She had recently been flogged, and had on some level enjoyed it. It was impossible for her to shake off the submissive feelings the flogging had stirred. Perhaps part of her longed for another beating. The tiny kernel of doubt and hesitation put a chink in her armor.

She was not powerful enough to make the Viscountess submit. As the knowledge washed over her, she swayed in her high heels. Escrava Lia stared at her mistress in surprise. As a wave of power came from the Viscountess, Dona Samara sank to her knees. A second later, her slave joined her.

The Viscountess rose regally to her feet and surveyed her new temporary acquisitions.

"I'm sorry you put your clothes back on only to have to take them off again. Tell your slave to strip you."

Dona Samara gave the order to escrava Lia in Portuguese. The slave peeled off the tight dress, again revealing the lush curves of her mistress. The Viscountess spent a few seconds drinking in the sight of the two naked women before she went to one knee in front of Dona Samara.

"I'm going to go to my room. If you follow me there on your hands and knees I'll know you wish to join me. We can discuss preferences, limits, and Safewords when we get there. Make sure your slave knows she is under no obligation to join us if she doesn't wish to."

The Viscountess rose and left the private lounge. By the time she reached the elevator she heard knees shuffling on carpet and didn't have to turn her head to know that both women were crawling very close behind her.

Chapter Thirteen

The Hospital Dominion was easily accessible from every major hospital and emergency room in the Real World. As Dominions went it was very small, only the inside of one building, but it served as both a functioning hospital for people who couldn't go to a regular doctor and a place where medical Scenes could be acted out with trained professionals. Severin had never been there, but he had heard about it, and their services came highly recommended.

Once he passed through the Gateway, it resembled a perfectly normal hospital waiting room with a few vending machines and old magazines scattered about, and posters on the wall warning about high blood pressure. The only unusual thing was the very skimpy outfits the nurses wore. Severin was almost certain that high heels, white stockings, and matching garter belts had gone out of fashion in the average hospital.

As he was waiting he saw the doors swing open two men rushed in, one with his shirt off, the other pressing a bloody cloth to the man's back.

"We were doing some cutting," the man with the cloth babbled to the nurse. He was on the edge of hysteria while the man who was bleeding looked perfectly relaxed. "I think the blade slipped and—"

Before he could even get the sentence out, two of the nurses came forward and took charge. As they vanished through swinging doors, moving deeper into the hospital, Severin heard one of the nurses say "Just come with us, it'll be all right, sir."

No sooner had they vanished than Severin felt a familiar surge of energy and turned to see the Viscountess enter the building. She was wearing a white blouse and leather skirt and didn't look as if she were exhausted from a long flight from Nevada. Overjoyed at seeing her again he threw himself to the floor and showered her boots with kisses.

"Hello, Severin, how was Venice?"

"Beautiful."

"And Bonaventura?"

"I can see why you like him."

"I can see you've brought me a letter. You'll have to tell me all about it."

She took a seat and pointed to a spot on the floor for him to kneel. He described everything that had happened to him and gave her the letter.

"I see." The Viscountess broke the wax seal and unfolded a letter. After reading it she frowned. "How was the whipping you received?"

"Very nice, quite stingy."

"Turn around and show me your back."

He did as she ordered and he felt her hands roaming across his skin.

"Does it hurt?" she asked.

"No." Severin paused. "Should it?"

"Are you aware that you were bleeding?"

"No, Viscountess."

"It's very shallow, no more than scratches really."

"From the flogging?" Severin frowned. He didn't think it hurt badly enough to have drawn blood.

The Viscountess sighed and leaned back in her chair. "According to the letter, D'Agostini's wife felt you deserved your punishment, however she didn't plan on drawing blood. She was using an unfamiliar instrument."

"The diamond flogger Manzoni gave her," Severin remembered. "Or possibly Red Lightning put that idea in his head."

"She apologizes in the letter and places herself entirely at my mercy for retribution if I come to Venice."

"Perhaps you should take her up on that. She's quite beautiful."

"It was a mistake for her to use something without seeing how it works. Still she seems genuinely contrite and since you both enjoyed it, I guess there's no harm done."

"How was Las Vegas?"

"Very nice. We shall have to go there sometime." The Viscountess mused. "I won the right to talk to Papillion in a poker game."

"Really? What did you have to gamble with?"

"Myself, of course."

"You risked yourself!" Severin exclaimed before he could stop himself.

The Viscountess glared at him.

"Kneel back, open your legs."

Severin's whole body shuddered as he dropped deeply into Subspace.

He obeyed, leaning backwards and lifting his hips to her. He felt her foot flick up his cock, pushing the sole of the boot against his balls.

"I don't need you telling me when I've made a mistake, is that understood?" She began to apply pressure.

"Yes, Viscountess."

"And you certainly don't have the right to raise your voice to me."

"No, Viscountess."

"Go ahead, apologize and ask me very nicely for your punishment." She increased the pressure enough to make him squirm.

"I'm very sorry that I spoke out of turn." Severin knew what was coming and tried to relax his muscles before he continued speaking. If he was tense it was just going to hurt more. "Please crush my balls."

"Again, with a little more sincerity this time."

"I'm so very sorry I spoke out of turn. I had no right to do so. Please, I beg you to crush me very hard to make up for my mistake."

"That'll do, I suppose."

She pushed down nice and hard, as if she were pressing on the gas pedal. Severin gave a gasp of pain and his whole body shook.

The Viscountess leaned back into the chair, releasing him. "I suppose you're right," she admitted. "It was risky, but it was the only plan I could think of. The important thing is that I got to talk to her."

She allowed Severin to sit comfortably while he took himself out of Subspace. She repeated what she had learned and they compared notes. They were obviously hearing the same simple conversations from several different points of view. So far no one had contradicted anyone else. There was nothing suspicious about the conversations so far and their hardest interview was still to come."

"So Blanca doesn't like us?" Severin said glumly.

"I'm afraid not."

As they were talking, a sexy nurse approached them. The nurse obviously sensed the energy in the air and was keeping a polite distance in case they were in the middle of a Scene.

"Excuse me for interrupting," the nurse said when she saw that they had noticed her. She was Asian and wore a long white lab coat over white bra and panties as well as the prerequisite white stockings. "You must be the Viscountess. We received your call earlier."

"I need to speak with Dr. Kingsly."

"She's in her office." The nurse paused and glanced down at Severin. "I noticed you examining his back. Is there anything wrong with him?"

"Nothing serious, just some scratches."

"Let me take a look at them. We can make sure there's no chance of infection."

"Really?" the Viscountess rose to her feet. "I thought we were protected from that sort of thing."

"It's a common misconception," the nurse smiled. "If you'll come with me, we can take care of him, and I can take you to the doctor."

"Thank you."

The Viscountess patted her thigh, signaling Severin to crawl behind her as they went deeper inside.

"When you're doing a Scene the energy in your body protects you from any harmful bacteria and viruses. That's why we don't need to worry about sexually transmitted diseases." The nurse informed them. "But once the Scene ends you can be left with an open wound and nothing to protect you from infection."

"He was flogged in Venice in the Europa Dominion. It's not exactly known for its cleanliness."

"I see."

The nurse stopped at a small examination area made by folding screens and gestured for Severin to sit on a bed. When he had done so she went behind his back and wet down some cotton balls with something from a bottle that Severin couldn't see.

"You'll like this," she told the slave. "It really stings."

She applied the damp cotton balls to his shoulder and as promised it stung a great deal. The nurse made sure to get everywhere before throwing the cotton away and turned to talk to the Viscountess.

"He'll be fine, I'm sure it won't scar. Try to keep from whipping him on the shoulders for a few days."

"I'll do my best."

"Also, it will help his immune system if he stays as aroused as possible." The pretty nurse smiled when she gave that order.

"I'll see what I can do." The Viscountess returned her smile. "Thank you so much, nurse."

"It's nothing. Let me take you to Dr. Kingsly."

The doctor occupied a fairly large office lined with books and anatomy charts. A strong woman in her mid-forties, she had a dominant air that seemed very natural and unforced. She shook hands with the Viscountess and glanced down to make eye contact with Severin when he was introduced. She neither ignored him nor gave him a foot to kiss.

The fact that she didn't feel the need to show her power over him spoke volumes about her self-assuredness.

"Thank you for seeing us on such short notice," the Viscountess said when she had settled into a chair with Severin sitting on the floor next to her. "As I said over the phone, I'm interested in speaking to the Kamen Girl that you hired."

"May I ask what this is about?"

"Severin and I have been asked by the Kamen Girls to look into something. We just have to ask her a few questions."

"I don't think that'll be a problem."

"Excellent. May I ask what you've hired her for?"

"Yes, well," Dr. Kingsly paused. "I suppose it's not really a secret. You have to understand that in addition to doing Medical Scenes we are a full-service medical facility, including a pharmacy. Unfortunately there's been some theft."

"That's a shame."

"Yes. It's comforting to think that everyone in the Scene is decent and honest, but some of the medications are worth a lot on the street. We're also chronically understaffed. There simply aren't enough kink-aware professionals. We have no security to speak of and it's obvious the honor system isn't working."

"So Blanca is working security?"

"Yes, she's been here a few days and so far there hasn't been any improvement."

"That's too bad."

Dr. Kingsly put a pair of glasses on and regarded the Viscountess. "Before you go, may I ask you a personal question?"

"If you wish."

"I noticed the male slave you have with you. Obviously you're very close. Have you ever thought about having him fixed?"

"Fixed?" the Viscountess frowned.

"Castrated. It's becoming very popular with female dominant couples. I did my husband a couple of years ago and I assure you we've never regretted it."

Severin tried to suppress a shudder, but didn't entirely succeed. Now that she mentioned it, he saw that all the medical charts on the wall were all anatomical drawings of male genitalia.

"Doesn't it affect his performance?"

"Oh no, if anything it enhances it. He can go for hours and it's much less messy." Dr. Kingsly clicked something on her computer. There was a screen on the bookshelf which lit up with a picture of a very sizable, very erect penis with no testicles and thin scars running the length of the shaft. "Of course if there's any problem in that department we can do a quick implant that will make his erection permanent."

"I see." The Viscountess sensed how tense Severin was and reached down to stroke his head.

"Of course, once you've done that, it's a simple matter to insert beads under the skin to give him a more interesting texture." The picture on the screen shifted to show the same penis, but now dotted with a pattern of raised bumps. Dr. Kingsly smiled and removed her glasses. "These are actually pictures of my husband. I did all the surgery myself."

"I have to confess I've never really considered it." The Viscountess said diplomatically.

"We have several options, either with or without anesthesia."

"The problem is, I enjoy cock and ball torture. In fact, I was crushing his balls just a few minutes ago."

"Of course. It's not for everyone. I'd suggest you try sex with a castrato before you make any decisions. Give me a call if you're interested and I can offer you my husband."

"That's incredibly generous."

"It's his pleasure, he loves showing off."

The two dominant women exchanged cards.

"I didn't mean to keep you," Dr. Kingsly apologized. "Let me take you to Blanca."

The doctor led them through the hallways. The Viscountess gave Severin permission to walk instead of crawl. Several of the rooms they passed were open to the public. They saw a rather forceful gynecological exam on a woman whose legs were splayed open, her feet in stirrups. Another room had a naked man getting a tooth drilled while a woman gave him oral sex.

The sound of the dentist's drill made Severin wince. He hated going to the dentist, though the woman's head in his lap was probably providing quite a distraction.

"This looks quite nice, we should get more medical work done here," the Viscountess commented to Severin.

"You're not actually planning on having me—"

"Castrated?" the Viscountess grinned wickedly. "Of course not."

"Thank you."

"Unless, of course you made me really angry. It's good to know that I always have this as an option."

"Thank you, Viscountess," Severin said meekly. He was almost certain she was teasing him, but he decided to be as submissive as possible just in case.

They entered another waiting room with a half dozen people sitting on chairs and couches, some of them in fetish outfits. There was a young woman dressed like a cheerleader with her arm in a sling and a man in a head-to-toe leather outfit who was sniffling and keeping a hanky to his nose. On the other side of the receptionist's window a very skinny brunette wearing a long white coat over white lingerie was sitting behind a desk.

A door opened to reveal an Indian man with a white coat draped over his three-piece suit.

"This is Dr. Bhandary," Dr. Kingsly introduced them. "He's in charge of the pharmacy and Blanca."

As Dr. Kingsly left, the dominant male doctor shook hands with the Viscountess and ignored Severin.

"I'm pleased to meet you," he said in a fairly heavy accent. "Let's talk in the supply room and you can speak with Blanca."

The supply room was the locked room he had just emerged from, packed with row after row of various pills and liquids. One wall was open, showing the back of the woman at the desk. In the middle of the room was a blonde woman in a rubber nurse's uniform and yet another white coat.

She was engrossed in her work, bending over a tray filled with pills and counting them out rapidly. She had a little metal tool sort of like a spatula and was rapidly sliding pills into a bottle, filling someone's prescription.

"We keep all the medicine in here," Dr. Bhandary explained. "Blanca's on duty, she should be around somewhere."

At that moment the Kamen Girl stepped out from behind a shelving unit where clearly she had not been a moment earlier. The woman who was filling the pill bottle jumped and made a little noise.

"Ah, there you are," the doctor smiled. "This is..."

"I know who they are," Blanca said coldly. She was tall and well built, with long, powerful legs. She could have been a ballerina, though her legs were well developed from martial arts rather than dance. Her white mask glistened with sequins under the cheap lights of the storage room.

"We've come to ask you—" the Viscountess started, but she was cut off.

"I don't care what you've come for. You need to leave."

"The Crone has asked us to investigate something. We need to ask you a few questions."

Blanca glared at them from under her mask. "When I go back home, if The Crone orders me to I'll talk to you. Until then I've got nothing to say to you."

Dr. Bhandary was looking back and forth between the two women and clearly had no idea what was going on.

The cheerleader with the injured arm approached the window on the other side. She handed her prescription to the brunette in lingerie who rose to fill it.

Apparently the two women took turns at the desk. The woman in rubber had recovered from her shock of seeing Blanca appear and brought the pill bottle to the desk, calling out someone's name. The leatherman got up for his pills.

"These two people are responsible for my friend Crimson Shadow being brutally punished by a client," Blanca explained to Dr. Bhandary. "I have nothing to say to them and I'd like them to leave so I can get on with my job."

"We aren't responsible for what happened to Crimson Shadow," the Viscountess insisted. "We helped her, even after she tried to kidnap Severin. We saved her life."

"I have no intention of getting involved in this." Dr. Bhandry raised his dominant energy, but neither woman seemed to notice. "The truth is she does have a job to do. We take this problem very seriously."

The Viscountess glanced at Severin and was surprised to discover that the slave was more interested in watching the brunette fill her bottle with pills. She was at the same station as the blonde, flipping pills into a bottle with a little metal instrument. Her back was to the other people in the room.

"I understand doctor," the Viscountess said calmly. "We also have a job to do and our job is also very serious."

Before the doctor could reply Severin surprised everyone by speaking up.

"Dr. Bhandry, we need to talk to you in private."

The doctor looked as if he was about to lose his temper, but he swallowed his anger.

"Come with me." He led them out of the storage room. He was probably going towards his office, but Severin started talking as soon as they were out of the pharmacy waiting room.

"Doctor, who are the women who work there?"

"That's Sandy and Jennifer. Sandy, the blonde, is pretty new, but Jennifer has been with us for about three years. They're college students majoring in pharmacy. We have six of them working for us. We have to have someone available all hours since we get people in from different time zones."

"Obviously you suspect one of the people who work there of being your thief."

Dr. Bhandry skidded to a halt, forcing the Viscountess and Severin to stop as well.

"Yes, I suspect them." He spoke the words carefully, making sure they were very clear even through his accent. "As I said we have six hard-working people in the pharmacy and I can't go around accusing people. I suggest you not accuse people either."

"I'm not accusing anyone," Severin shrugged, trying to look harmless. "I just wondered if you had noticed Jennifer's lab coat."

"She has a lab coat. So does Sandy and so do I. Half the building has them."

"Yes, but you and Sandy have a flap of material over the pocket to protect the contents in case something is spilled. Jennifer doesn't."

"So? That coat isn't hospital issue. It belongs to her."

"Of course, because hospital issue wouldn't have pockets that were sewn open." Both his owner and Dr. Bhandry stared at Severin. "It's an old magician's trick. The pocket looks normal, but it always hangs open so anything dropped will fall right into it."

Dr. Bhandry turned his glare on the Viscountess. "Did you notice this?"

"No," she admitted, "But then I'm not Severin. If he says it's true, then it's true."

"A few minutes ago Jennifer was filling the prescription for the cheerleader. Pain killers are worth a lot on the street. All it would take is a flick of her wrist to put some in her pocket."

"Why didn't Blanca see it? That's what I'm paying her for."

"I'm sure Blanca is very good at what she does," the Viscountess put in. "But this Jennifer seems to be a sleight-of-hand artist. Blanca isn't trained to handle that type of thief."

"And I suppose you are?"

The Viscountess and Severin glanced at each other. Severin lowered his head humbly to allow her to speak.

"As a matter of fact, solving mysteries is exactly what we do. Now, if you don't mind, we have to get back to Blanca, and you have a security problem to deal with."

"I've known this woman for a long time. I'm not going to accuse her just on the word of your slave."

"Severin is very reliable."

"He'd better be. If he's wrong, I want the two of you out of here, and don't come back with any more questions." Dr. Bhandry looked each of them in the eyes to make sure they saw how serious he was. "Now, let me handle this."

He went back towards the pharmacy, tension showing in every line of his body. The Viscountess and Severin trailed behind him.

It was obvious Dr. Bhandry intended to see Jennifer in action before doing anything. He waited in the storage room, along with the Viscountess and Severin. Blanca was presumably somewhere in the shadows observing them without being seen.

Sandy, the blonde in rubber filled the next prescription, but it was only about thirty minutes before Jennifer was at the desk and a woman in a pony girl harness on crutches hobbled up to her with a prescription. If Jennifer noticed that everyone was staring at her she gave no sign.

She took the appropriate bottle of pills from a shelf and poured out a large amount onto a tray. With rapid motions she slid the right number off to the edge of the tray where they could slide into the small pill bottle. The Viscountess made sure she was on the correct side to see everything.

She almost missed it. As Jennifer was filling the small bottle with her right hand, her left hand was on the tray with the extra pills. Her arm came down, dropping naturally to her side. There was nothing unusual about the motion at all, but when her hand left the tray she was making a fist and when her arm hung at her side the hand was open. As her hand had gone past the wide open pocket of the lab coat the fist had opened, depositing the contents into the pocket.

As Jennifer printed out a label for the bottle, the Viscountess slipped up to Dr. Bhandry.

"Did you see it?" she asked.

"No," the doctor said a little sharply. He caught himself and asked in a calmer tone. "Did you?"

"Yes, I saw it all. Severin is right."

That was too much for Dr. Bhandry. He caught Jennifer as soon as she handed the pills to the pony girl.

"Jennifer, I need to see your lab coat," he announced in an authoritative voice.

She jumped at his voice and instinctively tried to close the coat across her narrow lingerie clad form.

"I'm sorry, what?"

"Your coat. This will only take a moment."

"I don't understand." Jennifer's eyes betrayed some panic. She glanced past Dr. Bhandry to the Viscountess and Severin, sensing that they were to blame. Blanca had appeared beside them, adding one more pair of eyes accusing her.

Dr. Bhandry sent out a flare of dominant energy. Jennifer shuddered as it washed across her. It was clear to the Viscountess that Dr. Bhandry had topped her more than once. No wonder he was so reluctant to accuse her. If they were in a relationship it was going to look very bad for him.

The Doctor reached out and took the coat from her. Jennifer no longer offered any protest. When he reached into the pocket he drew out a handful of pills. The expression on his face went from anger to sorrow, then back to anger.

"Jenny, how could you do this?"

"I'm not taking that much. I just needed some extra cash."

"Can't you see what you've done? The pharmacy is one of the few parts of the Hospital that actually makes money. Are you trying to shut us down?" Anger was starting to win out over sorrow.

"Look, nobody's going to miss it. The stuff in here is worth a fortune."

That was the last straw. Dr. Bhandry's hand shot out, grabbing her by the arm. She gave a little squeal of protest as he forced her back over the desk. Sandy, the blonde in rubber, was keeping well out of the way.

"I'm ashamed that I ever allowed you in here," Dr. Bhandry growled. He began a very hard spanking, smacking his palm against her narrow ass. She screamed and writhed in his grip but she did not Safeword.

The Viscountess was worried that this was getting out of hand. The first rule of any Scene was that you do not punish someone in anger. On those rare occasions when Severin truly did something wrong and had to be punished for it, she always made sure that she was calm and collected before she struck the first blow.

Just then a pirate came up to the desk. He did not have a peg leg, an eye patch, or a parrot on his shoulder, but he was wearing a tricorn hat, sun bleached shirt, and knee breeches. One hand was resting on the hilt of his cutlass, the other hand held a prescription.

"Sorry," the pirate stammered. "I came to get something for scurvy, but I can come back if this is a bad time."

"I'm sorry," Dr. Bhandry apologized. He took hold of Jennifer and brought her away from the desk. Sandy slipped into the chair to continue doing her job.

"I didn't mean any harm," Jennifer protested. She was crying and trying to keep the tears from ruining her eye makeup.

"I don't want to hear any excuses. I have to talk to Dr. Kingsly and the rest of the board about you. In the mean time I want you to report to the animal testing lab."

Jennifer blanched at this pronouncement. "You can't..."

"Go!"

She left the room, shuffling her high heels on the floor.

"Animal testing lab?" the Viscountess immediately asked.

"It's not as bad as it sounds," Dr. Bhandry admitted. "People come here to try out a new punishment or a new sex toy before they use it on their partner. I'm sure she'll be fine."

Blanca was glaring at the Viscountess and Severin with a look of pure venom. If looks could kill, the two of them were already dead, cremated, and their ashes scattered.

"I hope you don't expect me to thank you," Blanca said pointedly.

"We were trying to help."

"I've had enough of your help. I'm sure your clever little slave can figure things out without talking to me. I plan on collecting my fee and leaving as soon as possible."

"Fee?" Dr. Bhandry interrupted. "As far as I'm concerned you've earned no fee. All you did was stand here for a week watching her steal right under your nose."

"You were watching her, too!"

"But I wasn't hired to catch her."

The tension in the room abruptly shifted when there was a knock on the door. It was so unexpected that everyone turned to look at the door as if the sound were a supernatural event. Dr. Bhandry went to the door and opened it, revealing Black Masque. The powerfully built masked beauty strode into the room as if she owned the building and was out collecting rent.

"I'm Black Masque," she announced. "I need to see Blanca."

"What are you doing here?" Blanca asked, stepping forward.

Black Masque glanced at the Viscountess and Severin, acknowledging them with a quick nod.

"Papillion sent me. She was worried about you. Tell me what's been happening here."

Blanca gave her a quick rundown ending with: "...and these two claim The Crone sent them to talk to me."

"I'm afraid The Crone did send them."

"What! That's ridiculous."

"I agree, but for now they work for us, and you should cooperate fully. Please go with them while I talk about your fee with the doctor."

Dr. Bhandry had his arms folded across his chest and did not look to be in much mood to negotiate. He did however unlock a small consultation room where the Viscountess and Severin could talk to Blanca in private.

The Viscountess sat in a chair while Severin took the floor next to her. Blanca declined the other chair and stood with her back to the wall. She had withdrawn behind her mask and her naked body was held rigid. She seemed determined to get this distasteful task over with as soon as possible.

"What do you want to ask?" Blanca demanded.

"You and some of the other Kamen Girls were in a lounge on the twenty-third floor. All of you had come back from various missions."

"If you say so."

This was obviously not going to be easy, even if Black Masque had told her to cooperate.

"How much of the conversations can you remember?"

"Not much. I was mostly killing time until Papillion showed up. When she arrived I was talking to her."

"What about Red Lightning?"

"What about her?" Blanca was defensive, but she still wasn't opening up to them.

Severin decided to go for broke.

"You accused her of lying about her injury," Severin said. "I'm curious why you said that."

Blanca's small breasts rose and fell as she drew in a deep breath. "All right, fine, I'll tell you what happened."

"We would appreciate it," the Viscountess smiled.

"You have to understand, Red Lightning has always been the best. She was top in her class, best ranks at everything. She was dammed near perfect and she didn't hesitate to tell everyone when they didn't measure up to her standards. Oh, she pretends to be nice about it, like she was giving you advice on how you could have done some job better, but all she was really doing was reminding you how much better she is."

"Go on."

"I know it's wrong of me, but when I heard she busted up her leg the first thing I thought was, thank goodness, she's not little miss perfect any more. I didn't say anything to her, though, until she went after Papillion."

"Was this about the pastry?"

"Yes. We all thought it was kind of funny, you know, some poor baker sees a pastry floating in the air for a second. Red Lightning just lit into her, about how reckless she was and a danger to the rest of us and she shouldn't even be allowed out on missions. I admit I blew my top. No one talks about Papillion that way. I told Red everyone makes mistakes and I wanted to know how robots that can barely climb stairs caught her in the first place."

"How did they catch her?" Severin asked.

"The way I heard it she had just stolen some blueprints from a safe and the Mariabots were following her. She raced onto the stairwell to lose them, because they couldn't possibly catch up with her on the stairs. Unfortunately there was already a group of robots on the landing of the floor below her and she was caught between them. They've got super strength and would have torn her up in close quarters fighting so she jumped over the railing and dropped a few floors to get away. That's when she hurt her leg."

"And you doubted her story?"

"No, not really," Blanca reluctantly admitted. "I'm sure she really did fight a dozen robots in a narrow stairwell and leap ten stories to the ground with only a sprained ankle to show for it. It's the kind of thing she does. I accused her of lying because I was mad and I wanted to get a rise out of her."

"And did you?" the Viscountess took over the questioning.

"I'll say! Red Lightning almost hit the roof. I thought she was going to punch me, but fortunately Black Masque was there to keep us apart. She made us apologize and shake hands. As soon as Papillion was done with her snack, we were off to my room."

"How long did you stay there?"

"Until the next day, the afternoon I think."

The Viscountess and Severin glanced at each other. Neither of them had any more questions.

"That's it?" Blanca stared at them. "That's all you wanted to know?"

"I'm afraid so."

"I don't get it. What's going on?"

The Viscountess glanced at Severin to see how much he wanted to tell her.

"Something was stolen that day from the ziggurat. The Crone has asked us to come in as outsiders and see what we can find out."

"You think I stole something?"

"We're talking to a lot of people," the Viscountess said smoothly.

"Great, that's just great. Can I go now?"

When they emerged in the hallway they found Black Masque waiting for them. Apparently she had concluded her business with Dr. Bhandry.

"Thank you for your help," the Viscountess told her. "I don't suppose you'd care to answer a few questions."

"I had a feeling you might ask me." Black Masque drew herself up to her full impressive height. "Very well."

Once the three of them were inside the small room the Viscountess immediately started on Black Masque.

"Apparently you were in that lounge. You had to break up a fight."

"So I did."

"But you didn't mention that when we were talking to The Crone."

"It was a minor squabble. I saw no reason to bother The Crone with it. Red Lightning and Blanca are two of our best. I'd trust my life to either of them."

"So tell me what happened in your own words."

Black Masque rolled her eyes up to the ceiling. She seemed to be watching it all happen inside her head.

"When I arrived the other women were already there, Skye, Tiger Mask, Red Lightning, Blanca, and Papillion. I had my back to the table and was getting ice water when I heard Papillion's story about the pastry shop in Paris. She made a mistake, but we've all done something like that. Red Lightning shouldn't have ridden her so hard about it."

"Have you had trouble with Red Lightning in the past?"

"I wouldn't say trouble. I admire Red Lightning. I've even taken her on as my protégé. She has a lot of discipline and holds herself to very high standards. Unfortunately she also tries to hold other people to those same standards and they don't always appreciate her input."

"That's a diplomatic way of putting it," Severin commented.

"Keeping the peace is part of my job," Black Masque admitted. "At any rate, Blanca overreacted. There was some shouting and clenched fists until I made them calm down. I wish it was more exciting, but that's all that happened."

"Did you see anything unusual?"

"Nothing," Black Masque snapped. "And before you ask, I didn't see anyone put anything into Skye's drink. She already had the cup when I got to the room."

"But you can't prove that," the Viscountess pointed out.

"Of course not. Now, are we done here?"

The Viscountess glanced at Severin who nodded.

"Thank you for your cooperation," the Viscountess smiled, but Black Masque did not return the smile.

"The Crone has ordered it, and I obey. I just hope some good comes from this. The Crone also told me to inform you that she wants a progress report as soon as possible."

"We can meet her tomorrow afternoon in Victoria at that place in Limehouse, if you'd like."

"That will be adequate. Until then."

Black Masque nodded her farewell and left the Viscountess and Severin alone.

"Severin," the Viscountess looked at her slave on the floor. "This would be a very good time for one of your brilliant deductions. Please tell me you know who stole the Sphere?"

"I'm sorry, I don't know yet."

"Do I have to call Dr. Kingsly and ask for her slowest, most painful castration technique?"

"It wouldn't help," Severin winced at the thought of the lovely doctor's scalpel. "We can't complete the puzzle until we have all the pieces, and I've got a feeling the most important piece is still missing. If we could figure out why the Sphere was stolen, we'd know who stole it."

Chapter Fourteen

The next afternoon in the Dominion of Victoria a hansom cab pulled by a well-built pony boy rattled through the streets of London. The Viscountess was dressed in one of her elegant Victorian outfits while Severin sat naked on the floor of the cab.

"So what do we tell The Crone?" the Viscountess demanded.

"Just tell her what we know."

"Which is what exactly? We still don't know who stole the Sphere. As far as I'm concerned it could be any of the four, or Black Masque for that matter," the Viscountess mused. "I believed what Papillion told me. Plus she and Blanca alibi each other."

"She could still be lying to protect her lover. There's also no way to be sure that Blanca didn't slip out while Papillion was sleeping."

"So they're both still suspects. What about Red Lightning? She certainly has a temper and she set you up for a nasty beating."

"True, but she also has the best reputation. She's little miss perfect, the last one who'd steal something so valuable. Plus she has a limp. Even if she stole Skye's mask, she's walking with a limp. The guardian they have chained to that stone would have seen the limp."

"So we can eliminate her?"

"Maybe. I'd know for sure if I could figure out why the Sphere was taken."

"While you ponder that, let's talk about Tiger Mask. We've heard from three other people what happened in that lounge, and her story was the sketchiest. She didn't remember Blanca and Red Lightning going at it. She didn't even remember Black Masque being there. What if she's trying to cover something up?"

"It's possible, but don't forget that everyone remembers things in different ways. She may have simply told us what happened as she recalls it. On the other hand, she did lie about being hired by Abraxus."

"So we're back to square one," the Viscountess groaned and leaned back into the seat. "We have to report to The Crone that we have nothing."

"We've made a start," Severin reminded her. "The thief knows that we're on to her. Now either the Sphere will miraculously turn up, one of the other Kamen Girls will take off, or one of our suspects won't return."

"And if none of those things happens?"

"Then the Sphere really was stolen to destroy the Kamen Girls or to be sold for money. It could be destroyed or sold by now and we may never get it back."

"Let's leave that last part out when we talk to The Crone. We'll pretend to be optimistic for now." The Viscountess glanced around at the street. "I think we've arrived, and just to make it a perfect day, it's started to rain."

Severin shivered as the cold rain washed over him. They had been issued an umbrella when they passed through the Gateway, which the Viscountess opened quickly, protecting herself from the drenching downpour. Severin followed her, but the leash was long enough that he was outside the protection of the umbrella.

Outside the Jade Pagoda the sudden shower had produced a rapidly moving torrent of filthy water that covered the sidewalk. It was wide enough that there was no easy way around it.

The Viscountess cleared her throat and pointed dramatically to the water.

"I don't intend on getting my boots dirty," she announced.

Severin was usually quick to obey, but he hesitated, still lost in thought.

"I'm waiting," she said icily, unclipping his leash.

Severin threw himself to the filthy sidewalk, making a human bridge for her to walk across. He consoled himself by remembering that this was much cleaner than Victorian London had actually been. It was probably cleaner than many streets in present day London, too, but that didn't make it any warmer or less muddy.

He felt the full weight of her, the crushing force that he found so pleasurable. Her low-heeled boots sank deliciously into his skin. She would never have done this if she were wearing her high-heeled boots; some of the spike heels could penetrate a man's skin.

The Viscountess had one foot on his shoulder and stepped onto the doorway of the Jade Pagoda. She reattached the leash and pulled Severin to his feet. Not surprisingly, he was filthy and shivering from the water. Some of the mud was even on his face, which he had been unable to keep out of the muck.

"Poor Severin," she chuckled. With one gloved hand she wiped clean a spot on his cheek, then leaned in to plant a kiss on him. "Come on, let's get you inside."

The Jade Pagoda was as empty of customers and as full of smoke as it had been the first time. On this occasion two white women lay on the floor, half-asleep. They were wearing only old and torn undergarments and were locked to a support pillar by chains around their necks. A sour-faced Asian who was well over six feet tall rose to his feet, fingering the hatchet stuck in his belt.

Before anything could happen Pain Toy appeared from a room behind the bar. She said something in Chinese which made the man shrug and sit back down on his bar stool. The woman who owned the Jade Pagoda was as beautiful as last time, her slender form encased in a sheath of silk so fine her belly button and nipples were visible. The long, blue-black hair cascaded down her sleek form.

"So, you have returned," Pain Toy stated. Her eyes took them in at a glance. "The old woman told me to expect you."

"We are supposed to meet with her."

"You will find her in a room at the back." She gestured towards a beaded curtain almost hidden in the shadows.

"Thank you. Do you have brandy?"

"We do."

"I would like one. Can you also provide hot tea and perhaps a towel for my slave?"

"Of course." Pain Toy gave a cruel little smirk. She seemed to know exactly how Severin had gotten in that condition.

Through the beaded curtain the Viscountess and Severin saw The Crone sitting at a table with Black Masque standing behind her, a silent sentinel. The Viscountess took a seat across from The Crone while Severin sat at her feet.

The sharp eyes of the old woman fixed them warily. "Do you have anything to report?" she asked sharply.

"We've talked to Black Masque and the four women who were with Skye in the lounge."

"And?"

The Viscountess paused while one of the white women came into the room, freed from her bondage to serve as their waitress. She put the brandy on the table and handed a cup of tea and a towel to Severin.

"Is there any other way I can serve you?" the prisoner asked. She did not have a lower class accent, and clearly showed signs of education. Pain Toy had implied on the first visit that her girls were upper class like the Viscountess, and apparently it was true.

It was also true that the two Kamen Girls made the slave girl very nervous.

The Viscountess dismissed her and waited until the beaded curtain had stopped swinging before she spoke. She described what they had heard from the Kamen Girls they had interviewed.

"Black Masque implied that you have learned nothing," The Crone stated. Behind her Black Masque stood with her powerful arms folded across her breasts, as impassive and unmoving as a statue.

"We have learned a great deal," the Viscountess glanced at Black Masque before continuing. "But it is true that we have not yet found the thief."

"What will you do now?"

The Viscountess looked down at Severin, who was still soaking up the muddy water that clung to him. Gently she took the towel from him and thoroughly cleaned his shoulders. The wounds from the diamond flogger were completely closed, but there was no sense in taking chances. Realizing this was his cue to speak, Severin looked up at the women.

"First, let me ask if all the suspects have returned to your home?"

"Blanca and Papillion have returned, but Tiger Mask and Red Lightning have not."

"Did they say why not?"

"Yes." The Crone looked up at Black Masque, giving her leave to make her report.

"Tiger Mask said that someone called Boss Man attacked, and she stayed for a few extra days to teach martial arts to a sexbot," Black Masque reported. "She told me you'd understand."

"Yes, it makes perfect sense." Severin remembered the tiny slip of a girl the sexbot appeared to be. Her wrestling style showed that she hadn't had any real combat training. She'd be devastating if Tiger Mask trained her.

"Red Lightning is still in Venice. Apparently Manzoni has an audience with the Doge and he's preparing some new pieces. She's under contract and he won't let her go until they have their showing at the Doge's Palace."

"That makes sense, too." Severin shrugged. "I take it none of the

Kamen Girls has gone on the run. By now the rumors must be spreading as to what happened."

"No one has run," The Crone informed them. "If that was your plan it has failed."

"It hasn't failed yet. I'm still expecting something to happen."

"What do you expect to happen?"

"I don't know yet," Severin admitted. Black Masque gave a little snort of contempt. "I don't think any of those women want to see the Kamen Girls destroyed. We have to be ready when the Sphere is used."

"Let us hope we do not have to wait too long." The Crone planted her staff and rose majestically to her feet, her long breasts swaying with the motion. "Our time is limited and we must prepare ourselves for the worst."

"Don't give up," the Viscountess reassured her. "I've found Severin is rarely wrong."

"I sincerely hope you are right. Please leave a message here if you need to contact us. One of us will check here on a regular schedule. We shall send a message to you if we need you."

The Crone left, followed by Black Masque who took a second to shoot the Viscountess a dark look. There was no doubt Black Masque still felt it had been a mistake to hire the Viscountess and Severin. On the other hand saying "I told you so" wasn't going to save them.

The Viscountess sat glumly and finished her brandy. She reached down and tousled Severin's hair.

"How are you feeling?"

"Fine. The tea is warming me up."

"What's our next move?"

"If I say there's nothing we can do but wait will you punish me?"

"Yes."

"There's nothing we can do but wait."

The Viscountess sighed.

"Very well. While we wait I'll take you down to Duchess and put you through the wringer."

"Thank you, Viscountess." Severin brightened considerably at the prospect of a visit to the pony girl farm.

As they went through the beaded curtain back to the main room they saw Pain Toy waiting for them.

"Leaving so soon?"

"Yes, I shall have to settle the bill."

"Don't bother." Pain Toy's voice was a seductive purr. "Why don't you stay for a while?"

"We must be going."

"But I insist." She had eyes like a cat. The jade green depths almost seemed to glow. "Make yourself comfortable. You must be so warm."

The Viscountess swayed slightly on her feet. Severin glanced up at her, wondering what was wrong. He hadn't felt any surge of power coming from Pain Toy, and yet it looked as if the Viscountess was slipping into Subspace.

It dawned on him what was happening. This was Limehouse in the Victorian era and Pain Toy was a dragon lady—an oriental temptress, they used to be called. He reached up and grabbed his leash, giving his strength to his owner.

The Viscountess felt the tug on the leash and remembered Severin. She blinked and shook her head, trying to knock herself loose from Subspace. She had fallen under so rapidly she hadn't even been aware it was happening.

"Don't try to resist," Pain Toy said. "You are under my power."

"I don't think so," the Viscountess glared at her. She was gratified to see Pain Toy curse softly and stamp her foot. "What exactly were you doing?"

"It is my preferred method of domination," the Asian beauty said defensively.

"I'm aware hypnosis and mind control are legitimate fetishes, but you should mention you have that ability before you challenge someone."

"I was going to give you a chance to Safeword." Pain Toy insisted.

"Oh really." The Viscountess stepped forward, her dominant energy spiking. Severin's cock hardened at once and Pain Toy took a step backwards as the Viscountess approached.

Pain Toy was a powerful dominant, but she wasn't raising her power to counter the Viscountess. Perhaps she felt she couldn't compete without the mind control trick, or possibly she felt guilty for trying the trick in the first place.

The Viscountess stood very close to her, drinking in her perfume.

"Are you going to formally challenge me?" the Viscountess demanded.

"No, Viscountess." A tiny shudder passed through her body as she switched from dominant to submissive.

"Good. Then I don't expect to have any problems with you in the future. That goes for my masked friends as well. They may be coming and going from this place quite a bit."

"They will be treated as honored guests," Pain Toy promised.

"Excellent. Now we must be going. I'm sure I will see you again."

Pain Toy bowed deeply and escorted them to the door.

Outside the sun had begun to shine through the clouds. The muddy stream that filled the sidewalk had been reduced to a trickle.

"It looks like a lovely day Severin. Let's walk back to the Gateway."

They made their way through the busy streets to one of the main intersections. They had their backs to the Thames, looking out at the stream of carriages that rattled past, each one pulled by a pony slave.

"Severin!" the Viscountess suddenly shouted, reaching back and grabbing his arm. She leaned into the street, staring at the back of a rapidly retreating carriage. Her focus was so great that she didn't see the heavy cart pulled by four burly men that was bearing down on her and Severin had to pull her back to the sidewalk.

"What's wrong?" the slave asked.

"It's her."

"Who?"

The Viscountess realized that the carriage she wanted was already lost in the sea of traffic.

"I saw St. Claire in the back of that carriage."

"Isn't she still at the Slut Box?"

"It's been a month. She must be free now."

Severin felt his stomach churn. He wanted to ask if she was certain, but he already knew what the answer would be. The Viscountess knew St. Claire as well as she knew anyone. They had been rivals for years. St. Claire had been sent into slavery as the result of losing a bet. Since St. Claire had been involved in covering up a murder, the Viscountess didn't feel sorry for her.

"Damn it, this is the last thing we need." The Viscountess clenched her fists in frustration.

"She can't have had anything to do with the theft of the Sphere, since she was locked up at the time," Severin reminded her. "St. Claire may have come here to mess with your head, but I'll bet she needs to lick her wounds for a while before she starts anything. In the mean time we still have a case to solve."

"You're right, of course," the Viscountess sighed. "But from now on we will have to be on our guard."

Severin suggested that they take a cab back to the Gateway, and the Viscountess agreed.

Chapter Fifteen

Thanks to the different time zones it was still early in the day when they returned to the Real World. They called Duchess who offered to send a cart to retrieve them, but it wouldn't be available until later in the day. To kill time the Viscountess and Severin went to the Boston Common to relax. When they returned home to rendezvous with the pony girl, a familiar face greeted them.

"Snuzzle!" the Viscountess exclaimed and hugged her. "How have you been?"

"Wonderful."

The woman was naked except for a body harness. She had dropped out of her pony Persona to wait for them. Her bit and bridle were set aside as well as the butt plug with her horse's tail. Sklavin had gotten her a snack.

While the Viscountess chatted with the pony slave Severin pressed kisses into her boots. The boots were heavy and had actual horseshoes attached to the soles.

"Let me grab a bag. Get yourself in character."

"Right," Snuzzle smiled her last human smile for the time being and began to center herself.

While the Viscountess went inside to pack, Severin sat on the pavement watching Snuzzle transform. He found the process fascinating. Although he could play the part of a pony, he didn't have her abilities. For him it was just following orders.

The slave girl flared her nostrils as she drew in a deep breath. She rolled her head, stretching every muscle. A sort of ripple passed through her. She stood straighter and looked faster and more powerful. When she looked down at saw Severin at her feet she gave a start and shied away from him.

"Easy, girl," Severin said softly, hoping she'd remember the sound of his voice.

The pony slave stamped her foot on the pavement, the metal horseshoe sounding like a bell being struck. She was clearly trying to establish her dominance over him, and Severin dutifully backed away from her. He tried to make her feel safe by staying as close to the ground as possible.

The Viscountess came from the house in time to see Severin scuttling away from Snuzzle.

"Is she giving you problems, Severin?" the Viscountess teased.

Snuzzle gave a whinny of pleasure at the sight of the Viscountess. She pranced in place, doing a sort of equine happy dance that made the bells on her nose and nipples ring merrily.

"Good girl," the Viscountess cooed. "That's my good girl."

Snuzzle whinnied softly as the Viscountess stroked her hair and ran her hands up and down the lean, well-muscled body.

"You want to run? Is that what you want?"

Snuzzle snorted and tossed her head.

"Good girl. Let's get you all buckled up."

Viscountess took the bridle and worked the rubber bit between Snuzzle's teeth. She had to lift the slave's pony tail hair to buckle it at the back of her head. Another strap went over the top of the head, holding everything in place.

Next came the butt plug. The body harness Snuzzle wore had a strap that went across her pussy, but was open in back so her ass was visible and there was room to insert the plug with its hair from a real horse dangling down. Viscountess made sure she was ready first, giving her flanks a few gentle strokes. The Viscountess had a good view of the small purple hearts that were tattooed on Snuzzle's ass and trailed down one leg.

Viscountess passed her hand under the strap in front, feeling how wet Snuzzle was before she began to slide the well lubricated plug into her ass. The pony slave shuddered with pleasure, bucking her hips against the Viscountess' hand.

"Good girl." The Viscountess rewarded her with a sugar cube—Domino brand, of course.

After the tail was in place it was simply a matter of attaching the reins to the bridle and backing Snuzzle between the poles. The Viscountess lifted the poles into the slave's hands and buckled the wrist cuffs to them.

Severin and her bag were placed on the floor of the pony cart. Once she took her seat, the Viscountess snapped the whip over Snuzzle's shoulders. The pretty pony slave pranced forward with a merry toss of her head, eager to be on the move.

"Don't wait up, I don't know how long we'll be," the Viscountess said to Sklavin, who was watching from the door.

From his place on the floor Severin could feel the cart rolling across the pavement and knew they were heading down the driveway to the street. He could hear the sounds of the afternoon traffic growing louder as they approached. Just when it seemed that they would enter the street Severin felt the familiar tingle of passing into the void.

The sounds of traffic faded and the substance under the wheels became smooth. When Severin looked up all he could see was a grey pearlescent sky that seemed to stretch forever. Just as Severin was making himself comfortable the void lightened and became a cloudy sky. With a slight bump the pony cart returned to earth and started moving across solid ground. Gravel was audible beneath the wheels. By using the void between Dominions as a shortcut, Snuzzle had brought them from Boston to rural Connecticut with only a few minutes of running.

Snuzzle had made the trip between Duchess' pony farm and the Viscountess' house so many times she could do it blindfolded. In fact, navigating the void blindfolded was one of the things Duchess trained her to do.

Duchess owned a large piece of land that she used for training pony girls. It was the fulfillment of a lifelong dream for her, one that she had pursued through years of being a professional dominant. Even with what she had saved, she had still needed the money from her slave husband to make the dream a reality. The once-wealthy man had signed over everything to the mistress he loved. Now he lived as a collared and leashed slave, naked except for the chastity device around his genitals.

By the time the cart had skidded to a stop on the driveway, Duchess was already out the door to greet them, slave in tow. She and the Viscountess embraced and kissed with the familiarity of old lovers, which they were.

It had been Duchess after all who had found the Viscountess when she was in the depths of her submissive period, when she was known as Desire and recognized her for the powerful potential dominant that she could become. She had taken Desire under her wing, molded her, trained her, and finally took her to Victoria where Desire had been given a new name and was from then on known as the Viscountess.

Duchess had to be older than the Viscountess, but it was hard to tell by looking at her. Her hair was stark white and hung down to her shoulders like spun silver. She moved with a beauty and grace that made men naturally want to serve her. The only real concessions she made to her true age were the crow's feet at the corners of her eyes and the laugh lines about her mouth.

She was accompanied by her slave Dickie, a man whose head was bald on top except for a fringe of white hair that gave him an oddly monk-like appearance. He'd put on some weight around his middle and was, as always, wearing nothing but his collar and chastity device. His balls dangled below the small tube that was locked around his cock.

It would have been hard for anyone from his old life to recognize him in his current state. Gone were the three-piece suits, the huge office, and control over a Fortune 500 company. In his day he was known as a ruthless tyrant of a boss, a hard-driving businessman who would stop at nothing to get ahead. Even then he had gone to Duchess on a regular basis to be beaten and humiliated. He wanted to lose the power that he had worked so hard to gain, wanted to suffer for all the decisions he made that hurt others.

While he had been her client, he had asked Duchess to marry him a dozen times over the years. She had always turned him down. Eventually, after the Viscountess had been trained and Duchess was seriously thinking about retiring from being a Pro-Domme, she decided to give her client his fondest wish.

It had taken the lawyers and accountants almost a year to figure everything out. He had to leave his company in capable hands and set money aside for his ex-wives and kids, even though he hadn't seen any of them in years. Everything he owned was put into the name of the Duchess. What she didn't want for herself, she sold. To the world at large Dickie had simply retired and left the rat race behind. Most of his old acquaintances believed he was living as a beachcomber on a Caribbean Island.

Dickie, or Richard as he had been known before marriage, had made love to his new wife exactly once. After their public wedding there had been a more private, more important ceremony, attended by Severin, the Viscountess, and a few of Duchess' friends. There, on the hotel bed, Richard had finally lived out all his fantasies with his imperious mistress. He had made love to her and she had responded enthusiastically. When he was finally spent, he had lain back on the sheets while his bride and the Viscountess locked the chastity device around his cock and balls.

Once that was in place, a formal collaring ceremony made Dickie, as he was now called, the property of Duchess in the eyes of the community. Severin thought about that night every time he was with the happy couple.

While their owners kissed and hugged, Severin and Dickie nodded to each other in the silent communion of slaves. They were interrupted by a furious barking as a naked woman on all fours raced past them. The dog slave ran to Snuzzle and got up on her haunches, licking at the tight strap across Snuzzle's pussy.

"Bad dog!" Duchess laughed. She reached down and grabbed a ring on the collar, pulling the slave back from Snuzzle. "Viscountess, this is Bright Eyes."

The dog girl barked excitedly and went to sniff the Viscountess.

"It's nice to meet you." The Viscountess extended her hand for the dog slave to sniff. When Bright Eyes made a high-pitched noise the Viscountess began to pet her. The dog slave was naked except for her collar and knee pads. Her light brown hair was in pigtails, keeping it from obscuring her face.

"I'm training her to be a companion animal to Snuzzle," Duchess explained. "Many race horses have dogs that keep them calm and relaxed.

"That sounds like an excellent idea."

"So what brings you down here?"

"We seem to have reached an impasse in the case we're working on. I thought I'd fill the time until something happens by torturing Severin."

"You know I can never resist torturing Severin." Duchess held out a boot for Severin to kiss. "Does he enjoy bastinado?"

"I'm pretty sure he hates it." The Viscountess held out one of her boots for Dickie to kiss.

"Oh, excellent, then this is going to be fun."

Severin found himself lying on his back in the large yard behind Duchess' house. His wrists were staked to the ground, his legs elevated by ropes from his ankles to two-foot-high posts. The soles of his feet felt very exposed.

Duchess had brought a picnic basket full of implements to torture Severin with and a blanket for her and the Viscountess to relax on. A few feet away behind a spilt-rail fence Snuzzle and Bright Eyes were playing, barking and running back and forth with the carefree abandon of animals at play.

"I have to confess, I don't have a lot of experience with bastinado," the Viscountess admitted.

"Don't worry, there's nothing to it. I've found most slaves aren't very fond of it, so it's a good lesson for them. Start with the flogger."

The Viscountess took Hornet's Sting from her belt and used it on Severin's right foot. The thin leather strands made an appealing sound as they struck the soles of his feet. Duchess used her own, heavier flogger on his other foot. Duchess' flogger had no name, but she had been using it for quite a while and it was building up a lot of power. There was a chance that soon it would be a Named item.

"The arch of the foot is the most sensitive," Duchess pointed out.

The Viscountess adjusted her swing, using an underhand stroke. Severin began to squirm in his bonds. The soles of his feet were starting to tingle and burn.

"That was just the warm up. Now the fun begins." Duchess gave a slender cane to the Viscountess. The two women struck almost at once. Severin gave a sudden cry and lurched against the ropes that held him. More rapid blows of the canes followed.

Through a haze of pain Severin heard a phone ring. Dickie picked up the phone in Duchess' bag as he had been trained to do.

"It's for you Viscountess," he said. "They say they got this number from Sklavin."

The Viscountess picked up the phone.

"Yes, this is the Viscountess." She listened for a moment. "Actually we're in the middle of a case right now.... I see.... Your niece has vanished from a sealed Dominion."

"We'll take the case!" Severin suddenly shouted from the ground. Duchess froze in mid-swing and stared at him, as did his owner. "This is what we've been waiting for," Severin explained.

The Viscountess continued speaking. "Actually it seems we do have time for your case. Tomorrow morning? Yes, we can be there."

The Viscountess turned off the phone and put it back in Duchess' bag.

"Explain," she demanded.

"There are only three reasons to steal that thing. One was to destroy it."

"Right, and if it's destroyed then there's nothing we can do."

"They could also sell it. It would be worth a fortune, but you can't just put something like that up on Ebay. I have a few feelers out with some of my contacts, but no one's heard of anything like this."

"And the third option," the Viscountess realized, "is that they needed it. They stole it so they could use it."

"It's only useful for one thing, getting in and out of Dominions."
Severin said. "I was hoping we'd hear about something unusual that happened in some hard-to-reach Dominion, but I never dreamed they'd just call us."

"I don't see what the connection is. This may still be a wild goose chase."

"I know," Severin sighed and laid his head back down in the grass. Now that his adrenaline surge was dying down his feet had begun to hurt.

"I'm terribly sorry," the Viscountess apologized to Duchess. "I know how rude this is, but—"

"You can't tell me anything about the case," Duchess finished the sentence for her. "I know."

"This could be the break we've been waiting for."

"I take it this means you won't be spending the night."

"I'm afraid not. We have some research to do and I just made a lunch date in Phoenix for tomorrow."

"So I guess you'll be borrowing Snuzzle again?"

"If I can have her."

"Let's see what she has to say."

Duchess put two fingers to her mouth and let out a whistle. Snuzzle and Bright Eyes immediately ran to the fence.

"Snuzzle, how would you like to have another jaunt with the Viscountess?"

The pony slave made a sort of a squealing noise and jumped up and down.

"There's your answer," Duchess smiled.

"Thank you for everything." The Viscountess leaned in and kissed her on the cheek. "Severin and I couldn't do it without you."

"That reminds me, I certainly hope we still have time to deal with him."

"Of course." The Viscountess glanced down at Severin. The phone call had brought him out of Subspace and he no longer seemed to be enjoying himself.

The Viscountess brought up her dominant energy, concentrating on the pleasure she got from punishing him. Next to her Duchess did the same thing. The twin waves of energy complimented each other, each one building on the other. Severin felt himself sinking back into Subspace. Submission washed over him like a warm bath. Sitting a few feet away Dickie felt the power as well. It made his cock twitch inside its locked prison.

"Now where were we?" Duchess ran her hand across the tender flesh of his feet. "Ah, right there."

She brought the cane down hard, continuing the series of strokes she had started moments before. The Viscountess lined up a shot and swung her cane. Between being with Duchess again and punishing Severin in such a delightful way, she was getting more than a little turned on. Unfortunately, instead of the evening of fabulous sex Duchess offered, Viscountess knew it would be better if they went home. Sadly, it was yet another case of business before pleasure.

Chapter Sixteen

Sappho's was a trendy upscale restaurant in Phoenix's Grandview neighborhood. It was a women's only—or as they spelled it *womyn's*—establishment. The person they were supposed to meet was a regular customer who had arranged Severin permission to enter. In order to avoid offending anyone, the Viscountess ordered him to wear clothes for the occasion.

The woman in charge of the parking lot took their cart and walked Snuzzle to an open space. There were already some empty carts parked there. The ponies rested at a chest-high watering trough under an awning while their owners had lunch. There was another trough filled with trail mix, nuts, oatmeal and so forth. Apparently pony cart was a popular way to travel in this part of the country.

"Would you like me to take her out of harness, Ma'am?" The pretty valet eyed Snuzzle with a lascivious smile.

"Yes, please, make her comfortable, but be careful with her."

"Don't worry, Ma'am, I'll treat her like she was my own."

"Don't treat her quite that well." The Viscountess gave the valet a five dollar bill.

"Yes, Ma'am, thank you, Ma'am." The valet tipped her hat.

Inside Sappho's the maître d, an elegant woman in a men's tuxedo curled her lip at the sight of Severin, but brightened considerably when the name of Lady Amanda was mentioned.

"Ah yes," the maître d purred. "Her ladyship's table is right this way, if you'd be kind enough to follow me."

They were led into an elegant dining room. Severin wasn't on his leash and was walking upright; his tortured feet ached with every step. Even while keeping his gaze on the floor he felt a ripple of surprise as women saw him enter the room.

Lady Amanda had a table that allowed her a full view of the room. She rose, smiled, and shook the Viscountess' hand.

"I've ordered a fruit platter," the lady announced, indicating the vast array of fresh fruit spread across a tray on the table. "Would you like something to drink?"

"Just water, thank you."

No one asked Severin if he wanted anything, or even acknowledged that he was there. As the Viscountess took her seat, Severin sat on the floor next to her, positioning himself so he could see Lady Amanda.

Lady Amanda was an attractive woman in her mid-forties. If she had been a building instead of a person Severin would say that she was well maintained. Her makeup, hair, and fingernails were perfect. She looked like she ate well and went to the gym on a regular basis. Severin thought she'd look even more attractive if she had no makeup on and was flushed and exhausted from whipping someone, but maybe that was just him.

"Thank you for coming on such short notice," Lady Amanda said. "I got your name from a friend in the Algophilia Society, and I really wasn't sure what to expect."

"I take it you have a problem that needs to be solved."

"Yes, and you're, what? Some sort of private investigator?"

"A few days ago I was called a super-hero, but private investigator is more accurate. Severin has a knack for solving puzzles." The Viscountess deliberately mentioned him just to remind her that there was someone else in the conversation. "We both have a number of contacts in the Scene and a great deal of experience in various Dominions. I hope we can help you."

"I hope so, too, as I'm not sure where to start."

"Try the beginning."

They paused as the waitress brought the Viscountess her water. It was bottled water, of course. The sound of classical music filled the air as a string quartet on a small stage started playing. All four of the women were nude.

"Well, I've known I was kinky and gay pretty much my entire life," Lady Amanda began. "I always hoped my little sister would turn out to be like me, but no such luck, she's plain vanilla and as straight as they come. I was delighted when one of her daughters turned out to be kinky, though. She recently turned eighteen and I've tried to be a mentor, to guide her."

"How did that work out?" the Viscountess asked, but she thought she could tell from the sound of Lady Amanda's voice.

"Amy has been difficult. She's still a teenager. We had a big blow up recently when she started dating someone from a motorcycle gang. I knew it was wrong of me to say so, but I didn't want my niece's first serious relationship to be with a diesel dyke with grease under her fingernails."

"I'm guessing Amy didn't take that too well."

"No, she didn't." Lady Amanda nibbled on a piece of cantaloupe as she searched for the right way to phrase her next statement. "Don't get me wrong, I love my niece and I respect her decisions, I just didn't want to see her wind up some biker's old lady when she can do so much better. She agreed to let things cool off for a while, and she wanted to get out of college for a semester, so I suggested I could enroll her at Blackbriar Academy. That way she could both continue her studies and get a glimpse of some different ways of playing."

"Does she enjoy school scenarios?"

"Apparently she never gave it much thought, but she was excited about visiting a different Dominion. I managed to get her signed up and sent her off to school."

The Viscountess took a piece of watermelon and swirled it in the yogurt dip. "What can you tell us about Blackbriar?" she asked Severin, holding the treat over his head.

"It's a very old and well established Dominion, but not very big, with one main building, some outbuildings and woods." He recited what he had learned on the internet the previous evening. "It's modeled after the classic boarding schools of the past. All the students are female while the teachers are a mix of male and female. The students are kept under very strict discipline with a great deal of caning and humiliation."

"I chose it partly for its security." Lady Amanda explained. "It's a private school and it's supposed to be very hard to get in or out."

"She's right," Severin agreed. "The only Gateways lead to the admissions office, and the way the Dominion is constructed, pony slaves can only enter at the front of the administration building. They're on watch twenty-four hours a day, so slipping in or out is practically impossible."

That earned Severin his watermelon. As he ate, Lady Amanda continued talking.

"She seemed very happy. The constant threat of discipline was very exciting. She made a new girlfriend, someone named Peggy. Then suddenly her letters stopped. I wrote to her and got no response. I tried to visit her and they wouldn't allow me in. I admit I pressured her into going there because I knew it would separate her from her leatherdyke girlfriend, but now I felt like something terrible has happened to her and it's my fault."

"So they wouldn't let you in to see her?"

"I'm the one who signed her in, so to them I'm her guardian. But when I asked to see her, they claim she refused to see me. I think they're lying."

"Are you sure Amy isn't simply mad at you?"

"If she was angry, why did I get happy, friendly letters for three weeks? I say something has happened to her."

"Do you think this biker has anything to do with it?"

"I don't know. I don't see how."

"What can you tell me about her?"

"She's in some club called the Roaring Girls. They have quite a reputation, and I'm afraid that's all I know about them."

"Did you at least get this woman's name?"

"I'm afraid not." Lady Amanda looked a bit guilty. "At first I didn't want to know her name, then when I did, Amy wouldn't tell me. When I couldn't reach Amy at Blackbriar I called the leader of the Roaring Girls, Nita Sloan. I guess I made a perfect fool of myself. Ms. Sloan called me a few choice names I haven't heard since college."

"I see." The Viscountess glanced down at Severin. "What can you tell me about the Roaring Girls?"

"It's Jacobean slang for prostitutes," the slave said brightly.

"Try something a little more recent." To encourage him she dangled a cluster of grapes over his head.

"They were one of the original S&M biker gangs back in the fifties. The group was founded by one of the Old Guard, but they've broken up and reformed several times since then. They have a reputation for being hell-raisers and breaking the rules. Also, according to some they have the largest collection of Named dildos in the country."

"You can see why I was worried about her," Lady Amanda put in.

"We may not be able to help you with that," the Viscountess explained. She rewarded Severin by breaking off some grapes and popping them in his mouth one at a time. "But if your niece is missing we will try to find her."

"And what will I owe you for this?"

"We can work something out if we're successful. Severin and I don't exactly charge by the hour."

"I'm not used to hiring people without knowing what it will cost me."

"Well, money is always nice, or we can work out a trade. The flogger and the single tail that I carry are both things I received for cases we solved. I investigated a murder for the Algophilia Society in return for a favor that I haven't used yet. I've also accepted sessions with submissives as payment." The Viscountess smiled reassuringly. "We're not trying to trick you. Severin and I will look into the situation, and if we can be of any help we'll contact you and we'll work out something to our mutual satisfaction."

"I guess I have no choice but to trust you." Lady Amanda hesitated, something still on her mind. "On the phone you also said you were in the middle of another case."

"Yes, well it's possible that your problem and our case are connected."

"In what way?"

"I'm not at liberty to say. I'm certain you understand."

"Yes, of course," Lady Amanda smiled, but something in her voice said that she didn't really understand. She was a woman who was used to getting her own way, and didn't appreciate curt responses to her questions.

The Viscountess glanced down at Severin. He made eye contact with her and shrugged. His body language said it sounded like a longshot, but they didn't have any choice but to follow the trail and see where it would lead.

Chapter Seventeen

The Viscountess and Severin took a take-out tray of fruit with them into the parking lot. The attendant had removed Snuzzle's bit to make her more comfortable, but the pony girl was still in full slave mode. Severin fed her some fruit while the Viscountess sat in the cart busying herself with her tablet and phone.

According to her Facebook page, Nita Sloan not only was the president of the Roaring Girls, but had her own body shop called Kustom Body. They seemed to specialize in high end, one-of-a-kind alterations to cars and motorcycles. The Viscountess called the shop and left a message. Next she checked her email and found that Lady Amanda had sent her pictures of Amy and a file with the school handbook for Blackbriar.

"How does it look?" Severin asked, glancing at what she was doing.

"Strict. I think Amy would have had an easier time breaking out of a prison Dominion."

"Yes, but then she'd have to worry about cat fights in the showers and that evil warden who always forces the girls into prostitution."

"That might be preferable." The Viscountess scrolled down the file. "According to this the school not only has discipline from the Headmaster and the teachers, but they also encourage the students to report on their fellow students and they get to participate in the punishments if the person is caught doing anything wrong."

"Lovely."

Her phone rang. The Viscountess engaged in a short conversation and hung up.

"We have an appointment in an hour."

"Where is this body shop?" Severin asked.

"Tucson, about a hundred miles from here. We could almost have Snuzzle run us down there without using the void."

Snuzzle heard her name and instantly perked up her ears. The Viscountess came to her and stroked her mane.

"Don't worry, honey, we're not going to make you run through the desert," the Viscountess assured her.

Snuzzle did a little happy dance, her horse shoes clanging on the pavement. The other pony slaves, who were still waiting for their owners glanced jealously in her direction.

"Severin, there's something I need your opinion on," the Viscountess unexpectedly announced.

"Yes, Viscountess."

"On the Facebook page for the Roaring Girls I noticed that they sent out an open invitation for male submissives. They apparently need one for a special party. The first person who responded to them warned everyone to stay away."

"Did he say why?"

"He made a lot of veiled accusations like 'out of control' and 'dangerous' without giving specifics. He doesn't come right out and say they're non-consensual, but the implication's there. Does any of this ring a bell with you?"

"Not exactly." Severin frowned. "I haven't done a lot of research on them, but I do try to keep up with the rumors. I know they've had some trouble with the law. There are a couple of assault charges and some vandalism accusations leveled against them, but nothing too serious."

"They've apparently done something to get someone upset."

"Perhaps we can ask Nita when we talk to her."

"I have a better question: what does a lesbian biker gang need with a man?"

Her question hung in the air unanswered. In the moment of silence Snuzzle shook herself, making the bells on her nipples ring.

"Looks like someone's anxious to be off." The Viscountess chuckled. "Finish giving her the fruit. I have one more call to make."

The Viscountess took out her phone and started to contact Blackbriar Academy while Severin offered a luscious piece of watermelon to Snuzzle. He knew how to feed ponies. He had the fruit on his palm, letting the slave take it herself. As Snuzzle ate he forgot himself and curled up his fingers, allowing her to snap at them.

"Watch it!" Severin exclaimed without thinking. His words drew an instant response from Snuzzle who snorted and gave an arrogant toss of her head.

"Now you're in for it. You know what a temper she has," the Viscountess teased.

Severin dropped to his knees on the pavement, hoping to calm the pony girl down. She threw back her head and neighed loudly, snapping her teeth together when she was done. Hesitantly Severin raised himself up and offered her a piece of cantaloupe. He held it in front of her mouth.

Snuzzle took the cantaloupe from him, but instead of biting, she caught his fingers in her mouth and sucked the juice off of them. The corners of her mouth twitched upwards in a very human smile for a split second as she did so.

Meanwhile the Viscountess had been on the phone to the Real World admissions center for Blackbriar Academy. Apparently the call was not going well.

"I just need to see your Headmaster for a few minutes about something quite urgent." She paused and listened. "Yes, I'm sure he is quite busy but—"

She scowled, listened to the receptionist for a few more minutes, then hung up.

"All right, my pets, it's time to go," The Viscountess announced. After buckling the bit into Snuzzle's mouth, she snapped her fingers and ordered Severin into the cart. He lay on the floor where she could rest her feet on him.

A peculiar fact of traveling through the void is that it is harder to make short journeys than long ones. The trip from Boston to Phoenix had taken only a few minutes in the void. Even with a pony of Snuzzle's ability it took two tries to get to the right city and then some navigation on the city's streets. A pony with less skill might have dropped them into China or Timbuktu.

They pulled up in front of a body shop in Tuscon that looked more like a converted warehouse than a garage. As she tied the reins to a rack that held several motorcycles, the Viscountess noticed that Snuzzle was sweating and gulping air from around her bit. She was going to need some rest soon and would have to drop out of her pony Persona to get some real human food. Viscountess loosened the bit and gave her some water before going inside.

The wide doors showed that Kustom Body was a beehive of activity with half a dozen cars and motorcycles being worked on. As they stepped out of the bright sunlight into the comparatively dark building the Viscountess and Severin felt a small surge of dominant energy strike them.

Nita Sloan threaded her way carefully through the maze of half-built vehicles in the shop she owned. She was a lean, hard woman with curves that looked as if they had been carved by the desert wind. Her skin was tanned and her dirt-brown hair had white streaks bleached by the sun. She was wearing leather chaps over tight jeans and a T-shirt with the name of her shop on it. She looked the newcomers up and down with a slightly wary expression.

"I'm the Viscountess, and this is my slave Severin. I believe you're expecting us."

"I'm Nita," she replied, not giving herself a title. She shook hands with the Viscountess and glanced at Severin. After a moment's hesitation she held out her hand to him as well. "I'd offer you my boot, but these things are filthy, and not in a good way."

Severin dropped to one knee and kissed her hand. He felt a trickle of dominant energy flow down her arm as she accepted his submission. He got the feeling that people didn't kiss her hand often and that she enjoyed it.

Nita had a flogger of knotted leather hanging openly from her belt, even though she hadn't been generating a Blindfold inside the shop. Seeing that the Viscountess had noticed the flogger, Nita smiled and rested her hand comfortably on the handle of the flogger.

"Everybody who works here knows I'm a leatherdyke. If they don't like it, they can work somewhere else."

As if in response to that one of the workers who had been welding a car frame flipped up his mask long enough to give the Viscountess a lascivious grin.

"Hey boss, you gonna whip her ass?" he called out.

"I just might. Get back to work!" Nita snapped. She turned to the Viscountess. "Why don't we talk up in my office?"

Nita's office turned out to be a sort of loft built over the main floor, high enough to escape the noise. It had a comfortable atmosphere with a faded carpet on the floor and wood paneling for walls. There was a coat rack that held her obligatory leather jacket decorated with the logo of the Roaring Girls as well as a single-tail whip. According to the pictures on the wall Nita raced motorcycles and was once crowned Ms. Leather Arizona.

"Want something cold to drink?" Nita asked, getting herself an energy drink from a small refrigerator.

"Water, if you have it."

"In the desert, always."

The Viscountess took the water and drank some, sharing the rest with

Severin. Nita sat across a desk piled high with paperwork.

"You said on the phone you wanted to talk," Nita began the conversation.

"Yes." The Viscountess tried to phrase her comments carefully. "Severin and I often are called upon to solve problems in the Kink community. We were investigating something when we heard about an incident that may be connected to the case."

"Incident?"

"A woman named Lady Amanda told us—"

At the mention of Amanda's name the atmosphere in the room changed and Nita cut her off.

"If auntie sent you here to hassle me, then this is going to be a really short conversation."

Nita's dominant energy spiked when she glared at them and Severin shivered in response. There was no doubt that Nita was a formidable woman.

"I'm not here to hassle anyone." The Viscountess continued coolly. She did not raise her own energy to challenge Nita. "I'd just like to find out what happened to her niece."

"She already called here and accused one of my women of making off with her precious niece and shacking up with her somewhere. She threatened to pull some strings and make things tough for me if I didn't roll over. I told her where to go."

"Yes, I've spoken with her; obviously tact isn't one of her skills. Do you have any idea if she's right about her niece?"

"I don't know. I don't monitor the personal lives of my people. Amy's over eighteen, right? The way I see it, if she's shacked up somewhere in a hotel room getting her pipes cleaned that's fine with me. If she's anything like her aunt, it'll be good for her."

The Viscountess had to smile at that.

"So you don't know anything about the Dominion Lady Amanda sent her to?"

"I don't do the whole Dominion thing. Frankly I get into enough trouble in the Real World."

"Do you think it's possible Amy did hook up with someone in your group?"

"Maybe. I don't know." Nita shrugged. "Supposedly it all started at this big rally in Nevada. We were raising money for a group that wants to pass gay marriage in the state so they had this huge fundraising party in the desert, like a gay Burning Man. There were a few thousand people there. The Roaring Girls had thirty or forty women there at various times. According to the aunt, Amy came down with some of her college friends and she hooked up with one of us. A lot of people got together that weekend."

"May I ask a question?" Severin said from the floor next to the Viscountess' chair. Both women glanced at him and gave their assent. "How many women are in the Roaring Girls?"

"We have eighty-two members paying dues. Of course some of them have moved away and never show up for meetings."

"You have regular meetings?"

"Sure, organizational meetings once a month, but we're lucky if we get ten people to show up for those. Of course I'm not counting any of the various girlfriends, slaves, and groupies that hang with us."

"Where do you have your meetings?"

"We own a bar outside of town. Legally, it's a private club. A few women live there full time and people show up a few times a week for drinks and to play pool." Nita laughed ruefully. "Hell, it sounds pretty quiet when I describe it that way."

"You do have quite a reputation," the Viscountess said carefully.

"And we earned it. The Roaring Girls are hell-raisers and shit kickers from way back, it's a big part of who we are. Of course we're a lot more than that. These days we've got jobs, we pay taxes, some of us are raising kids or taking care of elderly parents."

"So it's not all drinking beer and breaking the bottles over your enemy's heads."

"No, that's just on Saturday. The rest of the week we're pretty quiet." Nita laughed. She kind of snorted when she laughed. "What can I say, we were founded by one of the Old Guard, and we're proud of it."

"The Old Guard," Severin said wistfully. The people who had been kinky back in the fifties and sixties had discovered the Dominions and laid out the rules of S&M magic. No one had seen any of them for decades, but they left the entire Kink community as their legacy.

"If you want to understand us, you need to see our colors," Nita abruptly got up from her chair and went around the desk, rolling up her sleeve.

"We've seen your logo on the web site," the Viscountess explained, glancing at the leather jacket on the coat rack where the Roaring Girls symbol was also displayed.

"No, I mean the real thing, in the flesh."

Nita showed them the tattoo on her upper arm. The roaring Girls symbol consisted of a motorcycle tire surrounded by flames with the letters RG in bold black beneath. It was a simple, powerful symbol.

As the Viscountess and Severin stared at Nita's arm, they saw that the flesh was raised with scar tissue. Both the rim of the wheel and the spokes were actually made with a branding iron before the ink had been applied. Nita made a fist, flexing her arms so that the flames appeared to dance.

"Very impressive," the Viscountess said truthfully.

"Like I said, we take this shit seriously." Having made her point, Nita went back to her chair. "I work hard to keep my women out of trouble, so when auntie called me up and started making demands and threatens to stir things up, maybe I overreacted."

"It's understandable," the Viscountess admitted. "Perhaps if I could talk to some of your members I could find out if anything happened to Amy and one of your people."

"I don't think that's going to happen. We sort of have a problem with authority figures."

"I'm sure something can be worked out. I can be very persuasive."

"I'm sure that you can." Nita smiled. When she made eye contact with the Viscountess a spark of attraction jumped between them. The Viscountess was pleased to find that the biker was attracted to her.

But any hope she had that this would help her get more contact with the Roaring Girls was quickly dashed.

"Unfortunately," Nita continued, "right now we're in the market for a male submissive."

"Yes, I saw the Facebook posting."

"Yes, right." Nita hesitated. Clearly if her guest had seen the posting then they had also seen the negative responses to it. "It's just for one night, really. We need him for part of an initiation ceremony. Our new members are trained old school style. They have to start from the bottom as slaves and work their way up to being members. We have someone now who's ready, but we still need a man for the ceremony."

"I take it you're having problems?"

"You could say that. A while back we had a guy Safeword before the ceremony started. Last time we tried this we got halfway in and that guy suddenly Safeworded in the middle of it." She realized how that sounded and quickly added. "Don't get me wrong, he had every right to use his

Safeword. It's just that we'd built up so much energy and then all of a sudden it was over and we were just standing there with our dicks hanging out."

"So what exactly is this ceremony?"

"It's sort of a symbolic farewell to the male gender. You fuck one guy in the ass with our ceremonial dildo and it's as if you're fucking the whole male race. After the initiate is done, everybody takes a turn to bond the group closer. Then she gets her mark put on."

"That must be some dildo."

"It's been handed down from one leader of the group to another for years. No one knows where it originally came from."

"I'll bet it has a name," the Viscountess pushed her.

"We call it Boybreaker. It's not that big—just powerful—and it doesn't seem to like guys very much."

"I can see where you'd have a problem getting recruits."

"I have an idea," Nita said "If you need to ask some questions, why don't you give your slave to us for a few days? He can talk to people and take part in the ceremony."

The Viscountess glanced down at Severin. He was looking up at her with bright, eager eyes. This sort of situation was exactly like fantasies that he had for years.

"What if he Safewords?" the Viscountess asked.

"He can still talk to people. We're going to have folks coming in from all over for the ceremony. This may be the only time in years that ninety percent of our group will be there. If one of them shows up with Amy, then your problem's solved."

"What if Amy doesn't show?"

"I will tell people they have to talk to Severin on Sunday after everything is over."

"You've planned the ceremony for Saturday night?"

"Yes, it's been on the calendar for a while, but all our prospects for volunteers have chickened out. Ideally we'd like to have Severin stay with us starting Friday. That'll give him a chance to get the lay of the land, and we'll make sure he's in the right frame of mind for Saturday."

The Viscountess glanced down at Severin to see if this was all right. He nodded quickly.

"It seems we have a bargain."

"That's great. Um, normally if we have to borrow a slave we let the owner stick around, but the ceremony is strictly members only."

"I understand completely. I may be exploring other branches of the investigation anyway."

"Good. I hope you can find Amy."

"You don't have to pretend. I doubt you give a damn about her."

"You're right, I don't, but I care that my organization is getting its name smeared yet again."

"If you're innocent, I'll make sure everyone knows."

"Thank you, and thank you for the use of your slave."

"You're welcome." The Viscountess snapped her fingers and pointed to the door. "Severin go outside and water Snuzzle. I'll join you in a moment."

The Viscountess waited until Severin had left the room before she stepped very close to Nita.

"I just wanted to warn you that Severin has often fantasized about a scenario like this. I don't want things to get out of hand."

"He seems like a very good submissive," Nita reasoned.

"But you would have offered it even if he wasn't. You need a man, and since we need something from you, it was too good an opportunity to pass up." As the Viscountess spoke she took a step forward, letting her dominant energy flare up.

"It's his responsibility to use his Safeword."

"I'm making it your responsibility. If anything happens to him, I will come after you."

"Yes, Ma'am," Nita stammered. Without even being aware of it she had been topped by the Viscountess. "I'll make sure nothing happens to him, and he'll get his interviews, no matter what."

"Good." The Viscountess favored her with a smile. "It's been a pleasure meeting you. Don't worry, I'll see myself out."

Nita nodded. She was pushed back against the wall of her own office. When she looked down at herself she discovered a small circle of moisture on the front of her jeans.

Chapter Eighteen

The cool air of Boston felt good after the desert heat. Looking down the reins at Snuzzle's back, the Viscountess could see that the pony slave was drenched with sweat. She had been running long and hard and must have been exhausted.

With expert precision Snuzzle brought the cart onto the street outside the brownstone. The Viscountess tugged on the reins, pulling to the right to bring the cart down the driveway. Snuzzle brought the cart around in front of the garage and stopped when the Viscountess pulled back and cried "Whoa!"

Viscountess knew in theory that Snuzzle could be made to back the cart right into the garage where it normally sat next to the car. Unfortunately she had never had much luck making Snuzzle move backwards and knew from experience it was easier to take the bridle and tack off first and make Severin push the cart into place.

As the Viscountess removed the leather straps of the bridle, Snuzzle leaned into her.

"Good girl, you've earned your reward tonight." The Viscountess let Snuzzle's hair loose from the pony tail. Snuzzle twisted her hips, making the horse hair attached to her butt plug sway back and forth. "I know, you've had that in for a long time."

As gently as she could, the Viscountess slid the butt plug out. As her dilated anus shrank back to normal Snuzzle sighed. She lost her balance for a second and leaned against the Viscountess for support.

"Thank you, Snuzzle. You were wonderful, as always." The Viscountess kissed her on the cheek.

"Thank you," Snuzzle whispered. They were the first human words she had spoken in several hours.

Sklavin made pasta for dinner, knowing that Snuzzle would need carbs to replace what she'd lost while running. After showering, Snuzzle was offered the chance to put on clothes and sit at the table, but she refused. Even out of her pony Persona she was still too submissive to feel comfortable being treated as the equal of the Viscountess. She wound up eating her dinner from the floor naked and on all fours like Severin.

After dinner they gathered in the living room. Snuzzle knelt beside the large chair of the Viscountess and Severin was tied face down across a hassock so the Viscountess could rest her feet on him.

"Tomorrow won't be quite as difficult as today. I only want to visit one place, but it might be tricky," the Viscountess informed Snuzzle. "Have you ever heard of a place called Blackbriar academy?"

"No, Viscountess."

"Then you can't just take me there?"

"Not easily. Normally you have to visit a Dominion first. Once you've been there you get a kind of feel for the place and you can locate it when you go back to the void," Snuzzle explained. "When Duchess trains us, she has us travel in teams of two or three girls with a pony who already knows how to get to the destination. After they've been to each Dominion they have to go back on their own."

"What if they don't make it?"

"Every pony slave can jump into the void and reach Dominions, but doing it precisely, winding up exactly where you want to go, can take a lot of work. Many ponies are perfectly happy being draft horses, or racing at the track."

"I always wondered how that worked," the Viscountess admitted. She and Duchess had separated before Duchess opened her pony farm, so the Viscountess had never seen exactly how Duchess trained her charges. "Perhaps I won't have to take you into the void then. According to the school handbook there's a single Gateway to the academy. It's located at a real private school in upstate New York."

"Maybe I can help you," Snuzzle perked up at the information. "If I'm near a Gateway I should be able to sense its destination and take you there."

"That would be wonderful. I'd like to test their security a little."

"May I ask why?" Snuzzle shifted her slender, naked body to take some of the weight off her legs.

"Do you remember any of the conversation Severin and I had in the parking lot of the restaurant?"

"No, sorry, I must have been pretty deep in Ponyspace."

"We're on the trail of a young woman who may have been taken out of a Dominion that prides itself on its security. There's only one physical Gateway, and I'm sure she didn't get out that way."

"So you think someone took her out by pony?"

"Possibly. The school handbook says that ponies can only enter and exit the Dominion by the main gate on the administration building. I'd like to put that to the test."

"I've heard about places like that. Usually when you go to a Dominion there are always a few places where it's easiest to materialize. If a Dominion's small enough I can easily see that there might be only one way in or out, even for a pony."

"It's just a mile and a half across. There's nothing but the school, some woods, and a lake."

"I'll certainly test it out."

"Good."

The Viscountess rose from her chair and dropped to one knee beside Snuzzle. The hands of the dominant woman ran across the body of the slave girl, stroking her, touching her in all the places that she knew would make her respond.

"So what kind of reward do you want for today's service?" Viscountess asked, her voice a conspiratorial whisper. "Are you in the mood for pleasure or pain? Feeling a bit dominant perhaps? I saw you topping Severin earlier."

Snuzzle grinned and blushed slightly. "That's just my pony. She's got some Arabian in her blood. She can be very strong-willed sometimes."

"So long as she responds to the whip," the Viscountess purred, sliding her fingers between Snuzzle's legs. "So have you decided what you're in the mood for?"

"If it's all the same Viscountess, after that wonderful meal, I'd really like to just get some sleep. I know I'll be running more tomorrow."

"If that's what you want, but Severin and I will owe you one."

"Thank you, Viscountess."

As the Viscountess bent over to kiss her cheek the dominant noticed how exhausted Snuzzle was. After being in Persona all day she had been kept constantly aroused and run to exhaustion. She certainly deserved a treat, but perhaps it was better to rest for now.

"Sklavin! Get some blankets for our guest. She'll be spending the night in the garage."

Snuzzle smiled her thanks. If she slept next to her cart it would help her get into character faster in the morning. The Viscountess wondered if she should have part of the garage converted into a stall for Snuzzle. She had always felt that it was unfair to keep a pony slave in the city, since it was so hard to exercise her, but she and Severin were borrowing them more and more often. As their reputation grew it seemed likely that they would get more cases. Perhaps it was time to consider installing something permanent.

Hearing Snuzzle leave, Severin sighed into his ball gag. After dinner he had been bound, gagged, blindfolded. and left in a humbler, a wooden device that pulled his cock and balls back painfully between his legs. Lying on the floor a few feet from the pony slave he had heard the conversation and absorbed the information. If he had anything to add, he could have made a noise and the Viscountess would have freed his mouth from the gag.

Severin had been hoping to have some fun with Snuzzle before she retired for the night. He remembered the little thrill he had gotten when she unexpectedly dominated him while in her pony Persona and suspected that she would make a wonderful dominant. Unfortunately it was not to be, at least not for this night.

The Viscountess removed his gag and blindfold, allowing him to gaze upon her.

"Thank you, Viscountess," Severin said automatically.

"You're welcome, slave. I'd do a Scene with you, but I don't want to tire you out for your session with the Roaring Girls. Are you sure you're up to it?"

"Yes, Viscountess."

"Don't forget, these women have no reason to be gentle with you, and I'm not going to be there to help you."

Severin had served lesbians before. In some ways he preferred it, since they usually thought of him as a slave rather than a man and didn't expect the kind of intimate service that belonged rightfully to the Viscountess. Of course the vast majority of his time with lesbians they had been friends or acquaintances. Being with strangers was going to be very different.

"I think I can handle it," Severin said seriously. "At least I'd like a chance to try. It may be the only way to get the information we need."

"Promise me you'll Safeword if you have to. Nita promised that you can still ask your questions if you Safeword. I think we can trust her."

"Of course I'll Safeword."

Something in the way he said it set her off. Before he could say any more she was on top of him, her face inches from his.

"Do not talk like that, Severin," she said in a cool, steady voice. "You and I both know this is the sort of challenge you love. You've fantasized

about this sort of thing. If you can't convince me you're taking this seriously, I'll call Nita and cancel the deal."

Her concern touched Severin deeply. He took a deep breath before
answering.

"I'm sorry if I sounded flippant. I promise I'll be careful and Safeword if it gets out of hand."

"Good." The Viscountess kissed him on the forehead. "Don't forget,
every inch of your body belongs to me. You don't have the right to injure
yourself without my permission. And I don't give my permission."

"Thank you, Viscountess."

By this time Sklavin had returned from the garage. The German slave
helped the Viscountess with her clothes. When she was luxuriantly
naked, the Viscountess rewarded Severin by kneeling astride him and
pressing her pussy against his face. He had to lie on his back and curl
up his legs to keep the terrible pressure off his genitals.

His tongue found her clit as easily as if it was designed to do that
very task. As her sweet, warm fluids cascaded down his face, he brought
forth one delightful orgasm, then another, and finally a third before the
Viscountess was fully satisfied.

Chapter Nineteen

The Forsyth Academy was located in upstate New York. The students who were enrolled there—and certainly their parents—had no clue that it contained a permanent Gateway to another, much kinkier private school. The main building was an impressive structure of old stone, looking more like a fortress than a private school. Young people hurried back and forth, getting ready for the start of the school day. t. A few of them glanced at the horse cart, and may have wondered who would be at their school with a horse-drawn cart, but the magic of the Scene kept them from focusing on it for too long. The Blindfold prevented them from seeing the naked woman who had pulled it and her passengers, and they probably forgot that they had seen the cart at all a few seconds later.

Behind one of the doors in the perfectly normal Forsyth Academy was the receptionist who guarded the Gateway to Blackbriar as well as handling communications between the kinky academy and the outside world. She was the one who had been refusing the Viscountess an appointment with the Headmaster.

"How about it Snuzzle, can you feel the Gateway?" the Viscountess called out.

The pony slave gave a toss of her head.

"Good girl, now take me there."

As the cart lurched forward, Severin grabbed a handhold to brace himself. The Viscountess snapped her whip. Snuzzle accelerated and there was the familiar tingle of passing through into the void.

Almost as soon as they sensed they were in the void, the cart returned to reality. The wheels hit the pavement and the Viscountess pulled on the reins. They had reached their destination. They were still parked in front of a school, but instead of a stone fort they saw a brooding gothic exterior through the bars of an elaborate wrought iron fence. Atop the gates was an elaborate letter B surrounded by iron spikes. The gates were not locked but stood open showing the path to the door.

It looked inviting enough, but the Viscountess knew she had not been given an invitation. She hoped to test her theory and get out without being seen.

"Good girl, Snuzzle." The Viscountess leaned forward in her seat to make sure the pony slave could hear her. "Now let's try to get somewhere on the grounds. Do you see the open area in front of that side building? Take me there."

Snuzzle turned her head to mark the location, then nodded her head up and down. She ran forward and the world fell away from them again. For a second the void was all around them, then they were suddenly on solid ground.

Astonishingly they were not on the grounds of the school, but right back in front of the gate of Blackbriar Academy where they had begun. Snuzzle looked around wildly and realized that something was wrong. She cried out in a moment of panic, but the Viscountess calmed her by tugging the reins. The bit in Snuzzle's teeth pulled her head back sharply, bringing her to a halt before she bolted.

Once the cart was fully stopped the Viscountess leapt out, whispering soothing words under her breath. She stroked Snuzzle's mane, calming her. Snuzzle whinnied, upset about what had happened, but uncertain of what she could do.

"It's all right, it's not your fault," the Viscountess told her. "You did the best you could."

Snuzzle made eye contact with the Viscountess, something she almost never did while in her pony persona. The knowledge that she had failed her mistress seemed to be almost physically painful to her. She looked as if she might cry.

Throwing her arms around Snuzzle's neck, the Viscountess continued stroking her and whispering to her. Gradually the tension in Snuzzle's body faded.

"You did your best. Take us home now. Bring us to the farm."

Snuzzle tossed her head, anxious to be away from the place.

With a few quick steps the slave pulled the cart from the Blackbriar Dominion and into the void. Just as they were vanishing, the Viscountess caught a motion from the corner of her eye and saw a curtain draw back. It was possible that someone had spotted them.

When the world came back into focus around them they were in front of Duchess' house in the rolling hills of Connecticut. Since Duchess was not expecting them, the Viscountess had to ring the bell to summon her.

"I hope Snuzzle has served you well," Duchess said after they had exchanged greetings.

"Yes, of course, but now I'm afraid I have to ask a favor of you."

"Name it."

The Viscountess hesitated a moment before answering. "I'd like you to send me to school."

Attendants came forward to take care of Snuzzle and park the Viscountess' pony cart. Duchess ordered her chef to prepare a light brunch for herself and the Viscountess. They ate as their slaves looked on.

"I can't get an appointment with the Headmaster, and even Snuzzle can't get me past the front gates," the Viscountess explained.

"That's most peculiar," Duchess admitted.

"My best chance is to go in as a student. I have to be signed in by a superior. If I find something right away I'll try and contact you through the office in Forsyth. If not, you can sign me out again after a few days."

"You make this all sound terribly dangerous." Duchess grinned.

"It shouldn't be dangerous. Our theory is that this girl has given them the slip and they're covering it up. I just need to see if she's there, and if not, find out what's happened to her."

"Well, I look forward to having you under my charge again, albeit temporarily."

Duchess let her naturally dominant aura rise up. The Viscountess shuddered as the familiar power slid across her. She did not fight it, but fell naturally into a slightly submissive state. When the Viscountess was with Duchess it was easy to fall into that role of Desire again.

At her feet Severin shifted his position on the floor. Glancing down at him, the Viscountess sensed his agitation.

"Excuse me a moment, Duchess, I must speak with my slave."

"Of course, top secret investigations. I understand." Duchess waved them away.

They went to the back of the house to speak privately. The huge backyard was surrounded by the fields where the ponies played. Snuzzle and other fillies were playing and romping through the grass. In the corral they saw a blonde woman in a cowboy hat practicing her barrel racing. She was sitting on the shoulders of a tall, powerfully built woman who was running full speed around barrels set up in the dirt.

"You may speak freely," the Viscountess told Severin.

"Thank you, Viscountess, I was just wondering if this was the wisest course of action," he said humbly.

"I can't think of a better way to get in there. It certainly sounds less dangerous than being gang banged by the Roaring Girls."

"So it would appear," Severin said wryly. "Yet I think that school is worse. Everything there will be designed to take away your power. You might not even notice it happening."

"Then I shall have to be careful."

"When do you plan on enrolling?"

"As soon as possible." The Viscountess informed him. "According to the flier they accept students for any term from a few days up to a full semester. Since The Crone is still waiting to hear back from us I'd like to get started as soon as we can."

"I'm supposed to meet up with the Roaring Girls on Friday. By Sunday the ceremony will be over and I may have found the link we've been looking for."

"Or you may have found nothing. We can't afford to waste any time."

"I just don't like the idea of being out in the desert while you're—"

"Having naked pillow fights?" the Viscountess teased.

"You know what I mean."

"Of course I do, and it's very touching. We shall have to promise each other to Safeword if we have to and depend on Duchess to reunite us."

"I'd feel better if I were going with you."

"It's a lovely thought," the Viscountess laughed. "But I don't think Blackbriar allows pets. Bringing you in a pet carrier might attract attention."

She raised her dominant energy, turning serious again. Taking Severin's chin in one hand she raised his face up and gave him a stinging slap. This was followed by two more equally powerful slaps.

"Thank you, Viscountess," he said when she paused.

"That was just to remind you to take care of yourself. You're going to have your hands full with an entire bar of leatherdykes and I don't want you to get distracted worrying about me."

"Yes, Viscountess."

She slapped him a few more times, then made him follow her on all fours back to the house.

Duchess called the Real World office of the academy. She laid it on thick. Her "girl" was disobedient, disrespectful, and was probably cheating on her. The school offered to enroll her at once. Duchess agreed to deliver her the next day and fill out the paperwork.

Normally when Severin visited Duchess he looked forward to some wonderful punishments, but this time, things were different. Apparently the Viscountess and Duchess were too worried about wearing him out before his time with the Roaring Girls, so there would be no fun for him that night.

For her part the Viscountess pondered what she would find at Blackbriar Academy. Despite what Duchess had said, Viscountess knew her submissive Persona wasn't a Little or a Schoolgirl of any sort. When she allowed herself to become Desire she was a slave, an object to be used by her dominant. She hoped that it wouldn't be too obvious that she wasn't really a Schoolgirl. Her only consolation was that the school was often used by dominants who wanted to give their submissive a brief taste of school discipline. Surely she wouldn't be the only one "forced" to be a schoolgirl.

The Viscountess and Duchess retired early to the lavish bedroom. Severin and Dickie weren't even given the chance to watch the two women make love, which disappointed both slaves. Left to his own devices, Dickie immediately plopped onto the couch and started channel surfing. After a moment Severin joined him. Severin felt uncomfortable sitting on the furniture, but clearly the rules of the house were different from what he was used to.

As Dickie focused his attention on the sports channels, Severin was reminded of how little he had in common with the ex-CEO. Severin shifted uncomfortably on the couch. He looked forward to spending some time with the Roaring Girls, but he'd rather spend the night sleeping by the bed of the Viscountess than watching television and doing nothing.

Severin heard the sound of boots and spurs on the floor and saw the blonde cowgirl he had seen earlier enter the room. Her hair was pulled back from her face and braided. Her tight jeans were worn very thin and her T-shirt was plain. The woman hooked her thumb in her heavy leather belt and let her dominant energy wash over Severin, driving him to the floor, where he showered her scuffed riding boots with kisses.

"On your feet, boy," she curtly ordered in a sexy Texas twang. Severin scrambled to his feet and followed her out the door. They were heading to the barn. "I'm Tate," she said glancing over her shoulder. "It's short for Tatum, but you can call me Ma'am."

"Yes, Ma'am. My owner calls me Severin."

"I got a text from her to put you to work."

"Thank god, I was afraid I'd have to watch golf."

Tate gave a burst of laughter. She had a loud, braying laugh, as if she was used to laughing over loud music and the sound of beer mugs hitting the bar.

In the stables they found that most of the pony slaves had gone home for the night or were sleeping in beds. The only two slaves in the stable were Snuzzle and the powerful mare Tate had been riding earlier. Both of them were standing in the center aisle, held in place by ropes attached to their bridles.

Severin paused to admire the pony Tate had been riding. The powerful mare was in superb condition. Unlike most of the pony slaves, she was built for strength rather than speed or endurance. Even standing still it looked as if her hard body had been carved from stone. Her hair had been shaved into a Mohawk that became a braid which hung down between her shoulder blades.

"She's a beauty isn't she?" Tate's voice swelled with pride. "Her name's Roxy. I met her in a club a few years ago, and I've been training her ever since."

At that point Snuzzle snorted and tugged on her ropes, the noise instantly drawing their attention.

"You're beautiful too, Snuzzle," Tate grinned. "Severin, why don't you ease that tail out of her ass and put this cream on."

Severin got behind Snuzzle and slipped the butt plug with its pony tail out as gently as he could. She had been wearing it for hours as she played in the fields. Tate removed the somewhat larger plug from Roxy, then both slaves received a soothing cream for their aching backside.

Next, Tate handed Severin a brush with very soft bristles and assured him that it was Snuzzle's favorite.

"Just rub her down with it, nice and slow. She deserves a treat for all the time she spent as a pony today."

Severin started to do as she ordered, but when he faced Snuzzle she suddenly turned aggressive, trying to head butt him. Only the ropes kept her from cracking her forehead into his own. Severin jumped back in surprise.

"You got to show her who's boss," Tate explained. "Snuzzle's got a lot of spirit. You need to take a firm hand with her."

"If I could take a firm hand with women I wouldn't be a slave."

"All right, I'll give you that one. Try and calm her down. Just be gentle."

"Easy, girl," Severin said softly. He was trying to remember how the Viscountess talked to her. "You like the brush, don't you?"

Snuzzle looked at the brush and seemed to relax a little. He reached out with one hand and gently took her by the shoulder. With the other hand he started stroking her with the brush. He used long slow strokes, and soon he saw all the tension leave her body.

Severin could see Tate doing more or less the same thing with her pony. Tate had on a glove with rubber nubs on the palm which she used to give a gentle massage to her mare.

He saw Snuzzle smiling under her bridle and knew that she was coming out of her pony Persona. When he passed the brush across her flat stomach she twisted around, lifting herself up so the brush went a little lower. Severin didn't have to be told what she wanted. He drew the brush slowly across the tender flesh between her legs. The bristles had a very quick effect on her, soon she was bucking her hips. Severin pushed down a little harder, knowing her clit was against the bristles. Snuzzle bucked her hips rapidly, then sighed and let herself go limp so the ropes were holding her up.

Her excitement had gotten Severin hard. Tate glanced at him and grinned.

"Maybe you should take care of that little problem," she suggested.

"Can't. I'm not allowed to."

"Too bad." Tate shrugged and went back to work on Roxy.

Snuzzle was so completely out of Ponyspace that she reached up and undid the ropes attached to her bridle. Severin helped her and also unbuckled the bridle.

"Thanks," she smiled. "Is the Viscountess all right?"

"She's fine, Duchess is prepping her for her admissions interview."

"Duchess will probably want Blossom and me in the two-girl carriage."

"Where is Blossom? I saw her in the pen earlier."

"She's staying over at a friend's house."

Severin nodded. He glanced at the stall that had Snuzzle's name on the wall. It had straw on the floor, and a few blankets along with some personal items, bottled water, an MP3 player and a few books.

"Thanks Severin," Snuzzle said. She slid into the pile of hay and pulled the blanket over herself. She had literally been naked all day, but now that she was out of her Persona she felt the need to cover up.

Severin wasn't sure if she was thanking him for his attempt at grooming or something else. Before he could ask he saw that Snuzzle was already half-asleep.

"Come on," Tate interrupted his thoughts. She had already put Roxy away for the night. "Boss says you're supposed to sleep in the slave quarters tonight."

Severin sighed. The slave quarters were a shed in the back with a few cots. It was normally used for visiting slaves, or when Dickie needed some time alone for punishment. Severin would have much preferred to sleep on the floor next to the Viscountess, but apparently it was not to be.

Chapter Twenty

Wednesday morning Duchess and the Viscountess arrived for an interview in the admissions office of Blackbriar Academy. They took the two-pony carriage that Duchess preferred and had both Snuzzle and Blossom in harness. They had left the carriage in the Real World outside of Forsyth Academy just in case someone had spotted the Viscountess snooping around the day before. Inside that building a cheery blonde in a school uniform verified that they had an appointment and ushered them through a Gateway to Blackbriar. They were meeting with the assistant headmistress, Miss Krause.

The perky schoolgirl who introduced herself as Felicity looked almost young enough to have actually been a teenager, Viscountess thought, but perhaps she was simply very deep in her Persona.

Through a set of large glass doors Duchess and the Viscountess saw a beautiful rectangle of grass surrounded by buildings. It must have been between classes since a large number of women went back and forth on the sidewalk, all of them in uniform with books clutched in their arms. Apart from the stocks it looked a lot like any other all-girls school.

The Headmaster's office with its dark and foreboding door was at the end of the hall. They also passed a nurse's office on their way to Miss Krause.

Felicity hovered near the door as the two women went into the room. It was a large office with soft carpets, bookshelves, and a great deal of wood paneling, giving it a somewhat Victorian feel that made the Viscountess feel right at home. A schoolgirl stood with her nose pressed against the wall in a corner of the room. She was bent over slightly, her white cotton panties pulled down to her ankles, hands behind her back holding up her skirt. She had been well and thoroughly spanked, both cheeks a bright red. Although she made no sound, her shoulders rose and fell as if she were still crying.

Several instruments of punishment were prominently displayed on racks. There were paddles of various sizes and shapes as well as leather straps, both stiff and flexible. The woman who had used the paddles sat behind a large desk. She was a thin, brittle woman with a stiff, dominant air. Her cruel dark eyes showed little compassion.

"Please, take a seat. I take it you are the Duchess and this is the young lady in question."

"We call her Desire," the Duchess said airily as she slid into a chair. She glanced at the Viscountess, or Desire as she was now called, and made a gesture for her to sit as well. Duchess was a picture of elegance in leather skirt and silk blouse. The Viscountess had chosen jeans and a My Little Pony T-shirt.

"What a delightful child." Miss Krause smiled, but the smile did not reach her eyes. "But I understand there have been some problems."

"She has been very difficult lately," Duchess said, forming her words carefully.

"I see," Miss Krause nodded sympathetically. "Sometimes even the best girls need a firm hand."

"I try my best, but I just don't have the time or energy to give her what she deserves."

"I understand completely." Miss Krause smiled again. "Felicity dear, why don't you get us some coffee?"

"Yes, Ma'am," the perky schoolgirl chirped. Felicity had been trying not to stare at the girl in the corner and seemed grateful for a chance to get out of the room. She came back a few minutes later with fresh coffee for Duchess and Miss Krause. No one paid any more attention to the Viscountess than they did the crying girl in the corner.

Miss Krause and Duchess discussed the school and what it offered. Duchess was assured that she would get regular progress reports and that she could pick her young lady up at any time. There was a semester break coming up in two weeks which meant a three-week vacation for faculty and students. If Duchess felt Desire needed more work after that, she could send her back in the new semester.

"Hard work, rigid discipline, swift, firm punishments—it's really the only way to deal with young people these days," Miss Krause summed up her pitch.

"It sounds perfectly delightful," Duchess beamed. "I can't help wondering what that girl in the corner did."

"Oh nothing really," Miss Krause shrugged. "Disobeying her superiors, talking out of turn, that sort of thing. The important thing is that she's learned a lesson she won't soon forget."

"That sounds like just the thing/ Don't you agree, my dear?"

"Yes, Ma'am," the Viscountess replied dutifully. If a spanking like that was what students got for talking out of turn, it didn't bode well for her investigation.

"When can we begin?" Duchess asked.

"As early as tomorrow if you like. I can have a uniform drawn up for her at once."

"Splendid. Thursday will be wonderful."

The necessary paperwork was signed, handing over the girl known as Desire to Blackbriar Academy until such time as the school released her or her guardian took her back. They did not ask the Viscountess to sign since, after all, in the eyes of the school she was a minor.

After the paperwork was done, they all stood. Miss Krause shook hands with Duchess and assured her that she had made the right choice.

"And as for you, my dear," Miss Krause reached up and stroked a single finger across the Viscountess' cheek. "I'm certainly going to keep my eye on you."

The Viscountess hadn't been in a submissive state during the meeting. She wanted to keep herself alert so she could spot anything unusual about the academy. At the touch of Miss Krause's hand a shudder passed through her and she felt herself plunging into Subspace. She clenched her teeth together to keep from making a noise and reached out for the back of the chair for support.

Felicity guided them back to the Gateway.

"You're starting tomorrow!" the schoolgirl gushed. "Gosh, that's great, I can't wait."

"Is she always like that?" the Viscountess glanced over her shoulder at Miss Krause's office.

"She can be a little intimidating at first," Felicity admitted. She leaned in close to the Viscountess so they couldn't be overheard. "When you get punished, try to make it a teacher or another student. You don't want to have her on your ass."

"Thanks."

The Viscountess felt much better when she was back in the Real World sitting in the carriage. Blossom and Snuzzle had been waiting patiently for them to return.

"How are you, my dear?" Duchess asked.

"Fine. She just took me by surprise. I'll be more careful in the future."

"So long as you're submissive enough to pass."

"Being submissive enough won't be the issue." The Viscountess smiled. "Thank you again for the help."

"It was my pleasure. Do you think I'm cut out for undercover work?"

"You were superb. I'm sure she didn't suspect a thing."

It was true, the Viscountess mused, Duchess was a natural at this sort of thing, but then she had spent most of her life as a professional dominant. Her job required her to shift seamlessly from strict teacher to cruel nurse to imperious amazon to fit the needs of her clients. Playing the older partner to a stubborn brat was hardly a stretch.

They arrived back at the ranch in time to see Tate practicing her tie downs for the upcoming rodeo. A gate in the corral was open and a woman burst forth running as fast as she could. It was one of the young women the Duchess was training, not yet up to full pony status. Tate raced into the corral riding on Roxy's shoulders. The running girl got only a few steps before Roxy was on top of her. Tate hurled a lasso around the girl, yanking her to the dirt and then on top of her in seconds, quickly binding her in a hogtie.

One of the ranch hands, a grizzled woman, glanced at the stopwatch and shook her head.

"That's two seconds faster than last time," the old woman reported. "But you're a long way off the record."

Tate cursed and stamped her foot.

As the Viscountess left the carriage she glanced around for Severin. Dickie was in a small dog cage sitting in the shade of the big house. The cage next to him was empty and Severin was nowhere to be seen.

"I don't suppose you've seen my slave anywhere?" the Viscountess asked the ranch hands. The women looked around guiltily.

"We were just having some fun with him," the older woman said.

"Where is he?"

They looked at a corner of the corral where Severin lay in the dirt. He had been hogtied, the rope not only binding his wrists and ankles, but also his genitals.

"We didn't mean anything by it." A heavy woman wearing nothing but chaps and a vest along with the required boots and hat, came forward. "We were just talking about how some rodeos have a male calf roping competition. It's a little harder than the female because men have an extra attachment point. Anyway Tate said she'd never done a man before and when your boy said he wanted to try it, we figured what the hell, why not?"

"I see." The Viscountess could easily imagine how much Severin would enjoy being run down by the pretty cowgirl and her mare. "Can one of you let him go?"

The big woman introduced herself as Hoss and brought a Bowie knife roughly the size of her forearm from her belt sheath. Severin tried not to flinch as she sliced the rope off. A single slip could do serious damage, particularly when she went to work on the tight rope around his cock and balls.

Fortunately, Hoss was very skilled at this sort of thing. She cut the rope with a flick of her wrist and tugged it free with a few quick jerks. Severin was no worse for the wear except for marks where the rope had dug into him.

"There you go, good as new." Hoss tipped her cowboy hat, revealing that she had a shaved head.

"Thank you." The Viscountess prodded Severin with her boot. "But he was supposed to be resting?"

"I'm sorry Ma'am," Hoss ducked her head. "We didn't mean any harm."

"I understand, but I still didn't give permission for anyone to use my property."

"It will be dealt with," Duchess said sharply, glancing around at her ranch hands.

"Actually it was a very comfortable position," Severin said, not entirely convincingly. "How did it go at the academy?"

"Fine. Let's get you cleaned up and I'll tell you all about it."

She made him stand in the back yard while she hosed him down. The shock of the cold water hitting him almost made him cry out, but he knew that being sprayed with water barely counted as a punishment. If he was going to complain about a thing like that he wouldn't stand a chance with the Roaring Girls.

She sat in a lawn chair and described Blackbriar Academy while he dried off. When he was done she gave him the contract to read.

"It looks pretty normal," Severin admitted.

"It says Duchess can withdraw me at any time and they don't have the right to keep me from communicating with her. If they broke those rules they'd get Feedback."

Severin nodded. Feedback was the mysterious backlash that occurred when someone violated the rules of S&M play. If the academy really had lost Amy and was lying about it, it was bound to trigger severe Feedback.

"Wait a minute." Severin looked up, his eyes bright and the Viscountess knew he had thought of something. "This is signed by Miss Krause."

"She's the Headmistress, the assistant to Mr. Woodridge, the Headmaster."

"Did you see Woodridge at all?"

"No. Of course he might not come out for every new student." The Viscountess remembered the closed wooden door to the Headmaster's office.

"According to Lady Amanda he's the one who signed for Amy. If something's happened to her, he'll be the one suffering Feedback."

"Perhaps I'll add 'check on Woodridge' to my list of things to do."

"You have a big enough list already," Severin reminded her.

"At the top of the list is trying to find a link to the Kamen Girls." The Viscountess reminded him. "I still don't see a connection."

"It's too much to be a coincidence. I'm sure the Sphere was involved somehow."

"You just don't know how," the Viscountess teased him.

"I'm not beaten yet."

"Not yet, but when the Roaring Girls get through with you, I imagine you're going to be very well beaten."

Chapter Twenty-One

The next morning Duchess delivered the Viscountess to the real world Forsyth Academy and from there through the Gateway to the Dominion which housed Blackbriar Academy. Felicity, looking as bright and perky as ever, was on hand to greet her. Felicity took the Viscountess into the dressing room to help her with her uniform. The schoolgirl talked a great deal, but didn't seem to be saying much.

At one point when the Viscountess was wearing nothing but her bra and panties Felicity glanced at her and gushed, "Gosh, you're beautiful." She instantly turned red and stammered an apology. "I'm sorry, that's my big mouth. No wonder I keep getting punished."

"It's all right," Viscountess assured her.

"No, seriously, if you wanted to have me punished for that I would totally understand."

"Don't worry about it. Can you help me with these buttons?"

With Felicity's help Viscountess was able to get the rest of the school uniform on without any further incidents. They emerged from the dressing room in time to hear the conversation between Duchess and Miss Krause.

"I was hoping to speak with the headmaster," Duchess said, following the suggestion the Viscountess had given her.

"I'm afraid he's indisposed," Miss Krause said smoothly. "But I assure you, he pays close attention to all out students. Everyone here is very pleased to have Desire as our student."

Duchess glanced up and saw the Viscountess in all her schoolgirl glory; her crisp white blouse tucked into a dark skirt. The skirt came to just above her knees and below that she had on white socks with black patent leather shoes. Her hair was held back by a simple hair band.

"You look smashing." Duchess hugged her tightly and added suggestively, "They say we can keep the uniform."

The Viscountess smiled wanly. She would have been much more comfortable being paraded naked. She had crawled on all fours at the end of a leash and found it more empowering than the simple blouse and skirt.

Miss Krause ran her cold eye up and down the body of her new student. The Viscountess could feel the gaze of the older woman and knew that her awkwardness and hesitation had been noted.

"Yes, I think she'll do nicely," Miss Krause decided. "It's time to say goodbye, dear. We'll just give you a quick medical exam and then Felicity can show you to your room and get you set for classes."

"Yes, Ma'am."

"That's Headmistress to you, young lady."

"Yes, Headmistress," Viscountess shot back at once. The force of the rebuke was strong enough that Viscountess was unable to raise her eyes from the floor. Miss Krause chuckled, clearly amused at how quickly the Viscountess submitted to her.

Duchess stepped in at once, hugging the Viscountess a second time.

"Remember, I don't want any trouble, my dear. I'm sure you'll make your mommy proud. Don't forget to call every day."

"Yes, Mommy."

As the Viscountess spoke the words almost caught in her throat. In all her years as a submissive she had never actually called anyone mommy, or daddy for that matter. Somehow saying it out loud made it all real.

Miss Krause and Duchess went off to have an adult conversation. Felicity immediately squeezed her hand reassuringly.

"Don't worry, it's okay."

"I'm sorry."

"Don't worry," Felicity gushed. "Let me guess, you don't do this 24/7 do you?"

"Not really."

"And this is the first time she's left you alone when you're like this." The Viscountess nodded.

"You've got nothing to be afraid of. This place can be a lot of fun. The humiliation is awesome. Your mom's totally cool and I'm sure she'll take you back in no time."

"I have to call her every day."

"Right, that's from my office. I'm near the Gateway to Forsyth back in the Real World." Felicity explained. "You can actually get a cell signal."

"Great." Viscountess smiled. She didn't really think she would be in any danger here, even if Amy did somehow vanish. The daily phone call would allow her to pass information to Duchess every twenty-four hours. If she missed a call Duchess would come for her. They even had a secret code worked out so that the Viscountess could alert Duchess to trouble without tipping off anyone who might be listening in. "So Felicity, can I ask you a question?"

"Sure, that's kinda what I'm here for."

"You have an office, but you look like a student."

"Thanks." Felicity smoothed her skirt over her legs. "I guess you could say I'm a graduate student. I was here so long they didn't see any need to send me to classes, so I get to work in the office. Instead of paying me they just waive my tuition. Don't worry, I still get punished like the other girls—maybe more so."

"Telling tales again?" a sharp voice cut through the air. "You know what happens when you talk too much."

"Yes, Headmistress," Felicity squeaked. She went into a submissive position instantly, standing at attention, shoulders back, staring straight ahead, and arms at her side.

The Viscountess tried to imitate the posture. Miss Krause walked behind her, out of sight. The Viscountess could feel her tugging on her shirt collar and adjusting the position of her shoulders.

"Well your mother has left you to our care. I'm sure we'll get along famously, my dear."

Miss Krause crossed over in front of her. Years of training made the Viscountess lower her eyes to the floor. The Headmistress clicked her tongue disapprovingly.

"Eyes front, my dear. You stand at attention when one of your instructors is addressing you, understand?"

"Yes, Headmistress."

"Excellent. Now let us see what Nurse Kelly makes of you. Come along."

Miss Krause left, glancing back to make sure the Viscountess was following her. Felicity slouched gratefully as the Headmistress exited.

The nurse's office was just down the hall. The Viscountess noted that although much of the school had an almost Victorian feel to it, the nurse's office was straight from the 1950s. Everything was vintage, right down to the anatomy posters on the wall.

Nurse Kelly was dressed for the part with a perfect white uniform with cap and stockings. She had an air of brisk, efficient dominance about her.

"Hello Desire, I'm so glad to meet you," the nurse said, glancing at a clipboard to make sure she had the name right. "I'm Nurse Kelly, but you can call me Nurse."

"Thank you, Nurse."

"Now, let's see what we have here." Nurse Kelly checked the clipboard again.

The Viscountess became aware of another girl in the room. Someone was standing off to the side wearing a thin gown. There was an enema stand next to her and she had a pained expression on her face. The rubber tube from the empty bag disappeared under the edge of the gown.

"Having problems, Clara?" Nurse Kelly asked, glancing at the girl.

"I'm sorry, Nurse. I can't take any more."

"Don't worry, dear, it's all in. We just have to wait for it to settle."

"I'm not sure if I can hold it."

"Of course you can." Nurse Kelly smiled at the student. She crossed over and lifted the tube from the enema bag. It had a rubber bulb attached to it. The Viscountess recognized the equipment. She had something very similar in her bathroom back home. Nurse Kelly gave the bulb a few quick squeezes, watching the girl's eyes grow wide with discomfort. No doubt the bulb was inflating a balloon just past the sphincter that would seal the girl shut, not allowing her to expel so much as a drop.

"The teachers are tired of you interrupting class with your constant trips to the bathroom," Nurse reminded Clara. "If you can't learn to control your most basic bodily function we'll have no choice but to put you in diapers. I'm sure you don't want that."

Clara made a whimpering noise in her throat.

"That's what I thought. Now wait a few minutes while I see to our new student."

"Yes, Nurse," Clara said, not quite able to keep the strain from her voice.

The Viscountess noticed that despite the coldness in her tone Nurse Kelly checked her wristwatch as she stepped away from the girl. Clearly she was keeping track of the time so the enema wasn't held in too long.

"Desire, please step behind the screen and change into a gown so we can get started," Nurse Kelly ordered cheerfully.

Behind the screen the Viscountess wasn't surprised to find another paper gown exactly like the one Clara was wearing, incredibly flimsy and completely open in the back. She stepped out from behind the screen trying to hold the gown closed much to the amusement of Miss Krause.

Nurse Kelly gestured to the examination room. There was an ominous skeleton hanging there next to an old-fashioned exam table.

Once the Viscountess was sitting on the table the Nurse went to work. First she took the Viscountess' blood pressure, then she checked her pupils with a bright light. During the throat examination she deliberately triggered the gag reflex, noting how the Viscountess reacted to it. During the whole procedure the nurse kept up a stream of questions about the Viscountess' physical condition. Although the exam had its kinky aspects, it was professional enough that the Viscountess felt certain that Nurse Kelly really was a real nurse.

"Stand up and bend over the table. This won't hurt a bit."

The Viscountess saw a thermometer in her hands. The nurse shook it to get the mercury to settle in the bottom. It wasn't hard to guess what came next. As the Viscountess bent over the table she felt her gown open and cool air on her backside. The nurse applied some glycerin to the rectal thermometer and slid it gently into her ass.

"How does that feel?"

"Fine." The Viscountess shifted her position slightly.

"The glycerin is something of an irritant. It may not be as fancy as the lubricant you're used to, but I find the old fashioned ways work just as well, don't you agree?"

"Yes, Nurse," the Viscountess replied. There wasn't much else she could say in her position. The itching was beginning to get to her and she had to fight to keep from reaching back. No doubt Miss Krause was waiting for just such a mistake.

"I noticed from your entrance form that your mother has requested limited contact with the male teachers," the nurse said.

Viscountess wasn't sure how to answer. She hadn't been aware that was one of the options. Apparently it had been brought up in a private conversation between Duchess and Miss Krause.

"That's pretty common," Nurse Kelly continued. "Of course you realize the male teachers will still be able to punish you. You're only going to be exempt from the private lessons in their quarters. Most of the teachers are female anyway, and there's no limit on your interaction with them."

"I'm sure Desire is going to be a very popular little girl," Miss Krause put in.

"I agree." Nurse Kelly gave a gentle pinch on the ass as she withdrew the thermometer.

"Temperature normal," the nurse continued. She ordered the Viscountess to stand and slipped a stethoscope under the gown. "Heartbeat is a little fast. Get back on the table and put your feet in the stirrups."

The Viscountess knew this was coming. There was no way she was going to get a humiliating medical exam without some time in the stirrups. As soon as she had planted her feet, the nurse tightened leather straps around her ankles and positioned the stirrups so her legs were splayed open.

Nurse Kelly donned rubber gloves for the next part of the exam. She stretched the labia, poking and prodding, finally pressing a finger onto the clitoris which made the Viscountess let out an involuntary gasp.

Next came the speculum. Since the Viscountess couldn't see between her legs thanks to the gown across her elevated knees, the nurse helpfully held the instrument up for her inspection. With a touch of lubricant, the metal slipped easily into her. The steel instrument was cold enough that it made her jump. Before she could recover from the new sensation the nurse manipulated the lever, forcing it open widely and turning the screw to lock it into place. The Viscountess was fully on display now, every inch of her exposed and vulnerable. There was no way she could disguise how turned on she was.

The nurse looked over her shoulder at Miss Krause. "You're right. She is going to fit right in here."

"I had a hunch." Miss Krause gave a satisfied smile.

"We always check the students out during their first medical exam," Nurse Kelly explained to the Viscountess. "If they're not already aroused I make sure to stimulate them during the pelvic exam. If there's no response, we contact the parent and suggest that maybe this school isn't the best fit for them."

"I'll do my best to fit in, Nurse," Viscountess said. She was grateful that her old submissive Persona had helped her pass this test even if she was still having a hard time with the schoolgirl act.

"I'm sure you'll do just fine." Nurse Kelly leaned closer to her, making the conversation more intimate. "Don't forget you'll still have to deal with the female teachers and staff and there's no limit on what they can do. Are you all right with that?"

"Yes, Nurse."

"Your mother didn't put any limits on your punishments. If there's anything you'd like to remove I can add it to your permanent record right now and your mother never has to know."

The Viscountess hadn't been expecting this. It was tempting to try and have something removed from the list of punishments that inevitably awaited her, but she decided not to push her luck.

"I'm hoping the punishments won't be a problem."

"Good girl. Safeword if you have to, and I'm sure it'll be smooth sailing."

Nurse Kelly gently inserted a finger into her ass, which was still lubricated by the glycerin. The Viscountess tried to hold still, but it was almost impossible. The nurse added to her discomfort by lightly stroking her clitoris, bringing her close to orgasm, but not letting her come.

Miss Krause stepped closer to get a better look at the show the Viscountess was involuntarily putting on. She was squirming and gasping as the skilled fingers stroked her to the very brink repeatedly.

"We don't want her to enjoy herself too much," Miss Krause chuckled.

"You're probably right," Nurse Kelly agreed. She slowly removed the speculum and set it aside. "Get dressed and you can get to class. Don't be afraid to come to me if you need anything."

"Thank you, Nurse."

Back in the office Clara was still standing in her flimsy gown. She had her hands over her cramping stomach and her eyes were desperate. The nurse casually checked her watch and nodded.

"Very well Clara. Do you think you can show this much restraint the next time you're in class?"

"Oh yes, Nurse."

"Good."

When the bulb was deflated Clara came very close to losing control at once. As soon as Nurse Kelly gave her permission she rushed to the bathroom in a painful sort of waddle.

The Viscountess watched her go as she stepped behind the screen to dress. Once she was out of sight she reached back and scratched herself. The damned glycerin was driving her crazy.

As she dressed, the Viscountess reflected that the medical exam hadn't been very bad. Nurse Kelly seemed to be a concerned and caring dominant, but Miss Krause still seemed suspicious of her. Perhaps she was like that with all the students. It was something to ask Felicity.

The Viscountess was grateful to get away from Miss Krause when Felicity arrived to show her around. Leaving the administration building, they crossed the quad on the sidewalk. It was spring here. The sun was shining and the trees were heavy with leaves. The old buildings had ivy growing up the walls, making them look like a part of nature.

"Isn't Nurse Kelly great?" Felicity asked.

"Yes, she is." The Viscountess readily agreed.

"And so hot. I'd love to spend some time in her room, but she never seems to date students. Did you know she's actually a nurse?"

"I'm not surprised."

Felicity had already explained that there were two dorms, east and west. They were headed to the west dorm where a bed was waiting for her. The Viscountess was rolling a small suitcase behind her with some clothes.

"I don't think Miss Krause likes me very much," the Viscountess said experimentally.

"She's like that with everyone," Felicity assured her. "Although she's gotten worse lately."

"Why? What's happened lately?"

Felicity hesitated. She looked like someone who had a big secret. "It's no big deal."

"Does it have anything to do with Mr. Woodridge?" Viscountess guessed.

Felicity's mouth dropped open. The Viscountess sincerely hoped that Felicity never played poker.

"No," Felicity stammered, "I mean—"

"I don't want to get you into any trouble, but I noticed the Headmaster wasn't around. When my mom asked about him Miss Krause just blew her off."

"That's the thing. I haven't seen him for weeks. Miss Krause tells me not to worry but also not to tell anyone."

"So what happened to him?"

"I have no idea," Felicity bent closer so she could speak in hushed tones. The few students who were around weren't paying any attention to them, but it never hurt to be careful. "If you ask me, I think he quit."

"Why would he do that?"

"That's the crazy part. He loved it here. He was great with the cane and the strap, and he got to punish girls all the time. I can't imagine why he'd leave."

"That does sound strange," the Viscountess admitted.

"Miss Krause has been a real monster since he left. For once I'll be glad when the semester comes to an end."

"What do you do on your vacations?"

"I'm a consultant. I like to work financing startup companies."

"Really?" the Viscountess couldn't hide her surprise.

"Yeah," Felicity grinned and looked down at the ground. "I've got a business degree from Harvard, but I'd rather answer phones here and get spanked twice a week than get stuck in some office."

Looking at her closely it was easy to see that she was an adult. Felicity had to be in her twenties, possibly her thirties, but the Persona of the schoolgirl had been so strong the Viscountess had simply accepted her as a giggling teenager.

The west dorm had two floors and was divided into large rooms that each held ten students. The beds were lined up like in a military barracks. There was a single large bathroom for each floor. Felicity showed the Viscountess her bed and told her about the girl in the bed next to her.

"You'll love Peggy, she's really sweet. Most of your classes will be with her."

The Viscountess received a map of the school grounds, her schedule of classes, and the combination to the locker that held her school books. Everything about the classes seemed normal. In fact it brought back a rush of memories of her first days in college. Back then her growing awareness of the kinky side of her personality made concentrating on anything else nearly impossible and she was forced to drop out. It had taken her years to go back and finish her degree.

When she entered the Dominion she was unafraid of canes and paddles; those were things she could deal with. She found the thought of sitting in a classroom to be oddly panic-inducing.

"Relax, it'll be great." Felicity threw her arms around the Viscountess and hugged her. "Once you meet Peggy she can show you everything you need."

"I hope you're right." The Viscountess returned the smile.

Chapter Twenty-Two

The Viscountess had no trouble following the map to her locker, but opening the lock proved more difficult. Although she had been given the combination she spun the dial without any results several times. The hallway was full of girls with identical uniforms who flowed past her without paying any attention to her struggle.

"Let me help," a friendly voice said. The Viscountess turned to see a smiling face. The girl reached out and deftly spun the dial. "You have to turn it all the way around twice to clear it, and then do the numbers."

"Right." The Viscountess barely remembered how her high school locker had worked. "Thanks a lot."

"Sure, no problem. You must be the new girl. I'm Peggy." She enthusiastically thrust out her hand, which the Viscountess shook.

Peggy was a voluptuous beauty with a winning smile and curly brown hair that tumbled down her shoulders. Her full figure filled out the schoolgirl uniform nicely, but the Viscountess thought she'd look even better naked and chained up in her basement.

The thought of home made her think about Severin and she suddenly missed the weight of her whips on her belt. In the school uniform she didn't even have a belt.

"Felicity mentioned you," the Viscountess said, shaking off her dominant mood. "I think I've got the bed next to yours."

"Cool beans." The girl grinned. She seemed to be bubbling at medium perkiness compared to the more high-energy Felicity.

"Can you help me find my first class? It's history with Ms. Symons."

"I know, since we're in the same room in the same dorm, we have the same schedule."

"Convenient."

"You might not think that when you meet Monica."

"And she is...?"

"You'll know her when you see her." Peggy scrunched up her face as if she had just tasted something sour. "Come on, let's get going."

The hallway was a swirl of skirts and feminine energy. The

Viscountess was pleased to notice that she wasn't the only one having problems with her schoolgirl Persona. Many of the women she passed looked just as awkward and uncomfortable as she herself felt. Some of them looked as young as Felicity and Peggy, but others had signs of their real age, including a few schoolgirls with grey hair.

Peggy plowed through the sea of girls, leaving the Viscountess to scramble in her wake. They went around a corner and down the hall, breezing past a few stragglers to make it a minute before the bell rang.

The history room was well appointed with maps on the wall, a large globe and a set of encyclopedias. It was also complete with a school-marm, a beautiful woman of indeterminate age with her auburn hair in a tight bun and her make up perfectly in place. She gazed at the room through glasses with black plastic frames and radiated a sensuous dominance that made several of her students squirm in their seats.

The Viscountess slid into a seat in front of Peggy. She was directly across from a blonde with a slash of bangs across her forehead who glanced at her coldly. The blonde girl and the teacher were the only ones in the room wearing makeup and the only ones showing any sign of dominance. Although Ms. Symons had an approachable beauty, the blonde seemed to prefer keeping people at a distance.

After she glanced at the Viscountess, the blonde girl then gazed at Peggy for a few seconds, causing the voluptuous beauty to drop instantly into Subspace. Apparently the blonde girl was Monica.

"Students, we have someone new joining us today," Ms. Symons announced. "Why don't you stand up and introduce yourself to the class."

The Viscountess had just sat down, but she dutifully rose to her feet, feeling the eyes of everyone on her.

"Hello. My name is Desire," the Viscountess said. There was a snicker of laughter from somewhere, but Ms. Symons silenced the room with a look. The Viscountess slipped back into her seat at once.

"Now, let's get back to the subject of our last class."

Ms. Symons turned her back and began writing on the chalkboard. Everyone brought out their notebooks and began taking notes. The book that the Viscountess had been issued seemed like a standard high school level history text, but the topics Ms. Symons chose to lecture on seemed to follow a definite trend.

She chose to focus on slavery in the ancient world. There were rich and vivid descriptions of the slave harems of the kings of Persia. Somehow hearing about chains and whips and branding in Ms. Symons' calm, clear voice was unbelievably sexy. Several of the girls shifted in their seats, trying to resist reaching between their legs to touch themselves.

When the teacher turned to face the class she had a tight smile on her face, as if she were well aware of the discomfort that she was causing them.

"Now, we come to Rome. I'm sure all of you have read the books I assigned from the library." Ms. Symons scanned the room. "Who can tell me what SPQR stands for?"

A slender girl from India raised her hand at once and answered in a British accent. "It means the senate and people of Rome."

"Very good, and who would likely have that tattooed to them?"

The student hesitated and finally guessed, "slaves?"

"Not exactly. It was given to gladiators and soldiers whose lives literally belonged to the state. Now who can tell me what a slave girl was called in Rome?"

Several hands shot up, but she chose the blonde girl.

"Monica."

"Serva," Monica answered.

"Good, and do you know another Latin word for that?"

Monica shook her head helplessly.

"Anyone, what's another word for slave girl?"

"Ancilla," Viscountess said without thinking. Several girls stared at her and she realized that it must be against the rules to speak without permission.

"Very good," Ms. Symons beamed at her. Monica shot her a poisonous glare.

"Thank you." The Viscountess had only known the word because of the time they had been in a Roman Dominion. She and Severin had to rescue a woman from slavery after she had made a foolish bet on a rigged chariot race. Why couldn't Severin have gotten the school part of the mission? He'd be a whiz at it.

The rest of the class passed without incident. About halfway through the hour the Viscountess felt the need to relieve herself, but she decided to keep quiet. After what happened to the girl with the enema there was no point in risking any punishments until she understood the rules better.

As soon as the bell rang that ended class, the Viscountess was on her feet. Ms. Symons called her over to the desk.

"Where's the bathroom?" the Viscountess called to Peggy.

"Down the hall on the left," Peggy said cheerfully. "I have to go too, I'll meet you there."

As the rest of the girls filed out the Viscountess stood at Ms. Symons desk.

"I'm very glad to have you in my class," Ms. Symons said warmly. "But I have to warn you, there's a very big test coming up next week. It's going to cover everything we've been over this semester."

"I see," Viscountess answered, not sure what kind of response was called for.

"It's a policy in my class that the person with the lowest score on the test is punished in front of the class." The teacher glanced significantly at a slender but sturdy wooden paddle that hung from a hook on the wall. "I know it may seem unfair, but those are the rules."

"I understand."

"Good. As long as we understand each other."

Ms. Symons smiled and the Viscountess felt a subtle spike of dominant energy flow into her. The Viscountess realized that Ms. Symons was giving her a chance to beg for mercy, to make some kind of deal that would avoid the paddle. It was a tempting offer, but the Viscountess didn't see how it was going to help her find the missing girl, or the Kamen Girl's Sphere.

"May I go now?"

"Of course, and good luck here."

"Thank you, Ma'am."

The Viscountess left the room and hurried down the hall to the ladies room—there was no men's room. Inside she saw that a Scene was already in progress. Peggy was standing with her mouth open while Monica, along with the Indian girl and a rail-thin brunette smoked, depositing their ashes in Peggy's mouth.

Peggy didn't seem terribly happy about the situation, but she wasn't resisting them. The schoolgirl made eye contact as the Viscountess entered. Monica turned and gave her an icy glance. Monica had not forgiven the Viscountess for making her look bad in class.

The Viscountess went into a stall and immediately relived her bladder. Sitting there on the school toilet it was hard to believe she had eaten breakfast with Duchess while their respective slaves had serviced them. It seemed like a lifetime ago.

Before she was done on the toilet the Viscountess heard a Monica and her friends leave. A second later there was the sound of retching coming from the stall next to the Viscountess. Glancing over, the Viscountess saw Peggy on her knees in front of the toilet.

Hurriedly the Viscountess finished and went to her.

"Are you all right?"

"Fine," Peggy gasped, trying to catch her breath without throwing up again. "I was trying to swallow the butts and one of them broke open and got all over my tongue. I can't believe some people actually chew tobacco."

Her stomach started to go again. The Viscountess grabbed her hair as Peggy bent over the toilet and finished emptying her stomach.

"Why can't Monica and her friends just flush their butts like every other schoolgirl?"

"You know, my mouth, a toilet, same thing." Peggy shrugged.

The Viscountess winced at the self-deprecating joke. It might have meant nothing, but jokes like that were sometimes a sign of low self-esteem, which could be very bad in a submissive.

As she washed her face in the sink Peggy glanced up at the Viscountess with a smile on her face. "Thanks Dee, you're a brick."

The Viscountess couldn't help laughing. "Thanks, I've always wanted to be a brick."

Both of them laughed until suddenly they heard a sound that chilled their blood. The bell rang to signal the start of the next class.

Peggy squealed in horror and scooped up her books. She spilled into the hall with the Viscountess close behind. Their next class was very close by. Unfortunately, they got there just as the teacher, a heavyset, middle-aged man with a stiff mustache had closed the door.

There was no point in trying to sneak in. The teacher turned to look at them, as did every student in the room.

"I'm sorry, Mr. Henrickson," Peggy squeaked. "I lost track of time, I was—"

"It's my fault," the Viscountess said firmly, as she took a step forward. She hadn't actually planned on saying that, but somehow she didn't want to see Peggy suffer any more. The words were out of her mouth before she realized she was speaking.

"Well," Mr. Henrickson fixed his dominant gaze on her. She could tell just by looking at him that he was a spanker, the kind of man who wanted a woman over his knee. "You must be the new girl."

"Yes sir, I'm Desire. Peggy was kind enough to show me around and I guess I kept us from getting here on time."

"Normally I don't like to punish young ladies on their very first day in class. I don't want you to think that I'm some kind of a tyrant."

There was a bit of nervous laughter from the students as he said this. Apparently he was a bit of a monster.

"I'd be willing to accept any punishment you feel is appropriate," the Viscountess said, amazed at how brave she sounded.

Mr. Henrickson's eyes showed he was ready to punish her, but he made a show of thinking about it. He forced them to stand in front of the room for a few agonizing seconds while he stroked his chin in contemplation.

"Very well," he decided. "Since it's your first day I'll let you off with the stool. Peggy, if you'll get a seat for your new friend...?"

Peggy shot the Viscountess a sympathetic gaze. She still seemed a little stunned that the Viscountess had stepped up for the punishment.

Peggy went to a corner of the room and brought forth a high stool with a wooden seat and metal legs. The Viscountess saw that the seat was covered with countless small wooden projections. It looked like a meat tenderizer. The stool was tall enough that she couldn't put her feet on the floor, and there was no place for her feet to rest. She would have to sit with her full weight on the wooden spikes.

"There you are," Mr. Henrickson said magnanimously. "If you'll just lower your underwear and take a seat."

Several students laughed at her as she reached up under her skirt and pulled the white cotton panties down to her knees. The Viscountess could feel the weight of every eye on her.

Peggy supplied a short step so she could mount the high stool. The Viscountess put on a brave face and flipped up her skirt, settling her body onto the wood. It hurt right away. As her body settled she could feel every spike pushing into her. They weren't sharp enough to break the skin, but in a way this was worse. The sensation was overwhelming.

Despite her best efforts she started to squirm, trying to find a more comfortable position. Of course there was no comfortable position. There was no way to relieve her suffering. Every movement only increased the irritation of the wooden spikes. Her legs swung back and forth helplessly.

Mr. Henrickson smiled warmly as her. The front of his pants showed a noticeable bulge.

"Don't forget her hat," he said to Peggy.

Reluctantly Peggy went to his desk and brought over a large conical paper hat with the word "tardy" printed on it. She silently mouthed the word "sorry" as she placed it on the head of the Viscountess.

When the Viscountess saw the hat she almost laughed. The dunce cap was such a silly bit of business it hardly seemed to compare to the overwhelming pain coming from her bottom. When the hat was placed on her head the whole room erupted into gales of laughter. The Viscountess felt humiliation sink into every pore of her body. Here in the front of the class there was no way she could hide her shame, there was nothing she could do but sit there and suffer while her peers laughed at her.

Viscountess knew there was no rational reason why such a simple punishment was affecting her so deeply, but there was no question that it was. She had to fight to keep from crying. The only thing which held back the tears was the knowledge of how much more the class would laugh if she broke down so completely on her first punishment on her first day of school.

Putting on a brave face the Viscountess looked across the room. Everyone was looking at her and a few people were still laughing. She saw a few girls flick out phones to catch a quick picture. Peggy slid into a seat and started pulling out her books.

One person who was not laughing was Monica. The blonde was simply smiling, a cruel grin that stretched from ear to ear. Looking at her the Viscountess wondered if the tobacco that had gotten in Peggy's mouth was really an accident. Had the little minx set all this up?

One thing was for certain. The Viscountess had to learn to navigate the tricky waters of the school if she was ever going to find out if anything had happened to Amy and if she was linked to the Sphere.

Chapter Twenty-Three

Although Mr. Henrickson's science class did not discuss the theory of relativity, the Viscountess certainly learned that time was relative. It was the longest hour of her life. The pain was excruciating, bordering on unbearable. It was impossible to get comfortable, but every time she shifted her weight to relieve herself the pain only increased. To make matter worse, each time she squirmed the girls in the class would giggle and smirk at her. She burned with the terrible humiliation and it was only with an effort of self-control that she kept from crying.

Finally, the class came to an end. Peggy immediately rushed forward with the stool so the Viscountess could dismount from the cruel chair. The Viscountess almost made the mistake of getting down without permission. She caught herself just as the stern teacher approached her.

"Well, I hope you've learned your lesson," he announced.

"Yes sir," the Viscountess replied. She didn't have to pretend to be humbled. Monica and her two friends went past whispering and laughing at her.

"I'm sorry I had to do this, but the sooner you get used to the discipline around here the better off you'll be," Mr. Henrickson told her, sounding not at all sorry.

"Thank you, sir." The Viscountess could feel the dominant energy coming off of him and was trying not to respond to it, but an hour on the chair had put her into a very submissive state.

"Run along now, I think it's time for lunch."

Peggy helped her up and she managed to get to her feet and pull up her underpants. She thanked the teacher again and hurried out of the room, pausing only to grab her books.

Next came lunch. The Viscountess and Peggy dropped off their books at their lockers and headed for the cavernous room where meals were held. The high ceilings were supported by ancient wooden beams. It was filled with long wooden tables for the students used and a huge table at the front of the room for the teachers.

"Welcome to the refectory," Peggy announced cheerfully. "Lunch is pretty informal. Dinner is stricter."

Although the Viscountess had been expecting a cafeteria, Blackbriar was clearly more upper class than that. Servants came from the back room bearing plates of food. There were glasses and a pitcher of water on each table.

As she slid into the hard chair the Viscountess winced slightly.

"You should have let me take the punishment," Peggy insisted. "I've got more padding."

"I'll be fine. Believe me, I've been hurt a lot worse."

Many of the students were still milling around. Others were sitting down. The Viscountess estimated about two hundred students were in the room. The air was filled with the scent of furniture polish and the hum of dozens of whispered conversations.

Her attention was drawn to a low table where a dozen children sat. All though they were all fully grown adults they had such a carefree attitude that they seemed to be much younger than the other students. They were eating peanut butter and jelly sandwiched with the crusts cut off and drinking cartons of milk.

"That's the Littles table," Peggy explained. "It's kindergarten through sixth grade. They have their own separate classes and teachers. They don't sleep in the dorms; they get to go home at night."

They were certainly deeply in their Personas, the Viscountess mused. They stood out only because their Personas were younger than the rest.

At the head table sat the teachers, all on the side of the table facing the students. They had several freshly cooked chickens on the table which servants cut and placed on their plates. The center chair was conspicuously empty.

"Who sits there?" Viscountess asked, pointing to the chair.

"That's for the Headmaster, whenever he shows up."

"Where is he?"

"I don't know." Peggy shrugged. "He just stopped coming to meals and Miss Krause took over all the punishments."

"Weird." The Viscountess decided it would be a good time to ask her important question. "Hey that reminds me, do you know a student named Amy?"

Peggy was a much better liar than Felicity. There was only a second of hesitation to give her away before she answered.

"No, why do you ask?"

"A friend told me to look her up. She's supposed to be here."

"We got like two hundred students." Peggy looked around the huge room and shrugged.

The Viscountess looked down at the table for a moment so Peggy couldn't see her face. That hadn't been the answer she was hoping to hear. When Amy had written to her aunt she had mentioned her new friend Peggy. Now it looked like Amy was gone and her so-called friend was covering it up.

Servants arrived with food for both of them. Like Felicity, the servants appeared to be students who had stopped taking classes but still worked at the school. Everyone seemed to be from another Dominion, as if this world had no natives. It reminded the Viscountess of the world of the Kamen Girls. Without residents of its own, this Dominion would collapse, unable to sustain itself if everyone left it.

The food looked and smelled pretty good: roast chicken and mashed potatoes and gravy with peas. There was a small piece of cake on a side dish.

No sooner had the food arrived than they were suddenly joined by Monica and her two friends. Monica and the very thin brunette sat on either side of Peggy while the Indian girl flanked Monica.

"Hi. Desire is it?" Monica batted her eyelashes at the Viscountess. "That's such a cute name. I'm Monica and this is Raine."

"Hey," the Indian girl said somewhat noncommittally.

"And this is Cristall, with two 'll's. She's a teen model. You've probably seen her in Teen Vogue or Seventeen."

The Viscountess nodded, completely certain she'd never seen the emaciated girl before. On closer inspection Cristall with two 'll's was wearing subtle makeup that filled out her face and kept her sunken cheeks from looking too skeletal.

"See this?" Monica pointed to a small badge on her blouse with the letter P on it. "Do you know what this means?"

"No."

"It stands for Prefect. It means I kind of help out running the place. I have to make a report every time I see someone break a rule, and I get to help out with the punishments. Miss Krause really depends on me."

"We all get to help." Raine chimed in. Her high, childlike voice belied the cruel look in her eyes. She was flexing her hands as if she longed to have a cane at the table.

"I hear you're in our dorm, so I'll probably be seeing a lot of you." Monica promised, or perhaps threatened was a better word.

Their food arrived. Raine and Monica had identical plates to the Viscountess and Peggy, but Cristall received a plate of something pale and shapeless with a white sauce.

"It's soybean," she explained airily. "I have a macrobiotic vegan diet. My parents fly in meals daily. You won't catch me polluting my body with toxic meat."

"Actually, it's very good," the Viscountess pointed out.

"I see you've already met Piggy. Oops, I mean Peggy," Monica giggled. "Go ahead, show Desire your trick."

Peggy looked across the table at the Viscountess. Seeing the panicked look in her eyes the Viscountess immediately spoke up.

"That's okay, you don't have to."

"No really, it's hysterical," Monica gave Peggy an elbow to the ribs. "Go ahead, show her."

Peggy reached up and gingerly pushed her nose up, elongating her nostrils. She began making grunting, pig-like noises. Monica and her friends rocked with laughter.

"Oh god, that's priceless," Monica said when she got her breath back. "Go on; tell your new friend why you do that."

Releasing her nose, Peggy bit her lower lip nervously. "Well, when I get out of here, I don't exactly have a parent waiting for me. I'm probably going to put myself up for auction."

"And I'm going to have my Daddy buy her," Monica gushed. "He owns a whole bunch of really nasty porn sites. He's always looking for models, and I made him promise that he'll star her in his bestiality sites. Can you imagine her down on all fours in the mud while this huge male pig takes her from behind?"

Apparently Peggy had no trouble imagining it. She was breathing hard and her face was flushed. Monica and her friends had a good laugh at her expense.

The Viscountess considered remaining quiet. She was only going to be here a short time and she didn't want to make an enemy of someone who could make her stay miserable. On the other hand, a clash with Monica might well be inevitable, so she felt she should make the most out of it.

"I've always found bestiality to be problematic," the Viscountess mused. "It always looks rather awkward and uncomfortable, plus the animal can't really consent to it, since they can't understand how humans view the situation."

"That's too bad," Monica smiled sweetly. "My daddy has a whole kennel full of dogs that would love to get their paws on someone like you."

"Really?" the Viscountess returned her smile. "Does he have an Irish wolfhound? They're magnificent beasts."

Monica opened her mouth but for a second nothing came out. She was so used to girls being terrified of bestiality that she couldn't think of a comeback for the remarks of the Viscountess. While she fumbled for an answer Raine chimed in.

"Does he? That would be awesome?" the Indian girl asked.

Monica shot her a look that could melt ice and then rested her sights on Peggy again.

"Here, let me help with your diet."

She took the piece of cake away from Peggy. At the same time Raine leaned over and scraped her peas onto Peggy's plate. Peggy sighed and began to eat what they had left her.

Monica and her friends started concentrating on their food as well. None of them wanted to miss a meal. As they ate, they talked to each other as if the Viscountess and Peggy weren't there.

The trio took off as soon as they had cleared their plates, announcing "prefect duty." Watching them go, the Viscountess smiled.

"I have to admit, that was quite an experience." She said. "I've dealt with bratty bottoms before, but that's the first time I've seen a bratty top."

"Now I'm going to be wet all day." Peggy moaned. "I can't stand it."

"Why didn't you Safeword?"

"Yeah, right. Me using a Safeword with Monica? Never happen."

"Why not?"

"If I'm going to use a Safeword every time something happens to me, I might as well go home." Peggy hesitated, biting her lower lip. "At least that's what Monica says."

The Viscountess sighed. She could understand someone being attracted to the little blonde vixen, but she couldn't help but feel that Monica was taking advantage of Peggy's low self-esteem. If she hadn't come here to investigate Amy, she might be able to do something about it.

News that the first class after lunch would be gym gave the Viscountess images of Monica pelting her with missiles at dodge ball. As it turned out the gym was a large building off of the main quad connected by a dirt path. While the Viscountess, Peggy, and most of the other girls went into the building to change in the locker room, Monica and her friends split off to go towards a barn further down the path.

"If you're rich enough you can go riding for gym," Peggy explained. "The school provides the barn and horses, but your parents have to pay for the upkeep."

A riding mistress was leading the horses out of the barn and to the mounting blocks. They were actual horses and not pony slaves.

After donning their too tight T-shirts and very short shorts the students came out of the building and crossed to an area surrounded by a large oval track. The Viscountess was delighted to see that targets for archery had been set up. This was one of the few sports that she had experience in. When she had been training in Victoria, archery was one of the only activities that was recommended for young ladies. She had enjoyed it so much that she bought a bow when she got her house and set up a range in back of the garage. Of course she didn't practice as much as she should.

The gym teacher turned out to be a delight as well. Coach, as she was called, was a butch beauty with close-cropped hair and muscles that rippled when she walked. She wore sweat pants and a T-shirt with the school logo across one firm breast. The short sleeves displayed her well defined biceps.

"All right, ladies, it's time for archery," Coach announced after blowing her whistle. "Everybody grab a bow and pick a target."

They lined up as ordered. The Viscountess found she had a fiberglass bow that was a far cry from the six-foot wooden one back in Boston. Of course back home she also had Severin to fetch the arrows for her. While Peggy fumbled next to her, the Viscountess drew back the string and fired. It hit the target solidly, just inside the third ring.

"Wow," Peggy gasped.

Coach noticed and wandered over while the Viscountess took up another arrow.

"You have good form. Desire is it?"

"Yes, Coach." The arrow hit the target, but still far from the bull's-eye.

"Here, let me help."

Coach stepped in, very close to her. She reached out her arms so they lay along the arms of the Viscountess. Coach's hard body was pressed close. Her lips were just inches from the ear of the Viscountess.

"If you're a teenage girl I'm the Queen of Sheba," Coach whispered.

The Viscountess gave a start and the arrow went astray, missing the target entirely.

Coach gave her another arrow and again leaned into her.

"I don't know what you mean," the Viscountess said in a low tone.

"Would you like to run laps naked?" Coach gave a wolfish grin. "I can arrange it. I can even make you jump hurdles. Tell me what you're doing here."

Coach's physical presence was so overwhelming the Viscountess had to steady herself before she could formulate and answer.

"It was my mom's idea," the Viscountess said when she could think straight. "She sent me here."

"I see." Coach smiled. "All right then, back to work".

Coach left to look in on the other girls.

"You are so lucky," Peggy whispered when Coach was out of earshot. "Coach almost never hits on the new girls."

"Yep, that's me, lucky."

When the class was done they returned to the gym to change back into their uniforms. The Viscountess was in her underwear when she heard Coach bark out her name.

"Desire, my office!" When the Viscountess reached for her clothes Coach added, "Now!"

The Viscountess followed her in and the door was closed, cutting them off from the locker room and the showers. Standing in her bra and panties the Viscountess found herself crossing her arms across her chest to cover herself up.

"I'm sorry if I came on a little strong out there," Coach said unexpectedly.

"Uh, no."

"It's just that this place is very special to a lot of people. There are those who don't understand what we do here. They're always confusing it with pedophilia. If I thought for a minute that you came here to make crazy charges or make fun of us..."

"I wouldn't do that," the Viscountess said truthfully.

"I can see that now." Coach rose from behind her desk and approached the Viscountess. She slipped a finger into the elastic waistband of her underwear and slid it back and forth slowly. "As for making you run laps. I get the strangest feeling you'd rather be the one making me work up a sweat. Am I right?"

The Viscountess blushed and glanced away from Coach.

"That's what I thought," Coach let go of the underwear and stepped back. "You wouldn't be the first little girl who's tried to pull that trick. Although if your mother thinks you can learn to have a younger Persona and become submissive, she may be asking for the school to do too much. If you'd like I can write her a letter."

"No, that won't be necessary," the Viscountess assured her. "But thank you."

"Well, you'd better get back to class then."

As the Viscountess went out the door Coach gave her a quick pat on her ass.

"Lucky," Peggy repeated as the Viscountess grabbed her clothes and hurriedly put them on.

The Viscountess nodded. Coach had a good eye. She had known right away the Viscountess didn't have a proper Persona in place and wasn't submissive like three fourths of the other students. Fortunately, there were enough new students trying to form a Persona that Coach wasn't too suspicious. The Viscountess knew that she was lucky indeed.

Chapter Twenty-Four

The rest of the day was largely uneventful. Apparently even Blackbriar hadn't found a way to make geometry kinky. After classes there was some free time before dinner. Peggy used the opportunity to race to the bathroom in the dorm to play with herself. Monica and friends had been watching the bathrooms in the school too closely for her to risk trying it there.

Dinner was slightly more formal than lunch. The food was equally delicious and the meal was helped by the fact that Monica and her gang were nowhere to be found. There was an odd tension in the air that the Viscountess noticed.

"There's usually a punishment after dinner," Peggy explained. "It's always something big, in front of the whole school."

As the dished were cleared away the feeling of expectation rose. Miss Krause addressed the students, getting their attention. Her whip-thin body had a keen edge of dominance. She stood flexing a cane in her hands until the room became utterly quiet and she felt each eye turn to her.

"Monica, you may begin."

At Miss Krause's command Monica entered the room flanked by Raine and Crystall. Between them, carrying a bucket, was Felicity.

"Oh my god, it's Felicity. She works in the front office," Peggy gasped.

"I know, I met her this morning."

"Why are they punishing her? She never does anything wrong."

The Viscountess had a bad feeling she knew why Felicity was being punished.

It was a shock to see Felicity with all her bubbly energy drained away. Looking like a condemned woman, the schoolgirl poured the contents of the bucket on the floor. A ripple went through the room.

"Gravel. She's going to kneel on gravel," Peggy sighed. "I've been on gravel, but never in front of everybody. God I'll bet that hurts."

The Viscountess nodded sympathetically. She had an urge to rush down there and help Felicity, but what good would it do? She was being punished by the rules of the school, and wasn't going to Safeword.

Gingerly Felicity lowered herself to her knees. No one tried to help her. As her weight sank down on the gravel her mouth fell open in a silent O of pain.

"As many of you know Miss Felicity works in the office. Although she may not be taking classes anymore the rules of this institution apply to everyone. This morning she spoke out of turn. Since her tongue got her into trouble, I think it's only fair that her tongue take the punishment. Monica, if you will be so kind..."

"Of course Miss Krause." Monica smiled sweetly. She had a small bottle in her hand.

With her body shaking a little from the pain in her knees, Felicity opened her mouth and extended her tongue. Monica poured several drops from the bottle onto the tongue. The effect was instantaneous. Felicity made a gurgling sound and lurched. The sudden motion no doubt increased the pain in her knees.

"Hot sauce," someone in the room said. It was a sharp contrast to the classroom where everyone was laughing at the Viscountess. The students took the nightly punishments seriously.

Felicity was shaking so badly that she almost lost her balance. Raine and Cristall had to keep her upright. She still hadn't brought her tongue into her mouth. No doubt she was worried about spreading the hot sauce inside her mouth.

"Do you understand what you've done wrong, Felicity?" Miss Krause asked. Felicity nodded. "I can't hear you dear."

Monica laughed a little at that. Felicity had no choice but to pull her tongue in. The hot sauce in her mouth was so bad that tears began streaming from her eyes and her face began to turn red.

"Yes, Miss Krause," Felicity whimpered.

"And I'm certain you won't do it again."

"No, Miss Krause."

"Just as a reminder I have a copy of our student code of conduct for you to read aloud."

Felicity took the paper with a trembling hand and began to read. It was a simple declaration of diligence and obedience, but with her voice breaking it took her a few minutes to get through it. When she had swallowed all of the hot sauce Miss Krause ordered Monica to apply some more.

Eventually the ordeal was over. Felicity got to her feet with the help of Raine and Cristall. Gravel clung to her knees, driven so deeply into the flesh that Monica had to knock it clear. Finally, the sobbing girl had to pick up all the gravel with her hands and bring it back outside.

"It's not fair." Peggy whispered. "If they were going to punish her they should have done something awesome, like paddling or caning. Why pick punishments that nobody likes?"

"I think that was the point," the Viscountess said under her breath. Peggy looked at her with an odd expression.

The Viscountess was pretty sure that Felicity was being punished for talking to her. The purpose of the demonstration had been to send the Viscountess a message.

The woman in charge of the west dorm was Mrs. Abernathy, an attractive heavyset woman with salt and pepper hair. She had almost a hundred girls in her control, but she seemed to be more submissive than dominant. When the Viscountess saw Monica greet the dorm mother with a pinch on the older woman's full ass it became clear that the woman had no control over Monica.

Everything in the dorm room seemed very normal. The girls talked and read books, some listened to music. The Viscountess used the bathroom to change into her sleepwear. Pajama bottoms and a T-shirt that Duchess had bought for her. She was ready to settle in for a good night's sleep when Monica made an announcement.

"I almost forgot," the pretty blonde schoolgirl told the room. "We have a new student joining us. We need to give her a proper West Dorm welcome."

"Oh my god, I'm so sorry, I totally forgot," Peggy gasped. The Viscountess stared at her, not knowing what to expect.

"What should we do?" Monica asked.

"Indian burn!" someone shouted.

"London Bridge," another said.

"No, I've got it." Monica grinned mischievously and fixed her baby-blue eyes on the Viscountess. "Spanking machine."

There was a great chorus of cheers. Monica had all the girls in the room line up facing the Viscountess and spread their legs.

"Down on the floor, on your hands and knees," Monica helped the Viscountess to the floor.

When she looked up she was facing a tunnel of bare legs and pajama bottoms.

"All you have to do is crawl through," Monica teased. "Oh, and we'll be spanking you the whole time."

She gave the Viscountess a smack on her ass to get her started, then raced around to the end of the line so she would be the last person the Viscountess would have to pass, as well. Even Peggy was in the line.

Lowering her head, the Viscountess crawled forward. The first girl didn't really spank her, but yanked down her pajamas, forcing her to crawl with her pants down at her knees. That left her with only a thong for protection. The second girl laid in with swift spanks. The Viscountess crawled as fast as she could to get past. The blows irritated her bottom that had barely recovered from her ordeal on the spiked stool.

The Viscountess crawled through Peggy's chubby legs and got nothing more than a gentle pat. The girl after her however made up for it by not only spanking with one hand, but yanking off the thong with the other.

By the time she reached Raine, Cristall, and Monica at the end of the line the pain and humiliation had begun to get to the Viscountess. She was starting to cry and was having a hard time keeping herself focused. Monica made the last few inches as difficult as possible. She closed her legs on the neck of the Viscountess, pinning her in place. Monica reached down between her legs, spanking her not on her ass, but on her pussy.

It wasn't nearly as hard as some of the spankings had been, but the series of light blows was enough to make the Viscountess collapse. The worst part was, Monica could clearly feel how aroused she was.

"See, that wasn't so bad." Monica teased. "Now that you're officially one of us, if anyone messes with you, you come get me."

"Thank you, Monica," the Viscountess said automatically.

At that moment the dorm mother burst into the room.

"What is going on here? Desire, get off the floor and get your clothes on. I don't know what's gotten into you!"

"We were just telling her the rules, Mrs. A." Monica put in.

"Right now the most important rule is lights out."

Most of the girls chanted, "Yes, Mrs. Abernathy," and started heading for their beds. Peggy helped the Viscountess to her feet.

"I'm so sorry," Peggy whispered. "I should have known she'd pull that. I totally owe you a spanking. Anytime you want just take me over your knee."

"I might take you up on that."

"Really?" Peggy grinned, her eyes suddenly lighting up at the thought of the spanking. Her face was the last thing the Viscountess saw as the lights went out.

Chapter Twenty-Five

The next morning the Viscountess cut her breakfast short so she would have a chance to make her daily phone call. In the office, she found Miss Krause going over some papers, just out of earshot of the phone. Felicity was at her desk looking only slightly worse for the wear.

"How are you?" the Viscountess immediately asked.

"Oh, fine," she beamed. "My knees are super sore but I'm sure I'll be over it in no time. The worst part was missing dinner."

"Were you punished because of me?"

"Oh no, it's just one of those things, I guess I was due." As Felicity spoke she glanced at the open doorway, beyond which Miss Krause was standing. Felicity made a worried face and pointed to the Headmistress. Next she cupped her hand to her ear as if she was listening to something. The Viscountess stared, not entirely sure what Felicity's silent warning was trying to tell her.

Felicity opened her palm to reveal a hands free headset hidden there. Clearly Miss Krause was listening in on any phone calls.

"Here's the phone! You don't want to be late for class," Felicity said casually.

As the Viscountess dialed the phone she saw Felicity very carefully open up one of the schoolbooks the Viscountess had placed on her desk and slip a folded piece of paper in it. Neither woman said a word.

Duchess picked up the phone so quickly the Viscountess knew she had been waiting for her call.

"How is it, dear?" Duchess asked.

"I'm fine, and this place is just peachy."

"I see," Duchess said quickly. According to the code they had arranged, the word "peachy" meant that someone was eavesdropping. If the Viscountess had said it was "swell" that meant she was in trouble and needed help. "How are your classes?"

"Well, so far I've sat on a punishment stool with a dunce cap on."

"Well, we're certainly going to be talking about that when you get home."

"Have you been taking care of Severin? Does he miss me?"

"Don't worry, he's fine. I've been giving him lots of extra treats."

"Tell him I'll be home soon."

"I think a few more days may be enough for you," Duchess declared.

"I hope so," the Viscountess replied.

There wasn't much more they could say, particularly if Miss Krause was listening in. The Viscountess said goodbye to her "mother" and hung up.

"Bye, see you tomorrow!" Felicity chirped as the Viscountess ended her call. "If not sooner."

As the Viscountess left, she passed Miss Krause, who was still not in her office. Now she could see the Headmistress had a small electronic object in her ear.

The Viscountess waited until she was all the way out of the offices before she reached in and unfolded the paper. It was a note from Felicity asking to meet her after dinner behind the refectory.

Peggy caught up with her before she was finished reading and glanced at the note.

"That's so cool, you and Felicity. I've always had a thing for her, but she's so out of my league."

"Why don't you come with me?"

"I'm not invited."

"I don't think this is romantic. I think she wants to talk with me. I'd like to have you there."

"What for?"

"I just think something strange is going on here, and I'd like your take on it."

"Well, okay," Peggy said hesitantly.

For the Viscountess, her second day went much more smoothly than the first. She managed to avoid getting punished and witnessed a girl getting a quick over the knee spanking for talking in history class. Ms. Symons had an excellent hand, firm strokes, and a good follow through. Mr. Henrickson also rapped a student's knuckles with a ruler, a less exciting punishment, but not without its high points.

At lunch Monica and her companions returned to make veiled threats. The Viscountess refused to be impressed.

"You know," Monica said. "Maybe you don't understand how things work around here."

"I understand completely." The Viscountess smiled. Since she wasn't ever going to be friends with Monica she didn't see much point in engaging her.

With an angry scowl on her face Monica stormed off, followed by her friends. Raine wasn't through eating yet and looked mournfully down at the plate of spaghetti before following her mentor.

When the day's classes were over, they all gathered for dinner and a punishment. This time the dinner was meatloaf and the punishment was a hapless girl who had been caught playing with herself in one of the bathroom stalls. The girl was forced to stand on a chair where everyone could see her and demonstrate what she had done, reaching down under her skirt while the other students laughed and stared.

Raine and Cristall brought out a portable spanking bench which the girl had to mount. Her skirt was flipped up and her underwear pulled down, revealing the pale white cheeks of her ass. Monica provided the punishment with a stiff leather strap. The blows came hard and fast, not giving her time to process the sensation. She screamed and sobbed uncontrollably. Monica did not stop until both cheeks were a bright red.

After the beating Monica looked into the audience and made eye contact with the Viscountess. There was no mistaking the implied threat. The next time she punished someone, Monica planned on making sure it was the Viscountess.

After dinner the Viscountess and Peggy circled behind the building until they found Felicity.

"Hey," Felicity said brightly when she saw that Peggy was there.

"Hi," Peggy replied.

The Viscountess felt a spark of attraction pass between the two schoolgirls, but neither of them showed any visible sign of it. They wouldn't even make eye contact with each other.

"Okay, so, I'm glad you got my note," Felicity began. "I was thinking maybe we should sneak out and check on the Headmaster's house."

"He has a house?" the Viscountess asked.

"Yes. All the teachers get little cabins, but Miss Krause has a house, and the Headmaster has a regular mansion. It's one of the perks. He gets to have a lot of room when he, um, entertains students."

"If we get caught, this is really serious," Peggy said.

"Weren't you punished last night for merely talking about the Headmaster?" the Viscountess reminded her.

"Yeah, I know." Felicity glanced down at her knees, the pain from the previous night taking away a bit of her perkiness. "But that's what's got me thinking. Why is Miss Krause so upset? If we go there and the house is dark we'll know I'm right and he's away somewhere."

"What if we go and there's someone there?" Peggy asked.

"I don't know, maybe he's had some horrible accident and can't show his face. Maybe he has to walk around with a mask."

"Like the Phantom of the Opera," Peggy squeaked.

"Focus," the Viscountess said sharply, trying to bring them to heel. "You said we could sneak?"

"There are streetlights all along the path. There's enough light that we can sneak through the woods next to the path and no one will see us."

"Let's go."

As quietly as they could the trio left the sidewalk and went into the woods. It was exactly as Felicity had described it. There was just enough light from the streetlights spilling into the woods that they could creep along the trees and not trip on anything. The Viscountess pondered if it had been set up this way on purpose, to give students a chance to reach their teacher's home without being spotted.

The trail led them behind a series of cottages where there was less light, but they could still see well enough to make out the path. One cabin had the sound of whipping coming from it, another had the sound of enthusiastic lovemaking. They saw a girl walking towards Miss Symons' cabin. Her face was a mixture of excitement and fear.

The trail curved away from the modest dwelling of Miss Krause and towards the back of a large, two-story house. It wasn't exactly a mansion, but it certainly stood out. Most of the lights were lit on the first floor, casting rectangles of light onto the grass.

"Well, he's home. We can go." Peggy turned, but the Viscountess grabbed her sleeve.

"Wait. I want to get closer."

"I just realized," Felicity gasped. "This is exactly like Nancy Drew. Des is Nancy, I'm George, and Peggy is Bess."

"I'm not Bess. Bess is the fat one."

"Quiet," the Viscountess hissed. Both girls stopped talking at once.

Together they crept cross the lawn, staying low. There was someone moving in the house.

Crouching under a window, they heard a sound like a low moan. The three of them stared at each other, not certain what to make of it. They froze into position as someone leaned very close to the glass, staring out into the yard as if she had heard something. It was Nurse Kelly.

As soon as Nurse Kelly left the window they returned back the way they had come. They had so much adrenaline it was hard not to run and all of them wound up tripping a few times. Finally, they all stood in the light of a streetlamp.

"He's here, but he's sick," Felicity deduced.

"Sounds more like he's dying," Peggy put it.

"I think it's Feedback," the Viscountess announced.

They stared at her for a second.

"But isn't Feedback just for when you hurt someone?" Felicity asked. "He hasn't gone too far with anyone, at least not that I know."

"It can also happen when you break a contract," the Viscountess explained. "I have a feeling he's been like this since something happened to Amy and he started lying about her. He signed the contract with Amy's aunt Amanda, and now he's broken it."

"Yeah, what happened to Amy anyway? She didn't go out through my office."

Felicity addressed the question to Peggy, but the voluptuous schoolgirl just looked upset.

"I don't know anything," Peggy stammered.

"You have to know," Felicity continued. "She was like your best friend. She slept in the bed next to you."

"Ixnay on the amy-a."

"What?"

"That's pig Latin."

"I don't speak pig Latin. I don't even speak regular Latin."

"I do," the Viscountess interrupted. "Is there anything you'd like to tell me, Peggy?"

"I promised I wouldn't tell," Peggy sobbed, suddenly in tears. The Viscountess hugged her tightly.

"I know you made a promise to Amy, but I think she's in trouble and I need to know everything you can tell me."

"She's not in trouble," Peggy sniffed. "She ran off with her girlfriend."

"That's not possible," Felicity argued.

"I don't know how it happened," Peggy admitted. "All I know is Amy looked out the window one day in class and saw something. She ditched her next class. She didn't show up for it at all."

Felicity gasped in horror at this violation of the rules.

"I didn't see her until just before dinner," Peggy continued. "She was heading into the dorm, so I followed her. I saw her putting her clothes into a bag. She told me she was going off for a while and that she'd be back soon. She even said she'd be here by the end of the semester so she could get picked up by her aunt and there'd be no problem. Miss Krause made me promise not to tell anyone."

"Did Amy say how she was leaving?"

"No, just that she was meeting her girl in the clearing off the riding trail."

"It's a place kids go to drink, smoke, or make out," Felicity added helpfully.

"Can you take me there?"

"Not tonight," Felicity explained. "There's no lights on the trail. We'd need flashlights, and if we used those we'd be spotted for sure."

"There's got to be a way. What about tomorrow, do we have classes on Saturday?"

"No, just homework and cramming for the history test," Peggy said. Suddenly her face brightened. "Wait, there's going to be a field hockey game tomorrow afternoon. We can slip away from that and go while everyone else is busy."

"Look, maybe I should go alone," the Viscountess told them. "I don't want to get you two into any more trouble than you're already in."

Peggy and Felicity glanced at each other and both shrugged.

"I say we're in it together." Felicity held out her hand palm down.

"Me, too." Peggy placed her hand on top of Felicity's hand. They both turned to the Viscountess, waiting for her to complete the impromptu ritual.

"I guess we are all in it together." The Viscountess put her hand on top of theirs.

Suddenly they were all laughing and hugging.

"Thanks Des, you're the best," Peggy gushed, obviously relieved at having her secret burden now shared with others.

The Viscountess sighed. She had a nickname now. In the past when she had been Desire full time no one had thought to give her a nickname. Now suddenly she had become Des to these women who lived as teenagers. The name seemed to indicate she was adopting a new Persona, but she wasn't entirely sure who Des was supposed to be.

Chapter Twenty-Six

Duchess insisted on the four-girl carriage for dropping Severin off. Snuzzle was one of the lead ponies, since she had been to the Kustom Body shop in Tuscon before and could lead the way. Severin was not allowed to actually ride in the carriage, but had to run behind it, pulled by chains attached to his wrist cuffs.

Nita was leaning against her motorcycle smoking a cigarette when the carriage appeared from the void. As soon as the wheels hit the pavement, Duchess drew back on the reins and bid the four ponies to halt. It took them quite a few feet to bring the mass of the carriage under control.

The leader of the Roaring Girls looked very much like she was trying not to be impressed by the magnificent carriage and the four stunning pony girls. She nodded a greeting to Duchess and Severin. They had called ahead to explain that the Viscountess was going to be busy and Duchess would have to bring Severin to his appointment.

As the carriage stopped Severin sank to his knees, catching his breath. He was never able to keep pace with the powerful pony girls even when they were travelling through the void. Nita glanced at his naked body and shrugged.

"Thanks for bringing him," Nita dropped the cigarette and stamped it out. "I was worried he'd chicken out."

"The Viscountess told me to remind you of what she said," Duchess told her. There was a note of imperious command in her voice, as if she were a queen addressing a commoner.

"Not a problem," Nita assured her, refusing to notice the dominant tone Duchess used.

There was a van parked at the curb. A large, powerful woman got out of the driver's seat and ambled towards them. Nita unclipped Severin's wrists from the carriage and gave him a shove; he landed on the sidewalk in front of the woman.

"Slave, this is Momma Bear. Get to know her," Nita ordered.

Momma Bear was big all over, both tall and wide. She easily topped six feet and had broad shoulders and wide hips. Her grey hair was buzzed down into a flattop. She had on a classic biker vest revealing massive breasts barely contained by a leather bra. Below the waist she was encased in a leather kilt held up with an assortment of belts and straps. She was also packing; Severin could see a noticeable bulge in the front of the kilt.

"Hello, slave," she said cheerfully, reaching out one well-worn steel toed engineering boot for him to kiss. Severin did so. His tongue tasted dirt and sweat and the sweet after taste of many other tongues, most of them women who had licked this leather before him.

"Here's a bag with some clothes, in case he needs them. There's also a phone." Duchess handed Nita a small backpack.

"Thanks. Don't worry; he can call you or the Viscountess any time he wants. We'll let him go on Sunday one way or the other."

"Very good."

Severin noticed that Duchess did not tell her that the Viscountess was currently a schoolgirl. Perhaps some things were better left unspoken.

Momma Bear opened the back of the van and took out a leather hood that would cover Severin's entire head. He saw that the back of the van had chains and attachment points on the floor and ceiling.

"Are you all right with the hood, slave?" she asked, holding it up for him.

"Yes, Mistress."

"Just call us all Ma'am and you'll get along fine," Momma Bear explained. "If you don't mind, I'm just gonna call you slave. It's easier to do what we have to do if you don't have a name."

As she buckled the hood into place Severin suppressed a shiver of anxiety. When he was younger he had a friend who lived on a farm. His friend had said the same thing about naming animals that were going to be slaughtered.

Momma Bear buckled the hood tightly but left the zipper for his mouth open. Although his eyes and ears were blocked there was a hole for his nose that couldn't be sealed no matter how tightly it was zipped and buckled.

"How's that?"

"Fine, Ma'am."

"Good," Momma Bear chuckled. "Now stand up and just go limp."

Severin got to his feet, uncertain as to what was going to happen. As soon as he stood, Momma Bear scooped him off of his feet. She carried him effortlessly into the back of the van and put him on the carpet as if he were a sack of potatoes. Before attaching the chains to his wrist and ankle cuffs she leaned in so he could hear her through the hood.

"Make yourself comfy, you've got a ride." She locked him into position on his side using the chains. She also placed something on the floor next to him. Severin felt a plastic tube touch his lips through the opening in the mask. "This is a sealed plastic cup with a straw. It's fresh water, so when you're thirsty just drink. Let me know if you need a pee break. I don't want anything messing up my van."

Duchess and Nita might have had a longer conversation, but Severin couldn't hear it. They might as well have been miles away from him. Momma Bear started the van and drove away. Eventually Severin heard the sound of a motorcycle behind them and knew that Nita was following on her bike.

The trip was comfortable enough that Severin almost fell asleep. The time change between Boston and Arizona wasn't doing him any favors. He sipped warm but soothing water from the cup. The only issue he had was an itch on his testicles and he couldn't reach them to scratch.

Eventually they came to a halt. Momma Bear released him from his chains and took the hood off, giving him a few minutes for his eyes to adjust. They had driven far enough from the city that there was nothing around them but flat land with scrub brush and a few straggly trees. They had stopped in front of a low building that looked dusty and threadbare. Music came from inside and he could hear women laughing.

In the desert all around the building people had set up camps. There were a few RVs, but mostly tents with motorcycles, lots of motorcycles. Seeing him looking around Momma Bear offered an explanation.

"They've been coming in for days for the big ceremony. Tomorrow night you're going to be the popular girl in school."

Severin sighed. The women didn't look all that dangerous, but he was sure once their dominant energy was fired up, each of them would be formidable in her own right. Worst of all any of them could have Amy stashed in a tent or the back of an RV.

Nita arrived on her motorcycle. By the time she had put down the kickstand a naked woman with long chains linking metal bands on her wrists and ankles had emerged from the bar and dropped to her knees beside the bike. She carried a cloth, but mostly seemed to be cleaning the bike with her tongue. Severin saw that she did not have the Roaring Girl mark on her upper arm.

The leader of the Roaring Girls barely glanced at the slave so desperately cleaning her bike. She left her helmet for the slave to pick up and attached a leash to Severin's collar.

"Take his stuff to Squirt's room," Nita told Momma Bear. "Slave, you're with me."

Severin went from the bright sun into the darkened bar. He stumbled as his eyes adjusted and Nita yanked on the leash to keep him upright. Classic rock thundered from speakers with too much bass. There were about a dozen women in the room, most of them wearing leather or denim if they were wearing anything at all. Some were drinking at the bar, others playing pool. At the back of the room a woman pole danced on a stage to a small but appreciative audience. They were an interesting assortment of women, some who looked exactly like the rough-and-tumble sort who'd join a biker gang, others might well have been urban professionals blowing off steam on the weekend. The only thing the women had in common was the ubiquitous tattoo/brand on their arms.

Momma Bear hadn't been exaggerating when she said they were waiting for him. As he entered the room there was actually a small round of applause and someone gave him a very flattering wolf whistle.

They made their way through the bar to a back room. Severin was dragged past a naked woman who was hanging from the ceiling by her wrists and ankles, which had been locked together. She was curled into a ball with her face up. A group of laughing women were surrounding her, spinning her around and taking turns pouring beer into her mouth.

Nita lead Severin into her office. It was cluttered with too many small objects to keep track of and covered with a fine layer of sand that had filtered in through the cracks in the window. Nita produced a pair of reading glasses and wore them to spin the dial of a safe on the floor. The heavy, squat safe looked like it might have been from the Old West.

"Momma Bear will get you settled in a few minutes, but I thought you should see this before you go any further."

She took an object out of the safe gently unwrapped it from its blanket. Resting in her hands was a large, powerful dildo. There was no doubt that this was Boybreaker. It wasn't the largest Severin had ever seen. Not too long ago he had an exact double of the Black Jade Dragon dildo forced into him, and it had been bigger than this.

It wasn't the size that was intimidating, but the attitude that seemed to ripple off it. Boybreaker was made of black rubber, rigid and thick with veins that twisted around it like knotted vines. The bulbous head glared at him menacingly. It looked like a cock, but not a human one, something that should be slung under the body of a great beast.

Once he looked at it Severin couldn't look away. He reached out his hand slowly, almost as if he couldn't stop himself. When his hand brushed against the head of Boybreaker he felt a sudden snap of pain and he withdrew his arm. It was like an electric shock, as if it had bit him.

"Sorry, it does that sometimes." She hastily wrapped the dildo and put it in the safe once more. "Look, I'm not going to lie to you, this thing has seen some bad stuff."

"What do you mean?" Severin asked. He noticed that when they were alone in her office she spoke to him as an equal.

"Back in the day the Roaring Girls were a pretty rough bunch. They did things—things we'd never do today."

"What do you mean?"

"There was a time, like twenty, thirty years ago when they used Boybreaker on guys that they felt deserved it. They knew about Safe, Sane, and Consensual, but they used the same toy on their willing submissives that they used to punish guys who beat their wives or girlfriends. Stuff like that can leave a mark."

Severin nodded. Sex toys used in Scenes often had so much power flowing through them that they retained some of that power, gradually growing into a Named item. If Boybreaker had been used to rape men that would explain its arrogant and ruthless aura. It might also explain why the Roaring Girls had broken up and reformed so many times. The Feedback from using a Fetish item like that could be devastating. Tomorrow night's ceremony might be consensual, but Boybreaker wasn't going to make it easy.

Severin decided to ignore his worries. He had to focus on why he was really here.

"You still have no idea which of your members might be seeing Amy?" he prompted.

"No, not a clue." Nita shrugged. "We've got about forty women here now, more arriving tomorrow. It could be anybody."

Nita looked longingly at the pack of cigarettes on her desk, but didn't reach for them. The filled ashtray showed that she had no aversion to smoking in her office, but she was clearly trying to cut down. She immediately got back to business.

"Duchess, the woman in the carriage, told me about your limits. I'd like to hear them from you."

"No permanent marks," Severin said immediately. He added, "Also no breath play, no blood play, no needles, no scat or golden."

"If we hit you hard enough to break the skin, do you consider that blood play?"

"No, that just comes with the territory; I mean no knives or razors."

In actuality the no-permanent-marks rule was his only hard limit, and that was simply because only his owner had the right to mark him and she wasn't here. He had done everything on that list with other women whom he liked and trusted, but so far none of the Roaring Girls were in that category.

"Fair enough. I'll make sure everyone gets the word." Nita assured him. "You should know that tomorrow we're going to have a strict no alcohol rule at the ceremony. Nobody who's had a drink will be allowed near you."

Nita lead him back into the bar. While they had been gone, the dancing woman had stripped down to her sunglasses and the woman who had been hanging from the ceiling was now busy impaling herself on a dildo strapped to another woman's thigh. Nita carefully steered Severin away from the enthusiastic cries and moans as she bobbed up and down on the shaft.

"He's all yours." Nita shoved him toward where Momma Bear was waiting for him.

Momma Bear was sipping a bottle of lemonade and offered it to him.

"Thirsty?"

"Yes, Ma'am."

Instead of giving the bottle to him, she put it to his lips and tilted it, pouring it into his mouth. Two women at the bar next to them were watching. One of them, a middle-aged woman with short, stylish hair was glaring openly.

"I can't believe you're letting a man in here," she snarled.

Her attitude earned her a sharp response from Momma Bear. "He's for the ceremony tomorrow. You don't have to be here if you don't like it."

The woman looked like she wanted to say something else, but the glare that Momma Bear gave her was far too intimidating. The woman left, but was replaced by a slender brunette. The woman's leather jacket was well tailored and so black and shiny it was impossible to believe she'd ever ridden her bike long enough to get bugs plastered on it.

"Well, I think he's adorable," the brunette announced, sounding a little drunk. She pinched Severin's ass. "I can't wait to drill that cute little ass of his. Oh, has he seen Big Daddy yet?"

That last was directed at Momma Bear who shrugged. "Not yet."

"Go ahead and show him. I want to see the look on his face."

Momma Bear reached into her kilt and adjusted the straps of the dildo harness. When she opened the front of the kilt the pink head of a cock jutted through. For a split second Severin thought it was an actual penis, but no, it was only a realistic strap on.

Momma Bear was focusing all her dominant energy through the cock. Severin sank to his knees without being told and found himself face to face with it.

"This is Big Daddy. He's your new best friend," Momma Bear explained. "Go on, show him how much you like him."

Big Daddy was squat and thick and bristling with dyke energy. She took a step forward, feeding it into his mouth. For a split second Severin hesitated. The dildo was so realistic he almost couldn't put his lips around it. He thought about how much Bonaventura would laugh if the Venetian could see him now.

Severin took the mushroom-shaped head in his mouth and began to work it with his tongue. It was covered with something soft, but had a rigid core. Momma Bear sighed and bucked her hips. Severin decided not to risk choking on the dildo, but still wanted to entertain Momma Bear and the other woman. He ran his tongue up and down the length of the shaft, flicking it against the underside of the head so the dildo shook in its harness.

"Hold on, cowboy, save it for tomorrow." Momma Bear chuckled and lifted him to his feet. Severin noticed that she had big, calloused hands.

"I left Sebastian in my tent," the brunette said, obviously referring to her own dildo. "But don't worry, you can meet him tomorrow."

"So what do you think of the place?" Momma Bear handed him the bottle of lemonade. As if he had passed some kind of a test, she was now treating him with more respect.

"It's nice, very nice." Severin looked around, noticing some things he hadn't seen before. There was a metal cage on the floor beneath a block and tackle so it could be hoisted into the air. There were attachment points seemingly everywhere and chains that dangled from the ceiling ready for use.

"It was a dump when Nita found it. We had to fix it up. I installed the stage and stripper pole plus put a few rooms on in back. I live here pretty much full time with Squirt."

"Squirt?"

"She's our only full-time slave. You'll meet her."

"What about the woman who's being initiated?"

"Still at work, but she'll be by soon enough."

Severin pondered how he could slip a question about Amy into the conversation. He sensed Momma Bear had her finger on the pulse of the Roaring Girls even more than Nita. Unfortunately, he wasn't sure how to steer the talk in that direction. Nita had promised him that everyone would answer his questions on Sunday, but Severin saw no point in waiting. If he could find out the truth and call it in to Duchess he would have less stress when facing the ceremony.

As Severin was pondering he heard a series of high-pitched screams coming from the back of the room.

"Hey, that sounds like Squirt. Come on, you don't want to miss this."

Momma Bear took Severin by the arm and led him towards a door on the back wall. There was a hallway visible through the door which led to the new rooms that Momma had built. Two figures were coming down the hall towards the bar, a naked woman crawling on all fours with another woman behind her, squatting down and shuffling forward. When the woman behind moved her arm, the naked woman screamed a little and scuttled ahead a few more inches.

The room erupted into cheers at the sight of them. It took Severin a few seconds to process exactly what he was seeing. Only when he saw that the second woman had her arm buried deeply in the first woman did he understand. The woman behind had fisted the other and was now forcing her across the floor.

The naked woman was drenched in sweat, her breasts flopping wildly with each powerful thrust. Her face was a mask of pain and pleasure coated with tears, sweat, and drool. The way she was shuffling forward she seemed to be on her last legs.

The woman behind her had short hair and was stripped to the waist, revealing a lean body that shone with a thin coating of sweat. Her breasts were small and hard like clenched fists.

After one particularly savage thrust, the naked woman let out a howl and collapsed. A jet of fluid shot through the air and splashed on the floor. Most of the women watching applauded wildly. Severin didn't have to think very hard to figure out why they called her Squirt.

The dominant woman leaned over and talked to the submissive, but Severin couldn't hear what they said. Apparently Squirt gave her the all clear, for the butch immediately went into full dominant mode. She was wearing a long latex glove, like the kind vets use, all the way up to her elbow, even though most of it wasn't necessary. Instead of taking it off, she grabbed Squirt and pulled her to a sitting position.

"Look at the fucking mess you made, you worthless cunt!" She smeared the glove across Squirt's face, bathing her in her own come.

"She's called Sir," Momma Bear said to Severin, obviously referring to the dominant.

Sir grabbed a fistful of Squirt's hair and forced her head to the floor. "Look at that slimy trail you've left. Clean it. That's right, lick it up."

Squirt did as she was told, pressing her face to the floor and raising her ass to the audience. She ran her tongue across the wood, smearing the drops of ejaculate she had made.

"Mop it up with your hair," Sir decided. She helped by grabbing Squirt's hair again and using it on the floor.

Squirt had to keep her head low, shaking her head so she could mop up with her shoulder-length hair. She crawled out like that, giving everyone a good view of her. Severin saw that she had a full, well-rounded ass that had two tattoos on it. High on her left cheek, written in bold black letters, was the slogan "SLAVE 4 LIFE." On her right were the words "PROPERTY OF" above the same Roaring Girls design that everyone else had on their arms.

The two women went back down the hallway, but Severin noticed that as soon as they were out of sight of the bar Sir helped Squirt to her feet and gave her a hug.

"You should go wait in the kitchen for Squirt," Momma Bear said to Severin.

"Yes, Ma'am." Severin lowered his head and saw that he had a full erection.

"It's the first door on the left in the hall. And watch where you're pointing that thing, you don't want it to go off."

"Yes, Ma'am."

Severin immediately went to the kitchen. He found it was large enough to feed an army. Clearly this building had been a restaurant at some point in its past. There was a screen door that opened to the side of the building. Dusty shafts of sunlight shone through the screen as the desert sun slowly set.

Squirt came in, dripping wet. She grabbed a dishtowel from a shelf and patted herself dry. She grinned when she saw Severin in the room, the smile showing off her dimples.

Apparently giving up on being dry, she was still leaving a puddle on the floor when she went to the huge refrigerator and pulled out a sports drink. Twisting the cap off she chugged half the bottle.

"Sorry, electrolytes," she said by way of explanation. "You must be the new boy. Either that or you're really in the wrong place."

"Nita brought me in for the ceremony. I'm Severin."

"They call me Squirt, 'cause I do."

"I noticed."

"Oh yeah. Sorry, I was kind of hyper-focused."

Severin took the time to look at her more closely. She seemed to be composed mostly of circles. She had a pretty, round face, spherical bouncy breasts, and a bubble butt. The dimples when she smiled set it all off. If she had been fully clothed she might have been called cute, but no woman who was stark naked and still glowing from a harsh fisting should be called cute.

"I'm the same way when I do a Scene," Severin told her trying to start a conversation.

"Cool. Hey do you want some?" she finished off the sport drink.

"No, thanks."

Squirt got another bottle from the refrigerator and plopped into a chair.

"Okay, so ground rules," Squirt frowned, trying to remember the rules which were part of her everyday life that had to be explained to him. "First you should sit while you can. The kitchen is kind of a safe zone, but if somebody wants to fuck with you, they'll just drag you out. If you have any hard limits Nita will make sure everybody knows. Keep your head down, follow orders. Everybody here is Ma'am to you, except Sir. Sir is always Sir."

"I noticed her." Severin slipped into the chair across the kitchen table from the slave. "She seems pretty tough."

"Yeah, and I've got knuckle prints on my cervix that tells me she's in a pretty bad mood. Try to stay away from her, she's nasty even on a good day. Oh, and she doesn't have much use for guys."

"Thanks for the warning."

"You must have been expecting that, right? I mean, hello, lesbian biker gang, it's just what it says on the tin."

"I know, but Momma Bear seemed really nice."

"She's a sweetheart. She actually got married and had some kids before saying fuck it and becoming a leatherdyke. Nita's one of the good ones too, but she's the boss. She can't play favorites. If she has to come down on you, she will. Tycho is the best. I hope she shows up tomorrow."

"Tycho?"

"Yeah, she and Momma Bear saved my life once. Tycho is hot, you'll love her."

"She saved your life?"

"Yeah, long story."

"I've got time," Severin shrugged. He knew that it always helped if you could get people to talk about themselves.

"I don't want to go into details, but I've had a pretty fucked up life. I've always been submissive, but instead of running into someone who was into the Scene I just found a bunch of abusive assholes who made my life miserable. I wound up a stripper and I became the property of a coke dealer named Rico. He used to beat me up and tell me I was such a horrible freak no real man would ever touch me."

Severin opened his mouth, but Squirt waved him to silence.

"Yes, I know," she continued. "But Safe, Sane, and Consensual were just words I saw on the internet. When you've fantasized about getting raped your entire life it's hard to say no to a guy, no matter what he does to you. I figured I deserved it."

Severin was trying not to let it show on his face, but inside his heart was shriveling. It had been somewhat tough for him growing up a male submissive, but clearly for a female submissive the world was full of so much more danger.

"Anyway," she continued. "The Roaring Girls used to come into the club where I danced and flirt with me. One night I gave Tycho a lap dance. When I checked the money I saw a business card with a phone number on it. The back of the card said, "When you're ready, call." I don't know why, but I stared at that card until I memorized the number. I knew if Rico saw it he'd kill me."

She reached down and ran a hand across her ribs. Severin hadn't noticed it before, but the top two ribs on the right side seemed to sit oddly under the flesh.

"One night Rico just lost it. He called me all kinds of names and started working me over. Usually he'd do things that didn't leave bruises so I could still dance, but not that night. I was on the floor and he was kicking me. I felt my ribs go and it hurt so bad I couldn't breathe. I knew right then that it was over. He was really going to kill me. As soon as he turned his back on me I crawled to a phone and dialed the number. Rico went back to work on me. The next thing I know the door comes flying off its hinges and Momma Bear and Tycho come in like goddamn superheroes."

The thought of them made her smile wistfully.

"Tycho's an ex-Marine. She wrestled in high school and boxed in the Marines. Now she does semi-professional Unlimited Fighting matches. And Momma Bear is Momma Bear. They're the two people you most want in the world to kick down your door when somebody's about to kill you. I tried to warn Rico not to pull that knife, but he never listened to me."

"What happened?"

"It's not important. I mean it's not like they killed him or something. I hear he can even walk now with a cane."

Severin shook his head, trying to process it all. Squirt had traded a very real form of slavery for something that was actually a fantasy of slavery. It seemed like some sort of miracle that she could bounce back from that abuse and embrace a submissive life. Severin had always known that BDSM could be very healing, but this seemed like almost too much.

Severin focused on one thing.

"You said you hoped Tycho would show up tomorrow. Why, did something happen to her?"

"No, she just hasn't been around for a while. I figure she got her face busted up in a fight and she's too vain to show up with a black eye."

"How long has she been gone?"

"A few weeks. It's not like she lives here. She crashes in the spare room sometimes, but she's got a place in town."

Maybe she's got a black eye, Severin thought. Or maybe she's holed up somewhere with Amy. It dawned on him that the woman he was looking for might not even be here.

There was a commotion in the bar. Squirt jumped to her feet. "It's Tinashe! She's the new girl."

Severin followed her to the door.

Chapter Twenty-Seven

In the bar the newest Roaring Girl was being put through her paces on the last night before her initiation. Sir was barking orders at her and hitting her with a cane. Now that Severin got a better look at Sir he realized that the biker was barely over five feet tall. Somehow she packed the strength of a six-foot amazon into that little frame.

"Tinashe used to play ball in college. She doesn't work out any more, but I swear fat just doesn't stick to her," Squirt said to Severin.

Severin hated to hear the slight note of jealousy in Squirt's voice. It was true that the African-American woman was tall and lean, still retaining something of her athletic days, but that in no way made her sexier than Squirt's well rounded cuteness.

Tinashe had very dark skin and hair that was done in tiny dreadlocks close to the scalp. She had small, high breasts and a rib cage that was a shade too visible for Severin's taste. It was easy to guess that she'd been a basketball player, her arms and legs seemed slightly too long for the torso.

She was almost a foot taller than Sir, which seemed to put Sir in an even worse mood. Sir was ordering her to get on the floor, then stand up, then do jumping jacks. Tinashe always moved too slowly and was hit with the cane many times. The welts made dark shadows on her skin.

After a round of push-ups, Nita stepped in and ordered Tinashe to the kitchen. Sir glared at Nita, angry at the interruption, but she said nothing.

By the time Tinashe got to the kitchen Squirt was already there to hand her a sports drink.

"Thank you," Tinashe gasped when she had quenched her thirst. The workout had been harsh enough that she glistened with sweat. "I hate it when she does that drill instructor shit."

"She knows you hate it; that's why she does it."

"One more night of this," Tinashe sighed. "Then I'm back to being on top again."

"And you get to whip my ass?" Squirt said hopefully.

"You know it, girl."

The two naked women did a fist bump. Tinashe glanced at Severin.

"You must be the sacrificial lamb."

"I guess so. I'm Severin, but everybody here calls me slave."

"Funny, they call me slave, too. My name's Tinashe."

"That's a beautiful name."

"Thanks, my grandma gave it to me. It's African Shona, I think. It means 'God is with us.'" Tinashe gave a small laugh and looked down at herself. "Lord, how am I going to explain this to her. My mom knows I'm gay and kinky, we just have a don't ask, don't tell policy in my house. Grandma's different."

"In what way?"

"Look at me." Tinashe spread her arms. "I'm black, I'm a slave, and tomorrow I'm going to get branded. How am I supposed to explain that to a woman who fought police dogs just so she could vote?"

"They had gays and kinky people back then."

"Not in public they didn't, and that mark on my arm is going to be very public."

"If you don't want to do this..." Squirt went to her and put a hand on her shoulder.

"No, I want to. I thought about this for months. And I know you all want me to be a member." She looked at Severin and explained. "I passed the bar a year ago. I haven't had much luck getting a job with a big firm, but I do free work for the public defender. This bunch gets into trouble so often they just want a lawyer on permanent duty."

"That's not true; we wanted you for your body." Squirt hugged her until Tinashe laughed and hugged her back. They were still hugging when Nita came into the room.

"I hate to interrupt," the leader of the Roaring Girls announced, "but I need Tinashe. I'm taking you around to all the tents so you can meet people. Tomorrow will be too crazy for a lot of introductions."

"Yes, Ma'am." Tinashe squared her shoulders and took a deep breath, sinking back into her submissive role.

Nita attached a leash to Tinashe's collar and led her out. No sooner had they left than Momma Bear appeared at the door.

"Get ready, you two. We've got a crowd out there," Momma warned them.

Severin needed a bathroom break before facing the Roaring Girls.

The building still had the public bathrooms from its days as a restaurant, but the men's room had been turned into Squirt's bedroom.

Squirt had a bed next to the urinal. There was a bank of sinks and a single handicapped stall. She also had a small bed, a desk with a computer on it, and a small bookshelf.

"Sorry about the mess." Squirt kicked aside an ebook reader and a few magazines which skittered across the tiled floor. Severin saw his bag sitting next to her bed. "Normally I'd offer you a floor to sleep on, but I have a hunch neither of us are going to have a good night's rest."

Severin did his business in the stall, and then reported for duty. The sun had gone down and the bar had two dozen or more women in it. Momma Bear greeted him with a butt plug in her hand. It was a round bulb about the size of a walnut, already slick with lube.

"Come on boy. We need to start stretching you out for tomorrow."

Severin approached her cautiously. Momma Bear reached out and grabbed his cock and balls with one powerful hand. Her large calloused hands had a firm grip and she squeezed until she saw his eyes widen with pain. He was so busy thinking about the pain in his genitals that he barely noticed when she slipped the butt plug inside him. The round section went in and his sphincter closed on the narrow part, holding it in place.

A few women had paused to watch the proceedings. "Spank it in!" one of them shouted. Momma glanced at Severin. The slave nodded a silent agreement. Severin hadn't had a decent punishment in days and Momma Bear seemed like a good woman to start with.

Momma Bear pulled out a bar stool and sat on it, pulling Severin across her lap. She manipulated him as if he were a doll. His ass was pointed up and he had to touch the floor with his hands for balance while his legs kicked in the air.

When she brought her palm down the noise was so loud that it instantly attracted the attention of everyone. Severin was trying to keep his body limp to control the pain, but when her big hand came down the shock of it was enough that he involuntarily tensed up. The spanking from Momma Bear hurt as badly as the heavy paddle the Viscountess used on him days earlier.

Momma Bear alternated between his cheeks with a good hard rhythm. She didn't hesitate to hit the base of the butt plug with her hand. Each time it sent a delicious shockwave through his body which made him jump like a fish caught on a line.

His whole ass tingled and burned. As the sensation made its way through his body Severin could feel his cock start to grow. The leather of her kilt felt coarse against his sensitive head. Beneath the kilt he could feel the hardness of her own cock.

When she felt she was finished Momma Bear lifted him up and stood him on his feet again. The blood rush caused him to sway for a second while he blinked away tears. She held him by one arm to steady him.

"Thank you, Ma'am."

"Anytime," Momma Bear chuckled.

She walked Severin to one of the metal support poles and made him sit with his back to the pole. The pole was just big enough to be uncomfortable when she stretched his arms back and locked his wrist cuffs into place. From his position on the floor Severin had a view of half the bar as well as the pool table and the video games. Apparently the Roaring Girls liked Mortal Kombat—who would have guessed?

Momma Bear left for a moment then returned with a spreader bar and locked his legs into place. Severin shifted his weight to accommodate the new position and caused the butt plug to move. Severin gave a little gasp.

"Are you all right, slave?" Momma asked, sounding genuinely concerned.

"Yes, Ma'am," Severin assured her. "I'm just trying to get comfortable."

"Good luck with that." She grinned. "I'll be at the bar if you need me."

She went back behind the bar, leaving Severin to sit. The woman who had tended bar earlier was gone. Severin could see Squirt filling a cart with dirty glasses and wheeling it to the big industrial dishwasher in the kitchen.

The pain in his ass was a comfortable throb, although sitting on the floor with no way to move made it worse. As much as he had enjoyed the spanking from Momma, he couldn't help but wish it had been the Viscountess who had punished him. The sight of all the powerful leather-clad women just made him miss her more than ever. He'd give anything for a nice hard slap in the face from her or even a stomp on his foot.

Most of the women in the bar seemed relatively indifferent to him. Several of them didn't have the RG sign on their arms, which meant they were wives or girlfriends and wouldn't be able to participate in the ceremony.

After several minutes of listening to Melissa Ethridge from the juke-box Severin saw Sir saunter in from the back hallway. Squirt had said she was staying in one of the back rooms. Earlier Sir had thrown on a T-shirt to punish Tinashe, but now she had replaced it with a body harness that crossed between her breasts and bristled with spikes. Apparently she was not in a hugging mood.

Sir stood over him and lit a cigarette from a pack in her pocket. She crouched down until she was level with his face and exhaled smoke. Severin turned his face away. He wasn't concerned with the secondhand smoke, but he didn't want to risk making eye contact with her. She was like a wild animal poised to spring. If he looked her in the eyes she might take it as a challenge.

"Hello fuckmeat," she said by way of greeting. "That's what you are. How does it feel to just sit here and know that tomorrow night we're going to be drilling those two holes of yours?"

Severin wasn't sure if Sir was expecting an answer. She continued talking.

"Tomorrow's going to be a train pull, and you're the little engine that could. That's after Tinashe uses Boybreaker on you. Can you even imagine how bad that hard body is going to fuck you?"

Severin could imagine it. He found the thought both exciting and frightening.

"You're scared," Sir told him, easily reading his thoughts. She blew on the tip of the cigarette until it burned like a branding iron. "I don't blame you. I don't think you're scared enough."

She held the tip of the cigarette up to his nipple. She brushed it across the tender flesh, moving quickly enough that he felt only an instant of searing pain. Then she put the cigarette back in her mouth and puffed it back to life again.

"I hate guys that come in here and think they're all tough. They treat us like we're some kind of joke, and at the last minute they pull a Safeword so they can slink off and tell all their friends about how they pulled one over on the big bad leatherdykes. I fucking hate that."

She moved her arm and started to work on the other nipple. This time she didn't move the searing tip away until he cried out in pain.

"If you're going to Safeword I want to hear it now. I want to know what you're made of before tomorrow so we can start making other plans. If I were you I'd Safeword before I get to your dick. I can put out a whole carton on a guy's dick. Trust me, I've done it."

Severin blinked away tears and looked into her eyes. So far she had been careful not to make more than minor burns. If she was going to seriously torture him until he used his Safeword than he'd be foolish to let her continue.

The worst part was Severin could tell she wasn't really mad at him. From the way she was talking Sir was still pissed over the last guy who had backed out and then attacked them online. Severin knew he wasn't the kind of person who'd do that, but there was no way he could prove it to her.

Sir laughed a little and held the cigarette over his crotch. She made a circle with her wrist, slowly lowering it. There was so much dominant energy in the room that he hadn't fully lost the last erection. His cock lay half erect across his testicles.

Severin looked around and saw Nita coming through the door, followed by Tinashe and the slender woman with the metal bands on her wrists and ankles who had cleaned Nita's bike. When Nita stopped and put her hands on her hips the woman in metal sank to her knees. Clearly she was Nita's personal property. Tinashe stood respectfully, hands behind her back. All three women looked a little flushed, as if they had run to the bar.

"I thought I said no permanent marks," Nita said in a voice that cut through the music.

"He'll heal," Sir said. She glanced around the room to see if anyone thought that she was funny, but no one laughed.

Severin knew that Sir was actually right, no permanent damage had been done, at least not yet.

"Let it go," Nita said, taking a step closer.

Sir did not back down. Her body stiffened and her jagged dyke energy filled the room. It crashed into the wave of power that was coming off of Nita.

"I'm tired of this bullshit," Sir snarled. "He's going to fold just like all the others."

"He'll sure as hell fold if you keep fucking with him. We need to give him a chance."

"I'm just..." Sir's voice broke and her dominant energy wavered. "I don't want another bad ceremony. I gave the others a chance and look what happened."

There was raw emotion in her words. She desperately needed the ceremony to go well. It was clear how important the Roaring Girls were to her.

"Whatever happens will happen," Nita said gently. She had been stepping closer so the whole bar couldn't hear what they said. "Is that the only thing bothering you?"

"No, where the hell is Tycho?"

"She can take care of herself better than anyone. This isn't the first time she's flaked on us. Remember the trip to Mexico?"

"I remember," Sir's shoulders sagged. Her dominant energy began to flicker, then fade away. "It's just that whenever I spar with her it gets all my crazy out and I haven't seen her in weeks."

"If anything's happened to her, we'll find out," Nita promised.

Now that the crisis seemed to have passed, Momma Bear slipped up to stand on the other side of Severin.

"I have emergency keys to Tycho's place," Momma Bear said. "If you want we can check it out."

"We'll do it on Sunday, after the ceremony," Nita said firmly. "As for tomorrow night, no matter what happens at the initiation, we'll deal with it, right?"

Sir looked away. She took a deep breath and let it out before she answered.

"Right."

"Then kiss me and tell me everything's all right."

"It's all right," Sir said sheepishly. She went to Nita and planted a kiss on her cheek.

"What, you call that a fucking kiss?"

Sir gave a snort of laughter and came forward more boldly. She grabbed the front of Nita's vest with both hands and yanked Nita forward, forcing her head down to Sir's height. Sir planted a deep passionate kiss on her. Both their tongues were hard at work.

The kiss went on for quite a while. Several women in the bar cheered. By the time they broke off, both were flushed and out of breath.

While Nita and Sir hugged out their differences Momma Bear produced a salve and spread it across Severin's nipples. The cooling balm made him feel better at once.

"You'll be fine," she assured him.

"Thanks. I notice Tycho's name keeps coming up, Squirt mentioned her too."

"She's kind of a big deal around here. She and Sir are pretty tight."

"Then why do you have the keys to Tycho's place?"

"You ask a lot of questions for a guy with a butt plug up his ass," Momma Bear chuckled. "Relax. Nita said you were going to give us the third degree on Sunday. To answer your question, Ty and Sir are friends, not lovers. I get the keys because I'm the responsible one."

Nita and Sir went off together followed by Nita's slave. Tinashe was put to work entertaining on the dance stage. Surprisingly the former basketball player wasn't a very good dancer, despite being in superb physical condition. After she trudged her way through two songs Momma Bear took pity on her and sent Squirt to the stage to help.

Squirt had been working the bar all night and was eager to get away from it. The former stripper rushed to the stage and soon helped Tinashe grind her body against the pole. Being "forced" to make love to each other onstage looked like the most fun either of them had all evening.

Momma Bear eventually came and freed Severin.

"Nita says you can make it an early night," she explained.

"I'm fine with some punishment if you want."

"Don't worry, we'll beat the shit out of you tomorrow, I promise. For now, just get some sleep."

As he left the bar Severin looked back at Squirt and Tinashe. They were working a double ended dildo into themselves while a crowd gathered around the stage struck them with single tails. He couldn't help but feel jealous, even though he knew most of the Roaring Girls wouldn't have any interest in him. "Lesbian biker gang," Squirt had told him earlier. "It's just what it says on the tin."

Momma Bear insisted that he have another, larger butt plug inserted to sleep in. This one hurt more going in and had to be held in place with duct tape. "Trust me," she said. "You'll be glad you're stretched tomorrow."

He was allowed to go to the bathroom in Squirt's bedroom before the plug was put in. He took the opportunity to retrieve his bag. Since they had a shortage of beds, Severin was put outside on a concrete deck where a small nest of blankets had been prepared for him. They hadn't been able to scrape up a pillow, but he found that by bunching up one of the blankets he could make something soft to rest his head on. The desert at night was surprisingly chilly.

When Momma Bear left him Severin stared out at the sea of tents.

There was loud music playing and several women were dancing ecstatically around a bonfire. It looked like some wild pagan rite that he desperately wanted to be a part of.

I'll never sleep under these conditions, Severin thought.

He closed his eyes and when he opened them again it was morning.

Chapter Twenty-Eight

The day of the big field hockey game between east dorm and west dorm was bright and sunny. The students spent most of the morning washing their uniforms or hitting the books in the library. As she walked to the office to make her phone call the Viscountess saw yet another student heading to Miss Symons' cabin with her books for a mid-morning cram session. The history teacher would probably be too exhausted to even give the test if her whole weekend was booked that solidly.

Everyone gathered in the bleacher seats next to the grassy field marked off for the game. It looked to be a friendly but fierce rivalry between the two dorms. Coach had apparently trained both teams, which must have made strategy an interesting challenge.

Of course Monica and her friends were cheerleaders. The Viscountess wasn't a bit surprised to see them in their tiny skirts, waving their pompoms and showing off their flat stomachs in the abbreviated cheerleader uniforms.

The Viscountess knew very little about field hockey and she hoped she could slip away before she learned anything more. By the middle of the first quarter when the crowd was starting to get into the game, the Viscountess, Felicity, and Peggy took off. They crept to the back of the bleachers and onto the grass.

Two students were already making love on the grass, their skirts hiked up, their bodies pressed tightly together. Obviously they enjoyed living dangerously. Even if Monica was busy, every single teacher was in attendance at the game.

The trio went unchallenged past the gym and the barn with its horses. The riding trail was beautiful, winding its way through the woods. Peggy and Felicity stepped off the trail at a spot they recognized.

Just out of sight of the trail was a clearing about thirty feet wide, surrounded by an almost perfect circle of trees. There was evidence of past parties, some cigarette butts and a few empty bottles.

"This is it," Felicity said unnecessarily.

The Viscountess looked around. She wasn't sure what she was

looking for, but she felt that if there was a clue, it had to be here, where Amy and her mystery biker girl vanished. There didn't seem to be any sign of footprints.

There was, however, a round depression in the ground. It looked as though something the size of a beach ball had sat there. The sight of it stirred the Viscountess. She had to find more.

If Severin were here he would come up with something. The Viscountess looked around desperately. Severin would have just pulled some important clue out of thin air, like that arrow stuck in the tree.

The Viscountess blinked. An arrow stuck in a tree?

"Help me get that."

She pointed to the arrow. It looked nothing like the ones they had been shooting the previous day. Peggy obligingly got down on all fours so the Viscountess could have a platform to stand on. She reached the arrow and with some difficulty pulled it out.

The arrow was made of wood, not carbon composite. It had white fletching that seemed to come from an actual bird. Most interesting of all, there was something written along the shaft. The long curving letters looked vaguely like Arabic, but the Viscountess suspected that it wasn't any language from this world.

"So now we're trespassing," a curt voice said. Felicity gasped. Peggy gave a soft squeak of terror. Even the Viscountess felt her blood turn cold. It was Miss Krause and she was flanked by Monica, still in her cheerleading outfit. "This place is off limits to all students."

Peggy got to her feet, wiping the dirt from her knees. "I'm sorry, we were just, um."

"I know what you were doing—violating school rules. We've discussed this before." Miss Krause turned her powerful gaze on Felicity. The girl seemed to be having a hard time breathing, her eyes were riveted to the ground and she didn't dare look up. "After two days ago I thought you'd learned your lesson."

"I'm sorry," Felicity stammered. "I didn't mean..."

Miss Krause didn't even wait for her to finish her sentence. The Headmistress turned her gaze on Desire. Desire shuddered, feeling the dominant energy that flowed off the older woman. Miss Krause reached out with a thin hand and pinched her cheek.

"As for you, young lady, I've had quite enough of your lies. Did you really think you could fool me?"

Desire opened her mouth to speak, but the words caught in her throat.

"Someone tried to break in here with a pony cart," Miss Krause continued. "Then you showed up. Well, you wanted to be a student. Now you are one, how do you like it?"

Blinking away the tears from her eyes Desire managed to speak at last. "Please," she said, aware of how pathetic her voice sounded. "You can do whatever you want to me, but let them go. They had no part in this. It's all my fault."

"How noble," Miss Krause gave a dry laugh. "We'll see how noble you are when I'm done with you. We're going back to my office where I will show you how proper discipline is maintained. Tomorrow morning you will be expelled."

Peggy and Felicity started sobbing and hugged each other. Monica glanced over at Miss Krause.

"Your office? What about the assembly?"

"There will be plenty of time for that later. I want this done in private, but don't worry, your two friends will get to watch you." Miss Krause paused, seeing the arrow for the first time. "What is that?"

"It's nothing."

"Give it to me."

Desire held onto the arrow. It was her only clue, the very thing that she had come to the school for. Monica came forward. She wore her cheerleader's uniform like a leather corset, radiating cruelty from every pore of her lithe, nubile body. She yanked the arrow out of Desire's hands and gave it to Miss Krause.

"You will learn not to defy me," Miss Krause announced. "Now move, all of you."

The three girls were marched back to the administration building. They could hear the cheers from the crowd as they passed the playing field. Everyone was at the game. No one would even know what happened to them.

Desire knew she had to stand up to Miss Krause. Unfortunately she also knew that she had violated the school rules that she had promised to uphold. She really was guilty of trespassing and Desire doubted that she'd be able to resist Miss Krause until after the punishment. The important thing was she had to find a way to get the arrow back.

The three schoolgirls faced Miss Krause's large desk. Monica sat on the desk smirking. Nurse Kelly had been called in just in case she was needed, besides having her there added to the humiliation.

"Felicity, I am very disappointed in you. Clearly you are unworthy of the privileges we've bestowed on you. I fear I have no choice but to break you in the ranks and return you to regular classes."

Felicity sobbed while Monica gave a snort of laughter.

"As for you Peggy, no amount of punishment ever seems to improve your behavior, but I'm certain Monica here can come up with something. In fact, I'm certain Monica can come up with something suitable for both of you."

"It would be my pleasure, Miss Krause." Monica grinned and clasped her hands together.

"Before we begin, please fetch the bag from my refrigerator."

Desire saw Monica go to a small refrigerator located beneath a bookcase. What sort of punishment started with the refrigerator?

Monica brought a sealed plastic bag to Miss Krause. The older woman opened the bag and unwrapped an object about the size of her hand with long shafts sticking up like fingers. At the sight of it Desire felt her stomach knot in fear. Nurse Kelly stiffened.

"Miss Krause, that's been in there long enough to ferment," Nurse Kelly said, she seemed to be keeping her voice neutral to avoid causing concern to the students.

"So it has," Miss Krause said agreeably. "I think it will suitable accompaniment to Desire's punishment.

The scent coming off it was very powerful. Desire tried to keep her face blank, but her body language gave her away. Miss Krause looked at her and smiled.

"I can see you recognize this Desire. Why don't you explain it to your friends?"

"It's ginger root." Desire forced the words past her throat that had seemingly closed up on her.

"Figging," Felicity said in a hushed whisper, staring at the root as if it were an unexploded bomb. "I've heard of it, but I've never seen it done."

"Oh, I only save it for special occasions like this." Miss Krause donned rubber gloves and brought a paring knife from a drawer. She began to carve the root, peeling off the dark outer layer to reveal the paler heart of the root, glistening with beads of fluid that would burn and itch if applied to sensitive flesh. The scent of the ginger grew even stronger.

While the root was being prepared, Monica appeared bored. She picked up a black marker from the desk and crossed to Peggy.

"Just because you're not getting it in front of the assembly doesn't mean I can't have fun with you," she informed her victims. "I didn't get a chance to make you do your trick yesterday, so let's make up for that."

Monica took the marker and carefully wrote the word PIGGY across Peggy's forehead. The voluptuous schoolgirl made a sort of whimpering sound as she felt the marker touch her flesh. After a pause Monica decided one insult wasn't enough and wrote LOSER across Peggy's cheek.

Miss Krause barely glanced up from her work. Peggy's whole body shook slightly, as if the humiliation were physical blows that she could not endure.

Bypassing Desire, Monica went to Felicity next. The perky beauty had bangs that covered her forehead, but that did not spare her.

"You know, you were pretty stupid for getting involved in this," Monica informed her. "Let's make it official."

Monica wrote the word STUPID on Felicity's cheek. Tears sprang up in Felicity's eyes.

"Oh, and just in case anyone has forgotten your position on the social ladder," Monica added with a chuckle. She wrote LOSER on Felicity's other cheek. "Perfect. I can do this every morning for you two, so everyone will know what losers you are. Don't bother to thank me, it's all part of my job as Prefect."

By then Miss Krause had finished carving a serviceable butt plug from the ginger root. As Desire watched it take shape, the dread anticipation was almost too much to bear. Desire had seen it done when she was being trained in Victoria, but it had never been done to her. She knew that watching the instrument being prepared was part of the punishment, but knowing that did not help her.

"Monica, get the pillow."

As Miss Krause commanded, the blonde cheerleader went to the small couch and lifted a cylindrical pillow with a dark pillow case. It was exactly the right length to stretch across the side of the desk and could be secured in place with small straps.

The desk was cleared of all items. The last thing Miss Krause did was take the white shavings of the ginger root she had carved and sprinkle them across the pillow. It was obvious exactly what part of Desire's anatomy was going to be pressed against the fresh cuttings.

"Miss Krause I must protest," Nurse began, "This is inhumane."

"I shall be the judge of what is appropriate," Miss Krause said sharply. Her thin body bristled with dominant energy. "Unless of course you think you're above the discipline of this institution."

"No, I..." The voice of Nurse Kelly broke off as a shudder of submission passed through her. Despite being dominant with the students, Nurse was clearly a switch and Miss Krause knew how to keep her in line. "I'm sorry, Miss Krause."

"That's more like it." Miss Krause turned her powerful gaze on Desire. The schoolgirl was looking at the floor, unable to raise her head for fear of meeting Miss Krause's gaze, or even worse getting a better look at the root that had been shaped for her. "It's up to you now Desire. This is a very severe punishment, I won't lie to you. If you don't have the courage to face it, I'm sure your friends will understand. You're going to be expelled in either case, so it's up to you."

With some difficulty Desire raised her head. She swallowed and found that her mouth was very dry. She knew that using her Safeword was the smart thing to do. Unfortunately she also knew that she had broken the school rules and deserved the punishment. Worst of all, how could she show cowardice when she was leaving Felicity and Peggy behind at the mercy of Monica? Desire knew she had to show as much courage as them and face whatever was in store for her.

"I think I'm ready, Miss Krause," Desire announced when she was confident she could speak without having her voice tremble too much.

Miss Krause seemed almost surprised at the answer, but if that was so, she quickly recovered.

"Very well, please lift your skirt and approach the desk."

Desire walked around to the pillow roll sprinkled with ginger shavings. She raised her skirt all the way around, needing both hands to do it.

"Monica, will you do the honors please?"

"With pleasure." Monica grinned from ear to ear as she knelt beside Desire and began working her white cotton panties down her legs. She took her time about it, passing her fingers across the swollen lips of Desire's labia. When she felt the wetness there she laughed and teased, "Wow, your mom wasn't kidding when she named you. Why didn't she just call you Slut?"

"That's enough, Monica," Miss Krause admonished the girl. The time for verbal humiliation was past. Now they were moving on to more important things.

Monica yanked the panties all the way down, forcing her to step out of them so her legs could be spread. The Desire stood there awkwardly with Monica leering at her until she felt Miss Krause's firm hand between her shoulder blades, pushing her down. Her body pressed against the rounded pillow that lifted and displayed her as well as protected her from that hard edge of the desk. Her skirt was bunched in the small of her back.

Her tender flesh pushed against the ginger shavings. She felt a tingle, but it was not unbearable, not yet. Miss Krause put a dash of lubricant on her finger and inserted it into Desire's ass. When the finger was withdrawn it left enough lube behind to allow penetration, but not a thick enough coating to give her any protection from the ginger root.

The long white shaft was positioned against her sphincter. Desire knew that she had taken larger objects there, but somehow nothing quite as frightening as this. With a quick motion Miss Krause forced it in, driving the carved root deeply until the thick head was all that was visible.

Desire cried out and her whole body lurched, almost bringing her to her feet. The tight ring of muscle that had been violated convulsed, closing reflexively on the ginger, but as her muscle tensed she felt a slow burning make its way past the coolness of the object. In addition, the shifting of her weight had caused more of the shavings to push against her tender flesh. The tingling and itching was becoming intolerable.

The urge to reach down and touch herself was almost impossible to resist. Fortunately Desire needed no self-control, for the ever helpful Monica was already prepared. Apparently she had experience with girls bent across Miss Krause's desk. Monica tied hemp rope to hidden attachment points and drew the rope up to the desktop.

With a speed born of much practice, she knotted the rope about Desire's wrists and pulled it tight, stretching her arms out as much as she could. Desire found herself reaching for the other side of the wide desk with almost all her body's weight on the desktop. There was no way she could lift herself off the terrible pillow with only the balls of her feet on the floor.

There was no need to tie her legs. The insidious power of the ginger root was such that if she tried to close her legs, or even tried to tense her muscles the terrible burning instantly worsened. All she could do was stay as motionless as possible, her body open and vulnerable to the punishment.

Miss Krause took her time choosing a cane. She tried several, swinging them through the air with nasty hisses until she found one that was just right. She did not give Desire a chance to see the instrument that was to chastise her, but instead walked briskly to the desk.

"Are you ready, my dear?"

"Yes, Miss Krause," Desire managed to say, trying to sound brave for Felicity and Peggy's sake.

"Good." The older dominant woman gave a dry chuckle. "Normally I tell my charges that this will hurt me more than it hurts them, but in this case it's simply not true."

She raised her arm and brought the thin cane down on Desire's ass. It cut a line of agony across her, making her cry out and jump, held down by her outstretched arms. The pain also made her tense, causing the burning to sear through her. Desire tried to will her muscles to relax, but it seemed to do no good.

Miss Krause made sure the pain of the first blow had fully sunk in before she delivered the second stroke. For Desire the second was worse that the first. She had just managed to relax herself when she heard the cane whizzing through the air and immediately tensed. She regretted that at once for it caused the root to burn and throb so badly that she was already in pain when the cane struck.

The second welt appeared immediately above the first. Miss Krause aimed the third stroke lower, close to the sweet spot where the buttocks met the upper thighs.

There was another stroke, and perhaps a fourth, Desire could not tell. The agony was beyond words, it came from a raw, preverbal place deep within her. Desire was no longer even a teenager. The cane had reduced her to a bawling, sobbing infant.

Suddenly one of the cane strokes felt different than the others. There was a loud crack and the plug inside of her lurched painfully.

"You ungrateful child, look what you've done!" Miss Krause threw something on the desk. Desire tried to blink the tears out of her eyes long enough to focus on it. The cane had been broken when it hit the ginger root butt plug, "We'll just have to continue with a thicker cane."

"Give it to her! Make her pay for that," Monica taunted.

Desire made a sort of choking noise in an attempt to speak. On that last stroke she had jumped so hard that there was now a tiny shard of ginger pressing against her clitoris. She could feel it like a red hot needle in her flesh.

At that instant Desire knew that she was broken, that she had no choice but to use her Safeword. The thought of the torture continuing was too much for her, this woman had utterly and completely beaten her.

Before she could speak, or even form the Safeword in her mind, Felicity and Peggy must have sensed what was about to happen. The two schoolgirls ran to the end of the desk where Desire's arms were tied and they could see her face.

"Come on Des, you can do it," Peggy gushed.

"You can make it," Felicity added hopefully.

Desire looked at the shining faces of her school chums now marked with the humiliating writing. She thought about how much Monica would enjoy seeing her fold. If she gave up now Monica would never let anyone forget it.

"Well, what's it to be?" Miss Krause asked, giving her a few taps with the heavier cane.

Desire took a deep breath. She drew the strength from her friends to speak with a voice that was only a little shaky.

"Thank you, Miss Krause. Please continue."

Miss Krause said nothing. If there was an expression on her face, Desire could not see it. The cane came down hard on her quivering cheeks. Again she clenched and again the ginger burned through her. Desire saw her friends sobbing in sympathy for her, and then the sweat that ran from her brow blinded her to everything in the room.

If it was possible for cane strokes to show emotion it felt as if the new blows were more angry and frustrated than the first strokes. Miss Krause struck with her full strength. The thicker instrument did not cut as deeply, but it made harsh, bruising impact.

Miss Krause no longer waited for each blow to sink in before launching the next. As the strokes came faster and faster it became impossible for Desire to tell them apart. It was like an avalanche of pain, the agony of the cane and the burning of the ginger working together, each magnifying the other.

She had reached the sweet spot. Although it seemed impossible, the agony actually increased. Blows from the cane fell like rain. Desire could no longer feel her feet. The room spun about her and she burned as if she were waist deep in lava.

"Enough!"

The firm voice filled the room. From behind her Desire could hear some sort of a struggle, but she was too weak to turn her head. Felicity lifted Desire's head and wiped the strands of hair from her face where they had been plastered in place by sweat.

Desire saw that Nurse had grabbed Miss Krause's wrist and was physically stopping her from continuing. For a split second neither of them moved. Monica was sitting in Miss Krause's chair and had clearly been playing with herself. Her panties were down around her ankles and her fingers were sticky.

"That's enough and you know it," Nurse continued. There was nothing submissive about her now. There was a strange energy in the room and Desire realized with a shock that "enough" had to be Nurse's Safeword. She had called the Scene off when it had gotten out of hand.

"Of course. You're quite right." Miss Krause lowered the arm that held the cane. During the punishment she had been transformed. Her iron grey hair had come loose from the bun and tumbled down to her shoulders. She was flushed and excited, her nipples poking the front of her blouse.

Felicity and Peggy did not wait to be ordered before they set Desire free. With some difficulty she rose to her feet. Desire's legs didn't seem able to support her weight so her two friends put one of her arms over each shoulder. The ginger root slipped from her and fell to the floor. Desire almost whimpered at the touch of her dress sliding across the cheeks of her ass.

"You must forgive me, my dear," Miss Krause said to Desire, sounding very earnest. She was holding the cane as if it had suddenly become an unfamiliar object. "This was quite unprofessional of me. I have no excuse save that I am under a great deal of pressure."

"I'm sure you are," the punished girl smiled slightly. She did not actually forgive Miss Krause for her transgression. "Perhaps we should discuss it tomorrow morning. I'd like to get some rest."

"Certainly," Miss Krause said graciously.

"My office, now! Get her on a cot," Nurse ordered.

As they took their friend to the nurse's office Felicity and Peggy pondered the change in Desire's demeanor. When she spoke Desire had sounded more confident, more sure of herself, almost as if she were older.

The Viscountess took a deep breath, throwing off the last vestiges of her submissive Persona. Severin had been right as usual: this place was designed to take away her power. She had come into it as a confident adult, but she had been brought down to the level of a child by the simplest of means.

It wasn't the first time that the Viscountess had seen someone lose control during a Scene, but it had been a long time since she had been on the receiving end. She was grateful that Nurse had been there to intervene.

Interestingly the Viscountess felt that she had learned something from the experience. The guilt that Miss Krause felt when she lost her temper made the Headmistress's hidden submissive side bubble to the surface. Like the nurse, Miss Krause was a switch. The Viscountess felt that now that her own dominant side was back in place she would have no trouble turning the tables on the stern Headmistress.

In her office Nurse Kelly ordered the Viscountess to remover her skirt completely. Peggy was carrying her underwear, having made no attempt to give it back to her.

"Put her on the bed face down. That's right, girls." When the Viscountess was comfortable Nurse handed each girl some latex gloves and a small jar containing a white cream. "Put this on her, it'll help with the welts and take away the sting of the ginger."

The two schoolgirls eagerly donned the gloves and began to apply the soothing cream to their friend.

"I'm going to get some food for you. Stay here until I get back," Nurse continued. "Please throw the bolt on the door when I leave."

She's worried about Monica creeping back in to torment us, the Viscountess thought. It was a sign of how much the girl had terrorized the school.

Felicity and Peggy wasted no time getting to work on the Viscountess once the door was locked. Their quick, clever hands were all over her. The cream was soothing, and as the Viscountess settled into the bed she felt Felicity reaching down between her legs and slipping a finger inside her.

"Um guys," the Viscountess said. She wanted to tell them that they didn't have to do that, but the fact was it felt really good.

"Oh, you totally got some ginger here," Felicity teased as she continued stroking.

"And here." Peggy inserted a finger, slick with the soothing cream into the recently punished sphincter.

The Viscountess sighed and squirmed. She could no longer pretend it didn't feel good. The last few days had left her very aroused and frustrated, but she hadn't been aware of it until she felt the gentle touch. Of course this was strictly against school rules, which made it all the more exciting. Probably that was why Nurse had them lock the door.

By the time there was a sharp knock at the door announcing the nurse's return the Viscountess had already experienced two delicious orgasms. Peggy squeaked and jumped to her feet. She could not possibly have looked less guilty when she opened the door, but the nurse didn't seem to notice.

She brought so much food that she needed a wheeled cart for all of it. All three of the students stared at the feast. There was cold chicken and ham, and fresh fruit from the teacher's table along with freshly baked bread. There was an entire apple pie for desert.

"You missed lunch, and I felt going to supper probably wasn't a good idea," Nurse Kelly explained. "Dig in, ladies."

The Viscountess found she was famished. Peggy squealed with delight and began to pile meat on slices of bread. They both had quite forgotten the humiliating writing on their faces.

"Thank you for this," the Viscountess said, making eye contact with the nurse. "May I ask you a question?"

"Of course."

"Do you know what happened to the arrow Miss Krause took from me?"

"It's in a drawer in her desk."

"Please make sure nothing happens to it."

"I'll make certain of it." Nurse Kelly paused. "I'm sorry this happened."

"So am I," the Viscountess informed her. She felt the nurse gently slipping into Subspace. "Don't worry, it will all be straightened out tomorrow."

"Will there be anything else?"

The Viscountess looked her up and down from her starched cap to her long legs encased in the white stockings. If they were back home in her dungeon she would have no trouble thinking on things for the lovely nurse to do, but she had to remind herself she was still at school.

"That will be all, thank you," the Viscountess dismissed her.

As the nurse left the room Felicity watched her go with a sigh. "She is so hot."

Everyone agreed to that. As they ate, Peggy's face suddenly fell, her good mood vanishing.

"I just remembered," she said. "Tomorrow is Sunday. The worst punishments of the week are always saved for Sunday."

"She's right," Felicity sighed. "Monica always singles out someone for something special on Sunday."

Their unspoken dread filled the room. The student they knew as Desire was being expelled, but they would have to face the wrath of Monica by themselves.

"Brave heart, girls," the Viscountess said, settling into her pillow with a secret smile. "Maybe tomorrow something good will happen."

She heard Peggy and Felicity still fretting as she drifted off to sleep.

Chapter Twenty-Nine

The day of the initiation ceremony dawned bright and clear. Severin was sleeping near the outdoor showers that had been put in for the women in the tents. It was really just a water pipe with a few shower heads, obviously no hot water. Severin guessed that this was where Squirt had washed herself off after the marathon fisting session the previous night.

There was no form of privacy at the showers. Everyone would be able to see him, but Severin decided to bathe anyway. Most of the women in the tents were still asleep. By the time he was done he could smell a delicious breakfast cooking.

Momma Bear was at the stove making an enormous omelet. Bacon and sausage were on the grill. What Severin focused on was the huge pot of coffee.

"Help yourself," Momma Bear said. "This omelet's for you if you want it."

"Thank you, Ma'am," Severin remembered to say as he fixed his coffee. When he slid into his chair Momma Bear put the plate full of omelet in front of him and placed bottles of ketchup and salsa next to him.

"Enjoy it. This is the only meal you get today." Seeing the surprise on his face she quickly explained. "You can get snacks, but the less you have in your stomach for the ceremony the better. I speak from experience."

Squirt staggered in, her body marked with random patterns from a single tail. When she had her coffee she collapsed into the chair across from Severin.

"I see the condemned ate a hearty meal," she teased.

"Apparently it's all I get."

"Speaking as the one had to mop the floor after the last guy tossed his cookies, you have my thanks."

"Anything for the cause," Severin said between mouthfuls of the omelet.

Tinashe arrived looking exhausted, but well-scrubbed. It seemed that she had found one of the showers in the building that had hot water. She chose tea over coffee and settle into a chair.

"So, is everybody ready?" Tinashe asked.

"I think I am," Severin told her.

"Good, because I'm not so sure I'm ready."

"You'll be great," Squirt gushed. "Everyone already loves you."

"I know."

"I believe in you, come on, slave solidarity." Squirt held up her fist. After a moment's hesitation Tinashe gave her a fist bump. Abruptly Squirt turned to Severin. "Come on, you're one of us now. Slave solidarity."

She held up her fist to him and Severin gave her a fist bump. Squirt then made him do the same thing with Tinashe. Severin had seen other people do the fist bump thing before, but he had never actually done it himself. He found the little ritual oddly endearing.

For the slaves most of the day was spent cleaning up the building. Nita called Tinashe into her office for a conference that lasted over an hour. Squirt confided to Severin that this was the long talk about the future of the Roaring Girls that every potential new member got. She was also being given a chance to back out with no hard feelings.

In the early afternoon the Body Mod arrived who was going to put the mark on Tinashe. Severin always found the Mods quite interesting. Each of them had altered their bodies in some ways that was unique to the individual at the cost of a great deal of pain and discomfort. Despite this they made a great show of being uninterested in S&M. They considered the fact that they could see through the Blindfold to be a sign of their spiritual advancement and their multiple piercings, elaborate tattoos, and other even stranger modifications to be entirely artistic.

This particular Body Mod was named Serra Finn, Severin was told later. She was naked, which was to say that she was covered only by her tattoos. There were ram's horns inked on the sides of her shaved head and her torso was dotted with alchemical symbols. She rippled when she walked, the stark black tribal lines on her arms and legs accentuating her muscles whenever she moved. As she walked past Severin he saw that Serra had dragonfly wings tattooed on her back. A series of chakra points were marked with brightly colored ink, a definite contrast to the black ink that mostly covered her.

She had brought a bag containing her tools. Once she had set up she also spent time talking to Tinashe. She was no doubt explaining the procedure and quite possibly giving the young lawyer yet another chance to back out.

The bar was closed for the day, something that pissed off a good many women. As the day wore on more and more of them came up looking for a drink. Anyone with a Roaring Girl mark was turned away. If they insisted on drinking Momma Bear put an X on the back of their hand with a permanent marker which would deny them entry at the ceremony. Apparently Sir was on patrol at the tents to enforce the rules there.

Severin was grateful to see the no alcohol rule being enforced. The previous night several of the women in the bar were clearly drunk. Severin had noticed that none of the drunk women were giving or receiving punishment, but it made him feel better to see that Nita had decided to beef up security for the ceremony.

Later, Severin got a chance to speak with Tinashe while they were loading soft drinks into the refrigerator. She confirmed that she was going to go all the way with the ceremony.

"I'll try to be gentle Severin, but that dildo's a nasty piece of work," she told him.

"Do what you can and I'll handle the rest," Severin assured her. "By the way, I was wondering what you know about Tycho."

"Not much, what do you want to know?"

"Have you been topped by her?"

"Sure, lots of times. I even went to clean her apartment once."

"What was that like?" Severin gently pressed her for more details.

"Not bad, I dusted and scrubbed the floors. Also I washed dishes and got caned for leaving water spots on the glasses. There was one weird thing. She had the door to the guest bedroom locked. I could tell someone was in there. I could hear them, but Tycho said it was empty."

"Weird."

"Tell me about it. When you look at all the crazy shit they do in public, what the hell would they have to hide behind a locked door? I just figured it was some married woman or a famous actress or something and let it go."

"And this was a few weeks ago?"

"No, it was back when I started my training. Must have been five, almost six months ago."

Severin frowned. Five or even six months earlier would be well before the rally where Amy was swept off her feet by one of the Roaring Girls. It looked like Tycho's mysterious guest had nothing to do with the case.

Severin pondered if he had acted rashly in focusing on Tycho. The ex-marine seemed like exactly the person who would break into a closed Dominion to meet up with her girlfriend. The timing of Tycho's disappearance and Amy vanishing from the school couldn't be a coincidence. On the other hand, it was far from conclusive evidence. His focus on Tycho could be blinding him to other theories. He still had no way of being sure Amy and her girlfriend weren't in one of the RV's.

As the time grew closer Severin could feel the fear growing inside of him. If the Viscountess had been there he would have had no doubt he could do this. Without her he was afraid he would fail. He resolved to act as if she were constantly standing over him, watching him the entire time. Even her imaginary presence made him feel better.

Momma Bear removed the last of the series of butt plugs and cleaned him out with an enema so the ceremony wouldn't be too messy. She also gave him another chance to back out.

"Forget about what Sir said," Momma told him. "If you want to call it quits, we'll understand."

"No, thanks. I think I'm fine."

"All right then." She smiled. "Let's get started."

The bar was crammed with about fifty women. With that many people the temperature had skyrocketed, despite the air conditioner. Everyone was eerily quiet as Severin was led to a chain hanging from the ceiling. Momma Bear attached his wrist cuffs to the chain, stretching him up onto the balls of his feet. Severin found he much preferred the laughing and teasing of the night before.

As the crowd formed a circle around him, Nita stepped forth. She was wearing only her vest, chaps and boots. She looked as hard and solid as a rocky outcropping that had been carved by the wind. Her slave marched behind her in perfect rhythm to her steps. She was carrying a tray with various instruments on it.

Silently Nita selected a flogger. It was the thin, stingy flogger she had been wearing when Severin had first met her. It might not have been a Named item, but it was clearly one that she had great familiarity with.

Nita laid into him. The blows were hard and fast, but they were all on target. Severin twisted on the chain, his body going back and forth as he tried to avoid the blows. She compensated for his movements and hit him harder still. The stinging leather was everywhere; it felt as if a layer of skin was being slowly removed.

Momma Bear entered the circle, having changed into a corset that hugged her massive body tightly, lifting and displaying her huge breasts. She started on him with another flogger, this one bigger, heavier. Her skill was no less than Nita's. The two women whipped him back and forth. The combination of the stinging and thudding floggers was almost too much sensation for his brain to process.

Just as Severin thought that he could take no more, the blows came to a halt. While he was being punished Tinashe had slowly approached. She was naked except for the harness that supported Boybreaker. Her dark body radiated dominant energy so great that only his chains kept Severin from sinking to the floor to worship at her feet.

"Where do you want him?" Momma asked.

"Bend him over the table in front of the mirror. I want to watch his face," Tinashe replied. Her voice rang with confidence. She had successfully thrown off the submissive state she had been living in for months.

Momma Bear led him over to a table near the wall and forced him to bend over. The Roaring Girls obviously chose their furniture well. Every table in the room was at the right height to present someone for penetration.

His hips were pressed against a blanket folded over the edge of the table. Momma attached his ankle cuffs to the table legs. Sir attached his wrist cuffs to the legs on the other side of the table, holding his arms almost as wide as his legs. Sir worked with brisk efficiency and didn't make eye contact.

In this position his feet were still on the floor, but he was bent over so far that most of his weight was on his hips. Squirt arrived with a pillow and a small plastic bucket that looked about five inches deep. She put the pillow under his chin, forcing him to look up at his own face in the big mirror on the wall. He looked nervous.

"If you start to throw up I'll take the pillow away and give you this." Squirt showed him the pan. Severin nodded his understanding.

In the mirror he saw Tinashe looming behind him as proud and powerful as a pagan goddess. Her body seemed to glow with raw female energy. Someone had been teasing her while Severin was being flogged, building her close to orgasm but not letting her come. She was a loaded gun, primed and ready and the cock between her legs was the trigger.

Momma Bear bustled about; making sure everything was well lubed. Tinashe came forward, adjusting her position. Boybreaker's cruel head began to push at his sphincter. It was almost gentle at first, but it grew more insistent. She began to move closer and gradually the tight ring of muscle was forced open.

Severin tried to relax, even to push out a little which would make it easier for the dildo to slide in. He could feel the contempt Boybreaker had for him. Severin remembered the cruel nature of the thing even as it lay in Nita's office and the memory made it hard to relax.

It was in him now. He could feel the power of it. She took possession of him slowly, letting him feel every inch of it as the shaft slowly disappeared into his body. Pain blossomed like a flower. People began cheering and clapping as her hips grew closer to his body. Her clitoris throbbed against the base of the dildo. Her orgasm was coming. It had the inevitability of a runaway train.

Suddenly she was all the way inside him. Severin wasn't even sure it had happened until he heard the cheers. When he looked in the mirror he saw her bending over him, only the top of her head visible. She was gripping the edge of the table for support. Every muscle in her body seemed to tense as she moved against him.

She began to grind against his ass, twisting her hips. Even the smallest motions she made were magnified by the dildo. It seemed to twist inside of him like a snake.

She would not be denied. Her orgasm was coming, closer, closer. Severin squeezed his eyes shut. He tried to meditate, to make himself an empty vessel for her to fill.

Suddenly she cried out. It was a high, animal sound and her whole body shook. Severin cried out a second later, his own scream deeper and more raw. All the power in her body at the moment of orgasm was channeled down Boybreaker and into his body. Severin felt it like a white hot beam that cut a path through him straight down the middle and out the top of his head.

There was a moment of disorientation and Severin felt a wave of nausea. The room spun wildly. The sound of the crowd cheering was a roar like a waterfall. When his vision cleared Severin thought he saw his own body lying face down, bent across the table. There was a woman-sized ball of energy behind him, moving back and forth with small but powerful motions.

Severin seemed to see himself the way Boybreaker saw him. Pathetic, worthless, useless. A wave of self-loathing coursed through him. He was suddenly crushed by the weight of thousands of years of oppression. For a split second he felt the horror of every woman who had been raped, the pain of every woman who had ever been beaten by a man.

Severin felt as if he were drowning in that sea of pain. There was too much suffering for him to bear. He understood why so many others had Safeworded. The weight of history was too much. Severin focused on all his experiences with the Viscountess and the powerful objects that had been used on him. He knew there was a way to keep this from overwhelming him.

Severin clung to his conversations with Tinashe. She didn't hate him. In fact, she seemed pretty much at ease with the whole male/female thing. It hadn't bothered her a bit to be naked in front of him, or to see him naked. Momma Bear had been a wife and was a mother. Nita was way too professional to let her emotions get in the way of an important ceremony. Even Sir, who would have gladly branded him with her cigarette, didn't really hate him personally. She was a ball of anger and he simply made a good target.

The dark emotions weren't coming from any of them; they were coming from Boybreaker itself. It was a tool designed to hurt men. Possibly it had been used by women who believed that all men should be treated this way. It carried a nasty stain of hatred and resentment. The power of the dildo played on Severin's own guilt at being a male in a male-dominated world. It would be so easy to succumb to that self-loathing, but Severin refused to knuckle under to eight inches of rubber, no matter how much it might hate him.

He focused on the here and now. He was Severin. He was a slave who belonged to the Viscountess and he was here to serve these women. That was all that mattered. The only thing that was important in the world was the happiness of these women, particularly the one behind him.

"Are you still with us?" a woman asked. Severin hadn't noticed her, but she was between his head and the mirror. There was a stethoscope around her neck and she had been taking his pulse from the vein in his wrist near his wrist cuff.

"Are you all right?" the woman asked. She was a very pretty blonde with a Southern accent. Severin wondered if he had actually passed out or if he was simply concentrating so hard he hadn't noticed her checking up on him.

He tried to nod and say that he was fine, but he found that trying to lift his head from the pillow just caused neck strain and his voice was a little creaky.

"Do you need to stop?" the woman asked again. This time Severin managed to shake his head.

Momma Bear brought a squeeze bottle with a straw to his lips and squirted some into his mouth. As he drank the cool water Nita crouched next to the table and took his hand.

"You don't have to talk," she said. "If you want to stop now just squeeze my hand."

"I'm fine," Severin managed to say. It was easier to talk once his throat was wet. In the mirror he saw Momma Bear letting Tinashe sip from the same bottle he had just drunk from.

Severin felt like he was in a boxing movie. His trainer had just put his mouth guard in and when the bell sounded he was going in for the next round.

Tinashe hadn't withdrawn Boybreaker. All the time Severin had been contemplating his situation she had been slowly and steadily pumping the dildo in and out. A few seconds ago she had been like a runaway train, now she was a steam train, slow and steady. As the big dildo slid in and out there was another orgasm building.

She leaned back away from him, withdrawing Boybreaker until only the head was in him. They were suddenly looking at each other in the mirror. Rivers of sweat were running down her dark body. Severin realized he was drenched, and most of the perspiration wasn't his own. She laughed. It was the pure unbridled joy of a woman taking her pleasure to a higher level.

"You want more?" she called to Severin. "I got more if you want it."

By way of answering Severin lifted his hips to meet her. She grinned, giving him a few hard spanks before driving home the dildo.

In and out she went, faster and faster. Severin could feel the power of Boybreaker trying to destroy him, but he fought to ignore it. He kept his eyes open this time, so he could see her. He wanted to serve her, not Boybreaker. Her pain he could take—in fact he wanted to take it. By seeing Boybreaker as merely an extension of Tinashe he was able to resist its power when her next orgasm flooded through him.

She had been moving faster and faster, pumping her hips, eyes closed. When another orgasm ripped out of her she snarled like an animal and unexpectedly pounded both fists against his shoulder blades. The added pain surprised him, but made it easier to focus as the energy permeated him.

"Fuck!" Tinashe announced. She tried to ease gently out of him, but lost her balance and stumbled. Several people rushed forward and caught her before she could fall, but Boybreaker wound up being pulled out harshly and quickly. Severin was glad not to have to feel it any more.

With Boybreaker still in its harness Tinashe was lifted to the shoulders of the crowd who carried her around the room cheering. Severin saw this in the mirror as Squirt and Momma Bear set him free. He was immediately rushed to the kitchen.

Severin sat on a chair in the kitchen. Momma Bear put a bottle of some sports drink in his hand while Squirt plied him with peanut butter M&Ms. When he'd had enough of the bottle Squirt popped M&Ms into his mouth.

The beautiful blonde with the stethoscope was wearing a sports bra and black thong underwear. She had a large medical bag on the kitchen table. First she checked Severin's blood pressure. As the cuff inflated she smiled at him.

"Don't let the outfit fool you," she informed him. "I'm an EMT. Nita calls me in when she thinks... Well, you know."

"So how am I doing?" Severin was trying to read the dial on the blood pressure cuff, but couldn't make it out. While the cuff was tightened she pressed the stethoscope into the crook of his arm to check his heartbeat.

"You're doing better than the last two. You're fully conscious and you're speaking in complete sentences. How do you feel?"

"Pretty good."

"How's your ass?"

"Sore."

By the time she had finished with his temperature and blood pressure, Nita came into the kitchen. The bar outside was still a scene of wild celebration.

"So how is he?"

"He'll live," the EMT informed her. "I need to check for tearing and bleeding before I give a green light to continue."

Severin obligingly got up from his chair and bent over the table. The EMT donned gloves, lubricated her fingers and picked up a small flashlight with her other hand.

"He's pretty raw, but I don't see any actual blood."

When Severin stood up he saw Nita with her hands on her hips. She was trying not to radiate dominance, but she couldn't hold it back completely.

"It's entirely up to you, Severin." Nita reminded him. "The next part is the gang bang. If you're not up to it just say so."

"I think I can manage, if you'll give me a minute to catch my breath."

"All right," Nita glanced at Momma Bear. "Let's go. Whenever you're ready, Severin, just come into the bar."

He nodded. Momma Bear and Nita left, and after a moment the EMT followed them. Severin noticed that she did not have the Roaring Girls mark on her arm. The ceremony was supposed to be members only, but they apparently made exceptions for their medical team.

Squirt and Severin continued to snack. There were crackers and cookies as well as the candy. She asked him how it was and Severin found he couldn't really describe it. He wanted to have a long talk with Nita about Boybreaker, but that would have to wait.

The food went through him almost at once. Severin raced to Squirt's room to use the toilet. He returned to the kitchen feeling much better. In fact he felt ready for more.

Just as they were about ready to go back out, the door swung open and Tinashe came in looking exhausted and amazingly beautiful. They had a towel around her neck where she had made some attempt to dry herself off.

"Severin, you were great," she gushed. "I'm so sorry I hit you there at the end. I don't know where that came from."

"No harm done."

"Okay, I have to go. Serra's setting up her stuff."

Severin followed her out to the bar. It was turning into a pretty wild party. Music had started up again and women were dancing in various stages of undress. Several of them were already making love.

Severin turned to say something to Squirt, but someone grabbed a handful of her hair and dragged her away. She flashed a smile at him as she left, giving him a glimpse of her dimples.

Nita, Sir, and Momma Bear were all waiting for him. All of them had their strap-ons hanging from their dildo harnesses. Sir had stripped down to nothing but the spiked body harness and Doc Martens as well as the belts around her waist and thighs holding the dildo. Severin stared at her cock, not certain what to make of it.

Her dildo looked like a tentacle. It was long and slightly curved and the suction cups on its underside glowed in the dark. Severin was still staring at it when she reached up and grabbed his shoulders, pulling him to his knees.

"What are you looking at fuckmeat? Get to work!"

She rammed the tentacle dildo into his mouth. Severin realized that it wasn't as big or as powerful as many of the dildos he'd taken, but its shape made him oddly hesitant. He'd seen way too much Hentai to be entirely comfortable with the thought of a tentacle entering his body. Eventually his submission won out over his squeamishness and he started to lick and suck.

"That's right, baby," Sir sneered. She took a fistful of his hair and held his head still while she drilled his mouth with savage thrusts of her hips. He gagged and choked and tried to turn away, but she held him fast. "Look at me, bitch, look at me when I'm fucking your face."

He did as she ordered, but no sooner had he made eye contact than she seemed to change her mind. She yanked him off of it and tossed him to the floor. He let himself go limp as she gave him a few sharp kicks.

Sir surprised him by getting on the floor. She pointed to the tentacle that rose up from between her legs.

"Go ahead, fuckmeat, show us what you're made of," she thrust her hips up in the air to give him encouragement.

Positioning himself carefully Severin squatted over her and lowered himself down on the tentacle. He could feel the lubricated tip of it teasing its way past the opening, sliding easily into him. There was no way he could maintain his balance. He had to simply sit on her cock. It might have looked to an observer that he was dominating her since he was on top, but she twisted her hips and thrust upward every chance she got, reminding him who was in charge.

When Severin looked up he saw Big Daddy hanging in the air in front of him. Momma Bear had donned the dildo harness so that the fat little cock was slung under the corset. He leaned forward to take it in his mouth only to have her laugh and slap his face.

"Look at you, you're Daddy's little cock whore aren't you?" she teased.

Severin nodded and leaned forward, but she kept the dildo out of his mouth.

"Say it, tell me you're Daddy's little cock whore."

He said it, but it wasn't loud enough so she slapped his face. She slapped him again when he didn't say it clearly enough. Then he was finally allowed to take her into his mouth. His squirming around on the tentacle was having an effect on Sir who came very suddenly and quickly. Severin felt the power wash over him.

He managed to bring Momma Bear to orgasm by taking Daddy as deeply down his throat as he could and leaning forward, pushing the base of the dildo against her clitoris. Momma came with a soft sigh and Severin felt moisture trickle down from the dildo harness onto his chest, splashing her thighs.

Nita was next. Her cock was lean and hard, about the same size and shape as Penetrator back home. Thinking of the dildo made Severin instantly think of the Viscountess and he wondered what she was doing at that moment. Probably she was spending Saturday night painting her girlfriend's toenails or whatever it was they did in boarding schools.

Nita made him get on all fours. She tied a length of rope around the base of his genitals and attached it to a ring in the floor.

"This is Hippolyta," she said, allowing the tip of her cock to touch him. "It has the same name as an Amazon queen."

Severin realized that Nita was a modern day Amazon queen. The touch of the dildo crystalized for him what Nita had been trying to do for the Roaring Girls. She wanted to make them more than just a bunch of drunken brawlers. She wanted them to be warrior women.

Hippolyta slipped in easily, forcing its way deep inside him. Severin could feel the power and the passion behind every stroke of her hips. As she thrust forward he moved with her, punishing his own cock and balls which were still tied to the floor. It was gentle at first, but soon she was pushing harder and harder until he felt like his cock and balls were going to be pulled off.

Hippolyta also means horsewoman, Severin remembered from his Greek mythology classes. She was a horsewoman all right, riding him hard, faster and faster. The pain in his ass vanished when the pain in his genitals overwhelmed all other sensations. There was no need for any verbal humiliation; her control over him was too clear and obvious to need any words.

When she hit her first orgasm someone screamed. Severin realized that the sound didn't come from behind him, so it must have been him.

Other women took him next when Nita was done. He was bent over the table again, and later forced onto his hands and knees for another round. One woman put him on his back on the floor and shoved him into a ball so that his knees were at his shoulders when she took him.

During one of his breaks to rehydrate, he watched Tinashe get her mark. The newest member of the Roaring Girls was riding on a Sybian, lost in the ecstasy of stimulation as the machine hummed and throbbed under her. She barely seemed to notice as Serra Finn the Body Mod heated a small bit of metal with a propane torch.

When the metal was red hot she turned to Tinashe. Two of the Roaring Girls held on to her to keep her still as Serra pressed the red-hot metal to the flesh. Tinashe stiffened, but didn't make a sound. When the brand was pulled away there was a one-inch long brand on her upper arm.

Serra placed the iron back in the heat, and when it was ready she brought it back to the arm. Another mark was made next to the first, then another. Severin realized that the brands were forming the spokes of the motorcycle wheel. A tattoo would form the rim of the tire, and that would be followed by red flames and the initials RG.

Severin couldn't see any more since he was grabbed and made to bend over a chair so more women could have access to him.

He lost count of how many women there were, but he knew he didn't come close to serving every woman in the room. Several of them had no interest in him, even if this was a self-proclaimed bonding exercise. Others had simply exhausted themselves with their partners and didn't have any extra energy. At one point the EMT checked him and found blood. She called a halt to his activities.

Severin protested weakly that he felt fine and could keep going if he just got some rest. The pain had reached a point that he couldn't really tell what specifically hurt any more. It was almost like not being in pain at all.

"I can do it," Severin muttered as Momma Bear lifted him up and carried him to Squirt's room. They had set up a cot for him next to the urinal. The last thing he remembered before passing out was Momma kissing him on the forehead and telling him he had done well.

Chapter Thirty

Sunday morning the Viscountess rose and found that they had delivered all her clothes from the locker next to her bed. Nurse Kelly was at her desk, giving her some privacy as she changed. The Viscountess was happy to take the uniform off, even though she was changing into jeans and a T-shirt instead of her leather.

She took the time to examine her ass in the full length mirror. The marks were well placed and still very visible, but it appeared as if no blood had been drawn. The pain was just a distant echo of the day before.

When she was finished she went to Nurse and confirmed that Miss Krause was in her office. When the Viscountess reached the heavy oak door to the Headmistress's office she found it ajar. Miss Krause was behind her desk, as if waiting for her.

"Please come in, Desire. How do you feel this morning?"

"Still sore," the Viscountess admitted. She entered the office and swung the door shut.

"Once again I have to apologize for losing control yesterday." Miss Krause began fiddling with things on her desk, not making eye contact.

"That's not what I'm upset about," the Viscountess informed her. "I'm fairly certain that I know what's going on here, but I need you to answer a few questions."

There was no way to miss the note of command in the voice of the Viscountess. For a moment the iron will of the Headmistress asserted itself. She would not be dominated here in her own office by a mere girl. The Viscountess knew that if she were to waver even slightly Miss Krause would have the upper hand and she might as well bend over the desk again.

"I know what you've done," the Viscountess told her firmly. "I know what happened to the Headmaster."

The dominant energy coming from Miss Krause wavered, then collapsed at once like a house of cards. The headmistress felt guilty over losing control, but there was also a deeper guilt that made it impossible for her to take a stand. The Viscountess continued her questioning.

"What is your given name?"

"Helena."

"Very well, Helena, please leave the desk."

The older woman rose slowly from her chair and crossed to the front of the big desk. The Viscountess took her seat and quickly located the missing arrow. Helena Krause stood in front of her, head down and shoulders slumped.

"The Headmaster is suffering from Feedback, isn't he?"

Helena jumped a little, as if she had gotten an electric shock.

"Yes, but we didn't mean—"

"I know what you meant," the Viscountess cut her off. "You lost Amy and rather than admit it, you lied to her Aunt Amanda. That was a violation of the contract the Headmaster and Amanda signed. He must have suffered the Feedback as soon as he lied to her."

"It was only cramps at first. He said he could deal with it." Helena looked up at the Viscountess, her face a mask of regret and desperation. "The pain kept getting worse. He didn't dare leave his house. Nurse has been taking care of him."

"Why didn't you tell Amanda immediately?"

"We couldn't believe that she was really gone. We kept searching for her. By the time we knew she wasn't here it was too late. We couldn't tell anyone. Our reputation was at stake."

"Is your reputation more important than a girl's safety?"

"Peggy said she ran off with her girlfriend. It didn't seem possible, but we finally had to accept it. Amy also told Peggy that she'd be back before the end of the semester. We thought that if we just stalled long enough everything would be all right. No one need ever know."

"Maybe if you'd told Amanda things would have been different," the Viscountess said accusingly. "Amy's girlfriend was from a notorious motorcycle gang. She used a difficult and dangerous method to get to Amy. This arrow tells me that things didn't go according to plan."

When Helena looked up her eyes were bright with tears. "We had no way of knowing. We thought she'd just run off."

"If she were in the honeymoon suite at some hotel people wouldn't be shooting arrows at her."

It was clear that Helena really hadn't considered the idea that Amy was in trouble. Tears began flowing and it looked as if her knees would buckle.

"I had no way of knowing."

"Taking care of your students was your job. You not only have teenagers here, you have Littles. What do you think their parents are going to say?"

"Please," Helena sobbed. She dropped to her knees and clutched the desk for support. "You can't tell the parents. It will ruin us. If the students are pulled from here the whole Dominion will collapse."

The Viscountess hadn't considered that. It was possible Blackbriar would go the way of the Kamen Girl's home.

"Lady Amanda has to be told what happened."

"Yes," Helena agreed.

"Fortunately I may have a way of tracking Amy and her girlfriend. The truth is Lady Amanda hired me to investigate Amy's disappearance."

"I see that now. We should have cooperated. I should never have told Monica to go after you."

"That's another thing. Did you really think it was a good idea to give her so much power?"

"After I lost the Headmaster I was worried about keeping control of the students. Also I wanted any student who asked about Amy or the Headmaster to be discouraged."

"Is that why you made Monica a prefect along with her friends?"

"It seemed like a good solution. She's always been a bully, and a lot of the girls love being punished by her."

"But some of them don't," the Viscountess pointed out. "Monica has no self-control. She's a bad influence, particularly on you. I saw the way she was pushing you last night. Monica runs the entire school, including you."

Helena collapsed on the floor. The Viscountess couldn't even see her over the desk. She rose and went to the older woman, now a heap on the floor.

"I try to control her," Helena confessed, "But she knows too much. Can't you see, I've done everything for the sake of the school. You can do what you like, punish me any way you want, but please save the school."

The Viscountess felt it was the web of lies that she and the Headmaster had started that led them to this, but she couldn't help but feel touched by the pleading. She went to one knee and took Helena's chin in her hand.

"I don't want to destroy the school, but Amy has to be my primary concern."

"Of course."

"Tracking her down is my job. You need to redress the wrongs at this school. That includes restoring Felicity to her job in the office and putting Monica back in her place. You know the girls better than anyone; do you think you can handle that at today's punishment session?"

"Yes, of course."

The Viscountess was planning on staying to make sure everything was done properly, but she felt the action had to be taken by Miss Krause herself. Monica had to be removed from power in a way that restored order to the school and that would never happen if the Viscountess started throwing her weight around.

A few hours later the students all gathered for their mid-day meal and punishment. Several objects, including portable wooden stocks had been set up in front of the room. There was an odd buzz of excitement in the room. Rumors had been flying that something big was happening.

Felicity and Peggy, their faces freshly marked with humiliating slogans stared sullenly into their plates. The meal was lasagna, normally one of Peggy's favorites, but she had spent all morning being humiliated by Monica in front of the whole dorm. Monica had made it very clear that she and Felicity were going to "get it" at lunch.

Both girls were stunned to see Desire slip into the chair across from them. She was still wearing jeans and a T-shirt, the only girl in the room who wasn't in uniform.

"Des, I thought you'd gone!" Peggy exclaimed.

"Not yet. I have a ride coming, but I wanted to see this first."

"Well, at least we'll have one friendly face in the audience," Felicity said grimly.

When the dishes were cleared away, Miss Krause addressed the students. Monica, Raine, and Cristall were beside her, but from the expressions on their faces they had no more idea what was happening than anyone else.

"Before we begin, I'd like to welcome back someone after a long illness," Miss Krause announced. Mr. Woodridge, the Headmaster emerged from one of the back doors, accompanied by Nurse Kelly. He still looked a little weak, but he was back on his feet again. The students burst into applause at the sight of him. They may have lived in terror of his firm hand, but it was comforting to have him back in command.

The fact that his Feedback was going away meant that Miss Krause had called Lady Amanda and told her the truth. All the Viscountess and Severin had to do was recover Amy, her mysterious girlfriend, and the stolen Sphere and everything would be fine.

"I'd like to call on two students now. Would Felicity and Peggy please join me at the front of the room?"

One of the students hummed the Imperial March from Star Wars which made a few people laugh.

"If I don't survive, you can have my iPod," Felicity told Desire before she rose and followed Peggy.

As they nervously approached the front of the room the girls were unprepared as Miss Krause gave them a washcloth.

"Before we begin I want you two to clean your faces," Miss Krause told them sternly. "You are neither fat nor stupid nor a loser and I will not have my students marked in such a manner."

Peggy and Felicity took the washcloths and each helped the other clean their faces of the magic marker. Monica scowled at them, but said nothing. The students shifted nervously in their seats. This wasn't starting like any punishment they had ever seen.

"Excellent. Now we may begin. This school has seen some troubled times of late," Miss Krause told the assembled students. "But I believe those days are behind us. We will begin by addressing one of the chief causes of concern, Peggy and Felicity..."

At the sound of their names the two girls stiffened. They were unprepared for Miss Krause to continue her sentence.

"Would you be so kind as to remove the Prefect badges from these girls."

"What!" Monica exclaimed, glaring at the Headmistress. Student and teacher were locked together for a split second in a battle of wills, but it ended when Felicity plucked the Prefect badge from Monica.

Peggy, a little more hesitantly took the badges from the other girls. She turned to Miss Krause, confident that this was all a trick.

"Being a Prefect is a privilege that must be earned. It's a badge of honor, not an excuse to carry out personal vendettas."

Monica fumed. She glanced over at the teacher's table where people were still shaking hands with the Headmaster. The Viscountess had no trouble reading the thoughts of the pretty blonde girl. If the Headmaster wasn't incapacitated then whatever hold she had over Miss Krause had gone.

"You've been very eager to hand out punishments, Monica. I think it's time you paid for your excesses. I'm going to ask these two girls to put you in the stocks and paddle you."

"No, I won't do it," Monica gasped. She was trying to look confident, but not entirely succeeding.

"Of course I can't force you." Miss Krause smiled benevolently. "Why don't you join your friends over there? If you change your mind about the punishment please speak up."

For some reason there was a large piece of plastic on the floor. Miss Krause made Raine and Cristall kneel on the plastic. After a few seconds Monica joined them.

The three were kneeling so they were facing the students and their backs were to the head table. Miss Krause picked up objects from the table and gave them to Peggy and Felicity. The two girls didn't seem to know what to do, but some of the students had started to guess. There was a ripple of laughter that passed through the room. Monica and her friends were too nervous to even look over their shoulders.

Peggy had a squeeze bottle of chocolate syrup in her hand. At Miss Krause's instructions she held it over Monica's head and let the sticky dark mass flow over her. Monica's jaw fell open, but she snapped it shut to keep anything from getting into her mouth. The chocolate cascaded over her features.

At the same time two liters of soda descended on Cristall, completely destroying her hair, which she had spent an hour on and washing away her makeup. Raine got honey over her head.

The whole room roared with laughter. Once they understood what was going on Felicity and Peggy really got into it, grabbing things from the table and dumping them on their former tormentors. Raw eggs were next, then a dusting of flour. For the three girls it seemed like there was an endless supply of humiliating things on the table.

Cristall was the first to break. The former teen model literally couldn't take it and had to Safeword. She was led away to the showers. Raine and Monica endured for a few more minutes that must have seemed like hours.

"She made me do it! I didn't want to hurt anyone," Raine cried out. Her eyes were sealed with honey, but she groped around and indicated Monica. The audience booed and jeered her announcement.

Miss Krause was satisfied and let two students lead the sobbing sticky mess of a girl away. That left only Monica.

With a trace of her old arrogance Monica reached up and wiped the chocolate sauce from her eyes. When she looked back she saw Peggy with a bottle of molasses and Felicity with a bag of feathers from a pillow.

"I think I'll take that paddling now," Monica said in a hollow voice.

The room burst into cheers at the sight of Monica struggling to stand on the slippery plastic. Her uniform, once so immaculate, was ruined forever. Peggy and Felicity had to help her to her feet. At a command from Miss Krause two kitchen workers came in with a child's wading pool and two buckets.

"We don't want to ruin these beautiful stocks now do we?" Miss Krause asked Monica. The schoolgirl gave a little whimper in reply.

Monica stood in the wading pool as Felicity and Peggy poured the water over her. It was warm enough to keep the gooey mess from congealing and washed most of it away.

After the second bucket had been poured, the filthy mess was mostly gone but of course Monica was now soaked to the bone. Her dripping form was led to the stocks. It had been positioned so that she faced a wall and both the teachers and the students could see a side view of her as she was punished.

Peggy and Felicity helped her into position. Felicity lifted the wooden bar with holes for Monica's wrists and neck and lowered it again when Monica was in place. She was forced to bend over and there was another block of wood to hold her ankles in place.

As this was being done, Mr. Woodridge rose with magisterial splendor from his chair.

"Miss Krause, if I may... I'd like to get back in the swing of things. Would you do me the honor of giving me the first strokes?"

"Certainly, Headmaster."

The Headmaster took off his jacket and rolled up his sleeves. He was carrying what must have been his personal paddle. It was a foot long and made of solid wood with holes in the shape of stars cut through the wood. The Viscountess had seen paddles like that before. The holes would cut down on wind resistance allowing for a faster stroke, and it would no doubt leave distinct, star-shaped marks on the bottoms of the students.

"They say he can make a whole constellation on you," one of the schoolgirls breathed in a mixture of wonder and fear.

When the Headmaster lifted Monica's skirt and flipped it up the students could see that the white cotton panties were still marked by stains from the chocolate sauce even though they were also dripping wet. He scowled for a moment, unwilling to touch the soiled underwear, but Miss Krause helpfully provided him with a pair of scissors.

The students broke out in laughter and jeers as he snipped away the panties and made an elaborate show of taking the stained underwear with thumb and forefinger and tossing them aside.

From her seat the Viscountess had a good view of the show. Monica's dominant energy and self-confidence was normally so high that she could take a paddling like this with little problem and be back to her old self in no time. Miss Krause had chosen her punishments wisely. The humiliation of the splashing had worn away Monica's pride, leaving her defenseless.

The Headmaster raised his arm and brought it down. There was a loud smack of wood on damp flesh. Monica gave a little scream and lurched in her bonds. Water dripped freely from her onto the floor.

A second blow followed, then a third. Each one made Monica's whole body jump against the wooden stocks.

"Thank you, Miss Krause. You may continue." The Headmaster turned from Monica and went back to his seat. The students must have thought he was being merciful by limiting himself to three strokes, but the Viscountess suspected it was more likely he was exhausted from the exertion. Nurse Kelly helped him to his chair.

"Thank you, Mr. Woodridge. Now, since Peggy has been so severely punished by Monica I will give her the honor of finishing the punishment," Miss Krause said, her voice cutting through the noise of the students.

"I can't," Peggy stammered. "I mean I've never punished anyone before."

"It's easy silly, just swing the paddle," Felicity teased.

Hesitantly at first Peggy gave a few strokes with the paddle. It was longer and thinner than the one the Headmaster had used. This paddle was varnished wood about a foot and a half long and as thick as her finger. It made a distinct smack noise when it struck flesh.

"Harder!" someone in the audience shouted.

Peggy swung again, this time putting more of her body weight into it. There was a louder sound and Monica's whole body began to shake. The fact that Monica was reacting gave Peggy new strength. She kept hitting, increasing the force until after one very solid impact Monica howled in pain.

The sound of her cry sent another wave of laughter through the room. Miss Krause helpfully pulled Monica's stiff hair to one side so her face was visible, allowing the students to see the tears that fell from her eyes. Everyone seemed to be enjoying seeing the icy blonde brought down. Peggy kept hitting harder and harder. Standing where she was she couldn't see Monica's face, but she could see the pale flesh of her ass grow increasingly red.

"That's not fair," a girl shouted from the audience. "She framed me for cheating and had me paddled. I want a crack at her."

"Me too!" another girl shouted.

Suddenly everyone was on their feet and storming the front of the room. Several teachers at their table blanched at the sight of the students rushing forward. Fortunately, Miss Krause was able to exert her will over them.

"That's enough!" the Headmistress shouted to get their attention. The first student to reach the front of the room had tried to grab the paddle from Peggy, but Miss Krause took it away from her. "I believe the paddle has served its purpose. However if you feel Monica deserves a good old-fashioned hand spanking I won't stand in your way."

That led to a lot of cheering and clapping. Someone shouted "spank, spank" and soon the whole room was taking up the chant.

Trapped in the stocks, Monica could look only a little to the side where her fellow students were lining up. Once they were out of her field of vision she had no way of knowing how many of them chose to take a shot at her. "No, no," she begged, but the sound of her sobs was barely audible.

So the epic spanking began. One by one the laughing and giggling students had their way with Monica. Some were hesitant and barely hit her, others struck as hard as they could. Monica's ass, already raw from the paddle, turned a bright cherry red from the top of her thighs to the base of her spine.

The students would have gone on all day if Miss Krause hadn't stopped them. They were even talking about hanging Monica by her wrists from one of the tree branches and continuing the punishment outside. Miss Krause was delighted by this show of school spirit, but had to force them to calm down.

Eventually all the students had left except for the Viscountess, Peggy, and Felicity. Miss Krause unlocked the stocks and set Monica free. The girl, her once perfect blonde hair now a ratty mess, dropped to her knees and stayed there, squirming uncomfortably.

"Well, have you learned your lesson?" Miss Krause asked.

"Yes, Miss Krause, thank you for correcting me." Monica started to lick her lips, but immediately withdrew her tongue when she tasted what was plastered over her face.

"And what precisely was that lesson?"

"I had no right to abuse my position," Monica confessed. Her shoulders shook and she might have been crying, but the tears were lost in the dripping water that covered her.

"Are you still going to be mean to me?" Peggy asked.

"Um, maybe," Monica admitted truthfully. "But I won't be Prefect anymore, so you can always turn me in."

"I'm cool with that." Peggy grinned.

Miss Krause had gone to the Viscountess while the girls talked.

"It will take her a long time to recover from that, if she ever does," Miss Krause said.

"Another bully will take her place. It's the nature of these things."

"You could always stay and help. Desire would make a superb Prefect, and you already have two little deputies who worship you."

"I'm not sure I'm cut out for the life of a schoolgirl," the Viscountess chuckled. "It's too intense for me."

"A teacher, perhaps. There might be an opening next semester."

"Right now I have to try and find Amy. Plus, I have a naked man waiting for me back home."

"Ah," Miss Krause smiled and blushed. "I won't keep you, then."

Miss Krause didn't keep her, but Peggy and Felicity saw that their friend was going and showered her with hugs. It took some time for her to untangle herself and explain that she had to go.

"Thanks for helping," Felicity said.

"Gosh Des, you're the best," Peggy gushed, planting a kiss on her cheek.

Chapter Thirty-One

Severin opened his eyes and stared at the white porcelain urinal. It took him a second to remember where he was. Right—bar, women, dildos. He started to get up, but the cot was very low and it took him two tries to get to his feet. It didn't help that every muscle in his body was sore.

Squirt's bed was empty. Severin made his way to the bathroom stall. He definitely had to use the bathroom. He was looking forward to emptying his bladder, but having a bowel movement was another matter entirely. There was a dull throb coming from his backside and he wasn't sure how much damage had been done the night before.

Realizing he had to go to the bathroom eventually Severin sat gingerly on the toilet and did what he had to do. The pain increased, but not so much that he felt he was seriously injured. He checked the bowl before he flushed and was grateful to see no fresh blood. There were a few drops of red on the toilet paper, but not enough to be concerned.

The sound of flushing drew Squirt back to her room.

"Hey, how are you?"

"Fine, I think. How are you doing?"

"Every time we have one of these parties I say I never want to see a dildo again. Of course, I'll be back to my slutty ways in a day or two."

"I think I'm the same way."

"Um, was there any blood? We were told to take you to the emergency room if you were still bleeding."

"No, I'm fine."

"Sweet." Squirt grinned. "Everybody voted and you get to use the shower with hot water this morning. Oh, do you like waffles with walnuts?"

"Yes." His mouth watered instantly. Just the thought of waffles reminded him he was famished.

"Great. Get washed up and I'll tell Momma Bear to start cooking."

The shower felt good on his aching body. By the time he was in the kitchen he actually felt a little like his old self. A cup of coffee and a plate of steaming waffles loaded with butter and syrup put him on the top of his game.

"My turn to eat," Squirt announced with a wicked grin. She unexpectedly dropped to her knees and took his limp penis in her mouth.

"Um, excuse me," Severin said.

"Relax and enjoy it," Momma Bear told him. "It's the least we can do. Besides, Squirt's pretty good at this."

Squirt sucked as hard as she could and leaned back, stretching out his limp organ so much that it was almost painful. It left her mouth with a loud pop.

"Yep, still tastes the same," she told Severin.

"You don't have to do this."

"It's all right. I used to be blow job queen of my high school." Squirt drew the full length of him in, working the head of his cock with her throat muscles.

"No, I mean you really shouldn't do this," Severin told them. He paused and groaned as Squirt's active tongue went to work on him. "My cock and my balls belong to the Viscountess. I can't come without her permission."

"Can't we just call her and ask?" Momma Bear wanted to know.

"We can't reach her," Severin groaned. His cock was fully erect now. Squirt was making it dance with tiny flicks of her tongue.

"If this was going to be an issue you should have made it a hard limit."

"I didn't think it would be an issue. I didn't expect any of you would want to..." Severin broke off and gave a small scream of pleasure. Squirt had just the head of his cock in her mouth and was gently chewing on the sensitive flesh.

"You're really serious? Because the way I figure it, you've earned it."

"I'm sorry, I don't want to insult you but I don't feel right enjoying myself when I'm in the middle of a case and my Lady isn't here."

"All right," Momma Bear nodded. "I can see that. Come on Squirt, not today."

"But I was just getting into it," she protested. "I guess sucking cock is like riding a bike. You never really forget how to do it."

"I'm sorry, Squirt," Severin said with all sincerity. "What you offered me was very special. I wish I could accept it."

"It's all right. It just means more room for waffles."

"Right, waffles." Momma Bear turned back to the waffle iron.

While this had been going on another figure had entered the room like a ghost, silent but for the rattle of her chains. It was the woman who seemed to serve Nita. The slave paid no attention to anyone in the room and busied herself making coffee for her mistress.

"That's C," Squirt said very conspiratorially. "Nita's very old school and doesn't allow her to speak without permission."

"She's very well trained."

Now that he was seeing her up close Severin noticed that the metal bands on her wrists, ankles and the thin metal ring around her neck had been welded permanently into place. The chains that linked them could be removed, but she would wear the rest of the metal on her until someone cut it off of her. Severin imagined the welding being done in Nita's shop.

"Actually she's a CPA," Momma Bear said, adding another waffle to the stack she was making. "Nita hired her to balance the books on her garage, and one thing sort of lead to another. She saved us from a huge tax mess last year."

C didn't say a word, but Severin could make out just enough of her face to see a ghost of a smile flicker across her lips. A second later she was all business, shuffling out of the room in her chains, her face composed into a blank mask of submission.

Momma Bear joined Squirt and Severin for the next round of waffles.

"So are you going to want to talk to all of us? There must be sixty or seventy women here?" Momma asked.

"I'll talk to everyone if I have to. Right now I want to focus on you two, as well as Nita and Sir."

"So what do you think we've done?" Squirt asked hesitantly.

"Nothing. I'm not a cop. I'd like a chance to talk to Nita in private before I begin."

"She'll be up soon." Momma paused to swirl around the waffle in a generous coating of syrup before putting it in her mouth. "That was her coffee. She should be in her office in another twenty minutes."

Roughly thirty minutes later Nita met with Severin in her office. She was wearing tight leather pants and a T-shirt from her body shop. Instead of sitting in her chair she was perched on the edge of the desk, making her more approachable. C was nowhere to be seen.

"Before I begin talking to people I wanted to say something about last night," Severin told her.

"You were great last night. That's one of the best initiations that I can remember."

"Thanks." Severin took a deep breath. He was making an effort to speak to her as an equal, but it wasn't easy for him. Nita wasn't topping him in any way, but he couldn't help but be aware of how powerful she was. "But that's not what I wanted to talk about. It's about Boybreaker."

Nita instinctively glanced at the safe on the floor, as if were worried about the dildo escaping.

"What about it?"

"I know you're trying to make the Roaring Girls better. You want to leave their violent past behind. Surely you must realize that Boybreaker is a symbol of that past. It's been used to commit crimes and it still carries the taint of those days. I'm afraid it's going to poison everything you're trying to do here."

Nita's face hardened. Severin looked away from her and down to the floor, unable to meet her gaze.

"It's an incredibly powerful fetish object. It's been the symbol of the Roaring Girls since before I was born."

"Yes, Ma'am, but maybe you need a new symbol. That thing is evil. Is that really what you want your club to be associated with?"

Nita was angry now. Her breath came out from between clenched teeth, making a sort of hissing noise, dominant energy rolling off of her.

"We can't afford to look weak," she declared.

"I don't think Boybreaker makes you stronger, it makes you weaker. It knows you can't afford to give it up. It's depending on that so you'll keep feeding it victims and it can keep doling out punishments." Severin had to grip the arms of the chair to keep from falling to his knees, but somehow he managed to do it.

Nita abruptly got off the desk and paced for a moment.

"You're not the first one to mention this," she finally said. "Some of the women after the initiation have insomnia, bad dreams and that sort of thing. I figured it was just stress, or nerves."

"It's Boybreaker," Severin said simply. "When that thing was in me I felt the pain of every woman who had ever been abused or raped by a man. The guilt and anguish were overwhelming. I understand why the other men gave up. I almost did myself."

"Okay." Nita sighed. As her anger cooled her dominant energy faded. "Okay, I'll call a board of directors meeting so we can discuss it.

I don't think that dildo has any fans, so it's probably on the way out. Thank you Severin. I really mean that, thank you."

"Thank you for listening, Ma'am."

"Now I guess you get to give us the third degree. Squirt's hoping you'll beat her with a rubber hose."

"Let's hope it doesn't come to that."

When they returned to the bar, Momma Bear and Squirt were waiting, along with Sir and Tinashe. The new Roaring Girl still had the marks of the brand clearly visible as raised flesh on her arm. The outline of the rest of the wheel and the flames had been made, the full tattoo would be filled in later.

Sir had turned one of the chairs backwards and was straddling it. She was looking suspiciously at Severin, which did not help his confidence any.

"Nita told you I wanted to ask a few questions. My owner, the Viscountess and I have been asked to investigate the theft of a valuable object. I think the theft is linked to Tycho and the disappearance of a woman named Amy from a closed Dominion," Severin began.

"You'd better not be telling us you're trying to pin a robbery on Tycho," Sir growled.

"No," Severin said quickly. He still didn't have all the details of his theory worked out, but there was clearly no point in trying to accuse Tycho of anything in front of her best friends. "I think Tycho might have tried jumping between Dominions and got into trouble."

His theory seemed to calm Sir somewhat. "That does kind of sound like her," Sir admitted. She looked at the floor for a few seconds and Severin became aware that she had more to say. "Look, I don't know anything about Dominions, but was Amy the chick from the big rally?"

Nita got to her feet, directing her glare at Sir.

"I asked if anyone had heard of Amy," Nita reminded Sir.

"Look, when Ty falls for a girl it's usually only for a few weeks, then she moves on. I figured it's no harm, no foul," Sir shrugged. "Besides, I gave you plausible deniability when auntie called. You really didn't know anything."

Nita ground her teeth together. She looked like she wanted to have a long talk with Sir, but she wasn't willing to have it in front of Severin. Tinashe cut through the silence with a question.

"So these Dominions, they're like other worlds?"

"They're pocket universes," Severin explained. "Getting in and out of them can be tricky."

Momma Bear rose majestically to her feet and instantly had the attention of everyone in the room.

"I think we all agree that Tycho would be here if she wasn't in some kind of trouble," Momma Bear glanced around and saw the Roaring Girls nodding their agreement. She looked at Severin. "You seem to know what's going on."

"I just have a theory. I need facts to back it up."

"So what can we do?"

"I'd like to search her apartment. There may be a clue there as to what happened to her."

Severin tried to look confident, but he felt as if he were grasping at straws. If Tycho and Amy had gotten lost, the chances of finding them were very small. But every Dominion had entrances and exits. Even with no experience travelling between Dominions, they should have found a way to get home if they wanted to.

The biggest mystery was the one he couldn't share with them. What was the connection between the Roaring Girls and the Kamen Girls? Apart from a number of attractive members, there didn't seem to be a single thing linking them. Severin knew that he was banking a great deal on the two cases being related. If he was wrong, it might be too late to save the Kamen Girls.

Momma Bear went behind the bar and came back with a ring of keys.

"Let's go," Momma Bear said.

"We'll all go," Nita put in. "Tinashe, you stay here, the rest of us can go in the van."

"Shotgun!" Squirt shouted, jumping to her feet.

Tycho lived in an apartment in a stucco building about two miles from the Roaring Girls' bar. It was approaching noon and most of the neighborhood seemed to still be asleep or at church. Momma Bear noticed the mailbox was full and cleared it out. She glanced briefly at the mail, then shook her head. No clues there.

The door opened into a fairly large apartment. Severin could see a sizable living room dominated by a large television screen mounted on the wall. There was also a kitchen and a bathroom off to one side.

"Dusty," Squirt pointed out immediately. No doubt, like Tinashe, she had been forced to clean this place many times.

Sir went from room to room, her face tight with emotion. Severin realized she was looking for a body. Finally, she came back into the living room and shook her head.

"She's not here." Sir glanced at the table near the couch and saw something. "That's her phone. Why the hell would she go somewhere and not take her phone?"

"Relax." Momma Bear put a comforting arm around Sir's shoulder. "You know if someone tried to kidnap her every stick of furniture in this room would be broken."

"I know." Sir grinned, no doubt remembering some act of wanton destruction in the past.

"Tinashe told me that when she was here to clean there was a room she couldn't get into," Severin told Sir. "Is there a back bedroom or something?"

"Sure, end of the hall is a room with a fold-out couch. I've crashed there lots of times. I just looked, there's nothing there."

As she was speaking Severin started down the hall. He heard the rest of the women trailing after him. The room was small, and if the bed were pulled out there would be very little space to walk. Above the couch was a shelf that was loaded with various things.

Severin saw bandages on the shelf and a few lengths of wood. There were also many bottles of prescription pills, including tranquilizers and pain killers.

"There's a lot of medical supplies here," Severin said.

"Tycho was a medic in the Marines." Sir explained. "The pills all came from one of her ex-girlfriends. It's all meds that have gone stale; the pharmacy was just going to throw them out."

"I've got it," Severin said suddenly.

He turned to stare at the women. They stared back. They had no idea what he was talking about.

"I know who the thief is."

"Do you know where Tycho went?" Sir demanded.

Severin scowled. He wished the Viscountess were here. She would understand at once what was going on.

"I need to call Duchess, but my phone is back with my clothes." Severin was doing some calculations in his head. It was three hours earlier in Arizona, but he had missed the morning call home the Viscountess made from Blackbriar. Still, it was Sunday, so that meant no classes. Perhaps Duchess could get a call through if it was an emergency.

"I've got her number on mine. She gave it to me when you had the hood on in the van." Nita reached into her pocket for her phone.

Before Severin could take it there came a cry from the kitchen. Squirt hadn't followed the rest to the back hall. Everyone raced into the kitchen to see Squirt in the grasp of a masked woman. The woman had her arm wrapped around Squirt's neck in a choke-hold.

"Where is she!" the masked woman shouted.

"Don't hurt her." Nita spoke in a calm tone, trying to defuse the situation. Momma Bear and Sir spread out, one on either side of Nita in case they had to rush the attacker. They acted as if they had done this before.

"Where's Tycho?" the woman demanded.

"If we knew where she was, we wouldn't fucking be here," Sir snapped.

"Where is she?!"

Severin took a step forward. "Shouldn't you be with the Doge of Venice?" he asked gently.

Red Lightning stared at him, recognizing Severin from New Europa. She exhaled, making a little sound and her body seemed to sag. Squirt burst free and ran to Momma Bear's waiting arms. Nita and Sir immediately moved in.

Despite the limp, Red Lightning wasn't a woman to be taken lightly. Nita reached for her, but the Kamen Girl took her arm and managed to throw her to the floor. By the time Sir could reach her, Red Lightning had tossed a chair in her way.

Red Lightning vaulted over the kitchen table and raced out the door. Severin and Momma Bear were close behind. Severin knew that the Kamen Girls could become invisible. The apartment was on the ground floor. If she made it outside, she could vanish and they would never find her.

Just as Red Lightning threw the door open Severin felt a familiar surge of dominant energy which made his heart sing. From outside a whip cracked and they heard a thud as someone hit the ground.

Outside on the sidewalk Red Lightning lay face down. One ankle was imprisoned by the long bull whip in the hands of the Viscountess. The pony cart with Snuzzle in harness was at the curb.

"It looks like I got here in the nick of time," she commented dryly. "Perhaps I should be a super hero after all."

Chapter Thirty-Two

Severin prostrated himself on the ground and showered his owner's boots with kisses. Snuzzle did a little happy dance in her harness at the sight of him safe and sound. Red Lightning lay on the ground and did not seem to be in any hurry to get up. Having Sir standing over her might have helped to keep her quiet.

The Viscountess and Nita shook hands, reaching across Severin as if he wasn't there.

"It's good to see you again," Nita said. "Duchess warned me you might not be able to make it."

"I concluded my business early," the Viscountess explained. "When I got back I went to your bar to pick up Severin. Someone named Tinashe told me that you were here."

"Our newest member."

"I take it the ceremony went well."

"Yes," Nita glanced down at Red Lightning, "But I guess we have more important things to worry about."

The Viscountess had no desire to involve the Roaring Girls with the hunt for the stolen Sphere. She knew without asking that Severin had kept the details of the case secret, but unfortunately unforeseen events had altered their plans. The Roaring Girls now felt one of their own was in danger. They were a part of it whether the Viscountess liked it or not.

They went back inside the apartment. The Viscountess asked if Snuzzle could get some water. Nita ordered Squirt to take care of it. Red Lightning sat at the kitchen table looking around the room at her captors. Behind the mask her eyes flickered through many emotions. Severin saw anger, guilt, and fear.

"I think I already know what happened," Severin said when the Viscountess gave him the signal to start talking. "Just tell me if I'm wrong. This all started when you injured yourself. Were you really fighting Mariabots?"

"Yes," Red Lightning snapped. "They had me cornered and I decided to just jump out of the Dominion rather than fight."

"Isn't that dangerous?" the Viscountess asked.

"I've done it before." Red Lightning was defensive now. "I had to go to Earth anyway, so I just stepped through. Unfortunately, I got it wrong. I was miles from anywhere and about twenty feet in midair. When I hit the ground I busted up my leg pretty badly. There was nothing as far as I could see. I was in too much pain to try and jump again. I tried to walk out on one leg, but..."

She shook her head, looking down at her naked body, at the shattered leg that had put her in this mess.

"That's when Tycho found you," Severin guessed. Red Lightning seemed surprised that he knew. She nodded.

"Tycho was always riding dirt bikes out in the desert," Nita put in.

"She found me and brought me back. She's really very good. I couldn't ask for better treatment."

"Why didn't she take you to the Hospital Dominion?" the Viscountess asked.

"I asked her not to. We never go there unless we're practically dead. Kamen Girls take care of themselves. We have a whole medical wing in the Ziggurat, but I didn't want to go there until my leg was better. I didn't want anyone to know what I'd done, that I'd been so stupid."

Her voice broke. Tears welled up and glittered in the eye holes of her mask. Her hands resting on the table were clenched fists. When she finally looked up it was Nita that she looked at.

"Tycho saved my life," she explained. "She told me all about you guys. I told her she could ask me anything and I'd do it. I owed her. Do you know what that's like?"

"I do," Nita nodded.

"Then you understand?" Red Lightning looked around the room.

Nita shook her head; she refused to sympathize with Red Lightning. So it was Severin who spoke up.

"Tycho wanted to get her girlfriend Amy out of a sealed Dominion." He guessed. Red Lightning nodded. "Why didn't you just go in and get her yourself?"

"Tycho had to do it herself. She had something to prove to this girl's aunt. It was vital to her that she walk into that place and get the girl. She wanted me to make it happen."

There was a moment of silence as everyone digested what they had been told. The web of honor, pride and ego that trapped Red Lightning seemed to hang heavily in the air. Sir spoke first.

"I love her like a sister, but she's too stubborn for her own good." Sir's shoulders slumped. "Tycho once got into a fistfight with someone while one hand was tied behind her back. She said that she could do it, that she could beat them with one hand, so she actually had me tie one arm up while she fought. She won, but it was messy. She did it because she said she would."

"I told her about the way we travel between worlds," Red Lightning confessed. She was still being very careful with her words. "I knew I shouldn't have done it, but she saved my life. Besides I was on a lot of pain meds. When I went back to work I stopped by here. Tycho was upset about Amy and insisted I teach her how to travel the way the Kamen Girls do."

"We were told that kind of skill takes a great deal of time to learn," the Viscountess said evenly. She was careful not to sound too judgmental.

"It does. But Tycho is as strong and tough as any Kamen Girl. She actually was able to absorb enough energy to make a jump or two. The pain almost made her black out, but she wouldn't quit."

"When you went back to your Dominion you took some of the Rohynpol that Tycho had. I saw it on the shelf along with the pain killers and the splints and bandages. You had to hide in the room when Tinashe came to clean," Severin told her. "You used the drug to take out Skye. Did you actually expect to frame her for the theft?"

"No," the Kamen Girl said desperately. "She should have been out for hours. There was no reason I couldn't take it, let Tycho use it and bring it back. I just took the mask because Skye doesn't have the reputation I do. No one would notice her walking around, and if she wanted to pack in a side trip, it wouldn't get anyone talking. I planned on having everything back before she woke up. She never should have known her mask was missing."

"Is that why you took extra pain killers to hide your limp?" Severin asked.

"Yes, the door would have seen the limp and known it was me."

"Where is the mask?"

Red Lighting pointed to a kitchen counter. "I left it here. I kept coming back here when I could slip out of Venice waiting for Tycho to come back."

"So what went wrong?" Severin asked.

"I don't know." Red Lightning sobbed. "It should have been so simple. A few hours, tops. Tycho could handle at least two jumps, but she got nervous and wound up jumping with the Sphere instead of leaving it behind. I couldn't stop her. I was afraid to cause a scene in that school she was going to. Now she's taken it and I don't have any way of tracking her."

Sir looked as if she were about to say something, but Nita spoke for her.

"I don't think Tycho is a thief. It isn't in her nature."

"Then where is she! I finished my mission and came back here to wait. I've been waiting for days."

Red Lightning looked as if she were about to cry again. It was painful to see a woman so proud and so powerful brought so low.

"You of all people should know how many things can go wrong when you try to jump between Dominions. For someone with no experience whatsoever the number of things that can go wrong..." Severin let his sentence trail off. There was no point in finishing it.

"Then she's gone, and with her I've lost everything and I've destroyed my people."

Red Lightning sagged in her chair, her body wracked by sobs. Squirt returned from watering Snuzzle and knelt by Momma Bear's chair. Momma Bear reached over and scratched her head.

"Actually," the Viscountess said. "I might be able to help with that. I found this at the spot where Tycho took Amy away. I was hoping Severin could make something of it."

She reached into her boot and withdrew the arrow. When she gave it to Severin his eyes grew wide.

"Wow, I haven't seen one of these since college. This is an Elven arrow. It's from Dungeon."

"There's a Dominion called Dungeon?"

"Yes, it's based on the world's most popular tabletop role playing game. There was a time when I practically lived there."

"Is it a large Dominion?"

"Huge. It's an entire planet, plus it has a few other pocket dimensions of its own. I'll have to get this script translated, that might give us a clue where to start."

"Is Dungeon hard to get in and out of?"

"Not if you know what you're doing," Severin hesitated. "Of course, if you don't have any experience..."

"You see, this is why I hate Dominions," Nita cut him off.

"Rules," Sir added sourly. "I hate rules."

Red Lightning looked up. She had a hard time grasping that everyone wasn't as overwhelmed with despair as she was.

"Look, I don't know much about Dominions," Nita said to the Viscountess, "But if you need backup, I can make a phone call and have about sixty women here ready to kick ass. Tycho has a lot of friends."

"I'm hoping it won't come to violence. Right now I need you to take care of Red Lightning."

"I'm not going anywhere," the Kamen Girl said.

"Damn right, you're not," Sir snarled.

Severin glanced at the Viscountess. Since the Kamen Girls could all turn invisible and teleport to other Dominions it would be hard to keep one prisoner. On the other hand, Red Lighting seemed to have very little fight left in her.

"I want to go with you," Red Lightning said unexpectedly. "I have enough power left to get you there."

"No," the Viscountess said firmly, putting a trace of dominance in her voice. "You need to sit tight for now. We'll deal with you after we recover Tycho, Amy, and the object."

"We'll take good care of her," Nita promised.

Sir went to a closet and after some searching came back with a stiff leather belt that had handcuffs and leg irons attached to it. It looked very much like what was used to transport prisoners.

Nita folded her arms over her chest. "Why does that say property of Maricopa County Prisons?"

"Kind of a funny story." Sir grinned as she began to buckle the belt around Red Lightning. "Remind me to tell you about it sometime."

As the Roaring Girls were preparing to leave, the Viscountess went to the kitchen to retrieve Skye's mask. She stepped closer to Severin so she could speak without being overheard.

"Seriously Severin, how difficult will this be?"

"I'm not sure. Dungeon is full of monsters, trolls, Giants, Elves, Dwarves."

"Plus apparently a leatherdyke and a schoolgirl."

"And a magic orb," Severin reminded her. "We can't forget about the magic orb."

Chapter Thirty-Three

After returning to Boston the Viscountess elected to give Snuzzle a rest and take the Gateway to the Dungeon Dominion. Severin already knew where the Gateway was.

"It's in a little gaming store off of Mass. Ave. in Cambridge," he said as Sklavin removed Snuzzle's harness and the cart was put away in the garage.

"If it's your favorite Dominion and you know where the Gate is, why haven't you visited it in years?" his owner asked him.

"You know, I've been busy."

"No, I don't know," the Viscountess said sharply. "I demand an answer."

"I'm sorry," Severin stammered. It was very unlike him to act like this. "Back in the day I used to spend too much time there. I neglected a few of my classes. I even thought about just forgetting about the Real World and moving there full time. The Real World just didn't seem to have much to offer me."

"If you move to a Dominion you'll become a part of that world. You'll gradually forget who you used to be."

"I know, that's what stopped me. I didn't want to just fade away. I decided to give reality a try first."

"Will this be a problem for you? I know some Dominions can be addicting."

"I'll be fine," Severin reassured her. "Besides you need my knowledge."

"Good, then you can describe the Dominion to me on the way."

Snuzzle was left curled up on the couch. Sklavin drove them to the gaming store. In the back seat Severin tried to drag up any bit of knowledge that might be useful. It was fortunate that the Viscountess had read a great many fantasy books and knew something of what to expect.

"Time flows faster there," Severin told her. "If you're lucky you can have an epic adventure and still make it back in time for midterms. Once I was captured by Amazons, sold to their queen, got caught cheating on her, was sentenced to work in the mines and..."

"Short version."

"Time flows faster there so you can get more done. They've been there 24/7 for two weeks our time, it's probably been months for them."

"Probably? Isn't the time flow constant?"

"Not exactly. If you're doing something dull time flies by. It takes months of Dominion time to sail across the ocean, but it feels like hours unless you're attacked, then everything slows down. If you pop back to the real world you'll find it's usually just been minutes you've been gone."

"Like a dream," the Viscountess murmured. "I'm glad that you're comfortable with this place, but I can easily see how people can get lost there."

"If they've been there for months in local time they've had time to establish themselves. Somebody with experience in this world could have overthrown a king in that time. In their case I'm just hoping they've found a way to feed themselves."

"I take it this is a male-dominated Dominion?"

"In a lot of ways it is. Many of the women who are Denizens of the world are just there to be sex objects; I won't lie to you about that. They've got your basic haughty princesses that need to be humbled, slave girls that will be oh so grateful if you rescue them and so on."

"I have a feeling you didn't humble many princesses when you were there," the Viscountess smiled.

"Exactly. The world is also full of dominant women if that's what you're looking for. There are wicked queens, cruel nobility, and sadistic sorceresses. Every continent has different tribes of Amazons. Most of them are nomadic, with male slaves pulling their wagons. One time I—"

"Focus."

"Right, anyway," Severin shrugged off the happy memories. "A lot of visitors treat it like Ghore and gather a whole harem of slave girls, which is fine, but unlike Ghore this society allows for women to be very powerful. There are plenty of women rulers and some whole societies that are matriarchal."

"That's some comfort." The Viscountess glanced out the window. "We seem to have arrived."

The shop turned out to be called "Gateway to Adventure." Inside it was filled with racks of books for role playing games and numerous packs of collectible card games. Severin and the Viscountess made their way to the man behind the cash register in back. A few of his customers were kinky enough to recognize them for what they were, but they barely glanced up from the card game they were playing.

The owner of the store was a beefy man with a generous mustache. The top of his head was bald, but the rest of his red hair hung down to his shoulders. He hastily put aside the paperback he was reading when he saw the leather on the Viscountess and Severin's nakedness.

"I'm the Viscountess and this is Severin," she greeted him.

"My name's Bob, pleased to meet you." He shook hands with the Viscountess. She noticed the calluses on his hands. "Have you two come for a little adventure?"

"I believe so. First what can you tell us about this?" She handed him the arrow.

He looked at it and frowned. "You shouldn't take this out if its Dominion. You must know whatever spell was on it vanished once you crossed over."

"I didn't take it, I found it. Can you read what's written on it?"

Bob studied the flowing script for a moment, then nodded. "This arrow belongs to Lady Amaril in Cassomere, at least that's what it says."

"Can you get us to Cassomere?"

"Why, are you planning on taking her down? She's a high elf, very powerful, I wouldn't recommend it."

"We don't have a quest yet," Severin put in. "We'll find one when we get there."

"I'm sure the Gatekeeper can get you to Cassomere."

"Then you're not the Gatekeeper?" Viscountess asked.

"No, not exactly." Bob tossed on a battered felt hat and led them to a door marked "No Admittance" in the back of the store. Next to the boxes of books was a coat rack containing a leather jacket with chain mail sewn on it and a belt heavy with weapons. The mail on the jacket had broken rings and the sword looked as if it had seen some use.

Against one wall was a large circle that appeared to be carved from stone and had runes etched deeply in on its surface. It was so large it reached the ceiling and slightly lifted one acoustic tile. Severin and the Viscountess could walk through without ducking down. The air about the stone shimmered slightly.

"The real Gatekeeper is on the other side of that," Bob explained. "She can set you up with everything you need."

"How do you explain this to your Vanilla customers?" the

Viscountess asked, noticing that he hadn't shut the door and half the store could see them.

"Everybody's seen it. I just tell them it's a LARP prop, which in a way it is." Bob shrugged, but he did shut the door.

The Viscountess and Severin stared at the large object. It didn't just appear to be made of stone, it actually was stone. It must have weighed hundreds of pounds. It even had traces of moss growing on it, as if it had been dragged from Stonehenge and put up in a room with a door too small to possibly accommodate it. It was leaning against the wall, and on the other side was badly painted wood paneling.

Bob spoke a word in a language that the Viscountess had never heard. The energy in the room seemed to shift and a few of the runes glowed softly.

"There you go, step right through." He gestured to the stone ring.

"Thank you for your help."

"Good luck."

The Viscountess and Severin stepped through quickly. They had been through Gateways to Dominions many times, but to the Viscountess this felt subtly different. On the other side there was a round room empty except for a table in the center with a large bottle on it. Torches set in the wall flared to life as they stepped through. There seemed to be no other door or window except the stone ring, which existed on this side of the Gate as well.

The Viscountess looked around the room. She was trying to determine what was different about this place, but couldn't quite fathom it until Severin spoke up.

"We're entering a high magic Dominion," he explained. "You can sense the power here."

"It's like ozone in the air during a lightning storm," the Viscountess nodded.

As they spoke a peculiar thing happened. A trickle of smoke rose from the bottle. It twisted through the air on some wind they couldn't feel and dropped to the floor. Gradually the smoke began to grow thicker.

It became clear that there was a human figure in the smoke. In fact, it was a naked woman on her knees with her face pressed to the floor. A thick braid of jet black hair rose from the top of her shaved head and cascaded to the floor where it pooled like spilled ink. Female she might have been, but she clearly wasn't human. Her skin was bright blue and her ears were long and pointed.

"I am Yazmin the ever-obedient," she said in a voice thick with some exotic accent. "Kind mistress, gentle master, how may this worthless creature serve you?"

The Viscountess glanced at Severin who gave her the signal to start talking.

"We wish to travel to Dungeon," the Viscountess said firmly. "I was told that you can get us there."

"But of course. If beautiful mistress will allow this humble beast to rise I shall endeavor to be of service."

"You may rise."

"Thank you, my mistress."

The woman rose to her feet, looking more like she was drawn up by invisible wires than a person getting off their knees and standing. Once she was on her feet they could get a good look at her. She was impossibly beautiful. She wore nothing but rings in her nipples, nose, and labia as well as thin strips of silk that cascaded from her metal collar. The silk hid absolutely nothing and in fact it appeared to be so damp that it clung to her, showing off her curves.

She had a face that would make a supermodel weep with envy. Her body was full of sensuous curves, but somehow was also as well toned as a fitness model. Her breasts likewise were large but still perky in a way that would be impossible in the real world. Since she had no pubic hair her womanhood was prominently displayed. Her labia was the color of a plum, purple and dripping with fluid. The clitoris was a bright red. Yazmin lowered her large liquid eyes and looked at the floor.

"I apologize if the sight of my disgusting body offends you. If it pleases you to see me in another form, I shall be happy to change my shape."

"No." The Viscountess took a deep breath. "Your present form is just fine."

"I'll say," Severin murmured. The Viscountess glanced at him and saw that he had the beginnings of an erection. She gave him a quick stomp on the foot to bring him back to the task at hand.

"How may this worthless creature serve you?"

"We'll need clothes, I guess, and weapons."

"Of course. Clothes are not an issue; your selection of weapons is limited since part of the fun is finding your own equipment. Let's see, you are clearly the warrior of the party."

Yazmin made a languid gesture with one arm. The Viscountess

found her clothes vanishing. In the blink of an eye she was now wearing a chainmail bikini. Her belt with her flagellation instruments were the only thing remaining from her old ensemble.

"I'm supposed to fight in this?"

"It offers superb protection," Yazmin assured her. "If I give you more armor your defense will go down."

"I forgot to mention that," Severin said. "It works the opposite with guys. The more armor we wear the more protection we get, but with women the less they wear the better."

The Viscountess glared at him.

"Hey, I don't make the rules." Severin glanced at his owner and saw the curve of her ass, visible as the tiny chainmail covering swung freely. "My god, what happened to you?"

"I got caned. That's what happens to schoolgirls."

"You never said anything went wrong."

The Viscountess snapped her fingers and pointed at the floor. Severin immediately stopped speaking and dropped to his knees.

"I appreciate your concern for me, but this isn't the time or the place, Severin."

"Yes, Viscountess, I'm sorry."

"If I may be so bold." Yazmin held out one hand. A small bottle appeared there. "You don't want anyone to see those marks and get the wrong impression of you. This healing draught will assist you."

Severin nodded. "This place is full of healing potions."

The Viscountess took the bottle and removed the stopper. She drank it in one gulp.

"Minty," she declared. She felt an odd tingling and reached down to touch herself. The welts from the cane no longer throbbed and she felt only smooth skin under her fingers.

"Excellent," Yazmin favored them with a dazzling smile. "Perhaps a bit more leather would be appropriate for you, mistress."

She gestured again and the Viscountess was now wearing head to toe leather festooned with buckles and small spikes. It was not as constricting as leather would be in the real world, in fact it felt as smooth as silk.

Still on his knees, Severin fell to the floor. His lips were drawn to the leather of her boots that were like a black mirror. She allowed him to worship for a moment, then shifted her foot and placed it on the back of his head.

"This will do nicely," the Viscountess told Yazmin.

"And you shall need weapons."

There was suddenly a sword hanging from her belt along with her whips.

"If it's all the same I'd rather have a longbow."

"Please punish me, oh noble mistress. I shall correct my error."

The sword vanished. Now the Viscountess had a quiver of arrows slung across her back and an elaborately carved bow in her hands. She tested the tension on the string and found it had a perfect draw.

"This is excellent, thank you."

"You are too kind." Yazmin's eyes glittered as she took in Severin's naked form. "I see your slave is already properly attired for his station."

"Perhaps a bit of clothes wouldn't be amiss."

"Your merest wish is my command."

She gestured once again. Severin was now clad in a simple cloth vest and drawstring pants.

"Thank you for your service. We need to get to a place called Cassomere."

"You have but to step through the gateway a second time to be at your destination," Yazmin showed them the stone ring they had just come through. "Once you get there, ending your quest will be up to you. After you have accomplished your goal, you have but to think of returning and the gate will appear. When you return to this room I shall gladly restore your clothing and devices."

"You've been most helpful."

"It would be a kindness if you would mention my aid to he that owns me. Sir Robert, Lord of the Store of Gaming can be a cruel master."

"Yes, I'll make sure to mention it," the Viscountess promised. It was hard to imagine the man in the gaming store dominating this stunning beauty, but there was clearly a lot of magic in their relationship. For most people that was a metaphor, but for them it was a simple fact.

This time when they stepped through the stone ring they found themselves in a busy market. It looked like it was mid-morning in Cassomere. There were dozens of stalls selling all manner of goods. The air was an exotic mixture of horse manure, flowers, and spices. The Viscountess noticed that the air was still charged with the same magic she had felt in the chamber.

The Viscountess didn't want to appear like a tourist, so she tried not to stare at the tall slender elves, squat powerful dwarves, or the cute little halflings that passed her. They were all busy on their own errands in the thriving market. The crowd momentarily parted as a man about ten feet tall came striding past, leading cattle by a leash. The steers looked no bigger than dogs to the huge man.

"That's a giant," Severin said helpfully.

"Thank you, I'd guessed that." The Viscountess attached a leash to his collar. "It's a big city, where do we start?"

"Beggars are usually good for information."

"I don't see any beggars. Besides we have no money to bribe them with."

"That's easy; we find a monster to kill. We can turn dead monsters into gold."

"Delightful. Well, I do have a bow, and I'm a pretty good shot, but I don't want to waste a lot of time here."

"There isn't much time passing back in the Real World. We should have plenty of time to make it back and save the Kamen Girls."

"I still don't want to waste time."

The Viscountess began to walk the outdoor market, looking for anything that might guide them. On one side there was a wooden platform where a small slave market was being held. Some of the prisoners wore glasses or had tattoos that indicated they came from the Real World. None of them seemed too upset about their condition, so this was obviously their version of a fantasy adventure.

There was the sound of someone being beaten not very far away. The Viscountess felt someone watching her and felt a trickle of dominant energy from them. She turned and saw another raised platform where a husky woman with greyish-green skin and ill-fitting leather armor was taking a break from applying a large paddle to a naked man who was bent over on a kind of whipping horse. It was a long piece of curved wood shaped somewhat like an elongated letter S. His wrists were tied to the top of the wood and his feet to the bottom. He had nothing on below the waist and the curve of the wood made him stick his ass out for punishment.

The not-quite-human woman was leaning on her paddle and sipping water from a metal cup. When she was done she wiped her mouth and eyed both Severin and the Viscountess openly.

"She's a half-orc," Severin explained. "The badge on her armor probably means she works for the city guard."

"Sounds good, let's make a friend."

The Viscountess approached her. The big woman had a slightly overhanging brow and a flat nose, but she was not really unattractive. She exuded a raw sort of animal sensuality helped by the fact that one heavy breast was so poorly covered the nipple was visible. It was pierced with a small bone.

"Well met, strangers." The half-orc lifted the paddle. "Care to take a few strokes?"

"Don't mind of I do." The Viscountess lifted the paddle and found it a bit heavy for her taste. The woman had already left the man's ass bright red with little flecks of blood. Bracing herself, the Viscountess took a swing and lifted him to his toes, drawing out a loud cry.

"Ha! Good one," the half-orc chortled. "I'm Gorge."

"They call me the Viscountess."

"Pretty boy you've got there."

"Thank you."

The Viscountess tugged on the leash, drawing Severin to his knees. He placed a kiss on the muddy boots of the half-orc, which she seemed to enjoy.

"Is he available?"

"Possibly. We're here to find some friends. There are two women from our world we need to find. You look like the sort of person who likes to keep an eye on stray women."

"You may be right at that," Gorge leered at her, running her eyes up and down the leather-clad body of the Viscountess. "Tell you what, if your boy gets his tongue to work, I'll get mine to work."

"Sounds fair." The Viscountess only spoke after glancing at Severin to make sure he was on board with this exchange.

Gorge flipped up the flap of leather, which was all she had on below the waist. Between her meaty thighs her pussy was covered with thick, wiry pubic hair. As Severin went to work, the half-orc dropped the flap over his head and kept him in place with a powerful hand.

She had a deep, rich scent rolling off her. Under his tongue her clitoris swelled until it felt like it was as large as the tip of a man's thumb. The coarse hair rubbed against his cheeks, but he was rewarded with drops of warm, sticky fluid that flowed from inside her. When his tongue delved deeper he found that she had a metallic, slightly coppery taste.

"Two women from our world," the Viscountess went on, leaning against the large paddle. "They probably didn't come dressed for this place."

As the Viscountess described Amy and Tycho the half-orc sighed with pleasure. She adjusted her position so Severin could get better access. After a moment she gave a little gasp of pleasure and drew a deep breath.

"Damn," Gorge sighed. "That's good. Hey, I think I know the two you're talking about. They work at the Raven's Roost. It's a bar down past the wallows. The tough one's a bouncer. She's good. The cute one serves drinks. She'll be the one in the skirt. She's damned sexy, but don't touch her or the other one will have your arm off."

"That sounds like them." The Viscountess smiled at the description of the skirt. Apparently the power of the schoolgirl fetish was enough to cross even into this Dominion. She was glad she kept the outfit.

Gorge wouldn't let them go right away. She continued trying to make small talk while pressing Severin's head into her crotch with both hands. Severin licked and sucked and finally felt her whole body shudder with a powerful orgasm.

When she at last released him Severin fell back and had to make an effort to get back to his knees and kiss the half-orc's boots. He hadn't minded the scent of her, but he was grateful for more oxygen.

"Thank you, mistress," he said to her muddy boots.

"No, thank you, both of you." The big woman hesitated. "Us half-orcs don't get a lot of action. I really appreciate it."

"I'm sorry we have to leave so soon, but we have business."

Gorge's directions were fairly easy to follow. Just past the wallows, which was a muddy embankment where the river passed through town, the narrow streets widened into a much better part of town. The Viscountess was propositioned twice and challenged to one duel on the way there. Severin warned her that any interaction she became involved in could turn into some kind of epic quest, so she turned down all offers.

The Raven's Roost was a tavern which rented rooms on its upper floors. Gorge was of the opinion that the two women lived on the premises and rarely left the building. The glass in the door was too thick to reveal much of the interior and the window hadn't been cleaned in quite some time. The Viscountess opened the door and strolled right in.

"We're closed," a woman who was sweeping clumps of sawdust said without looking up. She was trim and fit with close cut light brown hair with a leather bodice that actually looked quite good on her. She had the symbol of the Marines tattooed on her well defined bicep.

"You must be Tycho."

Tycho stopped and stared.

"And you are..." she said suspiciously.

"I'm the Viscountess and this is Severin."

At that moment there was a little squeal and a younger woman with brown hair down her shoulders came running out of the back room. Amy still had her school dress on, but the blouse had been torn off to make a sort of bare mid-riff halter top for her. From the way it was buttoned it was clear that bras were not popular in this Dominion.

"Are you real? Are you from the Real World?" Amy demanded.

"Yes, we've come to take you two home,"

"Thank god. Say something real to me. Talk about The Apprentice, or American Idol, anything but swords and monsters."

"I don't watch a lot of television."

"You know what a television is," Amy gushed. She hugged the Viscountess.

They all sat a table while Tycho got them beer from the bar.

"I'd prefer water," the Viscountess said.

"No, you prefer the beer," Amy made a face. "You haven't tasted the water in this place."

"So who are you and why have you come here?" Tycho said, handing everyone their beer.

"Does it matter?" Amy snapped. Apparently the stress of living here had taken its toll on their relationship. "Every time we find someone from our world they're always here to kill some dragon, or drag gold out of some stinking underground hellhole."

"They invite us along sometimes," Tycho admitted. "But I don't want to move too far from the place where we appeared. I figure it's the best way to get back."

"Why don't you use the Sphere?" Severin asked.

It seemed to be the wrong question. Instantly the atmosphere in the room changed. Tycho grew more defensive and Amy's shoulders slumped.

"We lost it," Amy said.

"I lost it," Tycho declared bitterly. "I take full responsibility. Everything that happened was my fault. If I ever get out of here I'm going to throw myself on the mercy of those Kamen Girls and try to make up for what I've done."

The words seemed hard for her to say, but it was something she had to get off her chest. It was also clearly something she had been thinking about for a long time.

"What exactly do you mean you lost it?" the Viscountess asked diplomatically.

"Look, you know about the Sphere," Tycho explained. The Viscountess nodded. "I thought I had it down, but it got out of control. When I had Amy and was making the portal, the pain of using the sphere must have broken my concentration for a second. When we stepped through it was the middle of the marketplace and we were surrounded by, well, you must know what we saw."

"I freaked," Amy confessed. "I think I screamed."

"You screamed," Tycho assured her. "There was this crazy woman with pointed ears riding some kind of horse."

"Centaur," Amy interrupted.

"She shouted something and these guys in armor opened up with longbows."

"I take it, that's how this got to Blackbriar." The Viscountess laid the arrow on the table. I found it stuck in a tree."

"It was nearly stuck in my head. I could hear it go past my ear. It must have gone through the portal before it closed."

"So what happened next?"

"They roughed us up. I was so stunned I didn't even fight back. The woman said she wanted the magic globe and had her people drag the Sphere away."

"Didn't you try to get it back?"

"Eventually. We figured out where she lives, but it's a fucking castle. Her guards won't even open the gate to talk to us and shoot more arrows if we come close."

"Once we figured out how things were here we went to the city guard, but they pretty much laughed at us too," Amy admitted. "This Lady Amaril creep is way too rich for them to mess with."

"One of the guards was something called a half-orc." Tycho went on. "She managed to get us jobs here so we wouldn't starve. Of course that was after I'd spent some time with her."

Gorge was certainly good at getting her needs satisfied, the Viscountess thought.

"So you couldn't get it back?" she said aloud.

"What am I supposed to do?" Tycho demanded.

"Steal it," Severin said bluntly.

"I'm not a thief."

"That's too bad, because that's what you need here. Stealing here is against the law, but it's expected that people will do it. This place is based on a world where taking things is a necessary part of the game."

"Do I look like I play games!" Tycho exploded.

"No," the Viscountess said coolly, trying to calm Tycho down. "You look like someone trapped in a Dominion you don't know how to get out of."

"This is a world of epic adventures." Severin explained. "When you come here you can't go home until you've completed your quest."

"I don't have a quest."

"You have something you need to get back, and you have an enemy. It's a perfect set up. This world is waiting for you two to take on Lady Amaril and get the Sphere back. A lesser quest from some other party won't get you home until the Sphere is recovered."

"You're on a quest whether you like it or not," the Viscountess informed them. "Fortunately you have us to help. We're not going home either until we get the Sphere."

"I don't understand, what made you come here?" Tycho was suddenly defensive again. The Viscountess realized she hadn't answered Tycho's first questions.

"We were hired to find the Sphere," the Viscountess started to say, but she realized that was not what they needed to hear. "But we were sent after you two by Lady Amanda as well as Nita, Momma Bear, and Sir. They all miss you."

At the sound of her friend's names Tycho's face lit up, but her smile was quickly replaced by tears.

"I've screwed up so badly," she confessed. "Do you know how I got the Sphere?"

"Red Lightning told us."

"I don't know if I should try to go back. I don't know if I can."

"We've been here for about three months," Amy explained. "Although we weren't counting days at first and they don't have real calendars here. Anyway, it's been rough on both of us. I'm using my iPhone for a doorstop and I sold my bra for a gold nugget. I think I've forgotten what processed food tastes like."

"We'll get you home, I promise." The Viscountess glanced at Severin. "If I know the expression on Severin's face, he's already got a plan."

"It's simple," Severin shrugged. "All we have to do is break into a heavily fortified castle and steal the most powerful magical artifact in the world. Compared to satisfying the twelve insatiable goddesses of Kara-Thume, it'll be a piece of cake."

Tycho and Amy stared at him as if he were completely insane.

Chapter Thirty-Four

Under the theory of knowing one's enemy, Severin wanted to check out Lady Amaril. It turned out that she went on a morning promenade in the park two or three times a week. It was returning from one such a ride that Tycho and Amy had the misfortune to encounter her. The marketplace lay between the park and the lady's castle. It was also a perfect place to see someone without being seen.

The Viscountess, Severin, Tycho, and Amy went to the market and pretended to be browsing until they heard the clank of armor and the clatter of hooves.

"That's her," Tycho said.

Severin turned to get a good look. He tried not to be too impressed, but failed utterly. Lady Amaril and her mount were very impressive indeed. The lady was a full-blooded elf. She sat in the saddle with a grace born of centuries of life. She wore a riding cloak over white robes woven with silver and gold threads. Her ears looked as keen and sharp as a knife. There was an expression of distant cruelty on her perfect features, as if she could simply trample anyone foolish enough to get in her way and never notice that they were there.

Severin sensed she was capable of cruelty that was less distant as well. Her sleek body throbbed with dominant energy. Several people along her path fell to their knees as she rode past, but she didn't notice them. Severin felt his own legs grow weak and only the presence of the Viscountess kept him on his feet.

As impressive as she was, her chosen method of transportation was even more impressive. She was riding on the back of a female centaur. From the waist up the centaur was a beautiful woman, well-muscled and deeply tanned, with firm breasts and finely chiseled features. Her black hair was pulled away from her face and her skin gave way to the dark glossy coat of a horse. The equine part of her was powerful and sleek. She was larger than a pony, but not as large as a full grown horse.

She had been saddled so she could be easily ridden. There was a leather body harness around her torso and a full bridle with a bit between her teeth. The reins that were attached to the bit had short chains that lead down to her nipple rings. If Lady Amaril pulled back on the reins it would yank painfully on her nipple rings. The lady carried a riding whip and wore spurs on her boots and from the injuries visible on the centaur's flanks the lady didn't hesitate to punish her mount.

"Now that's a pony girl," the Viscountess admitted.

"Lady Amaril isn't bad either," Severin added.

"It was hard for me to notice the first time I met her," Tycho said ruefully. "I was too busy dodging arrows and being punched in the face."

Lady Amaril and her steed were escorted by six elves. Severin saw that they were in half plate and armed with Elven longbows. Their armor was polished to mirror perfection. They weren't quite able to keep up with the trotting centaur and so jogged close behind.

"She's got at least thirty men in that castle of hers," Tycho said.

"Show me the castle."

The four of them followed the entourage through the market and to a part of town where everything seemed to be carved from white marble.

"It's the Elven neighborhood," Severin said. He noticed street names and the names on stores were now in Elven script.

The castle of Lady Amaril took up the better part of a city block. There wasn't much they could see because of the two-story-high walls. The mansion inside the walls was a little taller than the walls themselves, but no part of the house touched the walls nor was it near enough to jump from the walls to a convenient balcony.

As soon as the last of the guards passed through the gate, a massive spiked barricade was lowered into place. Several guards were stationed just inside the gate. Probably there was someone there at all hours. Severin noticed that there was also a small door in the gatehouse big enough for a person to pass through. This would allow them to send one or two guards outside the wall without having to open the huge gate.

Severin insisted on walking all the way around the walls. He was rewarded by the sight of a wagon unloading sacks of grain at a back door. Guards in armor were on duty, but not paying attention.

"Let's see if I can get in there," Severin murmured. He was starting to feel like his old self again.

Before anyone could stop him, Severin walked to the cart and grabbed a sack which happened to contain flour. He put it on his shoulder and carried it through the door, following the driver of the cart who was right in front of him.

The Viscountess, Tycho, and Amy stared at the door that he had taken. They braced themselves for shouts of alarm; perhaps screams from Severin as arrows pierced him. All that happened was, rather anti-climactically, Severin and the cart driver both came back out and grabbed more sacks. They did this several times until the cart was emp-tied.

The cart driver shook Severin's hand enthusiastically and gave him something before getting in the cart and snapping the reins at the old horses to get them to move. Severin walked back holding up a few coins.

"I got some copper coins," he said brightly. "The old guy's son was hung over and couldn't help him. He was really grateful to have some assistance."

The Viscountess felt a flicker of annoyance at how cavalier Severin seemed, when she herself was on edge. "Well, did you find anything?" she demanded.

"A few things," Severin glanced around. The guards had closed and locked the rear door. There were no guards on the wall to overhear them. "Amaril lives on the second floor. No one can go up there without her permission. When I just looked up the stairs one of the servants looked as if he was going to have a stroke. Needless to say, the servants are all terrified of their mistress."

"How does this help us?"

"If she's storing anything valuable, it's going to be on the second floor. That reminds me, all her guards are Elves. The servants are various races, and from the brands and welts they're slaves in all but name. The point is, if we sneak in there we have to go in as servants. Even if we hit a guard on the head and steal his armor, none of us can pass for Elves."

"You and Amy could pass for servants," the Viscountess pointed out, "But Tycho and I would have to go in without our leather or our weapons."

"I'm better with my bare hands than with a sword," Tycho pointed out. "Everyone here loves to fight, but most of them haven't heard of martial arts, let alone boxing."

"I'd rather use stealth than fighting, but I doubt we're going to get out of here without some sort of trouble." Severin paused. The Viscountess could almost hear the wheels spinning in his brain. "Do you know if there are guards on the walls at night?"

"Yes," Tycho said. "I've seen them. At least one on each side of the wall."

"That makes it harder, but not impossible. We need a distraction, a good one."

The three women looked at each other.

"How good?" the Viscountess asked.

"Good enough to attract the attention of every guard in the place for a few minutes. I also need a padded grappling hook and about thirty feet of rope."

"We've got that back at the bar," Tycho said.

"It's in lost and found," Amy explained. "Somebody got drunk one night and walked off without it. We've had it there for weeks and no one has claimed it."

"Amazing coincidence," the Viscountess said to Severin. "Kind of like the first person we speak to knowing exactly where they were."

"It's that kind of a world." Severin shrugged.

Chapter Thirty-Five

It *was a good plan*, Severin thought, pacing back and forth in the Raven's Roost. It had the advantage of being very clean and simple. Of course there were still things that could go wrong. Every campaign went pear-shaped at some point. The trick was being able to recover without being caught.

While he paced, the bar had begun to fill with people. A group of Halflings was having an animated conversation in the corner. One lizard man had already drunk himself into a stupor and was passed out in a chair. Severin had to be careful not to step on his tail.

Tycho and Amy were breaking the news to their boss that they had to quit. The owner of the Raven's Roost was a gnome, a little man with a head that seemed too large for his body and wide expressive eyes. He spoke with what sounded to Severin like an eastern European accent.

"But you can't leave," the gnome stammered. "You're so popular, and your breasts, they are so round and firm."

"I'm glad you appreciate our hard work," Tycho snarled dangerously.

"We told you we'd leave as soon as we could," Amy reminded him.

"You two are irreplaceable," he groaned.

"Just put a sign in the window and find the next person who's stuck here and needs a job."

As they talked the Viscountess arrived, munching on some sort of kabob. She offered one to Severin.

"Do you have any idea what kind of meat this is?" he asked suspiciously.

"No, and I don't care. I think when we're in this Dominion we should have a don't ask, don't tell policy when it comes to food."

"That's probably very wise."

Amy and Tycho packed their meager belongings into a blanket and rendezvoused with Severin and the Viscountess at the back of the bar. The decision was made to wait until late at night for their break-in.

"It's a cliché, I admit," Severin told them, "But that's the best time to find bored guards."

"So this distraction you were talking about," Tycho said suspiciously.

"What did you have in mind?"

"I don't know, something to lure the guards away," Severin hesitated.

"I've got a better idea," Tycho sneered. "Why don't you have your mistress fuck you in the street and I can climb over the wall."

"Have you ever broken into a house before?"

"Have you ever been to boot camp? I can climb a wall in my sleep."

Her dominant energy flared and Severin backed down. The Viscountess immediately spoke up.

"Severin goes over the wall. He knows what the inside of the compound looks like. Besides you've had months to break into that place."

"I know, I just..." she stopped and scowled. "The way he was talking, like he wanted me and Amy to fuck in the street while some guys watch. I don't like the sound of that."

"Understandable," the Viscountess agreed. "I'd never ask you to do anything that makes you too uncomfortable. On the other hand we have to lure the guard away so Severin can climb over the wall without being spotted. I don't mind putting on a little show. How would you feel about a public Scene with me?"

Tycho made a great show of looking her up and down, as if she hadn't actually noticed the Viscountess before.

"I wouldn't mind doing a scene with you," Tycho admitted. "But I warn you, I don't bottom."

"That should make it more interesting." The Viscountess smiled. After a second Tycho smiled back.

"Just for the record," Amy spoke up. "I bottom."

"I'm sure we'll find something for you to do," the Viscountess promised.

"I don't want her to go inside with us," Tycho said defensively. "She should stay outside where it's safe."

"I'm not a child," Amy told her.

"She's also part of the quest. I think all four of us have to play a part," Severin explained.

"Once we've escaped with the Sphere we can summon the Gateway to take us home," the Viscountess reassured them. "But until then we're as stuck as you are."

They were interrupted when a party rolled into the bar with a great deal of shouting. Apparently they had just come back from an adventure. They looked battered and exhausted, but they were accompanied by a small harem of slave girls who were carrying gold and jewels. When the leader of the party announced that he was buying drinks for everyone the noise level in the bar practically raised the roof.

"We should get out of here before the jerk puts us back to work," Tycho warned. Amy's replacement, a chubby Halfling woman, was scurrying from table to table trying to get everyone's order.

They had time to kill until they could enact their plan. Tycho spent the last of her tip money on a well-crafted bullwhip. She couldn't afford one with an enchantment for accuracy or increased pain. It was just as well since the magic wouldn't have worked back in the Real World anyway.

The whip was a good companion to the sword that Tycho had already bought which was slung from her hip. Severin resisted the urge to get a weapon. He felt if it came to a fight they had already lost. He missed his old lock picks, but he had to pass as a slave, and a new set might be difficult to conceal.

They listened to drummers and flutists play in a park while satyrs copulated with nymphs in time to the music. As they headed towards Lady Amaril's castle, a handsome man suddenly stepped out of the shadow. He appeared so suddenly the Viscountess thought he might have been invisible a second before.

"Hello, my lady," he said in a well-modulated voice. He looked as if he had just stepped off the cover of a romance novel. He had dark, wavy hair down to his shoulders and keen blue eyes. His chest was bare except for a leather strap that passed over one shoulder. He had rippling muscles and absolutely no body hair. "Are you looking for a good time?"

"Not really," the Viscountess said politely. She couldn't believe someone that handsome was a street prostitute. In any event they didn't have the time to waste on him.

"Oh, I see." The man glanced past Severin and noticed Tycho and Amy. "Perhaps you prefer something different then?"

As he spoke his body began to shift and change. There was a slight blur and suddenly the handsome man was a strikingly beautiful woman. Her white blonde hair cascaded down to her shoulders. She had the hauntingly perfect face they had come to associate with elves, but this woman's body wasn't as slender as an elf. She had lush curves revealed by her tiny thong and her breasts were barely restrained by a thin sheet of silk.

The Viscountess started to speak and found nothing coming out. While she stood in shock Severin stepped up.

"I'm afraid we're in a hurry," he told the prostitute.

"Are you certain?" she smiled wickedly. "I can accommodate groups. I can be very accommodating."

As she spoke her thong suddenly bulged outwards. A very erect male member had now sprouted between her legs. A second later another penis sprouted just under the first.

"Intriguing," the Viscountess admitted. "But I'm afraid Severin is right, we must be going."

"Pity." The prostitute shifted yet again. Her whole body blurred and when she came back into focus she was exact double of the Viscountess.

With some genuine reluctance the group left the prostitute on the street.

"I can certainly see some of the appeal of this place," the Viscountess said to Severin. "How are you doing?"

"Fine," he told his owner. "I'm enjoying being back, but I'm also looking forward to leaving."

"I know what you mean." The Viscountess glanced back at Amy and Tycho. The two of them had fallen back and were talking in hushed tones, as if they still didn't trust their rescuers. "We've come too far to give up now. We'll get them back and recover the Sphere."

By one in the morning the excitement in the streets of Cassomere was reduced to only a few sword fights and random monster attacks. The neighborhood around Lady Amaril's was very quiet. Although many of the houses were well lit, Elves apparently weren't party animals. The streets around the castle were empty.

The streets were lit by glowing blocks of stone set in the wall. The moon was also full, which bathed everything in an odd, almost bluish light. Despite this, there were still shadows to hide in. Severin was pressed into the doorway of a closed shop that sold magic nipple and labia rings. The doorway provided him just enough cover as he slowly uncoiled the rope and waited for his cue.

From where he was he could see the guard pacing slowly across the walkway on the other side of the wall. There were also a guards on the east and west walls, plus five or six at the main gate. The best way in would be over the back wall. All he had to do was wait for the right moment.

Outside the west wall of Lady Amaril's castle, the Viscountess and Amy walked arm in arm. They were visible to the guard, but he didn't even glance at them. When they were at a point midway down the length of the wall, the Viscountess spun and pressed Amy back against the wall.

The schoolgirl gave a squeal as the Viscountess kissed her hard, forcing a tongue into Amy's mouth. Amy tried to twist away, but the Viscountess had her shirt open and was playing with her small breasts. She caused the nipples to stiffen with teasing strokes of her thumbs. Then when the nipples were good and hard and Amy was writhing with passion, the Viscountess bent her head and grazed a nipple with her teeth.

Amy cried out, her whole body twisting. The Viscountess reached a hand under the schoolgirl skirt. Her fingers found Amy wet and ready and she began to slide her fingers up against her clitoris.

While this was going on, Amy put up a mock struggle. As the two women twisted against each other the Viscountess turned her head and saw that the guard was indeed looking at them. That was one guard at least.

The Viscountess used her long whip as a makeshift rope and wrapped it around Amy's wrists. Amy obligingly stopped struggling then and allowed the Viscountess to reach under her skirt to continue her exploration.

The first clue the Viscountess had that Tycho had arrived was when the Roaring Girl's whip cut into her shoulder. The magical leather cat suit turned out to provide very little protection. In the time it took the Viscountess to untangle herself and her whip from Amy, she had been hit with two more blows from the whip.

"Leave her alone," Tycho announced, loud enough for the guards to hear.

"Don't hurt her," Amy sobbed, really getting into her part.

The Viscountess and Tycho circled each other, each with their whips out. The front of Tycho's bodice was open enough that both breasts were visible. The biker struck with smooth, even strokes of the whip. The Viscountess realized somewhat belatedly that Tycho was much better with a whip than she was.

They each struck out with their whips. The Viscountess managed to wrap her whip around Tycho's waist. It seemed like a good hit, but Tycho lashed out. Her whip tore off one of the buckles holding the leather outfit of the Viscountess in place. The fabric fell open, exposing her chest.

There was a snort of laughter from the wall. Now that the guards were making noise, the Viscountess had every reason to look up. She saw not one, or two, but three guards watching the fight.

Surely one of them has to be the guard from the back wall, the Viscountess thought. At that point Tycho's whip scored again, hissing over her shoulder and leaving a trail of fire across her shoulder blade. The Viscountess decided she had better focus on the task at hand.

Around the corner, Severin heard the crack of the whip and knew that Tycho had arrived. It took only a few seconds before the guard on the back wall headed over to join his friend. They might have thought the whip was the sound of someone actually attacking the building, but once they saw it wasn't, they stayed to watch.

Severin raced across the street to the base of the wall. At first glance it looked like an impossible task. In the Real World, Severin could never have made a throw like that. Of course this wasn't the Real World. Here he was a dashing thief. So long as he believed that he knew he could do it.

Even with strong belief, it still took two tries to get the padded grappling hook onto the wall. Severin scrambled up the coarse stone in exactly the way he would never have been able to do in the Real World. When he got to the top he was breathing hard and his shoulders were on fire, but he couldn't afford to stop.

He could see the backs of three guards watching the little show in the street. Not only was the guard on the west wall and the back wall watching, but another guard had come in with a ladder to climb up and see what was going on.

Severin found a good place to attach the hook and let the rope fall. He grabbed the line and dropped straight down into darkness. He descended too fast and the friction burned his hands. When he landed there was a jolt that took his breath away.

He fell to the ground, but was back on his feet almost at once. He was sore, but nothing was broken. Severin wiggled the rope until the hook came free. It came down, nearly hitting him in the head. He didn't try to coil it back up, but tossed it into the shadows of the wall.

As he had predicted, they weren't expecting any deliveries at night so there were no torches lit at the back door. The only torches were far enough away that they were of little use. The moon wasn't at the right angle to reach the wall, putting the entire length of it in darkness.

The back door didn't have a lock, but was held in place by a wooden beam. Severin felt around in the dark until he got his arms on the beam and slid it loose. This made a little bit of noise, but by this time the snapping of whips had given way to moans.

Severin felt a twinge of regret that he wasn't able to see what was going on.

With the door unbolted, Severin crept across the open area that lead to the garden. The plan was for everyone to meet in the shrubbery.

Apparently the distraction hadn't lasted quite long enough. He could hear the guards returning to their posts. If he tried ducking into the shadows now, it would only look suspicious. He had no choice but to continue walking as if he belonged there. He was almost at the garden when he heard the clanking of armor and two guards came around the side of the house.

"You there, boy!" one of them shouted.

Severin kept walking, as if he hadn't heard.

"You, stop!"

He had no choice but to stop. The guards came to him. He could see their slender, delicate features under the visor of the helmet. He tried to look meek and submissive, which fortunately came naturally to him.

"What are you doing?" the guard demanded.

"Nothing, sir," Severin blurted out. It was all he could think of to say.

"Good, get to the barn then."

Severin hesitated. The guard helpfully took him by the arm and spun him around so that he faced a wooden structure in the courtyard which was quite obviously a barn. Severin hadn't noticed it earlier.

The two guards were standing there talking. Severin had no choice but to go to the barn.

Outside, the Viscountess and Tycho were still engaged in battle. It was obvious the Viscountess was taking the worst of it. Tycho managed to yank the whip right from the hands of the Viscountess. Tycho's next stroke wrapped the whip around the Viscountess' waist. The triumphant Roaring Girl reeled her in like a fish.

The Viscountess did not pretend to fight back. When she was close to the biker she could smell the sweat and excitement coming off of her. Tycho was so excited that she had forgotten that she was putting on a show for some men.

They were suddenly inches apart. The Viscountess was careful not to raise her dominant energy. If Tycho thought the Viscountess was trying to top her, she'd fight back. The whole little scene could go south very quickly.

Instead of challenging her, the Viscountess leaned into her, kissing her passionately. Tycho moaned in spite of herself. Their two bodies came together. The Viscountess felt the muscles that could have torn her in half if this had been a real fight.

Apparently the guards had been hoping for a more violent ending to the struggle. After a few minutes of watching the two human women making out one of the guards made a disgusted noise and the men turned back to doing their job. One guard climbed down the ladder to the courtyard.

Although the guards probably thought that the three women were going off to a hotel room, in fact the Viscountess, Tycho, and Amy circled around the block and came to where they could see the back wall. The guard was back on duty, pacing the length of the wall. There in the center was the back door, which Severin had hopefully unlocked.

Tycho went first to make sure everything was okay. They had to wait until the guard had gone past the door, then move before he turned around and came back. It was a help that he couldn't see straight down onto the sidewalk without leaning dangerously over the edge.

Tycho gave the all clear sign before vanishing through the door. Amy went next, then the Viscountess. On the other side of the wall the Viscountess felt a moment of panic as she saw two guards near the house having a heated discussion. Then she realized that they were effectively blinded by the torches from the house. They couldn't see beyond the circle of light they stood in.

She crept across the open courtyard and made it to the garden.

"Severin?" she asked.

"He's not here," Tycho hissed. "He's vanished.

Chapter Thirty-Six

The big door to the barn was open so Severin went inside. The barn smelled, not surprisingly, like horses and fresh hay. It was a well-kept barn, lit by lanterns. There were probably a lot of things to see there, but the only thing he really saw was the centaur.

As impressive as she had looked earlier in the day she was much more impressive up close when she was free from the saddle and the bridle. She was tall enough that he naturally looked her in the pierced nipples. Her powerful arms were free and there was a riding whip in her hand. It was the same whip that had been used on her earlier.

She had something in her hand that she threw to the floor at his feet. It was a metal tool shaped like a hook. For a horrible second Severin thought it might be a dental tool and he wondered what he had gotten into.

"Don't just stand there, you idiot!" she snapped. "My hooves aren't going to clean themselves."

Severin picked up the metal hook. He had no real experiences with horses and less with centaurs, but how hard could it be to clean a hoof?

"Yes, Ma'am," he murmured as she lifted her right foreleg.

Abruptly she brought the hoof down again and lashed out with the riding whip. She gave him three hard strokes across his shoulders, the braided leather burning as if it were red hot.

"What did you call me?"

Severin realized that he had accidently fallen into the term of respect used by the Roaring Girls. In this Dominion Ma'am was only used with older, usually married women.

"It's Mistress," the centaur sneered. He noticed that her mouth was slightly wider than a human's mouth. Probably it was so she could draw more air into that huge equine body of hers.

"Yes, Mistress, thank you, Mistress."

Severin lowered his head in complete submission. That seemed to satisfy her, for she adjusted her stance and raised her right foreleg. He took the leg in his hands and saw that when she curled her leg he was looking down into her hoof. Inside the horseshoe there was a fleshy nub that looked very sensitive, but surrounding that was a cake of dried mud that she had picked up during the morning ride.

Gently he began to pick at it. He was happy to see the dirt cascade to the floor of the barn. Suddenly the centaur twisted her leg free. Horse's legs had always looked very thin to him, but when he actually had one in his hands he discovered that the muscles felt like steel cables.

"You've never done this before. Why did they send you here?"

"The guards told me to come here," Severin said truthfully.

She struck him a few more times with the whip while Severin cowered under her blows. She bent at the waist and unexpectedly lifted him to his feet. She tugged at the clothes he was wearing and examined his body. When she saw him naked the centaur burst out laughing.

"You haven't been branded. You're barely even bruised. You don't belong here, do you?" she asked. She didn't sound angry; she apparently thought it was funny. "I know who you are. I saw you at the market today, admiring my mistress. You're one of those pathetic slaves whose come here to beg for a place at her feet, aren't you?"

"Yes, Mistress." Severin was keeping his head down in submission and hoping it made his story more convincing.

"Very well," the centaur chuckled. Her thick fingers were on his nipples, squeezing with the force of a vice grip. "Go on, run to your new mistress. If there's anything left of you after she's done you may come crawling back and I'll find a stall for you."

She released his nipples and took him by the shoulders, spinning him around. Rearing back on her hind legs she planted both front feet into his shoulders, shoving him towards the open barn door. For Severin the double kick felt a little like being hit by a car. Of course she didn't use her full strength since she didn't break any bones.

Severin stumbled out of the barn. One of the guards on the wall glanced at him, but didn't seem to notice anything suspicious. The two guards who had ordered him to the barn were still talking, but were walking towards the front of the house and were soon around a corner.

He found the three women waiting for him in the shrubs by the garden.

"I was about to come after you," the Viscountess said.

"It was nothing I couldn't handle," Severin assured her.

"You've got hoof prints on your back. And you're missing your clothing."

As she wiped him clean they went over the plan. Two windows on the second floor overlooked the garden. Severin would go inside, get the Sphere and drop it out one of the windows, whichever room was the most convenient. Then they would catch it and head for the back door. Severin would follow as soon as he could.

The guards were checking the street for any sign of trouble, so they might not see them run through the courtyard. Even if they were spotted they should be able to cross to the door fast enough to escape.

The Viscountess wanted very much to join Severin, to offer him both moral and physical support, but she knew it wasn't a wise course of action. He would make less noise and attract less attention by himself. Plus if she went then Tycho would insist on going as well. Since they wouldn't leave Amy behind that meant all four of them would be traipsing through the house and they might as well bring a marching band.

She held out her arm so he could kiss the back of her hand. Crouching in the garden made offering her boot a little impractical.

"I know she's beautiful, Severin, but do not submit to her," the Viscountess said as his lips brushed her hand. "That is a direct order."

"Yes, Viscountess."

The door to the kitchen was unlocked. There were even a few servants still at work there, cleaning and preparing the next day's food. There were no guards watching them and they ignored Severin. He was just another human slave in a house that was filled with them. From what the centaur had said, new slaves showing up unexpectedly wasn't unusual.

Severin moved through the house with an aura of feigned casualness. He reached the wide staircase that he had glimpsed while delivering supplies. Once he was up there he would be in trouble if he was caught. Fortunately, he didn't hear a sound from the second floor. It was also equally fortunate that the interior of the house was well lit by a magic glow so the servants could work all night. There was no need to grope in the dark.

Once up the staircase he started searching. The first room was a library. Glancing at it quickly he couldn't see any hidden doors. With some difficulty he tore himself away. From the looks of some of the tomes Lady Amaril was something of a sorceress, which made her doubly dangerous.

The second room felt like a jackpot. It was a sort of combination lounge and torture chamber with a large chair, chains on the walls and a small cage. There was a large mirror on one wall with an elaborate gilded frame. Instead of reflecting the room it was clouded. Odd shapes and forms appeared in it, most of them flickering away before Severin could make out what they were.

The other wall was covered by a tapestry. On a hunch Severin lifted the heavy cloth and studied the wall. There was a simple stone wall behind it. There was also a small, almost impossible to spot hole in the wall that would take a key.

It was a classic hidden door. Severin felt that if the Sphere was anywhere it would be behind this door. All he had to do was open it. He didn't have any picks, besides it looked like it wouldn't be easy to open. His best bet was to find the key.

The next two rooms turned out to be a linen closet and a primitive bathroom. The third room was the bedroom.

Lady Amaril lay stretched out across her silk sheets completely naked. The lights were dimmed in this room and her pale flesh seemed almost to glow in the dark. Her small, round breasts rose and fell with her breathing. Her pubic hair was even more pale than the hair on her head. It was so colorless it seemed almost transparent, and although it was long and silky it hid absolutely nothing.

With a supreme effort of will Severin forced himself to look away. There was a small table next to the huge bed which had a dildo standing on its end. At its base were a number of small objects including a tiny, intricately wrought key on a chain. The sight of the key reassured Severin that he had been right in believing that no normal pick could have opened that door.

He reached for the key very slowly only to see a flash of movement. The dildo had shifted position. Suddenly it had the eyes and mouth of a viper. The dildo twisted around, protecting the key.

Severin looked into its beady eyes and saw the open jaws, the fangs dripping with venom. Although it made a small hissing noise, Lady Amaril was still sleeping peacefully.

Severin pondered if the dildo was like a real snake. Perhaps he could distract it. He placed his left hand off to the side, moving it fast enough to get the viper's attention. As the snake twisted around it left the key unprotected. By moving his right hand very, very slowly Severin was able to get the key and withdraw his hand while keeping the viper dildo entertained by wiggling his fingers.

As he made his way out of the bedroom Severin wondered if the dildo could come alive like that during sex. That would be a nasty trick to pull on someone.

Back in the room with the tapestry Severin checked the window. It was one of the windows that looked down into the garden. As he opened it he saw the Viscountess, Tycho, and Amy getting ready to catch the Sphere.

The door under the tapestry yielded easily to the key. Inside was a small room built of solid stone. The walls were lined with what were magic items, which were probably dangerous. On a table in the center was a globe the size of a beach ball glowing a soft blue and resting on a wooden stand. It looked like glass, but the Crone had assured them it was almost unbreakable crystal.

As Severin approached the Sphere, something moved inside of it. Small lightning bolts moved across its surface. Severin recalled that touching the Sphere charged you with energy and brought intense pain. He decided to exercise the better part of valor. Returning to the main room he pulled the tapestry from the wall and threw it over the sphere. The heavy cloth muffled its power allowing him to lift it and carry it to the window. It was heavy enough Severin was glad he didn't have to run while lugging it around.

This part of the plan went like clockwork. Severin hefted the Sphere through the window. Tycho and Amy caught it with a cloak. Tycho immediately slung it over her shoulder and headed for the back door. The hitch in the plan came when Severin heard an icy voice behind him.

"How dare you?"

He turned to see Lady Amaril. She had thrown on a robe and had a long, thin length of wood in her hand. Severin couldn't tell if it was a switch or a magic wand, probably it was both. There was so much dominant energy rolling off of her that it made her hair float up like a charge of static electricity.

"I'm going to have you flayed alive and dipped in pickling brine," she announced.

Severin heard the sound of men in armor heading for the room. He also heard a distant bell chiming. It was so quiet he hadn't noticed it at first. Apparently the alarm bell only sounded in her room. Severin had set it off and not even noticed.

As the dominant energy washed over him he felt his knees buckle. Submitting to her was the most natural and normal thing in the world. He wanted to serve her with every part of his being. The only thing that kept him on his feet was the words of the Viscountess.

I know she's beautiful, Severin, but do not submit to her. That is a direct order.

It was as if she were in the room, speaking to him. Bolstered by the thought of her, Severin did the only thing he could think of. He turned from Lady Amaril and jumped out the window.

In his prime Severin knew he could have made the jump with little difficulty. Now that he was years out of practice he landed hard and had to roll to absorb the impact. The Viscountess was on the ground waiting for him, her longbow already at work.

"Move, Severin!" she shouted.

As Severin scrambled to his feet he saw that Tycho and Amy were just going through the door to the street. One of the guards was still fumbling with his bow, but the other had already sent an arrow into the ground near where Severin landed. The Viscountess fired an arrow back at him, which didn't come close to hitting him, but it made him flinch and spoiled his next shot.

Severin felt his heart pounding as he raced out the door. They had done it!

His excitement cooled somewhat when he saw that Tycho and Amy had come to a halt in the middle of the street and were facing two people who were very familiar to the Viscountess and Severin.

Abraxus was there with his floating chair hovering a few inches off the cobblestones. Standing on the platform at the base of his chair was the stunning nude blonde slave Severin remembered.

"I have to confess, this is an interesting development," Abraxus said. His inhuman latex face slipped into an oily smile.

Tycho didn't hesitate. She drew her sword and went after them. The blonde slave simply plucked the sword form her hand. With a smug expression the blonde held the blade so that the tip was resting on her breastbone directly between her small, firm breasts. When she pushed, forcing the sword against her there was a terrible sound of creaking metal. The steel crumpled like paper. The slave smiled and returned the now useless lump of metal to Tycho's hand.

"Don't tell me you're behind this," the Viscountess said.

"Hardly. As I told you I merely observe."

"You've been following us." She observed. "I saw you two in Vegas."

"And I saw you in Venice," Severin added, "Although I thought I was hallucinating at the time."

"I admit, I was curious as to what your business was with the Kamen Girls. They are very mysterious. No one knows the true source of their power. When I noticed that Kamen Girls were being withdrawn back to their home I knew something had gone wrong and that somehow you two were involved."

Severin groaned. "Lady Amaril has a magic mirror that can reach other Dominions. I'll bet she was using it to find out more about the Sphere."

"Exactly," Abraxus said, sounding quite pleased with himself. "I suspected such an item would be very useful. If I can harness the power of the Sphere it will save wear and tear on dear Dhoia here."

He reached out and gently stroked the blonde slave. Looking at her, something clicked in Severin's mind.

"So you're here to steal the Sphere?" the Viscountess asked.

Abraxus looked offended. "Unlike you, I do not steal. I was arranging a complex series of transactions that would place her in my debt, leaving her no option but to give me what I want. Now you've rendered that somewhat meaningless."

"We have to go," Severin told his companions. "Abraxus is about to have other problems."

"My slave is more than capable of taking the Sphere from you," Abraxus assured them.

"No, she can't," Severin smiled. "I don't think she can leave your chair without losing her powers. She hasn't left it since we first saw you. She's very powerful, but only when she's next to you."

As soon as Severin spoke, Tycho and Amy both took a step back from Abraxus. The slave looked at her master for some direction.

"What makes you say that?" Abraxus demanded.

"Well, for one thing she hasn't walked over here and punched me. For another, I think your chair operates on both high magic and high technology. There's only one place it could have come from, the Comic Book Dominion. She's a super hero you've enslaved, but her powers only work in the special rules of your home Dominion. Somehow that chair carries a bubble of your world around with it."

Abraxus gritted his black teeth together. The slave looked seriously worried.

"Also," Severin added, "there's about to be a powerful Elven sorceress and a small army coming around that corner. There's magic in your world, which means she can attack you and I don't think your pet has any invulnerability to magic spells."

As Severin spoke, the sound of hoof beats got closer. Lady Amaril was on the back of her centaur, riding without a saddle. Her long wand was glowing with power. Behind her came her troops.

Severin, the Viscountess, Amy, and Tycho were already on the move. Abraxus must have known that the he wouldn't have time to use the pistons to excite his slave and open a path to another Dominion. He made the chair turn in the opposite direction from them.

Crouched down in an alley the four companions saw the armored Elves ride past. Severin sagged against the wall, exhausted. The Viscountess nudged him in the ribs and pointed.

At the end of the alley a stone gateway had appeared, its runes glowing softly. Their epic quest was at an end.

Chapter Thirty-Seven

The Viscountess elected to return Amy first. It was the least difficult of the things they had to do. After returning to the Real World, they went right to a restaurant. Tycho and Amy delighted in the first meal they had eaten in months in which all the ingredients were easy to identify. Severin sat on the floor and the Viscountess fed him chicken nuggets by hand.

A phone call to Lady Amanda made the agreement to meet at Sappho's in Phoenix. It was the place where she had first hired the Viscountess and more importantly it was someplace Snuzzle already knew how to reach. It was going to be tough enough on Snuzzle without making her find a new location.

After dinner Amy and Tycho hugged and promised to stay in touch. The Viscountess wasn't sure of either of them meant it. Possibly she was seeing them break up. In any event, it wasn't her business.

A short trip though the void with Snuzzle brought them to the parking lot of Sappho's which was sweltering in the sun. They had diplomatically left Tycho behind in Boston.

"I'm so sorry," Amanda told her niece. "I shouldn't have been so strict."

"It's okay." Amy hugged her again. "I promise not to run away again. That was a really bad idea."

When the reunion was complete Lady Amanda approached the Viscountess and shook her hand.

"I am deeply in your debt."

"It was really Severin who did all the hard work. If it wasn't for his skills, Amy would still be stuck in that Dominion."

Amanda's eyes flickered to Severin for a second, then she looked back to the Viscountess. "I hope that we can work out some way to repay you."

"We'll talk about that later," the Viscountess assured her. "I still have a great deal to do."

Snuzzle brought them back to Boston where they picked up Tycho. The Viscountess insisted that Snuzzle drink plenty of water and rest a few minutes before taking them back into the void.

About a half hour later the pony cart pulled into the street in front of the Roaring Girl's bar. By the time Snuzzle had skidded to a stop the door was flung open and women poured out to greet Tycho.

Severin saw that most of the campers and tents were still in the desert around the bar. They may have been waiting to see if Tycho could be rescued. On the other hand, they simply might not have left yet. Severin reminded himself that it was only Monday. It had been Sunday when he returned to Boston and went through the Gateway to the Dungeon Dominion. They had returned to the Real World on Monday morning.

Momma Bear lifted Tycho in a rib-crushing hug. As soon as she was released, Sir was hugging her.

"Don't ever fucking do that to us again," Sir declared. She had to break off the hug since her tears were completely ruining her butch image.

Nita shook hands with Tycho, and then wound up hugging her anyway.

"Are you all right?" Nita asked.

"Fine," Tycho replied. "Viscountess said you had Red Lightning here?"

"The woman in the mask, sure."

"I've got to talk to her."

Tycho brushed past Nita and went into the bar. Along the way she stopped to shake hands or hug several other women.

The Viscountess and Severin trailed behind her. Both of them wanted to see what happened when Tycho and Red Lightning were reunited. Nita spoke to them before they could get to the door.

"I owe you," Nita said.

"Not really," the Viscountess admitted. "We were hired to rescue Amy and Tycho just happened to be there."

"I still say we owe you. Besides after that last initiation we've had a lot to think about. Momma, Sir, and I have been brainstorming. We may come up with new ceremonies, a new dildo. If it wasn't for Severin none of that would have occurred to us."

"I'm glad it worked out." The Viscountess glanced at Severin. She absolutely had to hear what happened, but things had been moving so fast they hadn't had time to talk.

Inside the bar Tycho was confronting Red Lighting who was standing with her back to a support pole and held in place with stout chains.

"I'm going back with you," Tycho announced. "I have to testify at your trial. They need to know that it was all my fault."

"I don't think that's going to matter. It won't be that kind of a trial." Red Lightning seemed to have composed herself as she lay captive with the Roaring Girls.

"Damn it, that's not fair!"

"It's perfectly fair. I broke the rules and now I have to pay the price." Red Lightning spoke firmly but gently. "Remember that military group you used to be with and their motto? You told me what that means to you."

"The Marines. Semper Fi."

"Semper Fi. That's why I have to go back and face this alone."

"God damn it!"

There was a beer bottle left on a table. Tycho snatched it up and hurled it across the room where it shattered against the wall. Women with glasses or bottles at their tables quietly scooped them up. The Viscountess stepped close to Severin to shield his body from flying glass.

There was no more violence. Tycho ultimately left Red Lightning to her fate.

Red Lightning had to be aroused to open a portal and she readily admitted she hadn't been in the mood for days.

"That's all right," the Viscountess assured her. "We'll take the Sphere to Victoria and get picked up there."

They spent hours in Victoria waiting for the Kamen Girls to escort them to their Dominion. They passed the time catching each other up on their adventures. Severin got upset all over again when he heard about her caning. She was entertained by his description of the initiation ceremony. Soon, three masked women appeared. Their faces seemed grim even accounting for the masks.

By the time they got to the Dominion, the entire place was alive with activity. A small crowd followed the Viscountess as she marched toward the Ziggurat with the Sphere still wrapped in its blanket from Dungeon. With the help of Black Masque, it was placed where it belonged. The Sphere glowed brightly and sent off a small shower of sparks, apparently happy to be home.

Black Masque led the Viscountess and Severin to a private conference with the Crone while Red Lightning waited outside.

Before anything could be said, the Viscountess handed over Skye's mask.

"You have succeeded," The Crone said. She seemed to have withered in the time they were gone. There was a rasp in her voice and her long breasts dangled down her rib cage. "Now I offer you our reward for your services. You or your slave may call upon the Kamen Girls three times. We shall send our people to the establishment in Victoria each day. If you need us leave a message and someone will contact you. You may ask whatever you want of us and if it is in our power we shall grant it."

"That's most generous." The Viscountess bowed. "You should be careful though. Making that sort of promise is exactly how Red Lightning got into trouble."

"What do you mean?" Black Masque demanded. She had been unusually quiet since they got back. Red Lightning had been her protégé and she took Red's treason very personally.

The Viscountess explained everything that had happened, just as it had been told to her by Red Lightning and Tycho.

"What Red Lightning did was foolish and innocent people suffered for it, but she did it because she had to fulfill an oath, a promise that she had made. It's exactly like the promise you just made me," the Viscountess pointed out. "What if I asked you for the Sphere? You'd have to give it to me since it's in your power to do so."

"This is ridiculous." The Crone pounded her staff.

"I'm just pointing out a fact."

The Crone rose to her full height, her dominant energy washing over the room. Black Masque lowered her head. Severin felt weak in the knees and had to hold on to the Viscountess.

"I will do what must be done. This is not for outsiders. Black Masque, escort them from here and send them home."

Black Masque took them gently from the room. As soon as the door closed the Viscountess spoke.

"What is she going to do?"

"Exile and banishment," Black Masque explained. "She's going to take her mask away permanently. The energy of the Sphere that remains in her body will be removed. They say it's more painful that receiving the energy. The shock of it will leave her with partial amnesia. After that, she'll be sent into some Dominion to start over."

"She's sent somewhere naked and with amnesia?"

"That is our way."

The Viscountess ground her teeth in frustration but said nothing. She had no right to interfere with the way the Kamen Girls conducted their business. She hadn't even planned on defending Red Lightning, but she just couldn't help herself. Apparently arrogance was part of the training here.

Two hours later they were home in Boston, enjoying a delicious meal cooked by Sklavin. The slave had outdone herself preparing the mini-feast. As they ate the phone rang. It was Tycho.

"You won't believe what happened."

"Try me." The Viscountess said, putting it on speaker.

"One of the campers found a naked woman wandering through the desert and brought her to the bar. It's Red Lightning. She doesn't have her mask, but you can see the lines on her face where the mask had pressed into her skin."

"How is she?"

"A little confused. She doesn't seem to know much about the Kamen Girls. She remembers you and Severin, and she remembers me finding her in the desert."

"Take good care of her. You should be aware that her memory might not come back."

"All right. I'll deal with it." Tycho decided. "Maybe this way I can make up for getting her into this mess in the first place."

After she hung up the phone she glanced at Severin.

"Maybe that was The Crone being merciful," he guessed.

"There are certainly worse places she could have sent her."

"Like Dungeon," Severin chuckled. "She'd probably wind up leading college students on their first dungeon crawl."

"Don't lie, Severin. You enjoyed being back there."

"I did. I enjoyed it very much. There are a lot of great Dominions out there." He threw himself to the ground at her feet. His body ached from the wall-crawling and the sudden drops of the day before. "But I'd rather be home with you."

About the Author

Cameron Quintain is a shy, quiet librarian by day, and a swashbuckling superhero at night. His erotic vampire novella, *Familiar Places*, was a finalist in the 2014 Passionate Ink awards. *The Viscountess Interrogates* is his second novel.

The Viscountess Investigates
A Dominion Erotic Mystery

The regal Viscountess and her partner Severin are not your typical detectives, nor your typical mistress/slave pair from the BDSM subculture. They inhabit the magical and kinky world hidden by the powerful spell known as the Blindfold, and they travel from the Real World into magical Dominions that reflect every kink fantasy humans can dream of. When the powerful leader of the Algophilia Society is murdered, their path to track down the killer brings them through a Victorian London that never was, where "fox" hunts involve no animals, and a feudal Japan where a mysterious Jade carver creates terrifying magical dildos. Their loving bond as owner and slave is tested—and reinforced—as they whip, suck, and Scene their way to unraveling the mystery and confronting the culprit.

Familiar Places
A Tale of Vampires, Murder, and Submission
A Finalist in the Passionate Plume Awards!

Kenneth is a private detective on a case, and to solve it he needs help from the beautiful and dominant vampire he once loved, once served. A girl is missing, possibly kidnapped by vampires, and Dinaria is Ken's only ally in his old haunts. Twelve years earlier, Dinaria's temptations had ruled his life, until the moment he had finally rejected her to make a life for himself. But now, as they hunt for the missing girl, a world of temptations swirls around them both.

The House of Sable Locks
by Elizabeth Schechter

From Passionate Plume award winner Elizabeth Schechter comes a steampunk novel of dark passion and male submission. In a respectable neighbourhood, on the top floor of a beautiful house, crouches the Succubus; by design, and by temperament, she is all that men crave and fear. To the wealthy and privileged men of London, the Succubus is a test they must pass to gain access to the House of Sable Locks, the most exclusive brothel in town. However, to William, a wealthy young man born and raised in India, she is the very essence of his desires.

The Innocent's Progress and Other Stories
by Peter Tupper

In a steampunk society where sex is ritualized and marriage is sacred, the slightest misstep can bring your world tumbling down. In this collection, Peter Tupper explores the many facets of a time that never was, and a society that is all too familiar. Rich in eroticism, and immersive in its detail, *The Innocent's Progress and Other Stories* is a sterling example of what steampunk can be.

Circlet Press, Inc.
Erotica For Geeks
www.circlet.com